Can she

In the C

Three passionate and exciting romances from
three fabulous Mills & Boon authors!

In the Count's Bed

SARA CRAVEN

CATHERINE SPENCER

AMY ANDREWS

MILLS & BOON

First published in Great Britain 2011
Harlequin Mills & Boon Limited,
Eton House, 18-24 Paradise Road, Richmond, Surrey TW9 1SR

IN THE COUNT'S BED © Harlequin Enterprises II B.V./S.à.r.l. 2011

The Count's Blackmail Bargain, The French Count's Pregnant Bride and *The Italian Count's Baby* were first published in Great Britain by Harlequin Mills & Boon Limited.

The Count's Blackmail Bargain © Sara Craven 2005
The French Count's Pregnant Bride © Spencer Books Limited 2006
The Italian Count's Baby © Amy Andrews 2007

ISBN: 978 0 263 88430 2

05-0211

Printed and bound in Spain
by Litografia Rosés S.A., Barcelona

THE COUNT'S
BLACKMAIL BARGAIN

BY
SARA CRAVEN

Sara Craven was born in South Devon, and grew up surrounded by books, in a house by the sea. After leaving grammar school she worked as a local journalist, covering everything from flower shows to murders. She started writing for Mills & Boon® in 1975. Apart from writing, her passions include films, music, cooking and eating in good restaurants. She now lives in Somerset.

Sara Craven has appeared as a contestant on the Channel Four game show *Fifteen to One* and is also the latest (and last ever) winner of the 1997 Mastermind of Great Britain championship.

CHAPTER ONE

IT WAS a warm, golden morning in Rome, so how in the name of God was the city in the apparent grip of a small earthquake?

The noble Conte Alessio Ramontella lifted his aching head from the pillow, and, groaning faintly from the effort, attempted to focus his eyes. True, the bed looked like a disaster area, but the room was not moving, and the severe pounding, which he'd assumed was the noise of buildings collapsing nearby, seemed to be coming instead from the direction of his bedroom door.

And the agitated shouting he could hear was not emanating from some buried victim either, but could be recognised as the voice of his manservant Giorgio urging him to wake up.

Using small, economical movements that would not disturb the blonde, naked beauty still slumbering beside him, or increase the pressure from his hangover, Alessio got up from the bed, and extracted his robe from the tangle of discarded clothing on the floor, before treading across the marble-tiled floor to the door.

He pulled the garment round him, and opened the door an inch or two.

'This is not a working day,' he informed the anxious face outside. 'Am I to be allowed no peace?'

'Forgive me, *Eccellenza*.' Giorgio wrung his hands. 'For the world I would not have disturbed you. But it is your aunt, the Signora Vicente.'

There was an ominous pause, then: 'Here?' Alessio bit out the word.

'On her way,' Giorgio admitted nervously. 'She telephoned to announce her intention to visit you.'

Alessio swore softly. 'Didn't you have enough wit to say I was away?' he demanded.

5

'Of course, *Eccellenza*.' Giorgio spoke with real sorrow. 'But regrettably she did not believe me.'

Alessio swore again more fluently. 'How long have I got?'

'That will depend on the traffic, *signore*, but I think we must count in minutes.' He added reproachfully, 'I have been knocking and knocking...'

With another groan, Alessio forced himself into action. 'Get a cab for my guest,' he ordered. 'Tell the driver to come to the rear entrance, and to be quick about it. This is an emergency. Then prepare coffee for the *Signora*, and some of the little almond biscuits that she likes.'

He shut the door, and went back to the bed, his hangover eclipsed by more pressing concerns. He looked down at all the smooth, tanned loveliness displayed for his delectation, and his mouth tightened.

Dio, what a fool he'd been to break his own cardinal rule, and allow her to stay the night.

I must have been more drunk than I thought, he told himself cynically, then bent over her, giving one rounded shoulder a firm shake.

Impossibly long lashes lifted slowly, and she gave him a sleepy smile. 'Alessio, *tesoro mio*, why aren't you still in bed?' She reached up, twining coaxing arms round his neck to draw him down to her, but he swiftly detached the clinging hands and stepped back.

'Vittoria, you have to go, and quickly too.'

She pouted charmingly. 'But how ungallant of you, *caro*. I told you, Fabrizio is visiting his witch of a mother, and will not be back until this evening at the earliest. So we have all the time in the world.'

'An enchanting thought,' Alessio said levelly. 'But, sadly, there is no time to pursue it.'

She stretched voluptuously, her smile widening. 'But how can I leave, *mi amore*, when I have nothing to wear? You won all my clothes at cards last night, so what am I to do? It was, after all, a debt of honour,' she added throatily.

Alessio tried to control his growing impatience. 'Consider it cancelled. I cheated.'

She hunched a shoulder. 'Then you will have to fetch my clothes for me—from the *salotto* where I took them off. Unless you wish me to win them back, during another game of cards.'

This, thought Alessio, was not the time to be sultry.

His smile was almost a snarl. 'And how, precisely, *bella mia*, will you explain your presence, also your state of undress, to my aunt Lucrezia, who counts Fabrizio's mother among her closest cronies?'

Vittoria gave a startled cry and sat up, belatedly grabbing at the sheet. '*Madonna*—you cannot mean it. Promise me she is not here?'

'Not quite, but due imminently,' Alessio warned, his tone grim.

'*Dio mio.*' Her voice was a wail. 'Alessio—do something. I must get out of here. You have to save me.'

There was another knock at the door, which opened a crack to admit Giorgio's discreet arm holding out a handful of female clothing. His voice was urgent. 'The taxi has arrived, *Eccellenza*.'

'*Un momento.*' Alessio strode over and took the clothes, tossing them deftly to Vittoria who was already running frantically to the bathroom, her nakedness suddenly ungainly.

He paused, watching her disappear, then gave a mental shrug. Last night she'd been an entertaining and inventive companion, but daylight and danger had dissipated her appeal. There would be no more cards, or any other games with the beautiful Vittoria Montecorvo. In fact, he thought, frowning, it might be wiser, for the future, to avoid discontented wives altogether. The only real advantage of such affairs was not being expected to propose marriage, he told himself cynically.

He retrieved his underwear from the pile of discarded evening clothes beside the bed, then went into his dressing room, finding and shrugging on a pair of cream denim trousers and a black polo shirt. As he emerged, thrusting his bare feet into loafers, Vittoria was waiting, dressed but distraught.

'Alessio.' She hurled herself at him. 'When shall I see you again?'

The honest reply would be, 'Never,' but that would also be unkind.

'Perhaps this narrow escape is a warning to us, *cara mia*,' he returned guardedly. 'We shall have to be very careful.'

'But I am not sure I can bear it.' Her voice throbbed a little. 'Not now that we have found each other, *angelo mio*.'

Alessio suppressed a cynical smile. He knew who his predecessor had been. Was sure that his successor was already lined up. Vittoria was a rich man's beautiful daughter married to another rich man, who was all too easy to fool.

She was spoiled, predatory and bored, as, indeed, he was himself.

Maybe that had been the initial attraction between them, he thought, with an inner grimace. Like calling to like.

Suddenly he felt jaded and restless. The heat of Rome, the noise of the traffic seemed to press upon him, stifling him. He found himself thinking of windswept crags where clouds drifted. He longed to breathe the dark, earthy scents of the forests that clothed the lower slopes, and wake in the night to moonlit silence.

He needed, he thought, to distance himself.

And he could have all that, and more. After all, he was overdue for a vacation. Some re-scheduling at the bank, and he could be gone, he told himself as Vittoria pressed herself against him, murmuring seductively.

He wanted her out of the *appartamento*, too, he thought grimly, and realised he would have felt the same even if he hadn't been threatened by a visit from his aunt.

Gently but firmly, he edged her out of the bedroom, and along the wide passage to where Giorgio was waiting, his face expressionless, just as the entrance bell jangled discordantly at the other end of the flat.

'I'll get that. You take the *signora* to her cab.' Alessio freed himself from the clutching, crimson-tipped fingers, murmuring that of course he would think of her, would call her—but only if he felt it was safe.

He paused to watch her leaving, her parting glance both suspicious and disconsolate, then drew a deep breath of thanksgiving, raking the hair she'd so playfully dishevelled back from his face with impatient fingers.

The bell rang again, imperative in its summons, and Alessio knew he could hardly delay his response any longer. Sighing, he went to confront the enemy at the gates.

'Zia Lucrezia,' he greeted the tall, grey-haired woman waiting on his doorstep, her elegant shoe beating a tattoo against the stone. 'What a charming surprise.'

Her glance was minatory as she swept past him. 'Don't be a hypocrite, Alessio. It does not become you. I was not expecting to be welcome.' She paused for a moment, listening to the distant sound of a car starting up, and the rear door closing with a clang. 'Ah, so your other visitor has safely made her escape,' she added with a sour smile. 'I regret spoiling your plans for the day, nephew.'

He said gently, 'I rarely make plans, my dear aunt. I prefer to wait and see what delights the day offers.' He escorted her into the *salotto*, one swift, sweeping glance assuring him that it had been restored to its usual pristine condition. The tell-tale wine-glasses had been removed, together with the empty bottles, and the *grappa* that had followed had also been put away. As had the scattered cards from last night's impromptu session of strip poker.

And the windows to the balcony stood innocently open to admit the morning sun, and dispel any lingering traces of alcohol fumes, and Vittoria's rather heavy perfume.

Making a mental note to increase Giorgio's salary, he conducted the Signora to a sofa, and seated himself in the chair opposite.

'To what do I owe the pleasure of seeing you, Zia Lucrezia?'

She was silent for a moment, then she said curtly, 'I wish to speak to you about Paolo.'

He looked across at her in frank surprise. Giorgio's arrival with the tall silver pot of coffee, and the ensuing ritual of pouring the coffee and handing the tiny sweet biscuits, gave him a chance to gather his thoughts.

When they were alone again, he said softly, 'You amaze me, *cara Zia.* I am hardly in a position to offer advice. You have always allowed me to understand that my example to your only son is an abomination.'

'Don't pretend to be a fool,' the Signora said shortly. 'Of course, I don't want advice.' She hesitated again. 'However, I do find that I need your practical assistance in a small matter.'

Alessio swallowed some coffee. 'I hope this is not a request to transfer Paolo back to Rome. I gather he is making progress in London.'

'That,' said Paolo's mother glacially, 'is a matter of opinion. And, anyway, he is returning to Rome quite soon, to spend his vacation with me.'

Alessio's eyes narrowed slightly. 'The idea doesn't appeal to you? Yet I remember you complaining to me when we met at Princess Dorelli's reception that you didn't see him often enough.'

There was another, longer silence, then the Signora said, as if the words were being wrung out of her, 'He is not coming alone.'

Alessio shrugged. 'Well, why should he?' he countered. 'Let me remind you, dear aunt, that my cousin is no longer a boy.'

'Precisely.' The Signora poured herself more coffee. 'He is old enough, in fact, to be a husband. And let me remind *you*, Alessio, that it has always been the intention of both families that Paolo should marry Beatrice Manzone.'

Alessio's brows snapped together. 'I know there was some such plan when they were children,' he admitted slowly. 'But now—now they are adults, and—things change. People change.'

She looked back at him stonily. 'Except for you, it seems, my dear nephew. You remain—unregenerate, with your boats and your fast cars. With your gambling and your womanising.'

He said gently, '*Mea culpa*, Zia Lucrezia, but we are not here to discuss my manifold faults.' He paused. 'So, Paolo has a girl-friend. It's hardly a mortal sin, and, anyway, to my certain knowledge, she is not the first. He will probably have many more before he decides to settle down. So, what is the problem?'

'Signor Manzone is an old friend,' said the Signora. 'Naturally, he wishes his daughter's future to be settled. And soon.'

'And is this what Beatrice herself wants?'

'She and my Paolo grew up together. She has adored him all her life.'

Alessio shrugged again. 'Then maybe she'll be prepared to wait until he has finished sowing his wild oats,' he returned indifferently.

'Hmm.' The Signora's tone was icy. 'Then it is fortunate she is not waiting for you.'

'Fortunate for us both,' Alessio said gently. 'The Signorina Manzone is infinitely too sweet for my taste.'

'I am relieved to hear it. I did not know you bothered to discriminate between one foolish young woman and the next.'

As so often when he talked to his aunt, Alessio could feel his jaw clenching. He kept his voice even. 'Perhaps you should remember, *Zia*, that my father, your own brother, was far from a saint until he married my mother. Nonna Ramontella often told me she wore out her knees, praying for him.' *And for you,* he added silently.

'What a pity your grandmother is no longer here to perform the same service for you.' There was a pause, and, when she spoke again, the Signora's voice was slightly less acerbic. 'But we should not quarrel, Alessio. Your life is your own, whereas Paolo has—obligations, which he must be made to recognise. Therefore this—*relazione amorosa* of his must end, *quanta prima tanto meglio.*'

Alessio frowned again. 'But sooner may not be better for Paolo,' he pointed out. 'They may be genuinely in love. After all, this is the twenty-first century, not the fifteenth.'

The Signora waved a dismissive hand. 'The girl is completely unsuitable. Some English *sciattona* that he met in a bar in

London,' she added with distaste. 'From what I have gleaned from my fool of a son, she has neither family nor money.'

'Whereas Beatrice Manzone has both, of course,' Alessio said drily. 'Especially money.'

'That may not weigh with you,' the Signora said with angry energy. 'But it matters very much to Paolo.'

'Unless I break my neck playing polo,' Alessio drawled. 'Which would make him my heir, of course. My preoccupation with dangerous sports should please you, Zia Lucrezia. It opens up all kinds of possibilities.'

She gave him a fulminating look. 'Which we need not consider. You will, of course, remember in due course what you owe to your family, and provide yourself with a wife and family.

'As matters stand, you are the chairman of the Arleschi Bank. He is only an employee. He cannot afford to marry some pretty nobody.'

'So, she's pretty,' Alessio mused. 'But then she would have to be, if she has no money. And Paolo has Ramontella blood in his veins, so she may even be a beauty—this...?'

'Laura,' the Signora articulated coldly. 'Laura Mason.'

'Laura.' He repeated the name softly. 'The name of the girl that Petrarch saw in church and loved for the rest of his life.' He grinned at his aunt. 'I hope that isn't an omen.'

'Well,' the Signora said softly, 'I depend on you, my dear Alessio, to make certain it is not.'

'You expect me to preach to my cousin about family duty?' He laughed. 'I don't think he'd listen.'

'I wish you to do more than talk. I wish you to bring Paolo's little romance to an end.'

His brows lifted. 'And how am I supposed to do that?'

'Quite easily, *caro mio*.' She gave him a flat smile. 'You will seduce her, and make sure he knows of it.'

Alessio came out of his chair in one lithe, angry movement. 'Are you insane?'

'I am simply being practical,' his aunt returned. 'Requesting that you put your dubious talents with women to some useful purpose.'

'Useful!' He was almost choking on his rage. '*Dio mio*, how dare you insult me by suggesting such a thing? Imagine that I would be willing even for one moment...' He flung away from her. Walked to the window, gazed down into the street below with unseeing eyes, then turned back, his face inimical. 'No,' he said. 'And again—no. Never.'

'You disappoint me,' the Signora said almost blandly. 'I hoped you would regard it as—an interesting challenge.'

'On the contrary,' he said. 'I am disgusted—nauseated by such a proposal.' He took a deep breath. 'And from you of all people. You—astound me.'

She regarded him calmly. 'What exactly are your objections?'

He spread his hands in baffled fury. 'Where shall I begin? The girl is a complete stranger to me.'

'But so, at first, are all the women who share your bed.' She paused. 'For example, *mio caro*, how long have you known Vittoria Montecorvo, whose hasty departure just now I almost interrupted?'

Their eyes met, locked in a long taut, silence. Eventually, he said, 'I did not realise you took such a close interest in my personal life.'

'Under normal circumstances, I would not, I assure you. But in this instance, I need your—co-operation.'

Alessio said slowly, 'At any moment, I am going to wake up, and find this is all a bad dream.' He came back to his chair. Sat. 'I have other objections. Do you wish to hear them?'

'As you wish.'

He leaned forward, the dark face intense. 'This romance of Paolo's may just be a passing fancy. Why not let it run its course?'

'Because Federico Manzone wishes my son's engagement to Beatrice to be made official. Any more delay would displease him.'

'And would that be such a disaster?'

'Yes,' his aunt said. 'It would. I have entered into certain—accommodations with Signor Manzone, on the strict understanding that this marriage would soon be taking place. Repayment would be—highly inconvenient.'

'*Santa Maria.*' Alessio slammed a clenched fist into the palm of his other hand. Of course, he thought. He should have guessed as much.

The Signora's late husband had come from an old but relatively impoverished family, but, in spite of that, her spending habits had always been legendary. He could remember stern family conferences on the subject when he was a boy.

And age, it seemed, had not taught her discretion.

Groaning inwardly, he said, 'Then why not allow me to settle these debts for you, and let Paolo live his life?'

There was a sudden gleam of humour in her still-handsome face. 'I am not a welcome client at the bank, Alessio, so are you inviting me to become your private pensioner? Your poor father would turn in his grave. Besides, the lawyers would never allow it. And Federico has assured me very discreetly that, once our families are joined, he will make permanent arrangements for me. He is all generosity.'

'Then why not change the plan?' Alessio said with sudden inspiration. 'You're a widow. He's a widower. Why don't you marry him yourself, and let the next generation find their own way to happiness?'

'As you yourself are doing?' The acid was back. 'Perhaps we could have a double wedding, *mio caro*. I am sure honour will demand you ask the lovely Vittoria to be your wife, when her husband divorces her for adultery. After all, it will make a hideous scandal.'

Their glances met again and clashed, steel against steel.

He said steadily, 'I was not aware that Fabrizio had any such plans for Vittoria.'

'Not yet, certainly,' the Signora said silkily. 'But if he or my good friend Camilla, his mother, should discover in some unfortunate way that you have planted horns on him, then that might change.'

Eventually, Alessio sighed, lifting a shoulder in a resigned shrug. 'I have seriously underestimated you, Zia Lucrezia. I did not realise how totally unscrupulous you could be.'

'A family trait,' said the Signora. 'But desperate situations call for desperate measures.'

'But, you must still consider this,' Alessio went on. 'Even if his affair with the English girl is terminated, there is no guarantee that Paolo will marry Beatrice. He may still choose to look elsewhere. He might even find another rich girl. How will you prevent that?' He gave her a thin smile. 'Or have you some scheme to blackmail him into co-operation too?'

'You speak as if he has never cared for Beatrice.' His aunt spoke calmly. 'This is not true. And, once his disillusion with his English fancy is complete, I know he will realise where his best interests lie, and turn to her again. And they will be happy together. I am sure of it.'

Alessio sent her a look of pure exasperation. 'How simple you make it sound. You pull the strings, and the puppets dance. But there are still things you have not taken into account. For one thing, how will I meet this girl?'

'I have thought of that. I shall tell Paolo that I have workmen at my house in Tuscany putting in a new heating system, so cannot receive guests. Instead, I have accepted a kind invitation from you for us all to stay at the Villa Diana.'

He snorted. 'And he will believe you?'

She shrugged. 'He has no choice. And I shall make sure you have the opportunity to be alone with the girl. The rest is up to you.' She paused. 'You may not even be called on to make the ultimate sacrifice, *caro*. It might be enough for Paolo to discover you kissing her.'

He said patiently, 'Zia Lucrezia, has it occurred to you that this—Laura—may be truly in love with Paolo, and nothing will persuade her to even a marginal betrayal?'

He paused, his mouth twisting. 'Besides, and more importantly, you have overlooked the fact that she may not find me attractive.'

'*Caro* Alessio,' the Signora purred. 'Let us have no false modesty. It has been often said that if you had smiled at Juliet, she would have left Romeo. Like your other deluded victims, Laura will find you irresistible.'

'*Davvero?*' Alessio asked ironically. 'I hope she slaps my face.' He looked down at his hand, studying the crest on the signet ring he wore. 'And afterwards—if I succeed in this contemptible ploy? I would not blame Paolo if he refused to speak to me again.'

'At first, perhaps, he may be resentful. But in time, he will thank you.' She rose. 'They will be arriving next week. I hope this will not be a problem for you?'

He got to his feet too, his mouth curling. He walked over to her, took her hand and bowed over it. 'I shall count the hours.'

'Sarcasm, *mio caro*, does not become you.' She studied him for a moment. 'Like your father, Alessio, you are formidable when you are angry.' She patted his cheek. 'I hope you're in a better mood when you finally encounter this English girl, or I shall almost feel sorry for her.'

He gave her a hard, unsmiling look. 'Don't concern yourself for her, Zia Lucrezia. I will do my best to send her home with a beautiful memory.'

'Ah,' she said. 'Now I really do feel sorry for her.' And was gone.

Alone, Alessio went to a side table, and poured himself a whisky. He rarely drank in the daytime, but this was like no other day since the beginning of the world.

What the devil was Paolo thinking of—bringing his little *ragazza* within a hundred miles of his mother? If he gave a damn about her, he would keep them well apart.

And if I had an atom of decency, Alessio thought grimly, I would call him, and say so.

But he couldn't risk it. Zia Lucrezia had more than her full share of the Ramontella ruthlessness, as he should have remembered, and would not hesitate to carry out her veiled threat about his ill-advised interlude with Vittoria. And the fall-out would, as she'd predicted, be both unpleasant and spectacular.

Laura, he repeated to himself meditatively. Well, at least she had a charming name. If she had a body to match, then his task might not seem so impossible.

He raised his glass. '*Salute*, Laura,' he said with cynical emphasis. '*E buona fortuna.*' He added softly, 'I think you will need it.'

CHAPTER TWO

'WELL, it all sounds iffy to me,' said Gaynor. 'Think about it. You've cancelled your South of France holiday with Steve because you didn't like the sleeping arrangements, yet now you're off to Italy with someone you hardly know. It doesn't make any sense.'

Laura sighed. 'Not when you put it like that, certainly. But it truly isn't what you think. I'm getting a free trip to Tuscany for two weeks, plus a cash bonus, and all I have to do is look as if I'm madly in love.'

'It can't be that simple,' Gaynor said darkly. 'Nothing ever is. I mean, have you ever *been* madly in love? You certainly weren't with Steve or you wouldn't have quibbled about sharing a room with him,' she added candidly.

Laura flushed. 'I suppose I thought I was—or that I might be, given time. After all, we've only been seeing each other for two months. Hardly a basis for that kind of commitment.'

'Well, not everyone would agree with you there,' Gaynor said drily.

'I know.' Laura paused in her packing to sigh again. 'I'm a freak—a throwback. I admit it. But if and when I have sex with a man, I want it to be based on love and respect, and a shared future. Not because double rooms are cheaper than singles.'

'And what kind of room is this Paolo Vicente offering?'

'All very respectable,' Laura assured her, tucking her only swimsuit into a corner of her case. 'We'll be staying with his mother at her country house, and she's a total dragon, it seems. Paolo says she'll probably lock me in at night.'

'And she has no idea that you're practically strangers?'

'No, that's the whole point. She's pushing him hard to get engaged to a girl he's known all his life, and he won't. He says

18

she's more like his younger sister than a future wife, and that I'm going to be his declaration of independence. A way of telling his mother that he's his own man, and quite capable of picking a bride for himself.'

'Isn't that like showing a red rag to a bull? Do you *want* to be caught in the middle of two warring factions?'

'I won't be. Paolo says, at worst, she'll treat me with icy politeness. And he's promised I won't see that much of her—that he'll take me out and about as much as possible.' Laura paused. 'It could even be fun,' she added doubtfully.

'Ever the optimist,' muttered Gaynor. 'How the hell did you ever become part of this gruesome twosome?'

Laura sighed again. 'He works for the Arleschi Bank. We pitched for their PR work a few weeks ago, and Carl took me along to the presentation. Paolo was there. Then, a fortnight ago, he came into the wine bar, and we recognised each other.' She wrinkled her nose. 'I'd just split with Steve, so I was feeling down, and Paolo was clearly fed up too. He stayed on after closing time, and we had a drink together, and started talking.

'He wanted to know why I was moonlighting in a wine bar when I was working for Harman Grace, so I told him about Mum being a widow, and Toby winning that scholarship to public school, but always needing extra stuff for school, plus this field trip in October.

'Then Paolo got very bitter about his mother, and the way she was trying to tie him down with this Beatrice. And, somehow, over a few glasses of wine, the whole scheme evolved.'

She shook her head. 'At first, I thought it was just the wine talking, but when he came back the following night to hammer out the details I discovered he was deadly serious. I also realised that the extra cash he was offering would pay for Toby's field trip, and compensate Steve for the extra hotel charges he's been emailing me about incessantly.'

'Charming,' said Gaynor.

Laura pulled a face. 'Well, I did let him down over the holiday, so I suppose he's entitled to feel sore.

'However, when push came to shove, I honestly couldn't afford to turn Paolo down.' She sounded faintly dispirited, then rallied. 'And, anyway, I've always wanted to go to Italy. Also it may be my last chance of a proper holiday, before I seriously start saving towards the Flat Fund.'

'I've already begun.' Gaynor gave a disparaging glance around the cramped bedsit, a mirror-image of her own across the landing. 'There's an ugly rumour that Ma Hughes is all set to raise the rents again. If we don't find our own place soon, we won't be able to afford to move out. And Rachel from work is definitely interested in joining us,' she added buoyantly. 'Apparently, living at home is driving her crazy.'

She got up from the bed, collecting up their used coffee-cups. On her way to the communal kitchenette, she paused at the door. 'Honey, you are sure you can trust this Paolo? He won't suddenly develop wandering hands when you're on your own with him?'

Laura laughed. 'I'm sure he won't. He likes voluptuous brunettes, so I'm really not his type, and he certainly isn't mine,' she added decisively. 'Although I admit he's good-looking. Besides, I have his mother as chaperon, don't forget. And he tells me she strongly disapproves of open displays of affection, so all I really have to do is flutter my eyelashes occasionally.'

Laura gave a brisk nod. 'No, this is basically a business arrangement, and that's fine with me.'

Her smile widened. 'And I get to see Tuscany at last. Who could ask for more?'

But as the plane began its descent towards Rome's Leonardo da Vinci Airport she did not feel quite so euphoric about the situation, although she could not have fully explained why.

She had met up with Paolo the previous night to talk over final details for the trip.

'If we're dating each other, then you need to know something about me, *cara*, and my family,' he explained with perfect reason.

She'd already gathered that he occupied a fairly junior position at the bank's London branch. What she hadn't expected to hear was that he was related to the Italian aristocrat who was the Arleschi chairman.

'We are the poor side of the family,' he explained. He was smiling, but there was a touch of something like peevishness in his voice. 'Which is why my mother is so eager for me to marry Beatrice, of course. Her father is a very wealthy man, and she is his only child.'

'Of course,' Laura echoed. Who are these people? she wondered in frank amazement. And just what planet do they inhabit?

She thought of her mother struggling to make ends meet. Of herself, spending long evenings in the wine bar so that she could help towards her shy, clever brother having the marvellous education he deserved.

When Paolo used the term 'poor' so airily, he had no idea what it really meant.

Her throat tightened. She'd treated herself to some new clothes for the abortive French holiday, but they were all chain-store bought, with not a designer label among them.

She was going to stick out like the proverbial sore thumb in this exclusive little world she was about to join, however briefly. So, could she really make anyone believe that she and Paolo were seriously involved?

But perhaps this was precisely why he had chosen her, she thought unhappily. Because she was so screamingly unsuitable. Maybe this would provide exactly the leverage Paolo needed to escape from this enforced marriage.

'Anyone,' his mother might say, throwing up her hands in horrified surrender. 'Anyone but her!'

Well, she could live with that, because Paolo, in spite of his smoothly handsome looks and august connections, held no appeal for her. In fact, Laura decided critically, she wouldn't have him if he came served on toast with a garnish.

He was arrogant, she thought, and altogether too pleased with himself, and, although no one should be forced to marry someone they didn't love, on balance her sympathies lay with his would-be fiancée.

'I must insist on one thing,' she said. 'No mention of Harman Grace.'

'As you wish.' He shrugged. 'But why? They are a good company. You have nothing to be ashamed of by working for them.'

'I know that. But we're now the bank's official PR company in London. Your cousin must know that, and he'll recognise the name if it's mentioned. He may not appreciate the fact that you're supposedly dating someone who's almost an employee.'

'Don't disturb yourself, *cara*. I am nothing more than an employee myself. Besides, the chances of your meeting my cousin Alessio are slim. But Harman Grace shall remain a secret between us, if that's what you want.'

'Yes,' she said. 'I really do. Thank you.'

She was astonished to find that they were flying first class, proving that poverty was only relative, she thought grimly, declining the champagne she was automatically offered.

A couple of glasses of wine had got her into this mess. So, from now on she intended to keep a cool head.

She was also faintly disconcerted by Paolo's attempts to flirt with her. He kept bending towards her, his voice low and almost intimate as he spoke. And she didn't like his persistent touching either—her hair, her shoulder, the sleeve of her linen jacket.

Oh, God, she thought uneasily. Don't tell me Gaynor was right about him all along.

She was aware, with embarrassment, that the cabin staff were watching them, exchanging knowing looks.

'What are you doing?' she muttered, pulling her hand away as he tried to kiss each of her fingers.

He shrugged, not in the least discomposed. 'For every performance, there must be a rehearsal, no?'

'Definitely no,' Laura said tartly.

She was also disappointed to hear there'd been a slight change of plan. That instead of hiring a car at the airport and driving straight to Tuscany, they were first to join the Signora Vicente at her Rome apartment.

'But for how long?' she queried.

Paolo was unconcerned. 'Does it matter? It will give you a

chance to see *my* city before we bury ourselves in the country-side,' he told her. He gave a satisfied smile. 'Also, my mother employs a driver and a car for her journeys, so we shall travel in comfort.'

Laura felt she had no option but to force a smile of agreement. It's his trip, she thought resignedly. I'm just the hired help.

The Signora's residence was in the Aventine district, which Paolo told her was one of the city's more peaceful locations with many gardens and trees.

She occupied the first floor of a grand mansion, standing in its own grounds, and Laura took a deep, calming breath as they mounted the wide flight of marble stairs.

You've got your passport in your bag, she reminded herself silently. Also, your return ticket. All you have to do, if you really can't hack this, is turn and run.

When they reached the imposing double doors, Paolo rang the bell, and Laura swallowed as he took her hand in his with a reassuring nod.

It's only a couple of weeks, she thought. Not the rest of my life.

The door was opened by a plump elderly maid, who beamed at Paolo, ignoring Laura completely, then burst into a flood of incomprehensible Italian.

Laura found herself in a windowless hall, its only illumination coming from a central chandelier apparently equipped with low-wattage bulbs. The floor was tiled in dark marble, and a few pieces of heavy antique furniture and some oil paintings in ornate frames did little to lighten the atmosphere.

Then the maid flung open the door to the *salotto*, and sunlight struggled out, accompanied by a small hairy dog, yapping furi-ously and snarling round their ankles.

'Quiet, Caio,' Paolo ordered, and the dog backed off, although it continued its high-pitched barking, and growling. Laura liked dogs, and usually got on with them, but something told her that Caio was more likely to take a chunk out of her ankle than respond to any overtures she might make.

Paolo led her into the room. 'Call off your hound, *Mamma*,' he said. 'Or my Laura will think she is not welcome.'

'But I am always ready to receive your friends, *figlio mio*.' The Signora rose from a brocaded sofa, and offered her hand.

She was a tall woman, Laura saw, and had been handsome once rather than a beauty. But time had thinned her face and narrowed her mouth, and this, together with her piercing dark eyes, made her formidable. She wore black, and there were pearls round her neck, and in her ears.

'Signorina Mason, is it not so?' Her smile was vinegary as she absorbed Laura's shy response. 'You would like some tea, I think. Is that not the English habit?'

Laura lifted her chin. 'Now that I'm here, *signora*, perhaps I should learn a few Italian customs instead.'

The elegantly plucked brows lifted. 'You will hardly be here long enough to make it worthwhile, *signorina*—but as you wish.' She rang a bell for the maid, ordered coffee and cakes, then beckoned Paolo to join her on the sofa.

This, thought Laura, taking the seat opposite that she'd been waved towards, is going to be uphill all the way. And she was still inwardly flinching from 'my Laura'.

It was a beautiful room, high-ceilinged and well proportioned, but massively over-furnished for her taste. There were too many groups of hard-looking chairs, she thought, taking a covert glance around. And far too many spindly-legged tables crowded with knick-knacks. The windows were huge, and she longed to drag open the tall shutters that half-masked them and let in some proper light. But she supposed that would fade the draperies, and the expensive rugs on the parquet floor.

'I have some news for you, *mio caro*,' the Signora announced, after the maid had served coffee and some tiny, but frantically rich chocolate cakes. 'And also for the *signorina*, your companion. I regret that I cannot after all entertain you at my country home. It is occupied by workmen—so tedious, but unavoidable.'

Laura froze, her cup halfway to her lips. Were they going to spend the whole two weeks in this apartment? Oh, God, she thought, surely not. It might seem spacious enough, but she suspected that even a few days with the Signora would make it seem totally claustrophobic.

Paolo was looking less than pleased. 'But you knew we were coming, *Mamma*. And I promised Laura that she should see Tuscany.'

'Another time, perhaps,' the Signora said smoothly. 'This time she will have to be content with a corner of Umbria.' Her expression was bland. 'Your cousin Alessio has offered us the use of the Villa Diana at Besavoro.'

There was an astonished pause, then Paolo said slowly, 'Why should he do that?'

'*Mio caro.*' The Signora's voice held a hint of reproof. 'We are members of his family. His only living relatives.'

Paolo shrugged. 'Even so, it is not like him to be so obliging,' he countered. 'And, anyway, Besavoro is at the end of the world.' He spread his hands. 'Also, the Villa Diana is halfway up a mountain on the way to nowhere. It is hardly an adequate substitute.'

'I think Signorina Mason will find it charming.' Again the smile that did not reach her eyes. 'And not overrun by her own countrymen.' She turned to Laura. 'I understand that Tuscany has come to be known as Chiantishire. So amusing.'

'Has it?' Laura enquired with wooden untruthfulness. 'I didn't know.' Dear God, she thought. I'm going to be staying at a house owned by the chairman of the Arleschi Bank. This can't be happening.

'And Umbria is very beautiful,' the Signora continued. 'They call it the green heart of Italy, and there are many places to visit—Assisi—Perugia—San Sepulcro, the birthplace of the great Rafael. You will be spoiled for choice, *signorina*.'

Paolo cast a glance at the decorated ceiling. 'You call it a choice, *Mamma*?' he demanded. 'To risk our lives up and down that deathtrap of a road every time we want to go anywhere?'

He shook his head. 'If anything happens to my cousin Alessio, and I inherit, then the Villa Diana will be for sale the next day.'

There was another lengthier pause. Then: 'You must forgive my son, *signorina*,' the Signora said silkily. 'In the heat of the moment, he does not always speak with wisdom. And, even if it is a little remote, the house is charming.'

'And Alessio?' Paolo demanded petulantly, clearly resenting the rebuke. 'At least he can't mean to use the house himself, if we are there. Or he never has in the past.' He snorted. 'Probably off chasing some skirt.'

'Dear boy, the offer was made, and I was glad to accept. I did not enquire into his own plans.'

Laura had been listening with a kind of horrified fascination. She thought, I should not be hearing this.

Aloud, she said quietly, 'Paolo—isn't there somewhere else we could stay? A hotel, perhaps.'

'In the height of the tourist season?' Paolo returned derisively. 'We would be fortunate to find a cellar. No, it will have to be my cousin's villa. And at least it will be cooler in the hills,' he added moodily. 'When do we leave?'

'I thought tomorrow,' said the Signora. She rose. 'You must be tired after the flight, Signorina Mason. I shall ask Maria to show you your room so that you may rest a little.'

And so you can give your son your unvarnished opinion of his latest acquisition, thought Laura. But then this was only what she'd been led to expect, she reminded herself. She supposed she should be grateful that the Signora hadn't made a hysterical scene and ordered her out of the apartment.

The bedroom allocated to her was on the small side, and the bed was narrow, and not particularly comfortable. She had been shown the bathroom—a daunting affair in marble the colour of rare beef, but she was glad to find that the still-unsmiling Maria had supplied a jug of hot water and a matching basin for the washstand in her room.

She took off her shoes and dress, and had a refreshing wash. The soap was scented with lavender, and she thought with faint self-derision that it was the first friendly thing she'd discovered so far in Rome.

She dried herself with the rather harsh linen towel, then stretched out on top of the bed with a sigh.

The regrets she'd experienced on the plane were multiplying

with every moment that passed. Back in London, Paolo had persuaded her that it would be easy. A spot of acting performed against a backdrop of some of Europe's most beautiful scenery. Almost a game, he'd argued. And she'd be paid for it.

Well, she was fast coming to the conclusion that no amount of cash was worth the hassle that the next two weeks seemed to promise. Although most of her concerns about Paolo's future behaviour were largely laid to rest. The Signora, she thought with wry amusement, would prove a more than adequate chaperon. And if she had been in love with him, she'd have been faced with a frustrating time.

Her head was beginning to ache, and she reached down to her bag by the side of the bed for the small pack of painkillers she'd included at the last minute, and the bottle of mineral water she'd bought at the airport. It was lukewarm now, but better than nothing, she thought as she swallowed a couple of the tablets, then turned onto her side, resolutely closing her eyes.

The deed was done. She was in Italy, even if it wasn't turning out to be a dream come true.

Whatever, she thought wearily. There was no turning back now.

Dinner that night was not an easy occasion. Paolo had announced plans to take Laura out for a meal, but the Signora had pointed out with steely insistence that this would be unwise, as they would be making an early start in the morning to avoid travelling in the full heat of the day.

So they ate in the formal dining room, at a table that would have accommodated three times their number with room to spare. It did not make for a relaxed atmosphere, and conversation was so stilted that Laura wished Paolo and his mother would just speak Italian to each other, and leave her out of the situation.

She realised, of course, that she was being grilled. Remembered too that she and Paolo had agreed to keep her actual personal details to a minimum. As far as the Signora was concerned, she was a girl who shared a flat with several others, and who enjoyed a good time. Someone, she hinted with a touch of coyness, who had not allowed for the sudden entry of Mr Right into her life. And she sent Paolo a languishing look.

And whatever slights and unpleasantness might come her way, Laura knew she would always treasure the memory of the expression on the august lady's face as she absorbed that.

She had rehearsed the invented story of how and when she and Paolo had met so often that she was word-perfect. After all, she needed to give the impression that theirs was an established relationship of at least two months' standing, which deserved to be taken seriously, and might be ready to move on to the next stage.

For Steve, she thought with wry regret, substitute Paolo.

She even managed to turn some of the Signora's more probing queries into her background back on themselves by ingenuously asking what Paolo had been like as a small boy, and whether there were any childhood photographs of him that she could see.

She had to admit the food was delicious, although she'd had little appetite for it. And when dinner was over they returned to the *salotto*, and listened to music by Monteverdi.

And that, thought Laura, was by far the most pleasant part of the evening, not just because her late father had loved the same composer, but because conversation was kept to a minimum.

She was just beginning to relax when the Signora announced in a tone that did not welcome opposition that it was time to retire for the night.

Paolo wished her a very correct goodnight outside the *salotto*, but when Laura, dressing-gown clad, returned from the bathroom, she found him waiting in her room.

She checked uneasily. 'What are you doing here?'

'I wished to speak to you in private.' The grin he sent her was triumphant. 'You are completely brilliant, *carissima*. *Dio mio*, you almost convinced me. And *Mamma* is in such a fury.' He shook his head. 'I have just overheard her on the telephone, and she was *incandescente*. She must be speaking to her old friend Camilla Montecorvo, because she mentioned the name Vittoria several times.'

'Does that mean something?' Laura felt suddenly tired, and more than a little bewildered.

'Vittoria is the *nuora*—the daughter-in-law—of Signora Montecorvo,' Paolo explained, his grin widening. 'She causes big problems, and *Mamma* has heard all about them. Always, she has been the one to give advice to Camilla. But now it is her turn to complain,' he added gleefully. 'And she insists that her friend must listen, and help her.'

He almost hugged himself. 'It is all going as I hoped.'

'I wish I could say the same.' Laura bit her lip.

'You are regretting Tuscany?' Paolo shrugged. 'It was an unwelcome surprise for me also. And Alessio has other houses he could have lent *Mamma* that are not as remote as Besavoro,' he added, grimacing. 'For instance, he has a place near Sorrento where he keeps his boat, but no doubt he will be using that himself. He would not choose to stay anywhere near *Mamma*, so calm yourself on that point.'

'You're not a very close family,' Laura commented.

'Alessio likes to go his own way. *Mamma* tries to interfere.' He shrugged again. 'Maybe he is hoping she will stray too far from the house, and be eaten by the wolves.'

Laura stared at him. 'You mean there are such things..actually running wild?' Her tone held a hollow note.

'Yes, and they are on the increase. And there are bears too.' He laughed at her expression. 'But they are mainly found in the national parks, and I promise you that they prefer orchards and beehives to humans.'

'How—reassuring.' Laura took a deep breath. 'But it's not just disappointment over Tuscany, Paolo. Or the thought of moving to some Italian safari park either.'

She gave him a steady look. 'We shouldn't have started this. If your mother's so genuinely upset, it isn't a game any longer. I feel we should rethink.'

'For me, it has never been a game.' Paolo smote himself on the chest. 'For me—it is my life! I need my mother to know that my future is my own affair, and that I will not be dictated to by her or anyone. And that I am not going to marry Beatrice

Manzone.' He lowered his voice. Made it coaxing. 'Laura—you promised you would help me. We have an agreement together. And it is going well. Just two weeks—that is all. Then you will be free. You will have had your Italian vacation, and also been paid. This is so easy for you.'

He dropped a hand on her shoulder, making her move restively. 'After all,' he went on persuasively, 'what can possibly happen in two short weeks? Tell me that.' He smiled at her, then moved to the door. 'I tell you there is nothing to worry about.' His voice was warm—reassuring. 'Nothing in the world.'

CHAPTER THREE

LAURA did not sleep well that night. She was constantly tossing and turning, disturbed by a series of fleeting, uneasy dreams. Or, she wondered as daylight imposed itself at last, was she simply troubled by finding herself under the roof of a woman who cordially detested her—and with no reprieve in sight?

It was no particular surprise to find that the early start to Besavoro did not transpire. The car arrived punctually with Giacomo, its uniformed chauffeur, and there the matter rested while the Signora, after a leisurely breakfast, issued a stream of contradictory orders, made telephone calls, and wrote a number of last minute notes to friends.

Laura had discovered to her dismay that Caio was to accompany them and more time was wasted while Maria hunted the apartment for the special collar and lead he wore on holiday, and the new cushioned basket specially bought for the trip.

By the time the luggage was finally put in the car, Paolo looked as if he was about to become a basket case himself, Laura thought without particular sympathy.

It was one of the most luxurious vehicles she'd ever travelled in, but, seated in the back with the Signora and her dog in the opposite corner, she found it impossible to relax.

She'd expected another barrage of questions, and steeled herself to fend them off, but it didn't happen. The Signora seemed lost in thought, and, apart from lifting his lip in the occasional silent snarl if Laura glanced at him, Caio seemed equally detached.

There were numerous stops along the way—comfort breaks for Caio featuring frequently. But there were also pauses to buy coffee, chilled mineral water, and, once, some excellent rolls crammed with ham and cheese, at the busy roadside service stations. The Signora did not deign to leave the car on these occasions, but Laura was glad to stretch her legs in spite of the heat outside the air-conditioned car.

Her back was beginning to ache with the tension of trying to remain unobtrusive, she realised wryly.

She'd chosen her thinnest outfit for the journey—a loose-fitting dress in fine cream cotton with cap sleeves and a modestly square neckline. She wore low-heeled tan sandals, and a broad brimmed linen hat that could be rolled up in her bag when she was in the car. Apart from the obligatory sunblock, she'd put nothing on her face but a shading of mascara on her lashes, and a touch of light coral lustre to her mouth.

She tried to comfort herself with the reflection that the Signora might loathe her, but she couldn't truthfully complain about her appearance. Still it seemed small consolation.

The car didn't really need air conditioning, she thought ruefully. Paolo's mother could have lowered the temperature to arctic proportions with one look. And the cost of her brother's school trip was rising by the minute. He'd better enjoy it, that's all, she muttered under her breath.

But as they drove into Umbria she found herself succumbing to the sheer beauty of the scenery around her, all other considerations taking second place. Everywhere she looked seemed to be composed of endless shades of green, and every hilltop seemed crowned with its own little town, clinging precariously to its rocky crag.

Half an hour later they reached Besavoro, which seemed to be hardly more than a large village on the bank of a river, which Paolo told her was a tributary of the Tiber. The central point was the square, where houses and shops huddled round a tall, ornate church. There was a market taking place, and the cramped space had to be negotiated with care.

Once free of the village, they began to climb quite steeply, taking a narrow road up the side of the valley. They passed the occasional house, but generally it was rugged terrain with a steep rocky incline leading up to heavy woodland on one side, and, on the other, protected only by a low wall, a stomach-churning drop down to the clustering roofs, and the river, now reduced to a silver thread, below them.

She remembered Paolo's comment about a death trap, and suppressed a shiver, thankful that Giacomo was such a good driver.

'We are nearly there, *signorina*.' To her surprise, Laura found herself being addressed by the Signora. The older woman was even smiling faintly. 'No doubt you are eager to see where you will be spending your little vacation. I hope it lives up to your expectations.'

Any overture, however slight, was welcome, and Laura responded. 'Has the house been in the family long?' she enquired politely.

'For generations, although it has been altered and extended over the years. At one time, it is said to have been a hermitage, a solitary place where monks who had sinned were sent to do penance.'

'I know how they feel,' Paolo commented over his shoulder. 'I am astonished that Alessio should waste even an hour in such a place. He has certainly never repented of anything in his life.'

His mother shrugged. 'He spent much of his childhood here. Perhaps it has happy memories for him.'

'He was never a child,' said Paolo. 'And his past is what happened yesterday—no more.' He leaned forward. 'Look, Laura *mia*. You can see the house now, if you look down a little through the trees.'

She caught a glimpse of pale rose stonework, and faded terracotta tiles, and caught her breath in sudden magic.

It was like an enchanted place, sleeping among the trees, she thought, and she was coming to break the spell. And she smiled to herself, knowing she was being utterly absurd.

Impossible to miss the sound of an approaching car in the clear air, Alessio thought. His unwanted guests were arriving.

Sighing irritably, he swung himself off the sun lounger, and reached for the elderly pair of white tennis shorts lying on the marble tiles beside him, reluctantly dragging them on. For the past few days, he'd revelled in freedom and isolation. Basked in his ability to swim in the pool and sunbathe beside it naked, knowing that Guillermo and Emilia who ran the villa for him would never intrude on his privacy.

Now his solitude had ended.

He thrust his feet into battered espadrilles, and began walking up through the terraced gardens to the house.

Up to the last minute, he'd prayed that this nightmare would never happen. That Paolo and his *ragazza* would quarrel, or that Zia Lucrezia would love her as a daughter on sight, and withdraw her objections. Anything—anything that would let him off this terrible hook.

But her phone call the previous night had destroyed any such hopes. She'd been almost hysterical, he remembered with distaste, railing that the girl was nothing more than a gold-digging tart, coarse and obvious, a woman of the lowest class. But clever in a crude way because she obviously intended to trap into marriage her poor Paolo, who did not realise the danger he was in.

At the same time, she'd made it very clear that her threat to expose his fleeting affair with Vittoria, if he did not keep his word, was all too real.

'I want the English girl destroyed,' she had hissed at him. 'Nothing less will do.'

Alessio had been tempted to reply that he would prefer to destroy Vittoria, who was proving embarrassingly tenacious, bombarding him with phone calls and little notes, apparently unaware that her voluptuously passionate body in no way compensated for her nuisance value.

If she continued to behave with such indiscretion, Fabrizio and his mother might well smell a rat, without any intervention from Zia Lucrezia, he told himself grimly.

He'd been thankful to escape from Rome, and Vittoria's constant badgering, to this private hideaway where he could remain *incomunicabile*. He hoped that, during his absence, she would find some other willing target for her libido, or he might ultimately have to be brutal with her. A thought that gave him no pleasure whatsoever.

And now he was faced with another, worse calamity. This

unknown, unwanted girl that he had somehow to entice from Paolo's bed into his own. Probably, he decided, after he'd deliberately made himself very, very drunk...

If I emerge alive from this mess, I shall take a vow of celibacy, he thought moodily.

Guillermo was already opening the heavy wooden entrance door, and Emilia was hovering anxiously. He knew that his instructions would have been minutely carried out, and that the arrangements and the food would be perfect. But visitors at the villa were still a rarity, and the servants were more accustomed to their employer's own brand of casual relaxation. Zia Lucrezia's presence would prove taxing for all of them.

He stepped out of the shadowy hall into the sunlight. The car had halted a few feet away, and the chauffeur was helping the Signora to alight, while Caio yapped crossly from her arms.

But Alessio's attention was immediately on the girl, standing quietly, a little apart, looking up at the house. His first reaction was that she was not his type—or Paolo's, for that matter, and he found this faintly bewildering. In fact she fitted none of the preconceived images his aunt's fulminations had engendered, he thought critically as he observed her. Nearly as tall as Paolo himself, with clear, pale skin, a cloud of russet hair reaching to her shoulders, eyes like smoke, and a sweet, blunt-cornered mouth.

Not a conventional beauty—but curiously beguiling all the same.

Probably too slim, he mused, although the cheap dress she was wearing was singularly unrevealing.

And then, as if in answer to some silent wish, a faint breeze from the hills behind them blew the thin material back against her body, moulding it against the small, high breasts, the slight concavity of her stomach, the faintly rounded thighs, and long, slender legs.

Alessio, astonished, felt the breath catch suddenly in his throat, and, in spite of himself, he found his body stirring with frank and unexpected anticipation.

I've changed my mind, he thought in instant self-mockery. I

shan't get drunk after all. On the contrary, I think this *ragazza* deserves nothing less than my complete and sober attention.

He became aware that the Signora was approaching, her eyes studying him with disfavour.

'Is this how you dress to receive your visitors, Alessio?'

He took her hand, bowing over it. His smile glinted coldly at her. 'Ten minutes ago, Zia Lucrezia, I was not dressed at all. This is a concession.' He eyed Caio grimly. 'And you have brought your dog, I see. I hope he has learned better manners since our last encounter.' He looked past her to his cousin. 'Ah, Paolo, *come stai*?'

Paolo stared at him suspiciously. 'What are you doing here?'

Alessio gave him a look of mild surprise. 'It is my house, which makes me your host. Naturally, I wish to be here to attend to your comfort.'

'You are not usually so concerned,' Paolo muttered.

Alessio grinned at him. 'No? Then perhaps I have seen the error of my ways. And the house has enough rooms for us all. You will not be required to share with me, cousin,' he added blandly, then looked at the girl as if he had just noticed her. 'And the name of your charming companion?' Deliberately, he kept his voice polite rather than enthusiastic, noting the nervousness in the grey eyes under their dark fringe of lashes.

Paolo took her hand defensively. 'This is Signorina Laura Mason, who has come with me from London. Laura, may I present my cousin, the Count Alessio Ramontella.'

He saw that she did not meet his gaze, but looked down instead at the flagstoned courtyard. 'How do you do, *signore*?' Her voice was quiet and clear.

'Allow me to welcome you to my home, *signorina*.' He inclined his head with formal courtesy, then led the way into the house. 'Emilia, please show the ladies where they are to sleep. And the dog. Guillermo, will you take my cousin to his room?'

As he was turning away Paolo grabbed his arm. 'What is this?' he hissed. 'Where are you putting Laura?'

'In the room next to your mother's—at her request.' Alessio shrugged. 'I am sorry if you are disappointed, but you also know that she would never permit you to sleep with your girlfriend under any roof that she was sharing. Besides, if you even approach that part of the house, that little hairy rat of your *mamma's* will hear and start yapping.' His grin was laced with faint malice. 'Like the old monks, you will have to practise chastity.'

'A lesson you have yet to learn,' Paolo returned sourly.

'In general, perhaps, but I have never brought a woman here,' Alessio told him softly.

'Talking of which,' Paolo said, 'what do you think of my little English *inamorata*?'

'Do you need my opinion?' Alessio gave him a steady look. 'If she satisfies you, cousin, that should be enough.' He paused. 'Although usually you like them with more...' He demonstrated with his hands.

'*Sì*,' Paolo agreed lasciviously. 'But this girl has—hidden depths, if you take my meaning.' And he laughed.

It occurred to Alessio that he had never particularly liked his cousin, and at this moment it would give him great pleasure to smack him in the mouth.

Instead he invited him to make himself at home, and went off to his own room to shower and change.

Laura felt dazed as she followed Emilia and the Signora along a series of passages. The Villa Diana was a single-storey building, and it seemed to ramble on forever in a leisurely way. But she was in no mood to take real stock of her surroundings. Not yet.

That, she thought with disbelief, *that* was the Count Ramontella, the august head of the Arleschi Bank? That half-naked individual with the unruly mane of curling black hair, and the five o'clock shadow?

She'd assumed, when she first saw him, that he must be the caretaker, or the gardener.

She'd expected an older, staider version of Paolo, conventionally good-looking with a figure that would incline to plumpness in middle age. But the Count was fully six feet tall, with a lean, muscular golden-skinned body that she'd had every opportunity to admire. The shorts he'd been wearing, slung low on his narrow hips, just erred on the right side of decency, she thought, her face warming slightly at the recollection.

And he was nowhere near middle life—hardly more than in his early thirties, if she was any judge. Not, she supposed, that she was.

As for the rest of him—well, his face was more striking than handsome, with a high-bridged beak of a nose, a frankly cynical mouth, and eyes as dark as midnight that looked at the world with bored indifference from under their heavy lids. Or at least, she amended, that was the way he'd looked at her.

And he wasn't his aunt's greatest admirer either, as Paolo had suggested. She hadn't understood their brief exchange, but she'd detected a certain amount of snip, all the same.

But, if that was how he felt about his visitors, why was he here, when he wasn't expected and it was clear that he had better places to go? It seemed to make no sense.

Whatever, she could not imagine him being pleased to find he was entertaining a very minor cog from his London branch's PR machine. All the more reason, she told herself, for her connection with Harman Grace to remain a closely guarded secret. So— she'd continue to be the girl Paolo had met in a bar, and let his noble relative pick the bones out of that.

But her troubled musings ceased when Emilia, a comfortably built woman with a beaming smile, flung open a door with a triumphant, *'Ecco, signorina,'* indicating that this was her bedroom.

Laura took a step inside, and looked round, her eyes widening with delight. It couldn't have presented a greater contrast to the opulent and cluttered apartment where she'd stayed yesterday. For one thing, it was double the size of the room she'd occupied there, she realised, with a floor tiled in a soft pink marble, while the white plaster walls still bore traces of ancient frescos, which she would examine at her leisure.

But that was the only suggestion of the villa's age. For the present day, there was a queen-sized bed, prettily hung with filmy white curtains, which also graced the shuttered windows. A chest of drawers, a clothes cupboard, and a night table comprised the rest of the furniture, and a door led to a compact but luxurious shower room, tiled in the same shade of pink. The only other additions to the bedroom were a lamp beside the bed, and a bowl of roses on the chest.

She turned to Emilia. 'Perfect,' she said, smiling. And, managing to ignore Signora Vicente's disdainful glance, *'Perfetto.'*

When she was alone, she went over to the window, and pulled it wide. It opened, she saw, onto a three-sided courtyard, bordered by a narrow colonnade, like a medieval cloister, and she stepped through, gazing around her. There was a small fountain in the centre of the paved area, with a battered cherub pouring water from a shell into a shallow pool, while beside it stood a stone bench.

Directly ahead of her, Laura saw, the courtyard itself opened out into the sunlit grass and flowers of the garden beyond, and from somewhere not too far away she could hear the cooing of doves.

But it wasn't all peace and tranquillity, she realised wryly. From even closer at hand, she could hear the raised autocratic tones of the Signora, mingled with Emilia's quieter replies.

A salutary reminder that this little piece of Eden also had its serpents, not to mention wolves and bears, she thought, gazing up at the thickly forested slopes that brooded above her.

Suddenly, she felt tired, sticky and a little dispirited. She'd seen that there were towels and a range of toiletries waiting in the shower room, so decided she might as well make use of them.

She stood under the powerful jet of warm water, lathering her skin luxuriously with soap that smelt of lilies, feeling as if her anxieties were draining away with the suds and she were being somehow reborn, refreshed and invigorated.

Most of the towels were linen, but there were a couple of fluffy bath sheets as well, and when she was dry she wound herself in one of them, and trailed back into the bedroom.

While she'd been occupied, her case had arrived and was waiting on the bed, so she busied herself with unpacking. She hadn't brought nearly enough, she thought, viewing the results with dis-

favour, and very little that was smart or formal enough for someone who found herself staying with a count at his private villa.

The outfit that had survived with the fewest creases was a
wrap-around dress in a silver-grey silky material, and she decided
to try and create a good impression by wearing it for dinner that
night.

She had a solitary credit card, kept for emergencies, and maybe
she could persuade Paolo to risk the road from hell on a trip to
Perugia, so that she could supplement her wardrobe a little.

Whatever she wore, the Signora would sneer, and she accepted
that. But for reasons she could not explain, or even admit to, she
did not want Count Ramontella looking at her with equal disdain.

She wanted him to accept the fiction that she and Paolo were
an item. Perhaps to acknowledge, in some way she hadn't worked
out yet, that she was an eligible bride for his cousin, and welcome
her as such.

And pigs might fly, she thought morosely.

In the meantime, she wasn't sure what to do next. The whole
villa seemed enveloped in sleepy heat. There was even silence
from the adjoining room, the only sound being the faint soothing
splash of the fountain.

Laura felt she could hardly blunder about exploring her new
surroundings, alone and uninvited, in case she committed some
kind of social *faux pas*.

So, she decided, she was probably better off remaining where
she was until summoned.

She was just about to stretch out on the bed with her book
when there was a knock at the door.

Paolo, she thought instantly, wishing she were wearing something more reliable than a big towel. But when she cautiously
opened the door, and peeped round it, she found Emilia waiting
with a tray.

Beaming, the older woman informed her in halting English
that His Excellency thought the *signorina* might need some re-
freshment after her journey, then placed the tray in her hands
and departed.

Laura carried the tray over to the bed and set it down with

care. It held a teapot, with a dish of lemon slices, a plate of tiny crustless sandwiches containing some kind of pâté, and a bowl of golden cherries faintly flushed with crimson.

It was a kindness she had not anticipated, she thought with faint bewilderment. In fact the Count Ramontella seemed positively full of surprises.

But perhaps she was reading too much into this. Clearly his hospitality was primarily aimed at his aunt, and she'd been included as an afterthought.

Because her host didn't seem like a man who went in for random acts of kindness, Laura thought, remembering uneasily the faint curl of that beautifully moulded mouth.

So, she might as well make the most of this one, while it was on offer.

She ate every scrap of the delicious sandwiches with two cups of tea, then lay back with a contented sigh, savouring the cherries as she read. Later, she dozed for a while.

When she eventually awoke, the sun was much lower in the sky, and shadows were beginning to creep across the courtyard outside.

She donned a lacy bra and briefs, then sat down to make up her face with rather more care than usual, before giving her glossy fall of russet hair a vigorous brushing and fastening silver hoops in her ears. Finally, she sprayed her skin with the fresh, light scent she used, then slipped into the chosen dress, winding its sash round her slender waist and fastening it in a bow.

She'd brought one pair of flattish evening sandals in a neutral pewter shade—light years away from the glamorous shoes with their dizzyingly high heels that Italy was famous for. But even if she'd possessed such a pair, she wouldn't have been able to wear them, she conceded regretfully, because that would have made her slightly taller than Paolo, who was sensitive about his height.

Count Ramontella, of course, had no such concerns, she thought. The highest heels in the world would only have raised her to a level with his chin. And God only knew why such a thing had even occurred to her.

It was time she concentrated on Paolo, and the task she'd agreed to perform.

She let herself out of her bedroom, and started down the passage, trying to retrace her earlier steps. She had more time to observe her surroundings now, and she realised that the whole place was a series of courtyards, some completely enclosed, each of them marked by its own fountain, or piece of statuary.

And a good job too, because it's like a labyrinth, she thought, hesitating, totally at a loss, as the passage she was negotiating crossed another. To her relief, the white-coated manservant who had been at the entrance when they'd arrived appeared from nowhere, and indicated politely that she should follow him.

The room she was shown to was enormous, its focal point a huge stone fireplace surmounted by a coat of arms. It was also empty, and Laura hesitated in the doorway, feeling dwarfed by her surroundings, and a little isolated too.

Obviously, she had left her room much too early. The Italians, she recalled, were apt to dine later than people did in England, but she decided to stay where she was rather than attempt that maze of passages again.

She saw with interest that, in here, some restoration work had been done to the frescoed walls, and wandered round, taking a closer, fascinated look and speculating on their age. There were various hunting scenes, and, more peacefully, an outdoor feast with music and dancing, and the style of dress suggested the sixteenth century.

At the far end of the room, large floor-length windows stood open, leading out to a terrace from which a flight of steps descended, leading down to further gardens below.

Once again, furniture in the *salotto* had been kept to a minimum—a few massive sofas, their dimensions reduced by the proportions of the room, and a long, heavily carved sideboard were the main features. Also, more unusually, a grand piano.

It was open and, intrigued, Laura crossed to it and sat down on the stool, running her fingers gently over the keys, listening to its lovely, mellow sound.

She gave a small sigh. So many sad things had followed her

father's death, and the loss of her own much-loved piano was only one of them.

She tried a quiet chord or two, then, emboldened by the fact that she was still alone, launched herself into a modern lullaby that she had once studied as an exam piece.

Perhaps because it had always been a favourite of hers, she got through it without too much faltering, and sighed again as she played the final plangent notes, lost in her own nostalgic world.

She started violently as the music died to be replaced with the sound of someone clapping. She turned swiftly and apprehensively towards the doorway.

'Bravo,' said the Count Ramontella, and walked slowly across the room towards her.

CHAPTER FOUR

'OH CHRISTMAS,' Laura muttered under her breath, aware that she was blushing. 'I'm so sorry, *signore*. I didn't realise...' She swallowed. 'I had no right—no right at all...'

'*Nonsenso*. That was charming.' He came to lean against the corner of the piano, the dark eyes watching her coolly. He was totally transformed, she thought, having shaved, and combed his hair neatly back from his face. And he was wearing slim-fitting black trousers, which emphasised his long legs, offset by a snowy shirt, open at the throat, and topped by a crimson brocaded waist-coat, which he had chosen to leave unbuttoned.

He looked, Laura thought, swallowing again, casually magnificent.

'At last my decision to keep it in tune is justified,' he went on. 'It has not been played, I believe, since my mother died.'

'Oh, God, that makes everything worse.' She shook her head wretchedly. 'I must apologise again. This was—is—such an unforgivable intrusion.'

'But I do not agree,' he said. 'I think it delightful. Won't you play something else?'

'Oh, no.' She got up hastily, her embarrassment increasing, and was halted, the hem of her dress snagged on the protruding corner of the piano stool. 'Damn,' she added, jerking at the fabric, trying to release herself.

'*Sta' quieto,*' the Count commanded. 'Keep still, or you will tear it.' He dropped gracefully to one knee beside her, and deftly set her free.

She looked down at the floor. 'Thank you.'

'It is nothing.' He rose to his feet, glancing around him. 'What have you done with Paolo?'

'I—I haven't seen him since we arrived.'

44

'*Davvero?*' His brows lifted. 'I hope he is not neglecting you.' He sent her a faint smile. 'If so, you may be glad of the piano to provide you with entertainment.'

'Oh, no,' she said quickly. 'He isn't neglectful. Not at all.' She paused. 'Perhaps his mother wanted to talk to him.'

'If so, I think her revolting little dog would have told us all.' He was silent for a moment. 'Tell me, did you enjoy your afternoon tea?'

Her eyes flew to his dark face. 'You—really arranged that? That was very kind.'

He shrugged. 'We tend to have the evening meal later than you are used to in England. I did not wish you to faint with hunger.' He smiled at her pleasantly. 'You will soon become accustomed to Italian time.'

'I'll certainly try,' she said. 'But you can't make many adjustments in two weeks.'

His smile widened slightly. 'On the contrary, I think a great deal can change very quickly.' He walked over to the sideboard. 'May I get you a drink? I intend to have a whisky.'

'I'm fine—really.' She wasn't. Her throat felt as dry as a bone, and had done ever since she'd seen him standing there.

'There is orange juice,' he went on as if she hadn't spoken. 'Have you tried it with campari?'

'Well—no.'

'Then do so now.' He mixed the drink, and brought it to her. Touched his glass to hers. '*Salute.*'

'*Grazie,*' Laura said rather stiffly.

'*Prego.*' This time his smile was a grin. 'Tell me, *signorina*, are you always this tense?'

She sipped her drink, liking the way the sweetness of the juice blended with the bitterness of the campari. She said, haltingly, 'Not always, but this is a difficult situation for me.' She took a breath. 'You must be wondering, *signore*, what I'm doing here.'

'You came with my cousin,' he said. 'It is no secret.'

She took a deep breath. 'So, you must also know that his mother is not pleased about my presence.'

He drank some whisky, his eyes hooded. 'I do not concern

myself in my aunt's affairs, *signorina*.' He paused, and she saw that slight curl of the mouth again. 'At least, not unless they are forced upon my notice.'

She said rather forlornly, 'Just as I have been—haven't I?'

'Perhaps,' he said. 'But, believe me, *signorina*, now that we have met, I expect nothing but pleasure from your visit.' Before she could prevent him, he took her hand and raised it to his lips, kissing it lightly and swiftly.

The dark gaze glinted at her as he released her. 'Would it help you relax if we were a little less formal with each other? My name is Alessio, and I know that yours is Laura.'

She was aware that the colour had stormed back into her face. She said a little breathlessly, 'I think your aunt might object.'

His tone was silky. 'Then let us agree to leave her to her own devices, *sì*?'

'Yes,' she said. 'If you're quite sure.'

'I am certain.' He paused. 'Shall we take our drinks onto the terrace? It is pleasant there in the evenings.'

Laura followed reluctantly. She hadn't bargained for this, she thought uneasily. She'd expected Paolo to be hovering constantly, acting as a barrier between her and his family.

There was a table on the terrace, and comfortable cushioned chairs. Alessio held one for her courteously, then took the adjoining seat. There was a silence, and Laura took a nervous sip of her drink.

'You and Paolo aren't very alike—for cousins,' she ventured at last.

'No,' Alessio said, contemplating his whisky. 'There is very little resemblance between us. Physically, I believe he favours his late father.'

'I see.' She hesitated, then said in a small wooden voice, 'His mother, the Signora, is a very—striking woman.'

'She has a forceful personality, certainly,' he said drily. 'I understand that, when she was young, she was also considered a great beauty.' He leaned back in his chair. 'Tell me, Laura, how did you meet my cousin?'

'I work in a wine bar,' she said. 'He was one of the customers.'

'Ah,' he said. 'So you are not always as shy as you are with me.'

'But then,' she returned, 'I wasn't expecting to meet you, *signore*.'

'You have forgotten,' he said. 'We agreed it would be Alessio.'

No, she thought. I haven't forgotten a thing. I'm not ready to be on first-name terms—or any terms at all—with someone like you.

There was a loud sneeze from inside the *salotto*, and Paolo emerged, flourishing a large handkerchief. '*Maledizione*, I am getting a cold,' he said peevishly. 'Some germ on the plane, *indubbiamente*.'

Laura decided this was her cue. 'Darling.' She got up and went to his side, sliding her arm through his. 'How horrid for you. Summer colds are always the worst.'

For a second, he looked at her as if he'd forgotten who she was, then he pulled himself together, kissing her rather awkwardly on the cheek. 'Well, I must take care not to pass it on to you, *carissima. Che peccato*, eh? What a pity.' He slid an arm round her, his fingers deliberately brushing the underside of her breast.

Laura, nailing on a smile, longed to pull away and kick him where it hurt. Alessio drank some more whisky, his face expressionless.

If she'd hoped that the arrival of his mother a short while later would impose some constraint upon Paolo, Laura was doomed to disappointment. He'd drawn his chair close beside hers at the table, and appeared glued to her side, his hand stroking her arm and shoulder possessively, his lips never far from her ear, her hair, or her cheek, nibbling little caresses that she found positively repellent.

She knew, of course, that the Signora was watching, her mouth drawn into a tight line, because that was the purpose of the exercise. And there was nothing she could do about it. But she was also sharply aware that the Count was sending them the odd meditative glance, and this, for some reason, she found even more disturbing than the older woman's furious scrutiny.

She found she was silently repeating, 'Think of the money. Think of the money,' over and over again like a mantra, but it was not producing the desired calming effect, and she was thankful to her heart when dinner was finally announced, and Paolo reluctantly had to relinquish his hold.

The dining room was a long, low-ceilinged room, with a wonderful painted ceiling depicting some Bacchanalian revel, with people wearing bunches of grapes instead of clothes.

The scene below was much more decorous, the polished table gleaming with silver and crystal in the light of several elaborate candelabra. Alessio sat at the head of the table, with his aunt facing him at its foot, and Laura was seated halfway down, opposite Paolo, the width of the table putting her beyond the reach of any more amorous overtures.

Not that he seemed in the mood any longer. Instead he kept sighing, blowing his nose, and occasionally putting a hand to his forehead, as if checking his own temperature.

In spite of her concerns, Laura found she was really hungry, and tucked into the wild mushroom risotto, the veal in a rich wine sauce, and the creamy almond-flavoured dessert that she was offered with a good appetite. But she was far more sparing with the wine that Guillermo tried to pour into her glass, recognising that she needed to keep her wits about her.

Conversation was kept to general topics, and conducted in English. The Signora tried a few times to switch to Italian, but was forestalled by the Count, who silkily reminded her that she was overlooking the presence of their guest, so that she was forced to subside, glaring.

The meal was almost over when Paolo dropped his bombshell. '*Mamma*—the ring that my grandmother left me, which you keep in the safe at the *appartamento*. You will give it to me when we return to Rome, if you please?'

The ensuing silence was electric. Laura kept her eyes fixed on her plate. Oh, God, she wailed inwardly. What possessed him to say that—and why didn't he warn me?

Whatever she herself might think of the Signora, and no matter what disagreement over the future Paolo might be engaged in with her, the older woman was still his mother—and he was deliberately taunting her. Pushing his supposed relationship to new limits.

She thought, biting her lip, This is so wrong...

'It is a valuable piece of jewellery,' the Signora said at last, her voice shaking a little. 'It needs to be kept in security. But of course, *figlio mio*, it is for you to decide.'

'And I have done so.' Paolo sent her a bland smile. 'It is time it was in my keeping.'

Laura put down her spoon, unable to eat another mouthful. Across the candle flames, she sent Paolo a condemnatory look.

After that the conversation flagged, and she was thankful when the Count suggested that they have coffee in the *salotto*.

It was served black and very strong in small cups.

'*Grappa* for the *signorina*.' Guillermo proffered a tiny glass of colourless liquid, and she glanced across at Paolo, whose expression was so smug she could have slapped him.

'What is *grappa*?' she asked.

'A kind of brandy,' he said. 'Good for the digestion.'

For medicinal purposes only, Laura thought, raising the glass to her lips. She took one cautious sip, and nearly choked, eyes streaming.

'My God,' she said when she could speak, accepting the glass of mineral water that Alessio handed her. 'How strong is that?'

'About ninety-per-cent proof,' he told her, amused. 'You have never drunk it before?'

'No,' she said with feeling. 'I would definitely have remembered.'

The Count looked at his cousin. 'Paolo, you have neglected Laura's education.'

Paolo stopped mopping his face long enough to leer. '*Al contrario*, my dear Alessio, I've been concentrating on the things that matter.'

Alessio gave him a thoughtful look, but made no comment, while Laura sat, her face burning, wishing the floor would open.

The Signora, who had been sitting like a stone statue in a corner of the sofa, abruptly announced her intention of watching television, which, Laura discovered, was housed in a large carved cabinet in the corner of the room. It was some kind of current affairs programme, which she was unable to follow, so her interest soon waned.

Instead, she watched the chess game now in progress between the two men. She was no expert, but it was soon obvious that Paolo had got himself into an impossible position.

'I feel too ill to play,' he said peevishly as he resigned. 'I shall tell Emilia to make a *tisana* and bring it to my bedroom.'

He pushed back his chair and got up, kissing Laura on the cheek. 'Goodnight, *carissima*. If I sleep now, I shall be well tomorrow, so that we can spend some time alone together, and I can show you my beautiful country. Starting maybe with Assisi, hmm?'

Laura forced a smile, and murmured that it would be wonderful.

He kissed his mother's hand, ignored the basilisk glance she sent him, and disappeared.

Alessio moved the pieces back to the starting point and looked up at Laura. 'Would you like to challenge the winner?' he asked.

'After the way you dealt with Paolo, I don't think so.' Her tone was rueful. 'You need my young brother. He was school chess champion when he was six.'

'Your brother?' the Signora suddenly interrupted. 'I thought you were an only child, *signorina*.'

Laura realised too late that was what she'd agreed with Paolo. Not just an only child, but an orphan too. It would save them many problems if she was without family, he'd decreed. And she'd just blown it.

Which meant she would have to warn him first thing tomorrow about her unguarded words.

In the meantime: 'Is that the impression I gave, *signora*?' She made herself speak lightly. 'It was probably wishful thinking.' She paused. 'And now, perhaps you'll excuse me, too. It's been a long day, and I still have to negotiate the maze back to my room.'

Alessio rose. 'Permit me,' he said. He walked to the fireplace and tugged at the bell-pull that hung there. A moment later, Guillermo appeared, his face enquiring. 'The *signorina* is ready to retire. Please escort her,' he directed quietly.

Laura was still suddenly, aware of an odd disappointment. Then: 'Thank you,' she said stiltedly. 'And—goodnight.'

Alessio watched in silence as she followed Guillermo from the room.

As soon as they had gone the Signora was on her feet with a hiss of impatience. 'Are you mad? Why did you not take her to her room yourself? It was your chance to be alone with the little fool.'

His mouth tightened in the knowledge he had been sorely tempted to do exactly that, and had deliberately resisted the impulse. 'I know what I am doing,' he told her curtly. 'Or do you want her to take fright, and scuttle off to Paolo for sanctuary?'

'Take fright?' she echoed contemptuously. 'That one? What are you talking about?'

Alessio sighed. 'I merely wish to point out that she does not seem a girl one would pick up in a bar. I am—surprised.'

She gave a harsh laugh. 'So that look of mock innocence has deceived you, my worldly nephew, as it has my poor boy.' She spread her hand. 'Can you doubt how besotted he is with her? To ask for Nonna Caterina's ring so brazenly. The ring I planned for him to give to Beatrice. I could not believe it.'

'Neither, I think, could she,' Alessio said drily. 'Are you really so sure they are in love, or does he simply wish to sell the ring to pay off his gambling debts?'

'Love?' She almost spat the word, ignoring his jibe. 'What does that mean? She is attracted by my son's background—his position in the world. She believes he is also wealthy.'

'Then show her his bank statements,' Alessio said coldly. 'That will cure her, and save me a great deal of trouble.'

'But it will not cure him. You saw him this evening. He could not keep his hands off her.'

'So it would seem,' Alessio agreed slowly. 'It is as well, perhaps, that they are sleeping at opposite ends of the house.'

'You have forgotten this sightseeing tour tomorrow.' The Signora frowned. 'No doubt they will go only as far as the nearest hotel willing to rent them a room for a few hours.'

Alessio felt his mouth twist with sudden and profound distaste at the image her words conjured up, and denounced himself with silent savagery for being a hypocrite.

He said icily, 'Then I suggest, my dear aunt, that you too develop a sudden interest in the local attractions. You have not, after all, seen the Giotto frescos in the basilica at Assisi since their restoration. Go with them, and act as chaperon, if you think it is necessary. And take the dog with you. Teach him to bite Paolo each time he touches the girl.'

'Oh, there is no reasoning with you when you are in this mood.' The Signora swept to the door. 'I will bid you goodnight.' She turned and gave him a measuring look. 'But our agreement still stands. Be in no doubt of that.'

When he was alone, Alessio walked over to the piano, and stood picking out a few notes with one finger, his face thoughtful. He found himself remembering the delicate flush that had warmed Laura's pale skin when she'd looked up and seen him watching and listening in the doorway. Recalled even more acutely how her clean fragrance had assailed his senses as he'd knelt beside her to free her skirt.

The dress had been a beguiling one altogether, he thought. In other circumstances it would have been so simple to release the sash, and let it fall apart, revealing the warm sweetness beneath the silvery folds. So enticing to touch her as he wished, and feel her smooth skin under his mouth.

He found himself smiling, wondering if she would blush as deeply when she was aroused.

Not a wise thought to take to bed with you, he told himself wryly as he began to turn off the lights in the room. And he must be insane to indulge in this kind of adolescent fantasy about a girl he needed to keep, coolly and clinically, on the far edge of his life. But, then, only a fool would have allowed himself to be caught in this kind of trap in the first place.

And found he was sighing with unexpected bitterness as he walked to the door.

It was a long time before Laura fell asleep that night. She was tired, but aware of too many disturbing vibrations in the house to be able to relax completely. And her one recurring thought was that she was no longer sure she could go on with this charade, which was becoming far too complicated.

And, she suspected, unmanageable.

What was Paolo going to demand she did next? she asked herself, exasperated. Actually become engaged to him?

Once she'd got him to herself tomorrow, she would be able to talk to him seriously, she thought with determination. Persuade him that things had gone far enough, and his mother had been given sufficient shocks to last a lifetime. Surely the Signora must be convinced by now that her plan to marry him off was dead in the water—especially after that stunt he'd pulled at dinner, she thought grimly. They didn't need to take any more risks.

Now, somehow, she had to persuade him to take her away from the Villa Diana. Or, if she was really honest, separate her from its owner.

In spite of the heat, she found herself shivering.

She had been following Guillermo through the passages when it had suddenly hit her just how much she'd been hoping that the Count himself would offer to accompany her.

And how many kinds of madness was that? she asked herself with a kind of despair.

She'd been in his company for only a few hours, and already her awareness of him was threatening to spin out of control.

For God's sake, grow up, she told herself wearily, giving the pillows a thump.

Yes, there'd been times when the courtesy she knew he'd have shown to any guest under his roof had seemed to slip into kindness, but that could have been an attempt to make amends for his aunt's unfailing rudeness. And she'd be fooling herself if she thought otherwise, even for a moment.

The Arleschi Bank was considered a model of its kind, keenly efficient, highly respected, and superbly profitable, which was why Harman Grace were so keen to represent it. And it was clear that the bank's chairman played a key role in its achievements.

Count Alessio Ramontella lived in the full radiance of the sun, Laura thought, whereas she occupied some small, cold planet on the outmost edge of the solar system. That was the way it was, and always would be. And it was her bad luck that their paths had ever been forced to cross.

She closed her eyes against the memory of his smile, its sudden brilliance turning the rather ruthless lines of his mouth to charm and humour. She tried to forget, too, the warmth of that swift brush of his lips on her hand, and the way even that most fleeting of touches had pierced her to the bone.

It occurred to her that if Steve's kisses had carried even a fraction of the same shattering charge, he'd probably have been a happy man at this very moment, and Paolo would have had to look elsewhere for a partner in his scam.

I really need to get away from here, she told herself, moving restlessly, feeling the fine linen sheet that covered her grazing her skin as if it were raw. And soon.

It could be managed, of course, and quite easily. Paolo could pretend to take her on the visit to Tuscany they'd originally planned. Once they were alone, who would ever know if she slipped away and took an early flight back to London? And as long as Paolo kept a low profile, he could spend his vacation time exactly as he wished.

It wasn't what she wanted—it saddened her that she wouldn't see Florence or any of the region's other proud cities—but it was clear that she could no longer trust Paolo. And it was a way of dealing with a problem that was threatening to snowball into a crisis, entirely through her own stupidity.

Not that she could ever tell Paolo that. This was another truth that would have to be suppressed.

And he never wanted to come here in the first place, she thought. So he can hardly complain if I say I want to leave.

She turned over, burying her face determinedly in the pillow. And if her sleep was haunted by dreams, they did not linger to be remembered in the morning.

The determination, however, persisted, stronger than ever, and Laura sang softly to herself as she showered and dressed in a blue denim skirt and a sleeveless white top.

It was another glorious day, with the sun already burning off the faint haze around the tops of the hills. Probably her last day in Italy, she thought, and she would make the most of every minute.

She and Paolo would sort everything on the trip to Assisi, and by tomorrow they could be out of here, and life could return to normal again.

She would even learn to laugh about the last couple of days. Make a good story out of the Signora. Tell Gaynor, 'Hey, I met a man who was the ultimate sex on a stick, and fabulously wealthy too.' Let it all sound like fun, without a moment of self-doubt, she thought as she brushed her hair.

She had taken careful note of the route to the main part of the house the previous night, and found the dining room without difficulty, only to discover that it was deserted with no sign of food.

They eat dinner late, maybe breakfast is the same, she thought, slightly nonplussed. As she was wandering back into the entrance hall she was swooped on by Emilia, who led her firmly into the *salotto* and indicated that she should go out onto the terrace.

She emerged cautiously and paused in dismay, because Alessio was there alone, seated at the table, which was now covered by a white cloth. A few feet away, in the shade, a large trolley was stationed, and she saw that it held a platter with ham on the bone, together with a dish of cheese, a basket of bread rolls and a bowl of fruit. A pot of coffee was keeping warm on a heater.

'Buon giorno.' He had seen her, and, putting down the news-

paper he was reading, rose to his feet, depriving her of the chance to retreat back into the villa. 'You rested well?'

'Yes—thank you.' Reluctantly, she took the seat he indicated and unfolded her napkin, glancing at the table. 'Only two places?' Her brow furrowed. 'Where are the others?'

'They are breakfasting in their rooms,' Alessio told her. 'My aunt, because she prefers it. Paolo, because he is too ill to leave his bed,' he added sardonically.

'Too ill?' Laura echoed, taking the glass of chilled peach juice he'd poured for her. 'What do you mean?'

He shrugged. 'His cold. It has become infinitely worse. His mother is most concerned. Every lemon we possess is being squeezed to make drinks for him, and she has commandeered every painkiller in the house.'

'Oh.' Laura digested this, her dismay deepening by the second. She had not bargained for this development. She said, 'Perhaps I'd better go to him, too. See how he is, and if I can help.'

'A word of advice, *bella mia*,' Alessio said lazily. 'A wolf, a bear and my aunt Lucrezia—never come between any of them and their cubs. So, stay where you are, and eat. You will be much safer, I promise you.'

He got to his feet, lithe in cream denim trousers and a black polo shirt, and went to the trolley. 'May I bring you some of this excellent ham?'

'Thank you.' She watched him carve several slices off the bone with deft precision. As he placed the plate in front of her she said, 'Maybe he'll feel better later on, and be able to get up. We're supposed to be going to Assisi.'

'Paolo will be going nowhere for the foreseeable future,' Alessio said calmly. 'Unless his mother insists on my summoning a helicopter to take him to the nearest hospital, of course.'

'He has a cold in the head.' Laura's mouth tightened. 'It's hardly terminal.'

'It would be inadvisable to say so in front of Zia Lucrezia.' Alessio ate a forkful of ham. 'Not that we will see much of her either,' he added meditatively. 'Her time will be taken up with nursing the invalid, smoothing his pillow, reading aloud to him, and bullying my poor Emilia into creating little delicacies to tempt his failing appetite.'

Laura finished her peach juice, and set down the glass. She said slowly, 'You're really serious about this.'

'No, but my aunt is. However,' he added silkily, 'I gather that, with rest and quiet, the prognosis is generally favourable.'

In spite of her private concerns, Laura found herself laughing. 'It's just so absurd. All this fuss about a cold.'

'Ah, but it is the areas of fuss that matter in marriage, I am told,' Alessio said blandly. 'It is best to discover what they are before the ceremony, and you have now been given a valuable insight into Paolo's concerns about his health.'

He watched with interest as Laura began to cut her ham into small, careful squares.

'You plan to marry my cousin, of course?' he added after a pause.

Her eyes flew warily to his face. 'I—I think...I mean—there's nothing formal. Not yet.'

'But you are travelling with him in order to meet his family. And last night it seemed certain,' he said. 'For the Vicentes, as for the Ramontellas, the giving of a ring—particularly an heirloom—is a serious thing. A declaration of irrevocable intent. One man, one woman bound in love for the rest of their lives.'

'Oh.' She swallowed. 'I didn't know that. He—didn't tell me.'

'And now you must wait until he recovers from this trying cold,' Alessio agreed, adding briskly, 'Would you like coffee, or shall I tell Emilia to bring you tea?'

Her mind had gone into overdrive, and she had to drag herself back to the present moment. 'Oh—coffee would be fine.'

She took the cup he brought her with a murmur of thanks.

'You seem a little upset,' he commented as he resumed his seat. 'May I know the problem?'

'It's nothing, really.' She bit her lip. 'Just that I feel a bit useless and in the way with Paolo being ill.' She tried to smile. 'I shan't know what to do with myself.'

'Then I suggest you relax.' He pointed to the steps. 'They lead down to the swimming pool, a pleasant place to sunbathe—and dream about the future, perhaps.'

He smiled at her. 'And try not to worry too much about Paolo,' he advised lightly. 'He has about six colds a year. You will have plenty of opportunity to nurse him, I promise.'

She put down her cup, staring at him suspiciously. 'You're making fun of me.'

'Well, a little, perhaps.' The smile widened into a grin. 'Teasing you is almost irresistible, believe me.'

He pushed away his plate and sat back in his chair, regarding her. 'But allow me to make amends. I have to go out presently on a matter of business in the village. But if you came with me, we could combine it with pleasure by driving on to Assisi. There is much to see there, and a good restaurant where we can have lunch. Would you like that?'

There was a tingling silence. Laura's look of uncertainty deepened.

She said, 'You—you're offering to take me to Assisi.' To her discomfiture, she felt herself beginning to blush. 'That—that's very kind of you, *signore*, and I—I'm grateful. But I couldn't put you to all that trouble—not possibly.'

'But it would be no trouble,' he said. '*Al contrario*, I would find it delightful.' He paused deliberately. 'But I notice that you still have a problem calling me by my given name, so perhaps you feel you cannot yet trust me enough to spend a day alone with me.'

Or perhaps it is yourself you do not trust, *bella mia*, he added silently, watching the colour flare in her face. And if so—you are mine.

'N-no,' she stammered. 'Oh, no. It's not that—not that at all.' She cast around frantically for an excuse—any excuse. 'You see—it's Paolo. The Assisi trip was his idea, and maybe I should wait until he's better, and we can go together. I—I don't want to hurt his feelings. Can you understand that?'

'Of course,' he said. 'I understand perfectly, believe me.' More than you think or wish, my sweet one, he added under his breath.

He sighed with mock reproach. 'However, I am distressed that my shattered hopes do not concern you. Now that is cruel. But if I cannot persuade you, so be it.'

And when the time comes, he thought as he pushed back his chair and rose to his feet, some day—some night soon—then I will make you come to me. Because you are going to want me so much that you will offer yourself, my shy, lovely girl. Make no mistake about that. And I will take everything you have to give, and more.

Aloud, he said, '*Arriverderci*, Laura.' His smile was pleasant—even slightly impersonal as he looked down at her. 'Enjoy your solitude while you can,' he added softly.

And he walked away, humming gently under his breath, while Laura stared after him, still floundering in her own confusion.

CHAPTER FIVE

LAURA finished applying sun lotion to her arms and legs, and lay back in the shade of the big striped umbrella with a little sigh of contentment. Contrary to her own expectations, she was enjoying her solitude. The pool area occupied an extended hollow at the foot of the gardens, offering a welcome haven of tranquillity, with its marble tiles surrounding a large rectangle of turquoise water, and overlooked by terraced banks of flowering shrubs.

It was sheltered and very private, and, apart from birdsong and the hum of insects, it was also wonderfully quiet.

She put on her sunglasses and applied herself to taking an intelligent interest in her book, but the heroine's ill-starred attempts to pursue entirely the wrong man struggled to hold her attention, and at last she put the thing down, sighing impatiently.

In view of her current circumstances, it wasn't the ideal plot to engage her, she thought ruefully. In fact, *War and Peace* might have been a more appropriate choice. Especially as she'd just been totally routed by the enemy.

She'd managed to waylay a harassed Emilia, asking politely if she'd find out when it would be convenient for her to visit Paolo. But the reply conveyed back from the Signora was unequivocal. Paolo had a high fever but was now sleeping, so could not be disturbed.

If I were genuinely in love with him, I'd be chewing my nails to the quick by now, Laura thought indignantly.

But it was clear she had to start practising patience, and hope that, when his temperature eventually went down, Paolo would demand to see her instead.

She sighed. God, what a situation to be in, and all her own stupid doing, too. Why hadn't she remembered there was no such thing as a free lunch?

But the deep indolent heat was already soothing her, encouraging her to close her eyes and relax. Reminding her that it was pointless to fret, because, for the time being at least, she was no longer in control of her own destiny.

Che sera, sera, she thought drowsily, removing her sunglasses and nestling further into the soft cushions of the lounger. Whatever will be, will be. Isn't that what they say? So I may as well go with the flow. Especially as I don't seem to have much of a choice.

She closed her eyes. Oh, Paolo. She sent the silent plea winging passionately to the villa. For heaven's sake get well quickly, and get me out of here.

Alessio parked the Jeep in front of the house, and swung himself out of the driving seat. He needed, he thought as he strode indoors, a long cold drink, and a swim.

What he did not require was the sudden appearance of his aunt, as if she'd been lying in wait for him.

'Where have you been?' she demanded, and he checked resignedly.

'Down to the village. Luca Donini asked me to talk to his father—persuade him not to spend another winter in that hut of his.'

'He asked *you*?' Her brows lifted haughtily. 'But how can this concern you? Sometimes, Alessio, I think you forget your position.'

He gave her a long, hard look. 'Yes, Zia Lucrezia,' he drawled. 'Sometimes, I do, as the events of the past few weeks have unhappily proved. But Besavoro is my village, and the concerns of my friends there are mine too.'

She snorted impatiently. 'You did not take the girl with you?'

He shrugged. 'I invited her, but she refused me.'

She glared at him. 'That is bad. You cannot be trying.'

'No,' he said. 'It is better than I expected after such a short time.' His smile was cold. 'But do not ask me to explain.'

She changed tack. 'You should have told me you were going

to the village. You could have gone to the pharmacy for my poor boy. Last night he was delirious—talking nonsense in his sleep.'

'It is probably a habit of his,' Alessio commented curtly. 'Why not ask his *innamorata*?'

She gave him a furious look, and swept back to her nursing duties.

Alessio proceeded moodily to his room. The jibe had been almost irresistible, but he regretted it. There'd been no need to remind himself that Laura and Paolo had been enjoying an intimate relationship prior to their arrival in Italy. Because he knew it only too well already.

But what he could not explain was why he found it so galling. After all, he thought, he had never felt jealous or possessive about any of his previous involvements. For him, sex was usually just another appetite to be enjoyably and mutually satisfied. And there was nothing to be gained by jealousy or speculation over other lovers.

He'd awaited Laura's arrival at the villa with a sense of blazing resentment, even though he knew he had only himself to blame for his predicament, and, instead, found himself instantly intrigued by her. From that, it had only been a brief step to desire. And he strongly suspected this would have happened if he'd met her somewhere far from his aunt's interference.

He remembered, with distaste, icily promising to send her home with a beautiful memory. Now he wasn't sure he'd send her back at all. Certainly not immediately, he thought, frowning as he stripped and found a pair of brief black swimming trunks.

Maybe he'd whisk her away somewhere—the Seychelles or the Maldives, perhaps, or the Bahamas—for a few weeks of exotic pampering, with a quick trip to Milan first, of course, to reinvent her wardrobe. Buy her the kind of clothes he would enjoy removing.

And on that enticing thought he collected a towel and his sunglasses, and went down to the pool to find her.

He found her peacefully asleep, the long lashes curling on her cheek, her head turned slightly to one side. The sun had moved round, leaving one ankle and foot out in the open, vulnerable to its direct rays, and he reached up to make a slight adjustment to the parasol.

Having done so, he did not move away immediately, but stood for a moment, looking down at her. In the simple dark green one-piece swimsuit, her slender body looked like the stem of a flower, her hair crowning it like an exotic corolla of russet petals.

A single strand lay across her cheek, and he was tempted to smooth it back, but knew he could not risk so intimate a gesture.

Because he wanted her so fiercely, so unequivocally, it was like a blow in the guts. However, now was not yet the moment, so he would have to practise unaccustomed restraint, he reminded himself grimly.

Swallowing, he turned away, tossing his towel and sunglasses onto an adjoining lounger, then walked to the edge of the pool and dived in, his body cutting the water as cleanly as a knife.

Dimly, Laura heard the splash and came awake, lifting herself onto one elbow as she looked around her, faintly disorientated.

Then her eyes went to the pool, and the tanned body sliding with powerful grace through the water, and her mind cleared, with an instantaneous nervous lurch of the stomach.

Stealthily, she watched him complete another two lengths of the pool, then turn towards the side. She retrieved her sunglasses and slid them on, then grabbed her book, holding it in front of her like a barrier as Alessio lifted himself lithely out of the water and walked towards her, his body gleaming, sleek as a seal, in the sunlight.

'Ciao.' His smile was casual as he began to blot the moisture from his skin with his towel.

'Hello,' she responded hesitantly, not looking at him directly. Those trunks, she thought, her mouth drying, were even briefer than his shorts had been. She hurried into speech. 'You—you're back early. Did you settle all your business?'

'Not as I wished.' He grimaced. 'I had a battle of wills with a stubborn old man and lost.'

'Well,' she said. 'That can't happen too often.'

'It does with Fredo.' His face relaxed into a grin. 'He cannot forget that his son and I grew up together, and that he was almost a second father to me when my parents were away. He even took his belt to Luca and myself with complete impartiality when we behaved badly, and likes to remind me of it when he can.'

He shrugged. 'But he also showed us every track and trail in the forest, and taught us to use them safely. He even took me on my first wild boar hunt.'

'So why are you disagreeing now? Not that it's any of my business,' she added hastily.

'It's no secret. Even when his wife was alive, he did not like life in town, so when she died he moved up to a hut on the mountain to look after his goats there. He has been there ever since, and Luca worries that he is getting too old for such a life. He wants his father to live with him, but Fredo says his daughter-in-law is a bad cook, and has a tongue as sharp as a viper's bite, and I could not argue with that.'

'Absolutely not,' she agreed solemnly. 'A double whammy, no less.'

He laughed. 'As you say, *bella mia*. But the campaign is not over yet.'

'You don't give up easily.'

'I do not give up at all.'

He spread his towel on the lounger and stretched out, nodding at the book she was still clutching. 'Is it good?'

'The jacket says it's a best-seller.'

'Ah,' he said, softly. 'But what does Laura say?'

'That the jury's still out, but the verdict will probably be guilty. Murder by cliché.' She sighed. 'However, it's all I brought with me, so I have to make it last.'

'There are English books in my library up at the villa,' he said. 'Some classics, and some modern. You are welcome to borrow them. Ask Emilia to show you where they are.'

'Thank you, that's—very kind.' Her brows lifted in surprise. 'Is that why your English is so incredibly good—because you read a lot?'

'I learned English as a second language at school,' he said. 'And attended university in Britain and America.' His grin teased her. 'And it is fortunate that I did, as your Italian is so minimal.'

'But my French isn't bad,' she defended herself. 'If I'd gone on the holiday I originally planned, I'd have shone.'

'Ah,' he said. 'And what holiday was that?'

She was suddenly still, cursing herself under her breath. She'd let her tongue run away with her again. 'I thought of the Riviera,' she said. 'But then I met Paolo—and changed my mind, of course.'

'Of course.' She thought she detected a note of irony in his voice.

'Perhaps you should have stuck to plan A,' he went on. 'Then you would have avoided a meeting with Zia Lucrezia.'

'Indeed,' she said lightly. 'And Paolo might not have caught a cold.'

'Not with you to keep him warm, I am sure,' he said softly, and watched with satisfaction as the inevitable blush rose in her face. 'Have you been to see him?'

'I tried,' she admitted. 'But his mother wouldn't allow it. Apparently he's running a temperature.'

'Which you might raise to lethal limits.' He paused. 'And she may have a point,' he added silkily. 'But would you like me to speak to her for you—persuade her to see reason?'

'Would you?' she asked doubtfully. 'But why?'

'Who am I to stand in the way of love?' He shrugged a negligent shoulder, and Laura tried to ignore the resultant ripple of muscle.

Abruptly, she said, 'Do you know Beatrice Manzone?'

'I have met her,' he said. 'Why do you ask?'

'I was wondering what she was like.'

The dark gaze narrowed. 'What does Paolo say?'

She bit her lip. 'That she's rich.'

'A little harsh,' he said. 'She is also pretty and docile.' He grinned faintly. 'And cloying, like an overdose of honey. Quite unlike you, *mia cara*.'

She bit her lip. 'I wasn't looking for comparisons.'

'Then what do you want? Reassurance?' There was a sudden crispness in his tone. 'You should look to Paolo for that. And according to him, the Manzone girl is history.'

'His mother doesn't seem to think so.'

There was an odd silence, then he said, '*Mia bella*, if you and Paolo want each other, then what else matters?' He swung himself off the lounger, as if suddenly impatient. 'And now it is time we went up to the house for some lunch.'

Once again only two places had been set for the meal, which, this time, was being served in the coolness of the dining room. And her seat, Laura observed uneasily, had been moved up the table to within touching distance of his. It made serving the food more convenient, but at the same time it seemed as if she was constantly being thrust into close proximity with him—suddenly an honoured guest rather than an unwanted visitor—and she found this disturbing for all kinds of reasons.

But in spite of her mental reservations, her morning in the fresh air had certainly sharpened her appetite, and she ate her way through a bowl of vegetable soup, and a substantial helping of pasta. But her eyes widened in genuine shock when Guillermo carried the next course—a dish of cod baked with potatoes and parmesan—to the table.

'More food?' She shook her head. 'I don't believe it.'

Alessio looked amused. 'And there is still cheese and dessert to follow. You are going to be an Italian's wife, Laura. You must learn to eat well in the middle of the day.'

'But how can anyone do any work after all this?'

'No one does.' Alessio handed her a plate of food. 'Has Paolo not introduced you to the charms of the siesta?' He kept his voice light with an effort, knowing fiercely that he wanted to be the one to share with her those quiet, shuttered afternoon hours. To sleep with her wrapped in his arms, then wake to make slow, lazy love.

'We rest and work later when it is cooler,' he added, refilling her glass with wine.

'I think Paolo is used to London hours now,' she said, looking down at her plate.

'But he will not always work there, you understand.' He gave her a meditative look. 'How would you like living in Turin—or Milan?'

'I haven't thought about it.'

'Or,' he said slowly, 'it might even be Rome.'

She said, 'Oh, I expect I'd adjust—somehow.'

Except, she thought, that it will never happen, and began to make herself eat.

She wished with sudden desperation that she could confide in him. Tell him exactly why she was here, and how Paolo had persuaded her into this charade.

But there was no guarantee that he would understand, and he might not appreciate being made a fool of, and having his hospitality abused in such a way.

And although he and his aunt were plainly not on the best of terms, he might disapprove of the older woman being deliberately deceived.

Besides, and more importantly, thought Laura, it would render her even more vulnerable where he was concerned, and she could not afford that.

She'd come this far, she told herself rather wanly. She might as well go on to the bitter end—whenever that might be.

His voice broke across her reverie. 'What are you thinking?'

Quickly she forced a smile. Spoke eagerly. 'Oh, just how good it will be to see Paolo again. We don't seem to have been alone together for ages.' She managed a note of anxiety. 'You really do think you'll be able to persuade your aunt?'

'Yes,' Alessio said quietly, after a pause. 'Yes, I do.'

And they ate the rest of the meal in silence.

Siestas were probably fine in theory, thought Laura. In practice, they didn't seem to work quite so well. Or not for her, anyway.

She lay staring up at the ceiling fan, listening to its soft swish as it rotated, and decided she had never felt so wide awake. She needed something to occupy her.

Her book was finished, its ending as predictable as the rest of the story, and she had no wish to lie about thinking. Because her mind only seemed to drift in one direction—towards the emotional minefield presided over by the Count Alessio Ramontella.

And it was ludicrous—pathetic—to allow herself to think about a man who, a week ago, had been only a name on the paperwork from the Arleschi Bank's head office. A distant figurehead, and nothing more.

And no matter how attractive he might be, that was how he would always remain—remote. No part of any world that she lived in, except for these few dreamlike, unforgettable days.

Except that she had to forget them—and pretty damned quickly too—as soon as she returned to England, if not before.

She slid off the bed. She'd have a shower, she decided, and wash her hair. She'd brought no dryer with her, but twenty minutes or so with a hairbrush in the courtyard's afternoon sun would serve the same purpose.

Ten minutes later, demurely wrapped in the primly pretty white cotton robe she'd brought with her, and her hair swathed into a towel, she opened the shutters and stepped outside into the heated shimmer of the day.

She was greeted immediately with a torrent of yapping as Caio, who was lying in the shade of the stone bench, rose to condemn her intrusion.

Laura halted in faint dismay. Up to now, although he was in the adjoining room, he hadn't disturbed her too much with his barking. But she'd assumed that the Signora had taken him with her to the other end of the house to share her sick room vigil. She certainly hadn't bargained for finding him here in sole and aggressive occupation.

'Good dog,' she said without conviction. 'Look, I just want to get my hair dry. There's enough room for us both. Don't give me a hard time, now.'

Still barking, he advanced towards her, then almost jerked to a halt, and she realised he was actually tied to the bench. And, next to where he'd been lying, there was a dish with some dry-looking food on it, and, what was worse, an empty water bowl.

'Oh, for heaven's sake.' She spoke aloud in real anger. Caio would never feature on any 'favourite pets' list of hers, but he deserved better than to be left tied up and thirsty.

She moved round to the other end of the bench, out of the range of his display of sharp teeth, and grabbed the bowl. She took it back to her bathroom, and filled it to the brim with cold water.

When she reappeared, Caio had retreated back under the bench. He growled at her approach, but his heart clearly wasn't in it, and the beady, suspicious eyes were fixed on the bowl. She put it on the ground, then, to demonstrate that the suspicion was mutual, used her hairbrush to push the water near enough for the tethered dog to reach it. He gave a slight whimper, then plunged his muzzle into the bowl, filling the silence with the sound of his frantic lapping.

When he'd finished every drop, he raised his head and looked at her in unmistakable appeal.

I could lose a hand here, Laura thought, but Caio made no attempt to snap as she retrieved the bowl and refilled it for him.

'You poor little devil,' she said gently as he drank again. 'I bet she's forgotten all about you.'

The leash used to tie him was a long one, but Laura realised that it had become twined round the leg of the bench, reducing his freedom considerably.

She could, she thought, untangle it, if he'd let her. But would he allow her close enough to unclip the leash from his collar, without doing her some damage?

Well, she could but try. She certainly couldn't leave him here like this. She could remember hearing once that looking dogs in the eye made them more aggressive, so she seated herself at the far end of the bench, and moved towards him by degrees. When she was in his space, she clenched her hand into a fist and offered it to him, trying to be confident about it, and talking to him quietly at the same time. His initial sniff was reluctant, but he didn't bite, and she tried stroking his head, which he permitted warily.

'You may be spoiled and obnoxious,' she told him, 'but I don't think you have much of a life.'

She slid her fingers down to the ruff of hair round his neck and found his collar. As she released the clip Caio made a sound between a bark and a whimper, and was gone, making for the open space of the garden beyond the courtyard. And after that, presumably, the world.

'Oh, God,' Laura muttered, jumping to her feet and running after him, stumbling a little over the hem of her robe.

What the hell would she do if she couldn't find him? And what was she going to say to the Signora, anyway? She'd be accused of interfering, which was true, and coming back with a counter-accusation of animal negligence, however justified, wouldn't remedy the situation.

She had no idea how extensive the villa's grounds were, or if they were even secure. Supposing he got out onto the mountain itself, and a wolf found him before she could?

This is what happens when you try to be a canine Samaritan, she thought breathlessly as she reached the courtyard entrance, only to find herself almost cannoning into Alessio, who was approaching from the opposite direction with a squirming Caio tucked firmly under his arm.

'Oh, you found him,' she exclaimed. 'Thank heaven for that.'

'I almost fell over him,' he told her tersely. 'Where has he come from?'

'He was tied to the bench over there. I was trying to make him more comfortable, and he just—took off. I was terrified that I wouldn't be able to find him.'

'He was out here—in this heat?' Alessio's tone was incredulous, with the beginnings of anger. He glanced at the bench. 'At least he had water.' He looked at Laura again, more closely. 'Or did he?'

She sighed. 'Well, he has now, and that's what matters.' She was suddenly searingly conscious of the fact that she was wearing nothing but a thin robe, and that her damp hair was hanging on her shoulders. 'I—I'll leave him with you, shall I?' she added, beginning to back away.

'One moment,' he said. 'What made you come out here at this time?'

'I couldn't sleep. I thought I'd wash my hair, and dry it in the sun.' She forced a smile. 'As you see.'

His brows lifted. 'A rather primitive solution, don't you think? Why didn't you ring the bell for Emilia? She would have found you an electric dryer.'

'I felt she had enough on her plate without running around after me. And it is siesta time, after all.' She paused. 'So, why are you here, come to that?'

'I could not sleep either.' He glanced down at Caio, who returned him a baleful look. 'Under the circumstances, that was fortunate.'

'Just in time to spoil his bid for freedom, poor little mutt.' She offered the dog her hand again, and found her fingers being licked by his small rough tongue.

'You seem to have made a friend, *bella mia*.' Alessio sounded amused. 'My aunt will have another reason for jealousy.' He scratched the top of Caio's head. 'And I thought the whole world was his enemy.'

'He'll think so too, if we tie him up to that bench again,' Laura said ruefully.

'Then we will not do so. I will put him in my aunt's room instead, with his water. His basket is there, anyway, and he will be cooler,' he added, frowning. 'I cannot imagine why she would leave him anywhere else.' He sighed. 'Another topic for discussion that will displease her.'

'Another?'

'I have yet to raise the subject of your visit to Paolo.'

'Oh, please,' Laura said awkwardly. 'I've been thinking about that, and maybe I shouldn't persist. If she's so adamant, it will only cause problems.'

He said gently, 'But that is nonsense, Laura *mia*. Of course you must see your lover. Your visit can do nothing but good, I am sure.' His gaze travelled over her, from the high, frilled neck of her robe, down to her bare insteps, and she felt every inch of concealed skin tingle under his lingering regard. Felt an odd heat burgeoning inside her, which had nothing to do with the warmth of the day.

He smiled at her. 'And I will ask Emilia to bring you the hair-dryer,' he added softly, then turned away.

Laura regained the sanctuary of her room, aware that her breathing had quickened out of all proportion.

She closed the shutters behind her, then, on impulse, decided to fasten the small iron bar that locked them. It had clearly not been used for some time because it resisted, finally falling into place with a bang that resounded in the quiet of the afternoon like a pistol shot.

She could only hope Alessio hadn't heard it, because he'd be bound to put two and two together. And the last thing she needed was for him to think that he made her nervous in any way.

Because she had nothing to fear from him, and she was flattering herself to think otherwise.

Someone like Alessio Ramontella would live on a diet of film stars and heiresses, she told herself, pushing her damp hair back from her face with despondent fingers. And if he's kind to me, it's because he recognises I'm out of my depth, and feels sorry for me.

And as long as I remember that, I'm in no danger. No danger at all.

Her reunion with the dying Paolo was scheduled to take place before dinner. A note signed 'Ramontella' informing her of the arrangement had been brought to her by Emilia, along with the promised hair-dryer.

He'd certainly wasted no time over the matter, Laura thought as she followed Guillermo over to the other side of the villa. All she had to do now was pretend to be suitably eager.

She'd dressed for the occasion, putting on her other decent dress, a slim fitting blue shift, sleeveless and scoop-necked. Trying to upgrade it with a handful of silver chains and a matching bracelet.

She'd painted her fingernails and toenails a soft coral, and used a toning lustre on her mouth, emphasising her grey eyes with shadow and kohl.

The kind of effort a girl would make for her lover, she hoped.

She found herself in a long passageway, looking out onto yet another courtyard. The fountain here was larger, she saw, pausing, and a much more elaborate affair, crowned by the statue of a woman crafted in marble. She stood on tiptoe, as if about to take flight, hair and scanty draperies flying behind her, and a bow in her hand, gazing out across the tumbling water that fell from the rock at her feet.

'The goddess Diana for whom the villa is named, *signorina*,' Guillermo, who had halted too, told her in his halting English. 'Very beautiful, *sì*?'

'Very,' Laura agreed with less than total certainty as she studied the remote, almost inhuman face. The virgin huntress, she thought, who unleashed her hounds on any man unwise enough to look at her, and who had the cold moon as her symbol.

And not the obvious choice of deity for someone as overtly warm-blooded as Alessio Ramontella. Her dogs would have torn him to pieces on sight.

She looked down the passage to the tall double doors at the end. 'Is that Signor Paolo's room?'

'But no, *signorina*.' He sounded almost shocked. 'That is the suite of His Excellency. The *signore*, his cousin, is here.' He turned briskly to the left, down another much shorter corridor, and halted, knocking at a door.

It was flung open immediately, and the Signora swept out, her eyes raking Laura with an expression of pure malevolence.

'You may have ten minutes,' she snapped. 'No more. My son needs rest.'

What does she think? Laura asked herself ironically as she entered. That I'm planning to jump his bones?

The shutters were closed and the drapes were drawn too, so the room, which smelled strongly of something like camphorated oil, was lit only by a lamp at the side of the bed.

Paolo was lying, eyes closed, propped up by pillows. He was wearing maroon pyjamas, which made him look sallow, Laura thought. Or maybe it was the effect of the lamplight.

She pulled up a chair, and sat beside the bed. 'Hi,' she said gently. 'How are you feeling?'

'Terrible.' His voice was hoarse and pettish, and the eyes he turned on her were bloodshot and watering. 'Not well enough to talk, but Alessio insisted. I had to listen to him arguing with my mother, and my headache returned. What is it you want?'

'I don't want anything.' She bit her lip. 'Paolo, we're supposed to be crazy about each other, remember? It would seem really weird if I didn't ask for you.' She hesitated. 'I think your cousin feels that I'm stuck here in a kind of vacuum, and feels sorry for me.'

'He would do better to concentrate his compassion on me,' Paolo said sullenly. 'He refuses to call a doctor, although he knows that I have had a weak chest since childhood, and my mother fears this cold may settle there.' He gave a hollow cough as if to prove his point. 'He said he would prefer to summon a vet to examine Caio, and he and my mother quarrelled again.'

Laura sighed. 'I'm sorry if you're having a difficult time, but you're not the only one.' She leaned forward. 'Paolo, I'm finding it really hard to cope with being the uninvited guest round here. I need you to support me—take off some of the pressure.' She paused. 'How long, do you think, before you're well enough to get up and join the real world again?'

'When *Mamma* considers I am out of danger, and not before,' he said, with something of a snap. 'She alone knows how ill I am. She has been wonderful to me—a saint in her patience and care.' He sneezed violently, and lay back, dabbing his nose with a bunch of tissues. 'And my health is more important than your convenience,' he added in a muffled voice.

She got to her feet. She said crisply, 'Actually, it's your own convenience that's being served here. You seem to be overlooking that. But if you'd rather I kept my distance, that's fine with me.'

'I did not mean that,' he said, his tone marginally more conciliatory. 'Of course I wish you to continue to play your part, now more than ever. I shall tell *Mamma* that you must visit me each day—to aid my recovery. That I cannot live without you,' he added with sudden inspiration.

Her mouth tightened. 'No need to go to those lengths, perhaps. But at least it will give me a purpose for staying on.'

'And you can go sightseeing, even if I am not with you,' he went on. 'I shall tell *Mamma* to put Giacomo and the car at your service at once.' He coughed again. 'But now I have talked enough, and my throat is hurting. I need to sleep to become well, you understand.'

'Yes,' she said. 'Of course.' She moved to the door. 'Well—I'll see you tomorrow.'

Outside, she leaned against the wall and drew a deep breath. The daily visits would be a rod for her back, but, to balance that, being able to use the car was an unexpected lifeline.

It offered her a means of escape from the enclosed world of the villa, she thought, and, more vitally, meant that she would no longer be thrown into the company of Alessio Ramontella.

And that was just what she wanted, she told herself. Wasn't it?

CHAPTER SIX

EXCEPT, of course, it had all been too good to be true. As she should probably have known, Laura thought wryly.

Several long days had passed since Paolo had airily promised her the use of the car, and yet she was still confined to the villa and its grounds, with no release in sight.

Naturally, it was the Signora who had applied the veto. Paolo was still far from well, she'd pronounced ominously, and, if there was an emergency, then the car would be needed.

'If you had wished to explore Umbria, *signorina*, then perhaps you should have accepted my nephew's generous invitation,' she'd added, making Laura wonder how she'd come by that particular snippet of information.

But it was an invitation that, signally, had not been repeated, although she often heard the noise of the Jeep driving away.

And far from them being thrown together, after that first day, the Count seemed to have chosen deliberately to remain aloof from her.

He'd finished his breakfast and gone by the time she appeared each morning, but he continued to join her at dinner, although the conversation between them seemed polite and oddly formal compared with their earlier exchanges. And afterwards, he excused himself quickly and courteously, so that she was left strictly to her own devices.

So perhaps he too had sensed the danger of being over-friendly. And, having brought about her reunion with Paolo in spite of his aunt's disapproval, considered his duty done.

She should have found the new regime far less disturbing, and easier to cope with, but somehow it wasn't.

Even in his absence, she was still conscious of him, as if his presence had invaded every stone of the villa's walls. She found she was waiting for his return—listening for his footsteps, and the sound of his voice.

And worst of all was seeing his face in the darkness as she fought restlessly for sleep each night.

The evening meal, she acknowledged wretchedly, was now the highlight of her day, in spite of its new restrictions.

It was an attitude she'd have condemned as ludicrous in anyone else, and she knew it.

And if someone had warned her that she would feel like this, one day, about a man that she hardly even knew, she would not have believed them.

Yet it was happening to her—twenty-first-century Laura. She was trapped, held helpless by the sheer force of her own untried emotions. By feelings that were as old as eternity.

She'd soon discovered that he was not simply on vacation at the villa when she'd made herself take up his invitation to borrow something to read. His library, she saw, was not merely shelved out with books from floor to ceiling, but its vast antique desk was also home to a state-of-the-art computer system, which explained why he was closeted there for much of the time he spent at the villa.

Though not, of course, when she'd paid her visit. It had been Emilia who had waited benignly while she'd made her selection. She had just been hesitating over a couple of modern thrillers, when, to her surprise, she had come on a complete set of Jane Austen, and her choice had been made. She'd glanced through them, appreciating the beautiful leather bindings, then decided on *Mansfield Park*, which she hadn't read since her school days.

The name Valentina Ramontella was inscribed on the flyleaf in an elegant sloping hand, and Emilia, in answer to her tentative enquiry, had told her, with a sigh, that this had been the name of His Excellency's beloved mother, and these books her particular property.

'I see.' Laura touched the signature gently with her forefinger. 'Well, please assure the Count I'll take great care of it.'

However tenuous, it was almost a connection between them, she thought as she took the book away.

But, although the hours seemed strangely empty in Alessio's absence, she was not entirely without companionship as one day stretched endlessly into the next.

Because, to her infinite surprise, Caio had attached himself to her. He was no longer kept in the courtyard, but she'd come across a reluctant Guillermo taking him for a walk in the garden, on the express orders of his master, he'd told her glumly. Seeing his face, and listening to the little dog's excited whimpers as he'd strained on the leash to reach her, Laura had volunteered to take over this daily duty—if the Signora agreed.

Even more surprisingly, permission had been ungraciously granted. And, after a couple of days, Caio trotted beside her so obediently, she dispensed with the leash altogether.

He sometimes accompanied her down to the pool, lying under her sun lounger, and sat beside her in the *salotto* in the evenings as she flexed her rusty fingering on some of the Beethoven sonatas she'd found in bound volumes inside the piano stool. At mealtimes, apart from dinner, he was stationed unobtrusively under her chair, and he'd even joined her on the bed for siesta on a couple of occasions, she admitted guiltily.

'I see you have acquired a bodyguard,' was Alessio's only comment when he encountered them together once, delivered with a faint curl of the mouth.

Watching him walk away, she scooped Caio defensively into her arms. 'We're just a couple of pariahs here,' she murmured to him, and he licked her chin almost wistfully.

But she never took Caio to Paolo's room, instinct telling this would be too much for the Signora, who had no idea of the scope of her pet's defection to the enemy.

And I don't want her to know, Laura thought grimly. I'm unpopular enough already. I don't want to be accused of pinching her dog.

On his own admission, Paolo's cold symptoms had all but vanished, but he refused to leave his room on the grounds that he was still suffering with his chest.

Laura realised that her impatience with him and her ambiguous situation was growing rapidly and would soon reach snapping point.

These ten-minute stilted visits each evening wouldn't convince anyone that they were sharing a grand passion, she thought with exasperated derision. And if the Signora was listening at the door, she'd be justified in wagering her diamonds that she'd soon have Beatrice Manzone as a daughter-in-law.

But: 'You worry too much,' was Paolo's casual response to her concern.

Well, if he was satisfied, then why should she quibble? she thought with an inward shrug. He was the paying customer, after all. And found herself grimacing at the thought.

But as she left his room that evening the Signora was waiting for her, her lips stretched in the vinegary smile first encountered in Rome. Still, any calibre of smile was a welcome surprise, Laura thought, tension rising within her.

She was astonished to be told that, as Giacomo would be driving to the village the next morning to collect some special medicine from the pharmacy, she was free to accompany him there, if she wished.

'You may have some small errands, *signorina*.' The older woman's shrug emphasised their trifling quality. 'But the medicine is needed, so you will not be able to remain for long.'

Well, it was better than nothing, Laura thought, offering a polite word of thanks instead of the cartwheel she felt like turning. In fact, it was almost a 'get out of jail' card.

Saved, she thought, with relief. Saved from cabin fever, and, hopefully, other obsessions too.

She'd have time to buy some postcards at least—let her family know she was still alive. And Gaynor, too, would be waiting to hear from her.

In the morning, she was ready well before the designated time, anxious that Giacomo would have no excuse to set off without her. She still couldn't understand why the Signora should suddenly be so obliging, and couldn't help wondering if the older woman was playing some strange game of cat and mouse with her.

But that makes no sense, she adjured herself impatiently. Don't start getting paranoid.

Seated in the front, Laura kept her eyes fixed firmly ahead as the car negotiated the winding road down to the valley, avoiding any chance glimpse of the mind-aching drop on one side, and praying that they would meet no other vehicles coming from the opposite direction.

She only realised when the descent was completed that she'd been holding her breath most of the time.

Giacomo drove straight to the main square, and parked near the church. Pointing to the hands on his watch, he conveyed that she had fifteen minutes only to spend in Besavoro, and Laura nodded in resigned acceptance.

Well, that was the deal, she told herself philosophically as she set off. And she would just have to make the most of it.

She soon realised that Besavoro was in reality a small town, and not what she thought of as a village at all. The square was lined with shops, selling every sort of food, as well as wine, olive oil, hardware and clothing. It all had a busy, purposeful air, without a designer boutique or gift shop in sight.

But the little news agency she came to sold a few postcards, featuring mainly Assisi and the Majella national park, and she bought four, deciding to send one to Carl, her immediate boss at Harman Grace as well.

No one in the shop spoke English, but with great goodwill the correct stamps for Britain were offered, and her change was counted carefully into her hand.

A few doors away was a bar with tables on the pavement, and Laura took a seat, ordering a coffee and a bottle of mineral water.

She glanced across the square, checking the car, and then, carefully, her watch, before starting to write her cards.

At the same time she was aware that people were checking her, not rudely, but with open interest. English tourists were clearly a rarity here, she realised, turning her own attention back to the task in hand.

She was sorely tempted to put, 'Having ghastly time. Glad you're not here,' but knew that would involve her in impossible explanations on her return. Better, she decided, to stick to the usual anodyne messages. To Gaynor alone could she eventually reveal the grisly truth, and wait for her to say, 'I told you so,' she thought ruefully.

Although there were things about her stay at the villa that she wasn't prepared to talk about—ever. Not even to Gaynor.

Now all she needed was a postbox, she thought, rifling through her small phrase book for the exact wording. On the other hand it was probably quicker and easier to ask Giacomo.

She slipped her pen back into her bag, and felt for her purse, looking again towards the church as she did so.

But where the car had stood only minutes before, there was an empty space.

Laura shot to her feet with a stifled cry of dismay. It couldn't have gone, she thought wildly. There were still minutes to spare. And if Giacomo had just looked across the square he'd have seen her. So why hadn't he come across to her—or sounded his horn even? Why—simply drive off?

The bar owner came dashing out, clearly worried that she was about to do a runner, his voice raised in protest.

Laura pointed. 'My lift—it's vanished. I—I'm stranded.'

The owner spread his hands in total incomprehension, talking excitedly. She became aware that people were pausing—staring. Beginning to ask questions. Hemming her in as they did so. Making her uncomfortably aware of her sudden isolation, in a strange country, and unable to speak a word of the language.

Then, suddenly, across the increasing hubbub, cut a drawl she recognised. '*Ciao, bella mia.* Having problems?'

Alessio had come through the small crowd, which had obediently parted for him, and was standing just a couple of feet away, watching her from behind dark glasses, hands on hips. The shorts he was wearing today were marginally more decent than the first pair she'd seen him in, but his dark blue shirt was unbuttoned almost to the waist.

And if she was pleased to see him, she was determined that he wasn't going to know it.

She faced him furiously. 'Actually—yes. The damned car's

gone without me.' She almost stamped her foot, but decided against it. 'Oh, God, I don't believe it.' She bit her lip. 'I suppose this is your aunt's idea—to make me walk back up that hill, in the hope I'll die of heatstroke.'

He grinned. 'Calm yourself, Laura. This time Zia Lucrezia is innocent. I told Giacomo to return to the villa.'

'But why?' She stared at him. 'There was no need. We had a perfectly good arrangement...'

Alessio shrugged. 'I felt you needed a break. Also, that Besavoro deserved more than just fifteen minutes of your time. Was I so wrong?'

'Well, no,' she conceded without pleasure.

'Good,' he approved lazily. 'And when you have completed your sightseeing, I will drive you back in the Jeep.'

Laura suddenly realised that public interest in her activities had snowballed since the Count's arrival. The fascinated circle gathering around them was now three deep.

She said stiffly, 'I thought I'd made it clear. I don't want you to put yourself to any trouble on my behalf.'

'There is no trouble—except perhaps with Luigi here.' He indicated the gaping bar owner. 'So, why don't you sit down and finish your drink before he has a fit, hmm?'

He turned to the nearest onlooker, and said something softly. As if a switch had been pressed, the crowd began to melt unobtrusively away.

Such is power, Laura thought mutinously as she obeyed. She watched him drop into the chair opposite, stretching long tanned legs out in front of him as he ordered another cappuccino for Laura, and an espresso for himself from Luigi.

He'd caught her totally on the back foot, she thought. And she resented that swift painful thud of the heart that his unexpected appearance had engendered. Especially when he'd practically ignored her for the past week.

But I should want to be ignored, she thought. I should want to be totally ostracised by him. Because it's safer that way...

'Please do not let me interrupt.' He nodded to the small pile of cards. 'Finish your correspondence.'

'I already have done.' She smiled over-brightly. 'Just touching base with family and friends.'

'Ah,' he said. 'The family that, according to my aunt, does not exist.'

Laura groaned inwardly. Paolo had reacted with ill temper to her confession that she'd deviated from the party line.

She made herself shrug. 'I can't imagine where she got that idea. Perhaps it suited her better to believe that I was a penniless orphan.'

'Which, of course, you are not.'

'Well, the penniless bit is fairly accurate. It's been a real struggle for my mother since my father died. I'm just glad I've got a decent job, so that I can help.'

The dark brows lifted. 'Does working in a wine bar pay so well? I did not know.'

But that's not the day job. The words hovered on her lips, but, thankfully, remained unspoken.

Oh, God, she thought, hastily marshalling her thoughts. I've goofed again.

She met his sardonic gaze. 'It's a busy place, *signore*, and the tips are good.'

'Ah,' he said softly. He glanced around him. 'So, what are your impressions of Besavoro?'

'It's larger than I thought, and much older. I didn't think I would catch more than a glimpse of it, of course.'

'I thought you would be pleased that I sent Giacomo away for another reason,' he said, leaning back in his chair, and pushing his sunglasses up onto his forehead. 'It will mean that Paolo will get his medicine more quickly, and maybe return to your arms, *subito*, a man restored.'

'I doubt it.' She looked down at the table. 'He seems set for the duration.' She hesitated. 'Has he always fussed about his health like this? I mean—he's simply got a cold.'

'Why, Laura,' he said softly. 'How hard you are. For a man, no cold is ever simple.'

'Well, I can't imagine you going to bed for a week.'

'No?' His smile was wicked. The dark eyes seemed to graze

her body. 'Then perhaps you need to extend the scope of your imagination, *mia cara.*'

I am not—*not* going to blush, Laura told herself silently. And I don't care how much he winds me up.

She looked back at him squarely, 'I meant—with some minor ailment, *signore.*'

'Perhaps not.' He shrugged. 'But my temper becomes so evil, I am sure those around me wish I would retire to my room—and stay there until I can be civil again.'

He paused while Luigi placed the coffees in front of them. 'But I have to admit that Paolo was a sickly child, and I think his mother plays on this, by pampering him, and making him believe every cough and sneeze is a serious threat. It is her way of retaining some hold on him.'

'I'm sure of it,' Laura said roundly. 'I suspect Beatrice Manzone has had a lucky escape.' And could have bitten her tongue out again as Alessio's gaze sharpened.

'*Davvero?*' he queried softly. 'A curious point of view to have about your *innamorato*, perhaps.'

'I meant,' Laura said hastily, in a bid to retrieve the situation, 'that I shan't be as submissive—or as easy to manipulate—as she would have been.'

'*Credo,*' he murmured, his mouth twisting. 'I believe you, *mia cara.* You have that touch of red in your hair that spells danger.'

He picked up his cup. 'Now, drink your coffee, and I will take you to see the church,' he added more briskly. 'There is a Madonna and Child behind the high altar that some people say was painted by Raphael.'

'But you don't agree?' Laura welcomed the change of direction.

He considered, frowning a little. 'I think it is more likely to have been one of his pupils. For one thing, it is unsigned, and Raphael liked to leave his mark. For another, Besavoro is too unimportant to appeal to an artist of his ambition. And lastly the Virgin does not resemble Raphael's favourite mistress, whom he is said to have used as his chief model, even for the Sistine Madonna.'

'Wow,' Laura said, relaxing into a smile. 'How very sacrilegious of him.'

He grinned back at her. 'I prefer to think—what proof of his passion.' He gave a faint shrug. 'But ours is still a beautiful painting, and can be treasured as such.'

He drank the rest of his coffee, and stood up, indicating the postcards. 'You wish me to post these? Before we visit the church?'

'Well, yes.' She hesitated. 'But you don't have to come with me, *signore*. After all, I can hardly get lost. And I know how busy you are. I'm sure you have plenty of other things to do.'

'Perhaps,' he said. 'But today, *mia cara*, I shall devote to you.' His smile glinted. 'Or did you think I had forgotten about you these past days?'

'I—I didn't think anything at all,' she denied hurriedly.

'I am disappointed,' he said lightly. 'I hoped you might have missed me a little.'

'Then maybe you should remember something.' She lifted her chin. 'I came to Besavoro with your cousin, *signore*.'

'Ah,' Alessio said softly. 'But that is so fatally easy to forget, Laura *mia*.'

And he walked off across the square.

The interior of the church was dim, and fragrant with incense. It felt cool, too, after the burning heat of the square outside.

There were a number of small streets, narrow and cobbled, opening off the square, their houses facing each other so closely that people could have leaned from the upper-storey windows and touched, and Laura explored them all.

The shuttered windows suggested a feeling of intimacy, she thought. A sense of busy lives lived in private. And the flowers that spilled everywhere from troughs and window boxes added to Besavoro's peace and charm.

'So,' Alessio said as they paused for some water at a drinking fountain before visiting the church. 'Do you like my town?'

'It's enchanting,' Laura returned with perfect sincerity, smiling inwardly at his casual use of the possessive. The lord, she thought, with his fiefdom. 'A little gem.'

'*Sì*,' he agreed. 'And now I will show you another. *Avanti*.'

Laura trod quietly up the aisle of the church, aware of Alessio following silently. The altar itself was elaborate with gold leaf, but she hardly gave it a second glance. Because, above it, the painting glowed like a jewel, creating its own light.

The girl in it was very young, her hair uncovered, her blue cloak thrown back. She held the child proudly high in her arms, her gaze steadfast, and almost defiant, as if challenging the world to throw the first stone.

Laura caught her breath. She turned to Alessio, eyes shining, her hand going out to him involuntarily. 'It's—wonderful.'

'Yes,' he returned quietly, his fingers closing round hers. 'Each time I see it, I find myself—amazed.'

They stood in silence for a few minutes longer, then, as if by tacit consent, turned and began to walk around the shadowy church, halting briefly at each shrine with its attendant bank of burning candles.

Laura knew she should free her hand, but his warm grasp seemed unthreatening enough. And she certainly didn't want to make something out of nothing, especially in a church, so she allowed her fingers to remain quietly in his.

But as they emerged into the sunshine he let her go anyway. Presumably, thought Laura, the Count Ramontella didn't wish 'his' citizens to see him walking hand in hand with a girl.

Or not my kind of girl, certainly, she amended silently.

She'd expected to be driven straight back to the villa, but to her uneasy surprise Alessio took another road altogether, climbing the other side of the valley.

'Where are we going?' she asked.

'There's a view I wish to show you,' he said. 'It belongs to a *trattoria*, so we can enjoy it over lunch.'

'But aren't we expected back at the villa?'

'You are so keen to return?' He slanted a smile at her. 'You think, maybe, that Paolo's medicine has already worked its magic?'

'No,' she said stiffly. 'Just wondering what your aunt will think.'

'It is only lunch,' he said. The smile lingered—hardened a little. 'And I do not think she will have any objection—or none that need trouble either of us.'

The *trattoria* was a former farmhouse, extensively renovated only a couple of years earlier. Among the improvements had been a long wide terrace, with a thatched roof to provide shade, which overlooked the valley.

Their welcome was warm, but also, Laura noticed, respectful, and they were conducted to a table at the front of the terrace. Menus were produced and they were offered an *aperitivo*.

Laura found herself leaning beside Alessio on the parapet of the broad stone wall, holding a glass of white wine, and looking down onto an endless sea of green, distantly punctuated by the blue ribbon of the river and the dusty thread of the road.

On the edge of her vision, she could see the finger of stone that was Besavoro's *campanile* rising from the terracotta roofs around it.

Higher up, the crags looked almost opalescent in the shimmer of the noonday sun, while on the opposite side of the valley, almost hidden by the clustering forest, she could just make out the sprawl of greyish pink stone that formed the Villa Diana.

She said softly, 'It's—unbelievable. Thank you for showing it to me.'

'The pleasure is mine,' he returned. 'It is a very small world, this valley, but important to me.'

She played with the stem of her glass. 'Yet you must have so many worlds, *signore*.'

'And some I prefer to others.' He paused. 'So, where is your world, Laura? The real one?'

Her tone was stilted. 'London, I guess—for the time being anyway. My work is there.'

'But surely you could work anywhere you wished? Wine bars are not confined to your capital. But I suppose you wish to remain for Paolo's sake.'

She had a sudden longing to tell him the truth. To turn to him and say, 'Actually I work for the PR company your bank has just hired. The wine bar is moonlighting, and Harman Grace would probably have a fit if they knew. Nor am I involved with Paolo. He's renting me as his pretend girlfriend to convince his mother that he won't marry Beatrice Manzone.'

But she couldn't say any such thing, of course, because she'd given Paolo her word.

Instead she said, 'Also, I'm flat-hunting with some friends. We all want to move on from our current grotty bedsits, especially Gaynor and myself, so we thought we'd pool our resources.'

'Does Paolo approve of this plan?' Alessio traced the shape of one of the parapet's flat stones with his finger. 'Won't he wish you to live with him?'

She bit her lip. 'Perhaps—ultimately. I—I don't know. It's too soon for that kind of decision.'

'But this holiday could have been the first step towards it.' There was an odd, almost harsh note in his voice. 'My poor Laura. If so, how cruel to keep you in separate rooms, as I have done.'

She forced a smile. 'Not really. The Signora would have had a fit and I—I might have caught Paolo's cold.'

His mouth twisted. 'A practical thought, *carissima*.' He straightened. 'Now, shall we decide what to eat?'

A pretty, smiling girl, who turned out to be the owner's wife, brought a bowl of olive oil to their table, and a platter of bread to dip into it. The cooking, Alessio explained, was being done by her husband. Then came a dish of Parma ham, accompanied by a bewildering array of sausages, which was followed up by wild boar pâté.

The main course was chicken, simply roasted and bursting with flavour, all of it washed down with a jug of smoky red wine, made, Alessio told her, from the family's own vineyard in Tuscany.

But Laura demurred at the idea of dessert or cheese, raising laughing hands in protest.

'They'll be charging me excess weight on the flight home at this rate.'

Alessio drank some wine, the dark eyes watching her over the top of his glass. 'Maybe you need to gain a little,' he said. 'A man likes to know that he has his woman in his arms. He does not wish her to slip through his fingers like water. Has Paolo never told you so?'

She looked down at the table. 'Not in so many words. And I don't think it's a very fashionable point of view, not in London, anyway.'

The mention of Paolo's name brought her down to earth with a jolt. It had been such a wonderful meal. She'd felt elated—euphoric even—here, above the tops of the trees.

I could reach up a hand, she thought, and touch the sky.

And this, she knew, was entirely because of the man seated across the table from her. The man who somehow had the power to make her forget everything—including the sole reason that had brought her to Italy in the first place.

Stupid, she castigated herself. Eternally, ridiculously stupid to hanker after what she could never have in a thousand years.

Because there was far more than just a table dividing them, and she needed to remember that in her remaining days at the Villa Diana.

Apart from anything else, they'd been acquainted with each other for only a week, which was a long time in politics, but in no other sense.

So how was it that she felt she'd known him all her life? she asked herself, and sighed inwardly. That, of course, was the secret of his success—especially with women.

And her best plan was to escape while she could, and before she managed to make an even bigger fool of herself than she had already.

She was like a tiny planet, she thought, circling the sun, when any slight change in orbit could draw her to self-destruction. Burning up for all eternity.

That cannot happen, she told herself. And I won't let it.

He said, 'A moment ago, you were here with me. Now you have gone.' He leaned forward, his expression quizzical.

'''When, Madonna, will you ever drop that veil you wear in shade and sun?'''

She looked back at him startled. 'I don't understand.'

'I was quoting,' he said. 'From Petrarch—one of his sonnets to Laura. My own translation. It seemed—appropriate.'

She tried to speak lightly. 'You amaze me, *signore*. I never thought I'd hear you speaking poetry.'

He shrugged. 'But I'm sure you could recite from Shakespeare, if I asked you. Am I supposed to have less education?'

'No,' she said quickly. 'No, of course not. I'm sorry. After all, we're strangers. I shouldn't make any assumptions about you.'

He paused. 'Besides, the question is a valid one. Because you also disappear behind a veil sometimes, so that I cannot tell what you're thinking.'

She laughed rather weakly. 'I'm—relieved to hear it.'

'So I shall ask a direct question. What are you hiding, Laura?'

Her fingers twined together in her lap. 'I think as well as a good education, *signore*, you have a vivid imagination.'

He studied her for a moment, his mouth wry. 'And you still will not call me Alessio.'

'Because I don't think it's necessary,' she retorted. 'Or even very wise, you being who you are. Not just a count, but Chairman of the Arleschi Bank.'

'You could not put that out of your mind for a while?'

'No.' Her fingers tightened round each other. 'That's not possible. Besides, I'll be gone soon, anyway.'

'But you forget, *signorina*,' he said silkily. 'You are to become a member of my family. We shall be cousins.'

She paused for a heartbeat. 'Well, when we are,' she said, 'I'll think again about your name.' She gave him a bright smile. 'And now will you take me back to the villa, please? Paolo may need me,' she added for good measure.

As he rose to his feet he was laughing. 'Well, run while you may, my little hypocrite,' he told her mockingly. 'But remember this: you cannot hide—or not for ever.' His fingers stroked her face from the high cheekbone to the corner of her mouth, then he turned and walked away across the terrace to the restaurant's

main door, leaving Laura to stare uneasily after him, her heart
and mind locked into a combat that offered no prospect of peace.
And which, she suddenly knew, could prove mortal.

But only to me, she whispered to herself in swift anguish. Only
to me...

CHAPTER SEVEN

THE return journey was conducted mainly in silence. Laura was occupied with her own troubling thoughts, while Alessio was reviewing the events of the morning with a sense of quiet satisfaction.

She had missed him, he thought. Everything—including all the things she had not said—had betrayed it. So his ploy of keeping aloof from her had succeeded. And, now, she was desperately trying to reinforce her own barricades against him.

But it won't work, *carissima*, he told her silently.

After he'd got rid of Giacomo that morning, he'd stood for a while, watching her from the other side of the square.

She might not have the flamboyant looks of a woman like Vittoria, but her unselfconscious absorption as she wrote gave an impression of peace and charm that he had never encountered before.

And her hair had been truly glorious in the sunlight, the colour of English leaves in autumn. He'd found himself suddenly longing to see it spread across his pillow, so that he could run his fingers through its soft masses and breathe their fragrance.

Also, he'd noted, with additional pleasure, she was again wearing the dress that had so fired his imagination at their first meeting.

And soon, he thought, as he turned the Jeep onto the road up to the villa—soon his fantasies would all be realised.

Not that it would be easy, he mentally amended with sudden restiveness. She might have let him take her hand for a while without protest, but, in many ways, she still continued to elude him, and not just in the physical sense either.

Her relationship with his cousin was certainly an enigma. He didn't particularly share his aunt's opinion that the pair were in love and planning immediate marriage. But then, he admitted, he'd hardly seen them together. Although, that first evening, he'd observed that the little Laura had not seemed to relish her lover's advances. But that might have been because she preferred privacy for such exchanges, and not a family dinner.

Well, privacy she should have, he promised himself, smiling inwardly, and his entire undivided attention as well.

However, he still wondered if, given time, the whole Paolo affair might have withered and died of its own accord, and without Zia Lucrezia's interference.

Not that he'd been able to convince her of that, although he had tried. She'd simply snapped that she could not afford to be patient, and that Paolo's engagement to the Manzone girl must be concluded without further delay.

She'd added contemptuously that the English girl was nothing more than a money-grubbing trollop who deserved to be sent packing in disgrace for attempting to connect herself, even distantly, to the Ramontella family.

'And your part in all this should have been played by now,' she added angrily. 'You should have spent more time with the little fool.'

'I know what I'm doing,' he returned coldly. 'Precisely because the girl is far from a fool, or any of the other names you choose to call her.'

How, in the name of God, could he feel so protective, he asked himself ruefully, afterwards, when he might be planning the possible ruin of Laura's life? If, indeed, it turned out that she cared for Paolo after all.

But on one thing he was totally determined. When he took her, it would be out of their mutual desire alone, and not to placate his aunt. That, he told himself, would be the least of his considerations.

He could salve his conscience to that extent.

And, if humanly possible, it would happen well away from the Villa Diana, and Zia Lucrezia's inevitable and frankly indecent gloating.

Because he needed to make very sure that Laura would never know how they'd been manipulated into each other's arms.

Although that was no longer strictly true—or not for him, anyway, he reminded himself wryly. On his side, at least, the need was genuine, and had been so almost from the first. She was the one who required the persuasion.

Staying away from her over the past few days had been sheer torment, he admitted, to his own reluctant surprise. She had been constantly in the forefront of his mind, waking and sleeping, while his entire body ached intolerably for her too.

He was not accustomed, he acknowledged sardonically, to waiting for a woman. In his world, it was not often that he found it necessary. And it would make her ultimate surrender even more enjoyable.

He cast a lightning sideways glance at her, and saw that her hands were clenched tightly in her lap.

He said lightly, 'Is it the road or my driving that so alarms you, Laura?'

She turned her head, forcing a smile. 'It's the road, although I'm trying to get used to it. We don't have so many death-defying drops in East Anglia, where I come from.'

'Try not to worry too much, *mia bella*.' His tone was dry. 'Believe that I have a vested interest in staying alive.'

There was a movement at the side of the road ahead, and Alessio leaned forward, his gaze sharpening as a stocky, white-haired man wearing overalls came into view, carrying a tall cane shaped like a shepherd's crook. 'Ah,' he said, half to himself. 'Fredo.' He drew the Jeep into the side of the road, and stopped. 'Will you forgive me, *cara*, if I speak to him again about moving down to Besavoro? He has been avoiding me, I think.'

Laura sat in the Jeep and watched with some amusement. The old man stood like a rock, leaning on his cane, occasionally moving his head in quiet negation as Alessio prowled round in front of him talking rapidly in his own language, his hands gesturing urgently in clear appeal.

When at last he paused for breath, the old man reached up and clapped him on the shoulder, his wrinkled face breaking into a smile. Then they talked together for a few more minutes before Fredo turned away, making his slow way up a track on the hillside, and Alessio came back to the Jeep, frowning.

'Still no luck?' she asked.

'He makes his own goats seem reasonable.' He started the engine. 'Also, he says that the weather is going to change. That we shall have storms,' he added, his frown deepening.

Laura looked up at the cloudless sky. 'It doesn't seem like it,' she objected.

'Fredo is rarely wrong about these things. But it will not be for a day—perhaps two.' He slanted a smile at her. 'So make the most of the sun while you can.'

'I've been doing just that.' She paused. 'In fact,' she went on hesitantly, 'I was—concerned in case I'd kept you away from the pool. If you preferred to have it to yourself. Because I've noticed that you—you haven't been swimming for a while.'

'I swim every day,' he said. 'But very early. Before breakfast, when there is no one else about, but that is not through any wish to avoid your company, *mia bella*, but because I like to swim naked.'

'Oh.' Laura swallowed. 'Oh, I—I understand. Of course.'

'Although,' he went on softly, 'you could always join me if you wished. The water feels wonderful at that time of day.'

'I'm sure it does,' Laura said woodenly, all sorts of forbidden images leaping to mind. 'But I think I'll stick to my own timetable. *Grazie*,' she added politely.

'*Prego,*' he returned, and she could hear the laughter in his voice.

Furiously aware that her face had warmed, Laura relapsed into a silence that lasted until their arrival at the villa.

As she left the Jeep she thanked Alessio for the lunch in the tone of a polite schoolgirl taking leave of a favourite uncle, and went off to her room, trying not to look as if she was escaping.

Her clothes were clinging to her in the heat, so she stripped quickly and took a cool shower. Then, she put on her robe and lay down on the bed, trying to relax. But her mind was still teeming with thoughts and impressions from the morning.

It was weird, she thought, that Alessio—the Count, she amended hastily—should just turn up like that, out of the blue. And even more disturbing that she should have enjoyed being with him quite so much.

She'd been unnerved too by his suggestion that she was hiding something. He might have dressed it up in poetic language about veils, she thought ruefully, but basically he was issuing a warning that he was on to her.

And in turn she would have to warn Paolo, on her evening visit, that his lordly cousin was growing suspicious.

She found herself sighing a little. These visits were becoming more problematic each time. Quite apart from his obsession about his cold, it was difficult to hold a conversation with someone she hardly knew, and with whom she barely had a thought in common, especially when she suspected his mother was listening at the door.

I wish all this had never happened, she told herself vehemently. That I'd never agreed to this ridiculous pretence. And, most of all, that I'd never come here and set eyes on Count Ramontella. Better for me that he'd just remained a name on a letterhead.

Easy to say, she thought, but did she really mean it? Would she truly have wanted to live her life without having experienced this frankly dangerous encounter? Without having felt the lure of his smile, or reacting to the teasing note in his voice? Without realising, dry-mouthed, that he had simply—entered the room?

No, she thought sadly. If I'm honest, I wouldn't have wanted to miss one precious moment with him. But now the situation's getting altogether trickier, and I really need to distance myself. Put the width of Europe between us, and become sane again.

It's safer that way, and I'm a safety-conscious girl. I have to be.

She sighed again. Alessio Ramontella was just a dream to take back with her to mundane reality, she thought wistfully. A private fantasy to lighten up her fairly staid existence. And that was all he ever would, or could be...

Until one day, when he would become nothing but a fading

memory. And she could relax, lower her guard, and get on with her own life.

Perhaps, in time, she might even convince herself that none of this had ever happened.

She sat up, swinging her legs to the floor. She was obviously not going to sleep, so she might take the Count's advice, and exploit the fine weather while it persisted.

She changed swiftly into her swimsuit, slipped on the filmy voile shirt she used as a cover-up, and went down to the pool.

As she reached the bottom of the steps she was disconcerted to see that she would not be alone that afternoon either. That Alessio was there before her, stretched out on a lounger, reading.

He seemed deeply absorbed, and Laura hesitated, wondering if she should turn quietly and make a strategic withdrawal before she was noticed. But it was already too late for that, because he was putting down his book and getting to his feet in one lithe movement, the sculpted mouth smiling faintly as he looked at her.

'So you came after all,' he said softly. 'I had begun to wonder.'

'I—I decided to take your friend at his word.' She paused. 'I hope I'm not disturbing you.'

He said lightly, 'Not in any way that you think, *mia cara*.' He moved a lounger into the shade of a parasol for her, and arranged the cushions.

'Thank you.' She felt self-conscious enough to have stood on one leg and sucked her thumb. And he'd placed her sunbed far too close to his own, she thought with misgiving. However, it seemed unwise to make any kind of fuss, so she walked across and sat down, forcing a smile as she looked up at him. 'Heavens, it's hotter than ever.'

'Yes.' Alessio glanced up at the mountains with a slight frown. 'I begin to think Fredo may be right.'

Laura reached down and retrieved his book, which had slipped off his lounger onto the marble tiles between them. 'Francesco Petrarca' was emblazoned in faded gilt letters across its leather cover.

'Reading more poetry about veiled ladies, *signore*?' She

handed it to him. Literature, she thought. Now there's a safe topic for conversation.

'There is much to read,' he said drily. 'The great Francesco made his Laura's name a song for twenty years.'

'How did they meet?'

'He saw her,' Alessio said, after a pause. 'Saw her one day, and fell in love for ever.'

'And did they live happily ever after?'

'They lived their own lives, but not together. She—belonged to another man.'

She made a thing of adjusting her sunglasses. She said lightly, 'Then maybe he shouldn't have allowed himself to fall in love.'

'Ah,' he said softly. 'But perhaps, Laura *mia*, he could not help himself. Listen.' He found a page, and read aloud. '''I was left defenceless against love's attack, with no barrier between my eyes and my heart.'''

He put the book down. 'Is there a defence against love, I wonder?' The dark gaze seemed to bore into hers. 'What do you think, *bella mia*? Did Paolo travel straight from your eyes to your heart when you saw him first?'

No, she thought, pain twisting inside her. But you did—and now I'm lost for ever...

She made herself look back at him. 'Naturally there was—a connection. Why else would I be here?'

'Why indeed?' he said softly. He stretched slowly, effortlessly, making her numbly aware of every smooth ripple of muscle in his lean body. 'I am going to swim, Laura. Will you join me?'

'No,' she managed somehow. 'No, thank you.'

He smiled at her. 'You do not feel the necessity to cool off a little?'

'I'm a very poor swimmer,' she said. 'I don't like being out of my depth, and your pool has no shallow end.'

'Ah,' he said meditatively. 'Then why do you not allow me to teach you?'

There was a loaded silence, and Laura found she was biting her lip. 'That's—very kind,' she said, trying to keep her voice steady. 'But I couldn't—possibly—impose on you like that.'

'No imposition, *cara mia*.' His voice was a drawl. 'It would be my privilege, and my pleasure. Besides,' he added with faint reproof, 'everyone should be able to swim safely. Don't you agree?'

'I—I suppose so.' Except that we're not really talking about swimming, she thought wildly, and we both know it. So why—why are you doing this?

He said softly, 'But you are not convinced.' He walked to the far end of the pool, and dived in, swimming the whole length under water. He surfaced, shaking the water from his hair, and swam slowly to the edge, resting his arms on the tiled surround.

He beckoned. 'Laura, come to me.' He spoke quietly, but the imperative came over loud and clear. She realised, not for the first time, why he was a force to be reckoned with within the Arleschi Bank.

Reluctantly, she shed the voile shirt and walked over to the edge of the pool, reed-slender in her green swimsuit.

She said coolly, 'Do you always expect to be obeyed, *signore*?'

'Always.' The sun glistened on the dark hair as he looked up at her. He added softly, 'But I prefer compliance to submission, *signorina*.' He paused, allowing her to assimilate that, then smiled. 'Now sit on the edge,' he directed. 'Put your hands on my arms, and lower yourself into the water. I promise I will keep you safe.'

Her heart juddered. Oh, but it's too late, she thought. Much too late for that.

But she did as she was told, gasping as the coolness of the water made contact with her overheated skin, aware of Alessio's hands, firm as rocks, under her elbows.

'You can stand,' she accused breathlessly. 'But I can't reach. I'm treading water.'

'Then do so,' he said. 'You will come to no harm.' He added with faint amusement, 'And I can do nothing about the disparity in our heights, *bella mia*.'

He paused. 'You say you can swim a little?' And, when she

nodded without much conviction, 'The width of the pool, perhaps?'

'Possibly,' Laura said with dignity. She hesitated. 'But not without touching the bottom with my toe,' she conceded unwillingly.

He sighed. 'Then the true answer is no,' he commented austerely. 'So, we shall begin.'

It was one of the strangest hours of her life. If she'd imagined Alessio had lured her into the pool for his own dubious purposes, then she had to think again and quickly, because his whole attitude was brisk, almost impersonal. He really intended to teach her to swim, she realised in astonishment as she struggled to co-ordinate her arm and leg movements and her breathing, while his hand cupped her chin.

One of her problems, he told her, was her apparent reluctance to put her face in the water.

'What does it matter if your make-up is spoiled?' he said.

'I'm not wearing make-up,' she retorted, trying to catch her breath.

He slanted a faint grin at her. 'I know. Now let us try again.

'You lack confidence, no more than that, so you must learn to trust the water,' he directed eventually. 'Let it hold you, and do not fight it. Now, turn on your back and float for a while. I will support you.'

She did as she was bidden, feeling the dazzle of the sun on her closed eyelids.

She was not even aware of the moment he gently withdrew his hand from beneath her head until she heard him say, '*Brava*, Laura. You do well,' and realised he was no longer beside her.

Her eyes flew open in swift panic, to see him watching her from the side of the pool, and she floundered suddenly, coughing and spluttering. He reached her in a moment, and held her.

'You let go of me,' she gasped.

'About five minutes ago,' he told her drily. 'You stopped believing. That is all. But now, when you are ready, you will swim beside me across the pool, because you know you can. And remember to breathe,' he added sternly.

She gave him a mutinous look. '*Sì, signore.*'

But to her amazement she did it, and she felt almost euphoric with achievement when she found herself clinging to the opposite edge, catching her breath.

Alessio pulled himself out of the water, and stood for a moment, raking back his wet hair. Then he bent, sliding his hands under Laura's armpits, lifting her out to join him as if she were a featherweight.

'But I wanted to swim back,' she objected, smiling up at him as he put her down on the tiles.

'I think that is enough for the first time,' he said softly. He paused. 'After all, I do not wish to exhaust you.' His hands moved slowly to her shoulders. Remained there.

Laura was suddenly aware of a strange stillness as if the world had halted on its axis. Or was it just that her heart seemed to have stopped beating? He had told her to breathe, she thought confusedly, but it was impossible. Her throat was too tight.

In spite of the heat, she was shivering, an unfamiliar weakness penetrating the pit of her stomach.

He was looking down at her, she realised, watching her parted lips. He was smiling a little, but there was no laughter in the half-closed eyes, which studied her with frank intensity, as if mesmerised.

He bent towards her, and she thought, He's going to kiss me.

Deep within her, she felt a pang of yearning so acute that the stifled breath burst from her in a raw, shocked gasp. And with it came a kind of sanity as she realised exactly what she was inviting. And from whom...

She heard a voice she barely recognised as her own say raggedly, 'No—Alessio—please, no!'

The dark brows lifted wryly. He reached up, and framed her face with both hands, his thumbs stroking back the wet strands of hair behind her ears, then stroking gently along her cheekbones and down to the fragility of her jawline.

She felt him touch the corners of her quivering mouth, then the long fingers travelled down her throat to her shoulders again.

He said softly, 'No?'

He hooked a finger under the strap of her swimsuit, and drew it down, then bent, brushing his lips softly across the faint mark it had left on her skin.

Laura felt her whole body shudder in sudden heated delight at his touch. Knew, with dismay, that he would have recognised that too.

He said quietly, 'Laura, I have a house overlooking the sea near Sorrento. It is quiet, and very beautiful, and we could be there together in just a few hours.' His dark eyes met hers. 'So—are you still quite sure it is—no?' he asked.

Somehow, even at this stage, she had to retrieve the situation. Somehow...

She stepped back, out of range, lifting her chin in belated defiance. 'I'm—absolutely certain.' Fiercely, she jerked her strap back into place. 'And you—you—you have no right—no right at all to think—to assume...'

'I assume nothing, *carissima*.' He raised his hands in pretended surrender, his tone amused—rueful. 'But you cannot blame me for trying.'

'But I do blame you,' she flung back at him. 'And so would Paolo, if I decided to make trouble and tell him.' She swallowed. 'Do you think he'd be pleased to know you were—going behind his back like this?'

He shrugged. 'Paolo's feelings were never a consideration, I confess. I was far more concerned with my own pleasure, *bella mia*.' He smiled. 'And with yours,' he added softly.

She felt betraying colour swamp her face, but stood her ground. 'You still seem very sure of yourself, *signore*. I find that extraordinary.'

'Losing a battle,' he said, 'does not always alter the course of the war.' He paused. 'And you called me Alessio just now—while you were waiting for me to kiss you.'

Her flush deepened at this all-too-accurate assessment. She said through gritted teeth, 'The war, as you call it, is over. I shall tell Paolo I want to go back to England immediately. As soon as my flight can be rearranged.'

'And he may even agree,' he said. 'As long as it does not

interfere with his own plans. But if there are difficulties, do not hesitate to ask for my help.' He added silkily, 'I have some influence with the airline.'

Ignoring her outraged gasp, he walked across to his lounger, picked up the towel and began to dry himself with total unconcern. Laura snatched up her own things and headed for the steps.

'*Arrivederci.*' His voice followed her. 'Until later, *bellissima.*'

'Until hell freezes over,' she threw back breathlessly, over her shoulder, then forced her shaking legs to carry her up the steps and out of the sight and sound of him.

Alessio watched her go, caught between exultancy and irritation, with a heaped measure of sexual frustration thrown in.

He ached, he thought sombrely, like a moonstruck adolescent.

Stretching out on the lounger, he gazed up at the sky, questions rotating in his mind.

Why, in the name of God, had he let her walk away like that? He'd felt her trembling when he'd touched her. Why hadn't he pressed home his advantage—thrown the cushions on the ground, and drawn her down there with him, peeling the damp swimsuit from her body, and silencing her protests with kisses as he'd taken her, swiftly and simply?

Winning her as his woman, he thought, while he appeased the hunger that was tearing him apart.

Afterwards, he would have sent her to pack her things while he enjoyed another kind of satisfaction—the moment when he told Paolo, and his damnable mother, that he was taking Laura away with him. His mission accomplished in the best possible way.

Then, off to Sorrento to make plans—but for what? The rest of their lives? He frowned swiftly. He had never thought of any woman in those terms. But certainly the weeks to follow—maybe even the months.

At some point, they would have to return to Rome. It would be best, he decided, if he rented an apartment for her. A place without resonances, containing a bed that he'd shared with no one else.

But what was the point of thinking like this, he derided himself, when none of it had happened? When she'd rejected him, using Paolo's name like a shield, as she always did. And he'd let her go...

Dio, he could still taste the cool silkiness of her skin.

And now she wished to leave altogether—to go back to London. Well, so she might, and the sooner the better. Because he would follow.

In England, he could pursue her on his own terms, he thought. He'd have the freedom to date and spoil her exactly as he wished, until her resistance crumbled. And there would be no Zia Lucrezia to poison the well.

Yes, he thought with a sigh of anticipation. London was the perfect answer.

Unless... He sat up suddenly, mind and body reeling as if he'd been punched in the gut. Was it—could it be possible that he'd misjudged the situation completely? Might it be that she was genuinely in love with his weasel of a cousin after all? The idea made him nauseous.

Yet she'd wanted him very badly to kiss her. His experience with women left him in no doubt about that, while her own female instinct must have told her that, once she was in his arms, it would not stop at kissing.

She'd allowed Paolo to kiss her, of course, and all the other intimacies he dared not even contemplate, because they filled him with such blind, impotent rage that he longed to go up to the house, take his cousin from his sick bed, and put him in hospital instead.

He looked down at the book beside him, his mouth hardening. Ah, Francesco, he thought. Was that the image that haunted you every night—your Laura in her husband's arms?

He supposed in some twisted way he should be grateful to his aunt for persuading her malingering son that he was far more sick than he really was, and keeping the lovers apart. At least he didn't have the torment of knowing they were together under his roof.

Santa Madonna, he thought. Anyone might think I was jealous. But I have never been so in my whole life.

And I do not propose to start now, he added grimly.

No, he thought. He would not accept that Laura had any serious feelings for Paolo. Women in love carried their own protection like a heat-shield. No one existed in their private radiant universe but the beloved. Yet he'd been able to feel her awareness of him just as surely as if she'd put out her hand and touched his body.

So, maybe she really believed that, with Paolo, she would be marrying money—or at least where money was. The thought made him wince, but it now had to be faced and dealt with. Because it was clear that, living in one room and working in a bar, she was struggling near the bottom of the ladder.

And, if he was right, he thought cynically, then he would have to convince her that he would be a far more generous proposition than his cousin. That, financially, she would do much better as his mistress than as Paolo's wife.

A much pleasanter task, he resolved, would be to set himself to create for her such an intensity of physical delight that she would forget all other men in his arms. It occurred to him, wryly, that it was the least she deserved.

But what do I deserve? he asked himself quietly. And could find no answer.

'What is this? What are you saying?' Paolo's face was mottled with annoyance.

'I want to go home,' Laura repeated levelly. 'I—I'm totally in the way here, and it's becoming a serious embarrassment for me.'

'An embarrassment for which you will be well paid,' he snapped. He paused. 'But what you ask is not possible. My mother will become suspicious if you go home alone—think that we have quarrelled.'

'I fail to see how,' Laura said coldly. 'We haven't spent enough time together to have a row.'

He waved an impatient hand. 'I have worked too hard to convince her to fail now.' He thought for a moment. 'But we could leave earlier than planned, if we go together—in two or three days, perhaps.'

'Will you be well enough to travel?' Laura asked acidly, but her sarcasm was wasted.

He shrugged. 'We must hope. And *Mamma* intends me to take a little trip with her very soon, so we shall see.'

She said quietly, 'Paolo, I'm deadly serious about this, and I don't intend to wait indefinitely. In twenty-four hours, I'm looking for another flight.'

I can survive that long, she thought bleakly as she went to her room to change for dinner. But this time, I'll be the one adopting the avoidance tactics.

CHAPTER EIGHT

NOTHING happened. Nothing happened. The words echoed and re-echoed in Laura's head, matching the reluctant click of her heels on the tiled floor as she walked to the *salotto* that evening.

But even if that was true, she could hardly take credit for it, she acknowledged bitterly. Nor could she pretend otherwise for her own peace of mind. And she felt as guilty as if she and Paolo had been genuinely involved with each other.

She'd stayed in her room as long as possible, pacing restlessly up and down, frankly dreading the moment when she would have to face Alessio again.

She still seemed to feel his touch as if it were somehow ingrained in her. She'd been almost surprised, as she'd stood under the shower, not to find the actual marks of his fingers—the scar left by the graze of his lips on her skin.

But, invisible or not, they were there, she knew, and she would carry them for ever.

Guillermo was hovering almost anxiously in the hallway, emphasising how late she'd left her arrival, and he sprang forward, beaming, to open the carved double doors to admit her to the *salotto*.

She squared her shoulders and walked in, braced—for what? Mockery—indifference? Or something infinitely more dangerous...

And halted, her brows lifting in astonishment. Because she was not to be alone with Alessio as she'd feared after all. Paolo was there, reclining on a sofa, looking sullen, while the Signora occupied a high-backed armchair nearby, her lips compressed as if annoyed about something.

And, alone by the open windows, looking out into the night, was Alessio, glass in hand.

All heads turned as Laura came forward, and she was immediately aware of an odd atmosphere in the silent room—a kind of angry tension. But she ignored it and went straight to Paolo, who rose sulkily to his feet at her approach.

'Darling,' she said. She reached up and kissed his cheek. 'You didn't say you were getting up for dinner. What a wonderful surprise.'

'Well, I shall not be able to take the time I need to recuperate, when you are in such a hurry to fly home,' he returned peevishly, making her long to kick him.

'Signorina Mason—at last you join us.' The Signora's smile glittered coldly at her. 'We were just talking about you. We have a small predicament, you understand.'

'I can't see what that could be. Paolo's well again.' Laura slid a hand through his arm as she faced the older woman, chin up. 'That's all that really matters.'

'Then I hope you are prepared to be gracious,' said the Signora, her smile a little fixed. 'Because tomorrow I must tear him away from you. We are to pay a visit to my dearest friend, and remain for lunch. She is not aware of your presence here, so I regret that you have not been included in her invitation. You will, I hope, forgive our absence.'

She turned her head towards Alessio, who looked back, his face expressionless.

'And now it seems that you will also be deserted by our host,' she went on, her voice faintly metallic. 'My nephew tells me he has business in Perugia tomorrow that cannot be postponed. We were—discussing the problem.'

Laura found herself torn between relief and a sense of desolation so profound that she was ashamed of herself. She dared not risk a glance in the direction of the tall young man standing in silence by the window.

Once again, it seemed, he was—letting her go.

'It's kind of you to be concerned, *signora*,' she returned with total insincerity. 'But I'm quite accustomed to my own company. Besides, His Excellency has already given me far too much of his time. And I have my packing to do. The time will pass in a flash.'

The Signora gave her a long look, then addressed herself to her nephew. 'Camilla tells me that her son, Fabrizio, will be joining us tomorrow, with his beautiful wife—I forget her name. Do you wish me to convey any message to them on your behalf?'

There was another tingling silence. Then: 'No,' Alessio said icily. 'I thank you.'

'Then let us dine,' said the Signora. 'I have quite an appetite. Come, *signorina*.'

On the way to the dining room, Alessio detained his cousin. 'Why in the name of God have you agreed to go to Trasimeno tomorrow?' he demanded in an undertone.

Paolo shrugged. '*Mamma* has suddenly become more amenable on the subject of my marriage plans. I felt she deserved a small concession. Besides,' he added, leering, 'you heard her say that tasty little plum Vittoria Montecorvo was going to be there. I thought I might try my chances with her.'

A single spark of unholy joy penetrated Alessio's inner darkness. 'Why not?' he drawled. 'Rumour says the lady is—receptive.' He paused. 'Although there is an obstacle, of course.'

'Obstacle?' Paolo stared at him, then laughed. 'You mean the husband? No problem there. He's a total fool.'

'I was thinking,' Alessio said levelly, 'of Signorina Mason.'

'Ah—yes.' Paolo looked shifty. 'But we are not married yet, and a man should be allowed his bachelor pleasures.'

'I could not agree more,' Alessio told him softly. 'I wish you luck, cousin.'

If Laura had thought the presence of other people at the table would make the situation easier, she soon realised her mistake.

Only the Signora, who seemed to have belatedly rediscovered the laws of hospitality and chattered almost vivaciously throughout dinner, appeared to enjoy the lengthy meal. Paolo was lost in some pleasant day-dream and hardly said a word, while Alessio's responses to his aunt's heavily playful remarks were crisp and monosyllabic.

Altogether, the atmosphere was tricky, and Laura, to her shame, found herself remembering almost nostalgically the meals she'd eaten alone with Alessio.

Don't even go there, she adjured herself severely as the ordeal drew to a close.

They returned to the *salotto* for coffee, and it occurred to her that she ought to talk to Paolo privately, and make certain that he'd taken seriously her insistence on going home. And that he intended to call the airline and change their flight as soon as he got back tomorrow.

She said with feigned brightness, 'Paolo, darling, why don't we have our coffee on the terrace? It's such a beautiful night and we can—enjoy the moonlight together.'

For a moment, she thought he was going to refuse, then comprehension dawned. 'But of course,' he said. 'What a wonderful idea.'

As she walked out through the windows she was aware of Alessio's enigmatic stare following her. She paused, realising that she was breathing much too fast, and went to lean on the balustrade as she tried to regain her composure.

If she was honest, she thought, looking up at the sky, it was far from being a lovely night. The air was hot and stifling, and there was a haze over the moon. Wasn't that supposed to be a sign of bad weather to come?

Then, as she waited she heard somewhere in the distance the long-drawn-out howl of an animal, an eerie sound that echoed round the hills, and made the fine hairs stand up on the nape of her neck.

Gasping, she turned and almost cannoned into Alessio, who was standing just behind her.

She recoiled violently. 'Oh, God, you startled me.' She swallowed. 'That noise—did you hear it?'

'It was a wolf, nothing more.' He put the cup of coffee he was carrying on the balustrade. 'They live in the forests, which is one of the reasons Fredo likes to stay up there too—to protect his goats. Didn't Paolo warn you about them?'

'Yes,' she said. 'He mentioned them.' She added coldly, 'But he failed to tell me that they don't all live in forests.'

Alessio winced elaborately. 'A little unjust, *bella mia*. According to the experts, wolves mate for life.'

'The four-legged kind, maybe.' She paused. 'I've never heard any of them before this evening. Why is that?'

'They are more vocal in the early spring, when they are breeding,' he explained. 'Perhaps, tonight, something has disturbed them.'

'Perhaps.' She looked past him towards the lights of the *salotto*. 'Where's Paolo?'

'His mother decided that the night air would be bad for his chest,' he said solemnly. 'And, as they have a journey tomorrow, she has persuaded him to have an early night.' He indicated the cup. 'So I brought your coffee to you.' He added, silkily, 'I regret your disappointment.'

'Paolo's health,' she said stonily, 'is far more important.'

The howl of the wolf came again, and she shivered. 'That's such a—lonely sound.'

'Maybe he is alone, and lonely.' Alessio faced her, leaning against the balustrade. 'A wolf occasionally does separate from the pack, and find that he does not wish to be solitary after all.'

'Well, I won't waste too much sympathy.' Laura kept her tone crisp. 'Wolves are predators, and I expect there are quite enough stray females about to prevent them becoming totally isolated. What do you think, *signore*?'

He grinned at her, unfazed. 'I think that I would very much like to put you across my knee, and spank you, *signorina*,' he drawled. 'But that, alas, would not be—politically correct. So I will leave you before you draw any more unflattering comparisons.'

And that, Laura thought bleakly, when he'd gone and she was left staring into the darkness, was probably our last exchange. I insulted him, and he threatened me with physical violence. Tomorrow he'll be in Perugia. The day after, I'll be on the plane to London. End of story.

And she looked up at the blurred moon, and realised unhappily that she felt like howling herself.

Laura made sure she was around in the morning to bid Paolo an openly fond farewell.

'As soon as you get back,' she whispered as she hugged him, 'you must phone the airline and change our flights. Please, Paolo. I—I can't stand it here much longer.'

'You are better off here than lunching with Camilla Montecorvo. She is a bigger dragon than my mother,' he returned morosely. 'And at least you will have the place to yourself while my cousin is in Perugia on this mysterious business of his.' He gave her a knowing look. 'If you ask me, he has a woman there, so he may not come back at all.' Then, more loudly, '*Arrivederci, carissima.* Hold me in your heart until I return.'

Breakfast, as usual, was served on the terrace, although Laura was not so sure this was a good idea. It was not a pleasant morning. The air was sultry, and there was no faint breeze to counteract it. Looking up, she saw that there were small clouds already gathering around the crests of the hills, and realised that Fredo's change in the weather was really on its way.

She thought, Everything's changing... and shivered.

She also noticed that two places had been set at the table.

'His Excellency comes soon,' Emilia told her. 'He swims.'

Yes, thought Laura, biting her lip, fighting the sudden image in her mind. He—told me.

For a moment she let herself wonder what would happen if she went down to the pool and joined him there.

'I've come for my swimming lesson,' she could say as she slid down into the water, and into his arms...

She shook herself mentally. She would never behave in such a way, not in a thousand years, so it was crazy even to think like that. And futile too.

A woman in Perugia, Paolo had said.

The lone wolf off hunting his prey, she thought. Looking for a mate.

And that, she told herself forcibly, her mind flinching, was definitely a no-go area. How the Count Ramontella chose to amuse himself was his own affair. And at least she had ensured that she would not be providing his entertainment, however shamefully tempting that might be.

At that moment Alessio arrived, striding up the steps from the pool, damp hair gleaming and a towel flung over his bare shoulder. He was even wearing, she saw, the same ancient white shorts as on the day of her arrival.

'*Buon giorno.*' He took the seat opposite, the dark gaze scanning her mockingly. 'You did not join me in the pool this morning.'

'I hardly think you expected me to,' Laura retorted coolly, refusing to think about how close a call it had been.

'I expect very little,' he said. 'In that way I am sometimes pleasantly surprised.' His eyes sharpened a little. 'I hope you slept well, but it does not seem so. You have shadows under your eyes.'

'I'm fine,' she said shortly, helping herself to orange juice. 'But I think the heat's beginning to get to me. I'll be glad to go home.'

'Yet for Paolo, this is home,' he reminded her softly. 'So maybe you should try to accustom yourself to our climate, hmm?'

She glanced back at the hills. 'At the moment it seems a little unpredictable.'

'Not at all,' he said. 'We are undoubtedly going to have a storm.' He poured himself some coffee. 'Are you afraid of thunder, Laura *mia*?'

'No, I don't think so.' She looked down at her plate. 'And sometimes a storm can—clear the air.'

'Or breed more storms.' He paused. 'Did you say a fond goodbye to your *innamorato* this morning?'

'He's going for lunch with friends,' she said. 'Not trekking in the Himalayas.'

'Both can be equally dangerous. I suspect that my aunt may have arranged for Beatrice Manzone to be present.' He paused. 'Does that disturb you?'

She kept her eyes fixed on her plate. 'Paolo is old enough to make his own decisions. I—I simply have to trust him to do that.'

'How admirable you are, *mia cara*.' His tone was sardonic. He finished his coffee in a single swallow, and rose. 'And now I too must leave you. But, unlike Paolo, you are in safe hands.' He gave her a tight-lipped smile. 'Guillermo and Emilia will look after you well.'

But when are you coming back? She thought it, but did not say it. Could not say it.

She watched him disappear into the house, and pushed her food away untouched as pain twisted inside her. There was so much, she thought, that she dared not let him see. So much that would still haunt her even when the width of Europe divided them—and when she herself was long forgotten.

It was going to be, she told herself unhappily, a very long day.

In fact, it seemed endless. She didn't even have Caio's company, as the Signora had chosen to reclaim him that morning, announcing imperiously that he would be accompanying them to Trasimeno. Laura had seen him struggling, his small face woebegone as he was carried inexorably to the car.

She spent some time by the pool, but soon gave it up as a bad job. The clouds had begun to gather in earnest, accompanied now by a strong, gusting wind, and even a few spots of rain, so she gathered up her things and returned to the villa.

She'd finished *Mansfield Park* so she went along to Alessio's library and returned it, borrowing *Pride and Prejudice* instead. She knew the story so well, she thought, that she could easily read it before it was time for her to leave.

She lingered for a while looking round the room. It seemed to vibrate with his presence. Any moment now, she thought, he would stride in, flinging himself into the high-backed leather chair behind the desk, and pulling the laptop computer towards him, the dark face absorbed.

The desk itself was immaculately tidy. Besides the laptop, it held only a tray containing a few sheets of the Arleschi Bank's headed notepaper, and that leather-bound copy of Petrarch's poetry that he'd been reading.

She opened the book at random, and tried to decipher some of the lines, but it was hopeless—rather like the love the poems described, she told herself wryly.

From the eyes to the heart, she thought, the words echoing sadly in her mind. How simple—and how fatal.

To Emilia's obvious concern, she opted to lunch only on soup and a salad. The working girl's diet, she reminded herself, her mouth twisting.

Elizabeth Bennett's clashes with Mr Darcy kept her occupied during the afternoon, but as evening approached Laura began to get restive. The skies were dark now, the menacing clouds like slate, and Emilia came bustling in to light the lamps, and also, she saw, with faint alarm, to bring in some branched candlesticks, which were placed strategically round the room, while Guillermo arrived with a basket of logs and proceeded to kindle a fire in the grate.

Laura was grateful for that, because the temperature had dropped quite significantly, and the crackling flames made the room feel cheerful.

But as time passed her worries deepened. Paolo knew she was relying on him to organise their departure, she thought, so surely he must return soon, especially with the deterioration in the weather.

She could see lightning flashes, and hear thunder rumbling round the hills, coming closer all the time. She remembered nervously that, in spite of her brave words at breakfast, she really didn't like storms at all. And this one looked as if it was going to be serious stuff.

It was raining heavily by now, the water drumming a ceaseless tattoo on the terrace outside. She dared not think what the road from Besavoro would be like, and her feeling of isolation began to prey on her.

Think about something else, she adjured herself as she went off to change for dinner, even though it seemed as if she'd be eating alone. Don't contemplate Alessio driving back from

Perugia in the Jeep, because he almost certainly won't be. He has every excuse now, always supposing he needed one, to stay the night there.

She put on the silver dress and stood for a moment, regarding herself with disfavour. Her wardrobe had been woefully inadequate for the purpose from day one, she thought. And it was only thanks to Emilia's efficient laundry service that she'd managed to survive.

As for this dress—well, she wouldn't care if she never saw it again.

By the time she got back to the *salotto*, the storm was even closer, and the lamps, she saw, were flickering ominously with every lightning flash.

And then, above the noise of the storm, she heard the distant sound of a vehicle, and a moment later Guillermo's voice raised in greeting.

Paolo, she thought with relief. At last. They'd made it.

She was halfway to the doors when they opened and she halted, her heart bumping, a shocked hand going to her throat.

She said hoarsely, 'I—I thought you were in Perugia.'

'I was,' Alessio said. He advanced into the room, rain glistening on his hair, shrugging off the trench coat he was wearing and throwing it carelessly across the back of a chair. 'But I did not think it was right for you to be alone here in these conditions, so I came back.' He gave her a mocking smile. 'You are allowed to be grateful.'

'I'm used to weather,' she returned, lifting her chin. 'In England we have loads of it.' She hesitated. 'I thought—I hoped Paolo had come back.'

He said lightly, 'I fear I have a disappointment for you. The servants took a call from my aunt two hours ago. In view of the weather, they have decided to remain at Trasimeno for the night. Or that is the story. So—you and I are alone, *bella mia*.'

And as he spoke all the lights went off. Laura cried out, and in a stride Alessio was beside her, taking her hands in his, drawing her towards him.

'Scared of the dark, *carissima*?' he asked softly.

'Not usually,' she said shakily. And far more scared of you, *signore*, she whispered under her breath. 'It's just—everything happening at once,' she added on a little gasp, tinglingly conscious of his proximity.

Don't let him know that it matters, she ordered herself sternly. For heaven's sake, act normally. And say something with no personal connotations, if that's possible.

She cleared her throat. 'Does the power always go off when there's a storm?'

'More often than I could wish. We have a generator for backup at such times, but I prefer to keep it in reserve for real emergencies.' He paused. 'But Emilia does not like to cook with electricity, so at least dinner is safe.'

He let her go almost casually, and walked over to the fireplace, leaving Laura to breathe freely again. He took down a taper from the wide stone shelf above the hearth and lit it at the fire.

As he moved round the room each candle burst into light like a delicate golden blossom, and in spite of her misgivings Laura was charmed into an involuntary sigh of delight.

'You see.' He tossed the remains of the taper into the wide grate and smiled at her. 'Firelight and candle glow. Better, I think, than electricity.'

Not, she thought, aware that she was trembling inside, in these particular circumstances.

She steadied her voice. 'And certainly more in keeping with the age of the villa.'

Alessio inclined his head courteously. 'As you say.' He paused. 'May I get you a drink?'

'Just some mineral water, please.' Keep sane—keep sober.

His brows rose slightly, but he said nothing, bringing her exactly what she'd asked for and pouring a whisky for himself.

Laura sat on the edge of the sofa, gripping the crystal tumbler in one hand and nervously rearranging the folds of her skirt with the other.

Alessio added some more wood to the fire and straightened, dusting his hands. He sent her a considering look under his lashes, noting the tension in every line of her, and realising that he needed to ease the situation a little.

He said quietly, 'Laura, will you make me a promise?'

She looked up, startled, and instantly wary. 'I don't know. It—it would depend on what it was.'

'Nothing too difficult. I wish you to swear that when you are back in London you will go swimming at least once a week. You lack only confidence.'

'I suppose I could manage that,' she said slowly. 'There are some swimming baths quite near where I live.'

'Then there is no problem.' He added casually, 'Get Paolo to go with you.'

'Maybe,' she said, her mouth curving in such unexpected mischief that his heart missed a beat. 'If his health improves.'

He grinned back, shrugging. 'You can always hope, *carissima*.'

It had worked to some extent, he thought. She was no longer clinging to her glass as if it were a lifeline. But that strange intangible barrier that she'd built between them was still there.

Her reticence frankly bewildered him. He had once been forced to listen to Paolo's drunken boasting about his London conquests, and restraint had never featured as one of the qualities his cousin most favoured in a woman.

So what was he doing with this girl? His Laura, with her level smoky gaze and proud mouth? On her side, he supposed she might have been beguiled initially by Paolo's surface charm, but that must have been seriously eroded by the spoilt-child act of the past week.

And there was another factor that had been gnawing at him too. When he'd gone to post her cards that morning in Besavoro, he'd quickly noted down the names and addresses of the recipients, deciding they might prove useful for future reference. So who was the man Carl that she'd written to at Harman Grace, and what was their connection?

Could this whole trip with Paolo be simply a ploy to make her real lover jealous—provoke him into commitment, maybe? Was this what she was hiding behind that veil of cool containment?

No, he thought. I don't believe that—not in my heart. There's something else. And I have the whole night to find out what it is. To bring down the barrier and possess her utterly.

But first, he thought, he would have to get her to relax—to respond to him—to enjoy being teased a little. Perhaps tease him in return...

After all, he told himself with sudden cynicism, she would not be the first girl in the world to be coaxed into bed with laughter.

For one strange moment, he wished it were all over, and that she were joyously and passionately his, sitting beside him in the Jeep as they set off to some destination where his aunt's malice could not follow. Somewhere they could relax in the enjoyment of some mutual pleasure, he thought restlessly.

He longed, he realised, to fall asleep each night with her in his arms, and wake next to her each morning.

He wanted her as unequivocally and completely as he needed food and clothing. And he was going to wipe from his mind every vestige of the sordid bargain he'd been originally forced into by his aunt. From the moment he'd seen Laura, it had counted for nothing anyway.

But it could have been very different, he reminded himself grimly, so his amazing fortune was hardly deserved. And for a moment the thought made him disturbed and uneasy. And, he realised, almost fearful.

Pulling himself together, he picked up the nearest branch of candles and walked over to her, holding out his hand. 'Let us go into dinner,' he invited quietly.

Laura had made up her mind to plead a headache and go to her room directly after she'd eaten. But it was clearly ridiculous to express a wish for peace and quiet while the storm was still raging overhead, and might prompt Alessio to draw his own conclusions about her sudden need for seclusion. And that could be dangerous.

It was a strange meal. Conversation was necessarily sporadic. The flicker of the candles sent shadows dancing in the corners of the room, until they were eclipsed by the lightning flashes that illumined everything with a weird bluish glow. It seemed to Laura as if each crash of thunder was rolling without pause into the next, and it was difficult to concentrate on Emilia's delicious food when she was constantly jumping out of her skin. It was much easier, in fact, to drink the red wine that Alessio was pouring into her glass, and which made her feel marginally less nervous.

One particular thunderclap, however, seemed to go on for ever, with a long, rumbling roar that made the whole house shake.

Laura put down her spoon. 'Is—is that what an earthquake feels like?' she asked uneasily.

'Almost.' Alessio was frowning, but his gaze softened as he studied her small, pale face. 'My poor Laura,' he said. 'You came here expecting long, hot days and moonlit romantic nights, and instead—the storm of the century. But this house has withstood many storms, if that is any consolation. And it will survive this one too.'

'Yes,' she said. 'Yes, of course.' She bit her lip. 'But—I— I'm quite glad you decided not to stay in Perugia, *signore*.'

'Why, *mia bella*,' he said mockingly. 'What a confession. And I am also—pleased.'

She hesitated. 'Do you think it's this bad at Lake Trasimeno? They will be able to get back tomorrow? Paolo and I have all our travel arrangements to work out.'

He shrugged. 'As to that, I think we must—wait and see.'

'Maybe you could phone—and find out.' She tried not to sound as if she was pleading.

'Why, yes,' he said. 'If the telephone was still working. Guillermo tells me it went off not long after my aunt's call.'

'Oh, God.' She stared at him, unable to hide her shock and dismay. 'But you must have a cell phone, surely.'

'I have more than one, but there is no signal here. I regard that as one of the many pleasures of this house,' Alessio said, pouring more wine.

Lightning filled the room, and he smiled at her, his face a stranger's in the eerie light. 'So, for the time being, we are quite cut off, *mia cara*.' He paused. 'And there is nothing we can do about it,' he added softly.

CHAPTER NINE

THE fierce riot of the storm seemed suddenly to fade to some strange distance, leaving behind a silence that was almost tangible, and twice as scary.

Laura swallowed. 'Cut off?' she echoed. 'But we can't be.'

He shrugged again, almost laconically. 'It happens.'

'But how long are we going to be—stuck here like this?' she demanded defensively.

'Until the storm passes, and we can reassess the situation.'

She shook her head in disbelief. 'Don't you even care?'

'Why? There is nothing I can do, *mia cara*.' He smiled at her. 'So, I shall let you be agitated for both of us.'

Well, she could manage that—no problem, Laura thought grimly.

She picked up her glass, and drank again, aware that her hand was shaking, and hoping—praying—that he wouldn't notice in the uncertain light. She said huskily, 'There's the Jeep. We could—drive somewhere—some place with lights and a phone.'

'In this weather, on that road?' he queried softly. 'You are suddenly very brave, *mia bella*. Far braver than myself, I must tell you. So, do you wish me to give you the keys, because I am going nowhere.' He paused. 'You can drive?'

'I've passed my test,' she said guardedly.

His smile widened. 'Then the decision is yours. But you may feel it is safer to remain here.'

There was a silence, then Laura reluctantly nodded.

'*Bene*,' he approved lazily. 'And now I will make a deal with you, Laura *mia*. In the morning, when this weather has cleared, I will drive you anywhere you wish to go, but only if—tonight...' He paused again, deliberately allowing the silence to lengthen between them.

Laura's mouth felt suddenly dry. She said, 'What—what about tonight, *signore*? What are you asking?'

He said quietly, 'That you will again play the piano for me.'

'Play the piano?' Laura was genuinely taken aback. 'You're not serious.'

'I am most serious. You played the first night you were in my house. Why not the last? After all, you are going back to your own country. I may never have the opportunity to listen to you play again.'

Laura looked down at the table. 'I'd have thought that was a positive advantage.'

He clicked his tongue in reproof. 'And that is false modesty, *mia cara*. I have heard you practising each day. And once I found Emilia weeping in the hall, because your playing brought back memories of my mother for her also.'

'Oh, no.' Laura glanced up in dismay. 'Lord, I'm so sorry.'

'No need,' he said. 'They were happy tears. She loved my mother very much.' He rose. 'So, Laura *mia*, you will indulge me?'

Reluctantly, she followed him to the *salotto*, waiting while he carefully positioned more candelabra on top of the piano.

'There,' he said at last. 'Will that do?'

'Well, yes, I suppose...' She sat down at the keyboard, giving him a questioning look. 'What do you want me to play?'

'Something calming, I think.' Alessio sent a wry glance upwards as thunder rumbled ominously once more. 'That piece you have been practising, perhaps.'

'"Clair de Lune"?' She bit her lip. 'I'd almost forgotten it, and it's still not really up to performance standard.'

'But very beautiful,' he returned. He sat down in the corner of a sofa, stretching long legs in front of him. 'So—if you please?'

Swallowing nervously, she let her fingers touch the keys, searching out the first dreamy chords, only too conscious of the silent man, listening, and watching.

But, somehow, as she played her confidence grew with her concentration, and she found herself moving through the passionate middle section with barely a falter into the gentle, almost yearning clarity of the final passage. And silence.

Alessio rose and walked across to the piano, joining her on the long padded stool. He said softly, *'Grazie,'* and took her hand, raising it to his lips. He turned it gently, pressing his mouth to the leaping pulse in her wrist, then kissed the palm of her hand slowly and sensuously.

Her voice was suddenly a thread. 'Please—don't do that?'

He raised his head, the dark eyes smiling into hers. He said, 'I am not allowed to pay homage to your artistry—even when it has conquered the storm?'

The lightning was barely visible now, she realised, and the thunder only a distant growl.

'It—it does seem to have moved away.' She tried to retrieve her hand, and failed. 'Perhaps the electricity will come on again soon.'

'You don't like the candlelight?'

Laura hesitated. 'Oh, yes, but I wouldn't want to read by it, and I was really hoping to finish my book before tomorrow,' she added over-brightly, aware that his fingers were caressing hers, sending little tremors shivering down her spine. It seemed as if she could feel every thread in her dress touching her bare skin.

'Then we will have to think of some other form of entertainment that may be easier on the eyes.' Alessio paused. 'Do you play cards?'

She shrugged. 'The usual family games.'

'And poker?'

'I know the value of the various hands,' she said. 'But that's about all.'

'I could teach you.'

She stared at him. 'But don't you need more people?' she asked. 'Also it's a gambling game, and I—I haven't any money to lose.'

'It is possible to play for other things besides money, *carissima*. And one learns to make use of whatever is available. Sometimes that can be far more enjoyable than playing for mere cash.' He reached out, his fingers deftly detaching one of the small silver spheres on a chain that hung from her ear. He put it down on an ivory piano key, where it flashed in the candle flame. 'You see? Already you have something to stake.'

Strip poker, Laura thought numbly. Dear God, he's suggesting we should play strip poker...

She wrenched her hand away from his. 'Yes,' she said, her voice bitterly cold. 'And, no doubt, I'd have a great deal to lose, too. That's the problem with all your lessons, *signore*. They come at much too high a cost.'

He smiled at her, unruffled. 'How can you price the value of a new experience, *bella mia*?'

'Oh, you have an answer for everything—or you think you do.' She turned fiercely to face him. 'Why do you do this?' she demanded with sudden huskiness. 'Why do you—torment me like this?'

'Do I torment you, *mia cara*?' he countered harshly. One hand swept aside the silky fall of her hair to cup the nape of her neck, his thumb caressing the hollow beneath her ear, sending a sweet shiver along her nerve endings. 'Then why do you continue to deny what you know we both want?'

She could feel the heat rising in her body, the sudden, terrifying scald of yearning between her thighs, and was bitterly ashamed of her own weakness.

'I can't speak for you, *signore*,' she said, her voice shaking, 'but I just want to get out of here. Out of this house—this country—and back to where I belong. And nothing else.'

She paused, her chin lifting defiantly. 'And now that the storm's over, the telephone could be working again.'

He withdrew his hand with a faint sigh, letting one smooth russet strand of her hair slide lingeringly through his fingers. 'I think you are over-optimistic, Laura *mia*,' he told her drily.

'But could you find out for me—please? I really need to know the times of tomorrow's flights.'

He was her host, she thought with a kind of desperation. He couldn't—wouldn't—refuse her request, however stupid he might think it. She'd asked him to check something. Innate courtesy would take him from the room to do so.

And that would be her chance, she told herself feverishly. Because she needed to get away from him on a far more personal level—and tonight. The door to her room had a lock and key, she knew, and the window shutters had that bolt mechanism she'd used once before. She couldn't risk going through the house, of course, because he might intercept her, but she could cut across the gardens, and be safely locked in her room before he even realised she was missing.

Because she could not trust herself to be alone with him any longer. It was as simple and final as that. The necessity to go into his arms and feel his mouth on hers was an agony she had never experienced before. A consuming anguish she had not dreamed could exist.

And she dared not risk him touching her again. Not when the merest brush of his fingers could turn her to flame.

For a moment, she found herself thinking of Steve, and wondering if this was how he'd felt about her.

I hope not, she thought. I hope not with all my heart.

She watched Alessio walk to the door. Heard his footsteps receding, and his voice calling to Guillermo.

And then she ran across the room, tugging at the windows and their shutters to make a gap she could squeeze through.

She knew the route. She must have used it twenty times since her arrival. But always in the daytime. Never at night. And she had not bargained for the absolute darkness outside. The pretty ornamental lamps that dotted the grounds were out of commission, of course, but there wasn't a star showing, or even a faint glimmer of moonlight.

And, because the storm had passed over at last, she'd assumed the rain would have stopped too, but she was wrong. It was like walking into a wall of water, she thought, gasping.

Before she'd gone fifty yards she was completely drenched, her soaked dress clinging like a second skin, her feet slipping in her wet shoes, and her hair hanging in sodden rats' tails round her face.

She tried to peer through the darkness to get her bearings, but she could see nothing. She could only hope that she was going in the right direction—that somewhere ahead of her was the sanctuary she so desperately needed. She wanted to run, but her feet were sliding on the wet grass, and she was afraid of falling.

She was never sure of the precise moment when she realised that she was being followed. That Alessio was coming after her, running silently and surely in pursuit like a lone wolf from the hills.

She stumbled on, gasping, her heart pounding against her ribs, the words, 'No—please—no,' echoing their frantic rhythm in her brain.

But to no avail. He was suddenly beside her, taking her hand in an iron grasp and pulling her along with him as he ran, head bent.

She tried to drag herself free. 'Leave me alone...'

'Idiota,' he snarled breathlessly. 'Do you want me to carry you? Avanti!'

At last the sodden grass gave way to paving stones, and she saw a dim glow ahead of her and realised they must have reached her courtyard. Alessio dragged back the heavy glass doors, and pushed her inside ahead of him.

There were candles burning here too on the chest of drawers and the night table, and Emilia had also turned down the bed.

Laura stood, head bent, water running down her face and neck, and dripping off the hem of her skirt to form a forlorn puddle on the floor.

Alessio went past her into the bathroom, his sodden shirt adhering to his body like a second skin. He emerged, barefoot, carrying two towels, one of which he threw to her, using the other to rub his face and hair.

Laura stood motionless, the breath still raw in her lungs from that headlong dash. She held the towel against her in numb fingers, watching as he stripped off his shirt and began to dry his chest and arms. Her heart was beating wildly again, but for a very different reason.

He glanced up, and their eyes met. He said harshly, 'Don't just stand there, little fool. You are soaked to the skin, as I am. Take off your dress before you catch pneumonia.'

Her lips moved. 'I—can't...'

Alessio said something impatient and probably obscene under his breath, and walked over to her, his long fingers going swiftly and ruthlessly to work on the sash, which had tightened into a soggy and almost impenetrable knot. When it came free at last, he peeled the silver dress away from her body, and tossed it to the floor.

Laura made a small sound that might have been protest, but he ignored it anyway. He took the towel from her unresisting grasp and began to blot the chill dampness from her skin. Not gently. She gave an involuntary wince, and felt his touch soften a little. His expression, however, did not, even though the scraps of lace she was wearing were hardly a barrier to his dark gaze.

There was no sound in the room except their own ragged breathing. The shadows dancing on the walls seemed to reduce the room to half its size, closing them into the small area of light provided by the candles.

At last, Alessio threw the towel behind him, and stood looking down at her.

'So,' he said quietly. 'What in the name of God, Laura, did you think you were doing?'

'Running away.' Her voice was barely audible.

'Well, that is plain,' he said with sudden harshness. 'So eager to escape me, it seems, that you could not wait until tomorrow. That you were even prepared to risk damaging your health by this folly tonight. But why, Laura? Why did you do this?'

'You—know.'

'If I did,' he said, 'I would not ask. So, tell me.'

If there were words, she could not think of them. If there were arguments, she could not marshal them. There was her body's need roused to the brink of anguish by the rough movement of his hands on her skin as he'd dried her.

And there was candlelight and the waiting bed...

Oh, God, she thought with desperation. I want him so much. I never knew before—never realised that this could ever happen to me. And I—cannot turn back. Not now. I must have—this night.

Her throat was tight as she swallowed. As she lifted her hands and placed them on his shoulders, reaching up on tiptoe to kiss him shyly and rather clumsily on the mouth.

For a heartbeat, he was still, then his arms went round her, pinning her against him with a fierce hunger he made no attempt to disguise. He said her name quietly and huskily, then his lips took hers, exploring the soft, trembling contours with heated, passionate urgency, his heart lifting in exultation.

She was his, he thought, and she had offered herself as he'd once promised she would. Not that it mattered. The only essential was Laura herself—here at last, in his arms, her lips parting for him eagerly as their kisses deepened into sweet, feverish intimacy, allowing him to taste all the inner honey of her mouth.

He began to caress her, his fingers lightly stroking her throat and neck, then sliding the straps of her bra from her slender shoulders, so that when he found and unclipped its tiny hook the little garment simply fell away from her body. He caught his breath as he looked at her, his eyes heavy with desire, then pulled her closer, so that the tips of her small, perfect breasts grazed his bare chest with delicate eroticism.

He recaptured her mouth, burying his soft groan of pleasure in its moist fragrance, teasing her tongue with his as his hands continued their slow quest down her slim body.

When he reached the barrier of her briefs, he eased his fingers inside their lacy band, gently pushing them down from her hips to the floor.

He'd expected to feel her hands on him, discarding what remained of his clothing, wanting to uncover him in her turn, but, to his faint surprise, she made no such attempt. So he allowed himself a hurried moment to strip naked, before lifting her and putting her on the bed.

He followed her down, taking her in his arms, murmuring husky endearments, glorying in the cool enchantment of her quivering body against his.

He kissed her again, his hands cupping her breasts, stroking the nipples gently until they stood erect to his touch, his inward smile tender as he heard her small, startled sigh of pleasure. He bent his head and caressed the hard, rosy peaks with his mouth, the tip of his tongue drawing circles of sweet torment round the puckered flesh.

He was hotly, achingly aroused, but even in the extremity of his desire for her some remaining glimmer of sanity in his reeling mind warned him that, apart from her kisses, her response was more muted. That she still maintained some element of that reserve that had always intrigued him. Was it possible that, even now, when she was naked in his arms, she could be shy of him?

He wanted her to match him in passion—to be equally enraptured. He longed for the incitement of her hands and mouth on his body, which, so far, to his faint bewilderment, she'd withheld.

Was she scared, perhaps, of the moment when all thinking ceased and the last vestiges of control slipped away?

If so, he would have to be careful, because he could not lose her now.

Very gently, he began to kiss her body, caressing every shadowed curve, each smooth plane as the sweet woman-scent of her filled his nose and mouth.

He rested his cheek against her belly as his hand parted her thighs, finding the scalding moisture of her need.

He heard her gasp, her breathing suddenly frantic as her body arched involuntarily towards him in surrender to the sensuous pressure of his fingers. But he would offer her another kind of delight, he thought, smiling, as he bent to pleasure her with his mouth.

Yet suddenly she was no longer yielding. She was tense— even struggling a little, her hands tangling in his hair, trying to push him away.

'No—no—please.' Her voice was small, stifled. 'You mustn't—I can't…'

'Don't be afraid, *carissima*,' he whispered as he acceded reluctantly to this unexpected resistance. 'I will do nothing you don't like.' Or that I cannot persuade you to like, in time, *mi amore*.

Instead, his fingers sought her tiny hidden bud, stroking it rhythmically—delicately—while his mouth returned to her breast, suckling the engorged peak until she moaned in her throat.

'Touch me,' he breathed, starving for her. He took her hand and carried it to his body, clasping her fingers round his hardness while he moved over her, positioning himself between her thighs, waiting for her to guide him into her, to surrender to the first deep thrust that would make her his at last.

She was trembling violently, her movements almost awkward as she obeyed his silent demand, taking him to the heated threshold of her womanhood.

But as he began to enter her slowly, gently, prolonging the exquisite moment quite deliberately, he felt the sudden tension in her once again. Realised that the cry of pleasure he'd expected was one of pain instead, and that this time the resistance seemed to be physical.

'*Mi amore*—my sweet one,' he whispered urgently. 'Relax for me.'

And then he looked down into the wide frightened eyes, and he knew.

The hurting—the shock of that tearing pain—stopped almost as soon as it had begun. Laura, her fist pressed to her mouth, was aware of Alessio pulling back. Lifting himself away from her altogether.

She turned away too, curling into the foetal position, her startled body shaking uncontrollably.

She closed her eyes, but she couldn't shut out the sound of his harsh breathing as he fought for control. For an approximation of calm. The passing minutes seemed to stretch into eternity as she lay, waiting.

But for what?

Eventually, he said, 'Laura, look at me. Look at me, now.'

He was sitting up in the bed, the edge of the sheet pulled across his loins. His dark face was a stranger's as he looked at her.

He said, his voice flat, 'This was your first time with a man.' It was a statement, not a question, but he added sharply, 'Do not attempt to lie. I want the truth.'

'Yes.' The single word was a sob.

'You did not think to tell me?'

'I didn't know I needed to.' She bent her head wretchedly. 'It never occurred to me that it might—hurt...' She swallowed convulsively. 'I thought I could pretend—so that you wouldn't know that I hadn't—that I'd never...'

He said very wearily, *'Dio mio.'* There was a long silence, then she felt him stir, and braced herself for the inevitable question.

'Paolo,' he said quietly. 'You—and Paolo—you let me—you let everyone think that you were lovers. Why?'

'Paolo and I decided—to travel together. To see how it worked out.' Even now she had to try and keep the secret. 'Oh, God, I'm so sorry.'

'You have nothing to regret.' His voice was expressionless. 'The blame is mine entirely.'

She felt the mattress shift as he moved, looked up quickly to see him standing beside the bed, pulling on his clothes.

'Alessio.' She lifted herself onto her knees, reaching out a hand to him. 'Where are you going?'

'To my own room,' he said. 'Where else?'

'Please don't go,' she whispered. 'Don't leave me.'

'What you ask is impossible.' The back he kept turned to her was rigid, as if it had been forged out of steel.

She touched her tongue to her dry lips. Her voice was ragged. 'Alessio—please. What happened just now doesn't matter. I—I want you.'

'No,' he said. 'It ends here. And it should never have started. I had no right to—touch you.'

'But I gave you that right.'

'Then be glad I have the strength to leave you,' he said.

'Glad?' Laura echoed. 'How can I be—glad?'

'Because one day you will come to be married,' he said, the words torn harshly from his throat. 'And your innocence is a gift you should keep for your husband. He should have the joy of knowing he will be your first and only lover.'

He took a deep raw breath. 'It is far too—precious an offering to be wasted on someone like me.'

'Not just—someone,' she said in anguish. 'You, Alessio. You, and no one else.'

His need for her was a raw, aching wound, but he could not allow himself to weaken now. Because, one day, he needed to be able to forgive himself.

He bent and picked up his damp shirt from the floor, schooling his expression into cynicism.

'Your persistence forces me to be candid,' he drawled as he faced her. 'Forget the high-flown sentiments, *signorina*. The truth is that I was in the mood for a woman tonight, not an inexperienced girl.' He added coolly, 'Please believe that I have neither the time or the patience to teach you what you need to know in order to please me.'

He saw the stricken look in the grey eyes, and knew it was an image that would haunt him for the rest of his days.

He added, 'In the morning, we will deal with your departure. I am sure you have no wish to linger. Goodnight, *signorina*.' He inclined his head with cruel politeness, and left.

She watched the door close behind him, then looked down at herself with a kind of numb horror. It was the worst humiliation of her life—kneeling here naked—offering herself—pleading with a man who'd just made it brutally clear that he no longer desired her.

It had never occurred to her, she thought blankly, that losing her virginity would be anything but simple. She was a twenty-first-century girl, for God's sake, not some Victorian miss. And it seemed to her bewildered mind as if Alessio, in spite of what he'd just said, had been gentle. Yet, it had still hurt her in a way that she'd found it impossible to disguise.

But that, she thought wretchedly, was nothing compared with the aching agony of his subsequent rejection of her, both physically and emotionally. Her body still burned from its unfulfilled arousal.

Worst of all, she had almost, but thankfully not quite, told him, 'I love you.'

And in the morning she was going to have to face him somehow—with this nightmare between them. And she couldn't bear it—she couldn't...

With a little inarticulate cry, she dived under the covers, dragging them up to her throat, her whole body shaking uncontrollably as the first white-hot tears began to spill down her ashen face.

Alessio stood, shoulders slumped, one hand braced against the tiled wall of the shower, and his head bent against the remorseless cascade of cold water.

If he could manage somehow to numb his body, he thought starkly, then maybe he could also subdue his mind. But he knew already that would not be easy.

How many cold showers would it take to erase the memory of her eager mouth, her warm, slim body stretched beneath him in a surrender that should never have been required of her?

How could you not see? he accused himself savagely. You blind, criminal fool. How could you not realise that she was not merely shy, but totally inexperienced, when everything you did—everything she would not allow you to do—told you that more plainly than any words?

But that first sweet, awkward kiss offered of her own volition had wiped everything from his mind but the assuagement of his own need.

He paused and swore at himself. Was he actually daring to blame her, even marginally, when he had manoeuvred and manipulated her to a point when she had been no longer prepared to resist him?

The fact that his sense of honour had forced him to abandon the seduction in no way diminished his feelings of guilt.

He found himself remembering something his father had once said to him just as he'd been emerging from adolescence. 'Like most young men, you will find enough unscrupulous women in the world, Alessio, to cater for your pleasures. So, treat innocent girls with nothing but respect.' He'd added drily, 'Or until your intentions are entirely honourable.'

It had seemed wise advice, and until now he had followed it.

He had simply not dreamed that Laura could be still a virgin. At the same time, he was shamingly aware of a fierce, almost primitive joy to know that she had never given herself to Paolo.

But she did not belong to him either, he reminded himself with a kind of sick desolation. And, after that last act of necessary cruelty, she never would...

With a groan, he slid down the wall to the tiled floor of the shower, resting his forehead on his drawn-up knees, letting the water beat at him. He had done the right thing, he told himself. He had to believe that.

Yet, he had ignored his father's other piece of worldly wisdom, he realised with a flash of weary cynicism—that a gentleman should never leave the lady in his bed unsatisfied.

Well, his punishment and his penance would be to drive her to Rome tomorrow, and watch her walk away from him at the airport, through the baggage check and passport control, and out of his life.

'Laura,' he whispered. 'My Laura.' He had not cried since his father's funeral, but suddenly, at the sound of her name, he could taste tears, hot and acrid in his throat, and it took every scrap of control he possessed to stop him weeping like a child for his loss.

Swallowing, he lifted himself to his feet and turned off the shower. It was time to pull his life together, he commanded himself grimly, deciding, among other things, how he should deal with his aunt on her return. And, if she made good her threats, how he should handle the aftermath of her revelations.

I should have stood up to her at the start, he thought, his mouth tightening in cold anger as he reached for a towel. Told her to do her worst, then dismissed her from my life, together with Paolo.

But that I can still do, and I will.

It is the wrong that I have done Laura that can never be put right. And somehow I have to live with that for the rest of my days.

CHAPTER TEN

SHE'D cried herself to sleep, but Laura still found no rest. She spent the remainder of a troubled night, tossing and turning in the wide bed, looking for some sort of peace, but finding only wretchedness.

Alessio's hand on her shoulder, shaking her, and his voice telling her curtly to wake up just seemed part of another bad dream, until she opened unwilling eyes and saw him there, standing over her in the pallid daylight.

She snatched at the disarranged covers, dragging them almost frantically to the base of her throat, and saw a dark flush tinge his cheekbones and his mouth tighten to hardness as he registered what she was doing.

He was fully dressed, wearing jeans and a black polo shirt, but, as one swift glance under her lashes revealed, he was also unshaven and heavy-eyed, as if he too had found sleep elusive.

'What—what do you want?' She kept her voice as brusque as his own.

'There has been a serious problem,' he said. 'That noise we heard last night was, in fact, a landslip. Guillermo tried to get down to Besavoro earlier, and found the road to the valley completely blocked with rocks, trees and mud.'

'Blocked?' Laura repeated, her heart missing a beat. 'You mean—we can't get out?'

'Unfortunately, no.' He shrugged. 'But the emergency generator is now working, so you will have hot water, and electric light, which should make your stay more comfortable.'

'But how long am I to be kept here? I—I must get to the airport...'

'Heavy lifting equipment has been requested from Perugia,'

he told her expressionlessly, 'but it may not arrive until tomorrow at the earliest.'

'Not until then?' She digested the news with dismay. 'And how long will it take to clear the road after that?'

Alessio shrugged again. 'Who knows?'

'You don't seem very concerned that we're practically imprisoned here,' she accused, her voice unsteady.

'I regret the inconvenience,' he said icily, 'but at the moment I find Fredo a much greater worry. He is missing, and it is thought that his hut was in the path of the landslide.' He paused. 'I am going down to give what help I can.'

She bit her lip. 'I see—of course.' And as he turned away: 'Alessio, I—I'm really sorry.'

'Why?' At the door, he halted. The backward glance he sent her was unreadable. 'You do not know him.'

'No, but he's your friend, and he obviously means a great deal to you.' She added swiftly, 'I'd be sorry for anyone under the circumstances.' She hesitated. 'Is there anything I can do?'

His smile was faint and brief. 'Perhaps—if you know how to pray.' And was gone.

She lay, staring across the room at the closed door, her instinctive, 'Please take care,' still trembling, unspoken, on her lips. And quite rightly so, she told herself. To have indicated in any way that his well-being mattered to her would be dangerous madness.

So—it had happened, she thought. She had seen him, spoken to him, and somehow survived. She supposed the fact that he'd come to tell her there was an emergency had eased their meeting to a certain extent. It had had a purpose and an urgency that an embarrassed encounter across the breakfast table would have lacked.

But it also meant that she'd been deprived of her only shred of comfort in the entire situation—the knowledge that she was leaving. That she would not have to spend time alone with him, or pass another night in the vain pursuit of sleep under his roof.

All she wanted, quite simply, was to go far away, and try to forget the appalling humiliation of the past twelve hours. If that was, indeed, possible.

Yet now the trap had closed on her again, and she was caught. And there was literally nothing she could do about it except— endure.

It was a very small consolation to know that he would be equally reluctant to have her around after last night's wretched debacle.

Somehow, she reflected painfully, she must have given the impression that she possessed a level of sophistication that was beyond her. A willing female body ready to provide Alessio with the level of entertainment he expected from his sexual partners. Discarded when he realised the truth.

She would carry the stark cruelty of that for the rest of her life, like a scar, she thought.

She turned onto her stomach, burying her face in the pillow. So, when she'd opened her eyes just now and seen him there beside the bed, how was it possible that her body had stirred for one infinitesimal moment in hope and desire?

Because it had done so, she admitted painfully. It might be pathetic and shameful, but it was also quite undeniable.

Which meant that, even now, and in spite of everything, she— wanted him.

Dear God, she thought in angry self-derision, had the totality of his rejection taught her nothing?

Yet it might have been even worse if he'd persuaded her to go away with him. Made what amounted to a public statement of his desire for her, and then, almost in the next breath, dismissed her. At least, hidden away here at the Villa Diana, no one else would know of her humiliation.

She sat up, with sudden determination, pushing her hair back from her face. If she continued thinking along those lines, she could end up feeling grateful to him. And she wasn't.

But lying here, brooding, was no answer either. She had to get up and prepare for the rest of her life. Something that never had included Alessio Ramontella, and never would.

Somehow, she had to put this brief madness behind her, and become sane again.

And I can, she promised herself, lifting her chin with renewed pride. I can, and I will.

It was a strange day. The sky was still heavy with cloud, revealing the sun only in fitful bursts, yet at the same time it was stiflingly hot. The heavy air was filled with the almost jungle smell of wet earth and vegetation, and, although Guillermo had gone down and patiently cleaned out the pool, Laura was not tempted to spend much time out of doors.

In spite of her brave resolution, she found herself prowling round the house, restless and ill-at-ease, as if she were a caged animal.

Alessio did not return, and when Guillermo came back from taking midday food and wine down to those trying to clear some part of the landslide he could only say that Fredo had not yet been found, and the search was continuing.

She wanted to ask, 'Is the Count all right?' but bit back the words. This was not a question she had any reason or any right to ask.

She read the rest of her book and returned it, but did not allow herself to choose another, although *Emma* tempted her. On the one hand, she didn't want to think she might be around long enough to finish it. On the other, she hated the idea of leaving it half unread.

She spent some of her time exploring the house in greater detail, especially the older parts, examining the restoration work that had taken place on frescoed walls and painted ceilings. With a building of this age, careful renovation would always be needed, she thought. A labour of love that would last a lifetime.

And she could understand its attraction. The remoteness that aggravated Paolo had an appeal all its own. She could see how Alessio would regard it as a sanctuary—a much-needed retreat. What she couldn't figure so well was why someone, so very much of the world, should require such a place. Why he should ever want to escape.

But then the entire way the Count conducted his life was an enigma, she thought, or as far as she was concerned anyway. A mystery that had already caused her too much unhappiness, and which she could not afford to probe.

I have to begin to forget, she told herself. However hard that is. However long it takes.

As always, music was her solace. She had no idea when, if ever, she would have access to such a wonderful piano, but she was determined to make the most of it.

She found the book of Beethoven sonatas again, and glanced through them looking for those she'd learned to play in her younger days. She realised for the first time that there was an inscription inside the collection's embossed cover, and that even she could translate this brief message—'To my dearest Valentina from the husband who adores her. My love now and for ever.'

She turned the page swiftly, feeling with embarrassment that she should not have read the message—that she had somehow intruded on something private and precious.

She chose a page number totally at random, and, after loosening up with a few preliminary scales, began to practise.

It was only Emilia's quiet entry with another batch of candles that alerted her to the passage of time since she'd first sat down to play.

'Heavens.' Laura looked almost guiltily at her watch. 'It's nearly time to change for dinner. I didn't realise.' She paused. 'Has—has His Excellency come back yet?'

Emilia pursed her lips. 'No, *signorina*. But do not concern yourself,' she added encouragingly. 'He will return to you very soon.'

Laura was infuriated to find she was blushing again, and hotly, too. 'I just meant that we should maybe—hold dinner until he arrives.'

'But of course, *signorina*.' Emilia's smile was serene but also openly sceptical. Pull the other one, it seemed to advise drily. We are not blind, or deaf, Guillermo and I, and we have known Count Alessio all his life. So you cannot fool us—either of you.

But this time you're wrong, Laura wanted passionately to tell her. And I'm the one who was fooled.

Instead, she bent her head and concentrated on the passage she'd just stumbled over.

Alessio came home half an hour later, walking straight into the *salotto*. Laura glanced up, her hands stilling on the keys as she looked at him. His face was grey with weariness, and his clothes were heavily stained with mud and damp.

She swallowed. 'Did—did you find Fredo?'

'*Sì, alla fine.*' He walked to the drinks table and poured himself a whisky. 'We traced him because his dog was beside him barking.'

She gasped. 'Keeping the wolves away?' she asked huskily.

'Perhaps. It is all too possible.' He drank deeply, then brushed his knuckles across his mouth. 'Fredo is now in hospital, with a badly broken leg.' The words were hoarse and staccato. 'But he was also out all night, lying in that storm, and that is regarded as far more serious. Luca is with him, but his father has not yet regained consciousness.'

He did not tell her of the nightmare journey made by the search party, carrying the badly injured old man on an improvised stretcher across the side of the mountain unaffected by the landslide to the place on the road where the ambulance was waiting.

Nor did he say that the mental image of her face had gone with him every step of the way. That the sight of her now filled him with an illicit joy he could neither excuse nor condone.

Her voice was quiet. 'You said—we could try prayer.'

He walked slowly back and stood by the empty hearth, staring ahead of him. 'I have,' he said. 'I went to the church in Besavoro, and lit a candle.' His smile was twisted. 'I have not done that for a long time.'

As she looked at him Laura caught her breath. 'Your hands—they're bleeding.'

His own downward glance was indifferent. 'It is not important.'

'But you need to take care of them,' Laura insisted. 'Those cuts could easily become infected...'

Her voice tailed away as his brows lifted coldly.

'Your concern is touching, but unnecessary,' he said. 'I can look after myself.'

He spoke more brusquely than he'd intended, because he was fighting an impulse to go and kneel beside her, burying his face in her lap. He saw her flinch at his tone, and cursed himself savagely under his breath.

Yet it was for her own protection, he thought grimly. He dared not soften. He could not take the risk of going near her, or allow himself even the fleeting luxury of touch.

He finished the whisky and set down the glass. 'I had better bathe and change quickly,' he said, striving for a lighter tone. 'No storm will be as bad as Emilia's mood if her dinner is spoiled.'

Laura watched him go, then made her way slowly to her own room. She showered quickly, but made no attempt to dress afterwards. Instead, she sat on the edge of the bed in her cotton robe, staring into space, a prey to her own unhappy thoughts.

She was aroused from her reverie by a tap on the door, and Guillermo's voice telling her that dinner was served.

She got up quickly, and opened the door a fraction. 'I'm not very hungry tonight, Guillermo,' she said. 'I—I think it's the weather. It's so sultry. Will you—explain to His Excellency, please?'

Guillermo's face said plainly that he would prefer not to, and that his wife might also wish to know the reason for the *signorina* being absent, but he gave a small bow of reluctant acquiescence and departed.

But a few minutes later he was knocking again, and this time he presented her with a folded sheet of paper.

The words it contained were terse. 'Laura—do not force me to fetch you.' And it was signed 'Ramontella'.

'*Scusi, signorina.*' Guillermo spread his hands apologetically. 'I tried.'

'Yes,' she said. 'I'm sure you did. Tell the *signore* that I'll be there presently.'

The silver dress was out of bounds, and probably ruined anyway. She was sick of the sight of the blue shift, so she dressed almost defiantly in one of the few outfits she hadn't worn before—a pair of sage-green linen trousers, and a sage and white striped blouse, which buttoned severely to the throat.

Last night's rain hadn't done the pewter sandals any favours either, but they were all she had, so she slipped her feet into them and set off mutinously for the dining room.

Alessio was leaning on the back of his chair, waiting for her.

She lifted her chin, and met his gaze without flinching. She was trying to play it cool, but inside she was melting—dying. The day's wear and tear had been showered away, and, apart from a dressing on one hand, he looked his lean, dangerous self again.

He was wearing the usual black trousers and snowy shirt, and another of those amazing waistcoats—this time in black and gold.

Alessio's own first thought was that if she'd dressed deliberately to disguise her femininity, she had seriously miscalculated. The cut of the linen trousers only accentuated the slight curve of her hips and the length of her slim legs, while the wide waistband reduced her midriff to a hand's span. As he would have had pleasure in proving under different circumstances, he thought with a pang of longing.

And now that he had seen her naked, the prim lines of that blouse were nothing more than a tease. An incitement to remember the delicate beauty beneath.

He felt his heart thud suddenly and unevenly, and snatched at his control, straightening unsmilingly as she walked to the table and sat down.

'Prayer is one thing,' he said softly as she unfolded her napkin. 'Fasting, however, is quite unnecessary.'

She gave him a defiant look. 'I'm just not hungry.'

He shrugged as he took his own seat. 'And I do not care to eat alone,' he retorted. 'Besides, when the food arrives, your appetite will soon return.'

'Is that an order?' she inquired in a dulcet tone.

'No,' he said. 'Merely a prediction.'

She bit her lip, knowing that an icicle had more chance in hell than she had of turning up her nose at Emilia's cooking. 'I notice we're dining by candlelight again.'

'There is not much fuel for the generator,' Alessio returned casually. 'Guillermo wishes to conserve what is left.' His smile was swift and hard. 'Be assured it is not a prelude to romance, *signorina.*'

She met his gaze squarely. 'I never imagined it would be, *signore.*'

'But I understand that work to restore the electricity supply has already begun,' he went on. 'Also the telephones.'

'And the road?'

'I am promised that digging will commence at first light. As soon as there is a way through, you will be on your way to Rome. Does that content you?'

'Yes,' she said quietly. 'Of course.'

'Bene,' he commented sardonically. There was a silence, while his dark eyes dwelled on her thoughtfully, before he added, 'Believe me, *signorina*, I am doing all I can to hasten your departure.'

Laura stared down at the polished table. 'Yes,' she said, 'I do—believe it.' She swallowed past the sudden constriction in her throat. 'And I'm—sorry that you're being put to all this trouble, *signore*. I realise, of course, that I—I should never have come here.'

'Well, we can agree on that at least,' Alessio said with a touch of grimness. She thought she was being sent away for all the wrong reasons, he told himself painfully. But how could he possibly explain that he was, for once in his life, trying to do the right thing?

He could not, so maybe it was better to let matters rest as they were. To allow her to go away hurt and hating him—just as long as she did not turn to Paolo instead. The very idea sent a knife twisting inside him.

He found himself trying to hope that she would wait instead for someone decent and honourable who would treat her gently, and with tenderness, when the time came. But he knew that was sheer hypocrisy. That the thought of his Laura in any other man's arms was intolerable anguish, and would always be so.

It was a largely silent meal. Both of them, locked into their own unhappiness, ate just enough of her delicious food to appease Emilia, but without any real relish.

Afterwards, they went to the *salotto* for coffee, but more for convention's sake than a desire to endure more awkward time in each other's company. There were altogether too many no-go areas to avoid, and they both knew it.

Alessio, physically and mentally exhausted by the events of the past twelve hours, was tortured by his longing to have the right to go with Laura to her room, crawl into bed beside her and sleep the clock round in the comfort of her arms.

For her part, Laura felt as if she were suspended in some wretched limbo, waiting for a death sentence to be carried out, but not knowing when the blow might fall.

Everything that occurred tonight—each word, each action— might well be for the last time, she thought, and the knowledge that she would soon go from here and never see him again was almost destroying her.

I can't leave like this, she thought suddenly. Not when, even now, I want him so terribly. I know I don't have the experience he wants, but surely there must be something—*something*—I can do to capture his interest...

'May I offer you something with your coffee?' His tone was coolly formal, and Laura looked up with a start.

'Thank you,' she said. 'May I have *grappa*?'

His brows lifted. 'If that is what you wish.' He paused. 'I did not think you cared for it.'

Dutch courage, Laura thought, but did not say so.

'I certainly found it a shock the first time,' she said with assumed calm. 'But I'd like to—try again. If I may.'

Their eyes met in an odd tingling silence, then Alessio turned away abruptly, and went to the drinks table, returning with two glasses of the colourless spirit.

He handed her one and raised the other, his mouth twisting slightly. *'Salute.'*

She repeated the toast, and drank, hoping that her eyes wouldn't water or her nose bleed. That was hardly the impression she wanted to make.

She was sitting on one of the sofas, but Alessio had gone back to stand by the fireplace, she noticed—which was about as far away as it was possible to get without leaving the room. It was not a promising beginning.

Taking a deep breath, she swallowed the remainder of the *grappa* and held out her empty glass, trying for nonchalance. 'I think I'm developing a taste for this.'

'I do not advise it.' His tone was dry.

'It's my last night in Italy.' Her glance held a faint challenge. 'Maybe I should take a risk or two.'

His mouth tightened, but he refilled her glass without comment and brought it back to her.

As he turned away she said, 'Alessio...'

He looked down at her, frowning slightly. '*Cosa c'e?* What's the matter?'

'Last night, you asked me for a favour,' she said. 'You wanted me to play the piano for you.'

'I have not forgotten.'

'I was thinking that tonight it's my turn—to ask you for something.'

His sudden wariness was almost tangible.

'I am sorry to disappoint you,' he said with cool courtesy. 'But I do not, alas, play the piano.'

'No,' she said, feeling the swift thud of her heart against her ribcage. 'But you do play poker—and you offered to teach me—if you remember.' She took a breath. 'I would like to—take you up on that offer—please.'

He was very still. 'Yet, as you yourself pointed out, *signorina*, a poker school requires more people, and you have no money to lose. Nothing has changed.'

She said softly, 'Except I think you had a very different version in mind.' She detached one of her earrings and held it out to him on the palm of her hand. 'Isn't that so?'

'Perhaps.' The dark face looked as if it had been carved from stone, and his voice was as austere as an arctic wasteland. 'But it was a disgraceful—an unforgivable suggestion, which it shames me to think of, and I must ask you to forget that it was ever made. Also to excuse me. I wish you goodnight, *signorina*.'

He made her a slight, curt bow, and made to move away. She caught at the crisp sleeve of his shirt, detaining him, all pride gone, swept away by the starkness of her need.

Her voice was low, and shook a little. 'Alessio—please. Don't leave me. You—you made me think you wanted me. Wasn't it true?'

'Yes,' he said harshly. 'Or, true then, certainly. But—situations change, and now I wish you to go back to your own country, and get on with your life, as I must continue with mine. Tell yourself that you were never here—that this never happened. Forget me, as I shall forget you.' He released himself implacably from the clasp of her fingers.

'I recommend that you get some sleep,' he added, with chilling politeness. 'You have a long journey ahead of you when tomorrow comes.'

'Yes,' she said. 'And I'll make it without fuss—tomorrow. I swear it. I—I'll never even ask to see you again. But—oh, Alessio, won't you please give me—tonight?'

'I cannot do that.' His throat felt raw, and a heavy stone had lodged itself in his chest. 'And one day, Laura *mia*, you will be grateful to me. When you can look into the eyes of the man you love without shame.'

She watched him go, mind and body equally numb.

'The man you love,' she whispered, brokenly. 'The man you love. Is that really what you said to me? Oh, God, Alessio, if you only knew the terrible irony of that.'

And she buried her face in her hands, sitting motionless in the corner of the sofa, unconscious of the passage of time, until, one by one, the candles guttered and burned out.

Somehow, in the small hours, she got herself back to her own room, undressed and crept into bed, pulling the covers over the top of her head as if she wanted to hide from the coming day.

Or at least from the man she'd be forced to share it with. The man to whom she'd humbled herself for nothing.

No, she thought wretchedly. Not for nothing. For love.

Had he guessed? she wondered yet again. Had he realised that even this brief time in his company had been long enough for her to fall hopelessly, desperately in love with him? To build a pathetic fantasy where some kind of happy ending might be possible?

And was it the knowledge that he could break her heart, rather than his discovery of her inexperience, that had made him turn away from her?

He could hardly have expected such an outcome, after all. And it had clearly turned her from an amusing diversion into a potential nuisance.

And no amount of assurances on her part, or pleading, would convince him otherwise. She was now a serious embarrassment and he wanted her gone. That was totally clear.

I must have been mad, she thought, fighting back a dry sob. What part of 'no' did I not understand?

But that was history now. It had to be, whatever inner pain she was suffering. She would deal with that—somehow—when she was safely back in England.

There could not be long to wait. She would be on her way just as soon as a path to accommodate the Jeep was cleared through the debris. He'd told her that.

Now all that remained to her was to behave with as much dignity as she could still muster for the final hours of her stay at the villa.

And maybe Alessio would be merciful too, she thought unhappily, and leave her to her own devices.

Her packing was almost completed by first light. All that remained to go in the case were the robe she was still wearing and her toiletries.

It was going to be another very hot day, so she decided again to travel in the cream cotton dress, once more immaculately laundered by Emilia.

It's as well I'm leaving, she told herself, trying to wring some humour out of the situation. I could get thoroughly spoiled.

She opened the shutters and stepped out into the courtyard. The storm might never have happened, she thought, viewing the unclouded sky. Yet its aftermath still lingered in all kinds of ways.

It was still very early, and she doubted whether anyone else in the house was even stirring.

In the distance, coming to her through the clear air, she thought she could hear the sound of heavy machinery, but perhaps that was just wishful thinking. A longing to be able to leave the past behind and escape.

Except it might already be too late for that.

She felt suddenly very tired—and strangely defeated. She went slowly back into her room and lay down on top of the bed, stretching with a sigh.

After all, she told herself, she needed a sanctuary, and this was as good as any other. Alessio had no reason to come to this part of the house, and would certainly not be seeking her out deliberately, so she could feel relatively safe.

Presently, she would get showered and dressed, she thought, but not yet. Already the warmth of the sun spilling into the room was making her feel drowsy, and perhaps in sleep she might even find the peace that would be denied her in her waking hours.

So, almost gratefully, Laura closed her eyes, and allowed herself to drift away. But before she had taken more than three steps into the golden landscape before her, she became aware of a voice saying, *'Signorina!'*

She opened reluctant eyes to find Emilia bending over her. She sat up slowly. 'Is something wrong?'

'No—no,' Emilia assured her. 'But it is time to eat, *signorina*. Come.'

'I'm fine—really. I—I don't want any breakfast.'

'Breakfast?' The other woman's brows rose almost comically. 'But it is the *seconda colazione* that awaits you, *signorina*.'

'Lunch?' Laura queried in disbelief. This implied she'd been asleep for hours, when she knew she'd only just closed her eyes.

She peered at her watch, and gulped. 'My God, is it really that time already?'

'*Sì—sì.*' Emilia nodded vigorously, her face firm. 'The *signore* ordered that we should not disturb you from your rest, but you cannot sleep all day. You also need food.'

Laura hesitated. 'I—I have to get dressed first.'

'No need, *signorina.*' Emilia allowed herself a conspiratorial twinkle. 'No one here but you,' she added. 'The *signore* is at the *frana* speaking to engineers about how to make the road safe. He told me he will not come back until late, so you may eat in your *vestaglia.*'

'I see.' Laura got up from the bed, shaking out the crumpled skirts of her robe. He was doing her a kindness, she thought, and she should feel thankful, not sick and empty. Or so lonely that she wanted to weep.

If she'd expected some kind of scratch meal because the master of the house was absent, she was soon proved wrong.

A rich chicken broth was followed by pasta, grilled fish, and a thick meaty stew with herbs and beans, and, after the cheese, there was a creamy pudding tasting of blackcurrant.

I won't want another meal for a week, thought Laura, reflecting wryly that Emilia must have heard about airline food.

She guessed that as soon as Alessio returned she would be leaving, and she wanted to be ready. So she used the siesta time to shower and wash her hair. Emilia, beaming, had told her that the electricity had been restored, but Laura still chose to dry her hair in the sun, sitting on the bench in the courtyard. Last time she'd done this, Caio had been here, she thought idly, then stiffened.

Paolo, she thought. Paolo and his awful mother down at Lake Trasimeno. She hadn't given them a single thought. But then she doubted whether either of them had spared much time to consider her plight either.

Whatever, she would have to leave a message with some excuse to explain her abrupt departure alone. Paolo would probably not be pleased, but that couldn't be helped. And she'd probably done enough to convince his mother that the Manzone marriage was a non-starter, so some good might come out of the bleak misery of this ill-starred visit after all.

But three long hours later she was still waiting. She tried to occupy some time at the piano, but was too irritated by her own lack of concentration to continue, so she put the music away, and closed the lid gently. Another goodbye.

She wandered restlessly round the heated stillness of the garden, trying not to look at her watch too often, and failing. She still had no idea what flight she'd be able to catch. Maybe there wouldn't be one until the next day, now, and she would have to spend the night at the airport, but even that could be endured.

Anywhere, she thought with sudden passion. Please, God, anywhere but here. I can't be with him for another night. I can't...

The sun was setting when she at last heard the sound of the Jeep. She'd been curled up in the corner of the sofa, but now she stiffened, sitting upright, her eyes fixed painfully on the open doorway. She heard his footsteps, his voice in a brief exchange with Guillermo.

Then he came into the room and stood looking at her, in silence, a strange intensity in his dark gaze that parched her mouth and made her tremble inwardly.

She found words from somewhere in a voice she barely recognised as hers. 'The road—is it ready now? Can we go?'

'*Sì,*' he said quietly. 'It is open.'

She touched the tip of her tongue to her dry lips. 'Then—I'd better get—my things.'

He said something soft and violent under his breath, then came to her, his long stride swallowing the distance between them. He took her wrists, pulling her to her feet in one swift, almost angry movement.

Then he bent his head, and kissed her on the mouth with a searing, passionate yearning that made her whole body shake.

'Forgive me.' The words were forced from him hoarsely as he looked deeply, hungrily into her eyes. 'Laura, forgive me, but I cannot live one more hour without you.'

She should stop this now, a small sane voice in her head kept repeating as Alessio kissed her again. Stop it, and step back, out of harm's way. Anything else was madness.

Madness, she thought as coherent thought spun out of control, leaving nothing but this terrifying frenzy in her blood that demanded to be appeased.

Madness, she told herself on a small sobbing breath as she slid her arms round his neck, and let him carry her out of the room.

CHAPTER ELEVEN

THE whole villa seemed hushed, its only sound his footsteps as he strode swiftly with her along the shadowed corridor to his bedroom.

Alessio kicked the door shut behind him, then crossed the vast room, putting Laura down on the canopied bed. For a long moment he looked down at her, then he bent and quite deliberately took the neckline of her dress in both hands, tearing the thin cotton apart like paper.

She gasped, her eyes dilating in sudden uncertainty, and saw his swift, crooked smile.

He said softly, 'Do not be frightened, *carissima*. I have wanted for so long to do that, but now I will be gentle, I promise.'

He released her from the tangle of fabric, tossing it to the floor behind him, before stripping off his own clothing with unhurried purpose. Then, at last, he lay down beside her, framing her face in his hands as he kissed the lingering doubt from her wide startled eyes, then moved down to her mouth, his lips moving almost languorously on hers until he felt the tension leave her, and her slender body relax trustingly into his arms.

He let the kiss deepen, opening her mouth so that his tongue could seek the moist heat of hers, while his fingertips stroked her face and throat, and the vulnerable angles of her slender shoulders, his touch light and almost undemanding. Almost—but not quite.

He felt the growing tumult of her breathing as he began gently to caress her small, eager breasts.

Her rosy nipples were already hard with desire when he freed them from their lace cups, and bent to adore them with his lips and tongue. She gave a tiny whimper, her head moving restlessly from side to side, colour flaring along her cheekbones.

Her shaking hands went to his body, seeking his hardness, driven by the harsh flowering of her own need, but Alessio stopped her, clasping her fingers, and raising them swiftly to his lips.

'Not yet, my sweet one,' he whispered. 'It is too soon for us to enjoy each other as lovers should. This time, *mia cara*, these first moments must be for you alone.'

His hands traced a slow golden path down her body, brushing away her last covering as if it had been a cobweb. And where his hands touched, his lips followed, warm and beguiling. Luring her on.

Telling her—promising her that, this time, there would be no turning back. That the passionate covenant of his nakedness against hers would be fulfilled.

Laura's breathing rasped fiercely in her throat as her aroused senses responded with renewed delight to his caresses, to the physical fact of his nearness, and the warmth of his bare skin brushing hers.

His mouth returned to her breasts, suckling them tenderly as his hand slid between her thighs. She gasped a little in mingled excitement and apprehension, remembering that first time, but discovered at once there was to be nothing painful or threatening in this delicate exploration of her most intimate self.

She found herself sinking into a state of almost languid relaxation, aware of nothing but his fingertips moving on her softly and rhythmically at first, then increasing the pressure into a pattern of deliciously intense sensations. His thumb was stroking her tiny silken mound, coaxing it to heated tumescence, while, at the same time, the long, skilful fingers eased their way slowly into her moist inner heat, forcing the breath from her lungs in a sigh of totally voluptuous pleasure.

His lips moved back to hers, kissing her unhurriedly, his tongue stroking hers, thrusting softly into her mouth, mirroring the frankly sensual play of his hands.

Her earlier languor had fled. There were small flames dancing now behind her tightly closed eyelids. She could not hear, or make a sound, her whole being concentrated on this relentless, exquisite build of pleasure that he was creating for her.

Her body was writhing against his touch, begging mutely for some surcease from this incredible, unbearable spiral of delight that had become almost an agony.

She heard a voice she barely recognised as hers crying out hoarsely as he brought her at last to the peak of consummation, and held her there for an endless moment, before releasing her, and allowing the first uncontrollable spasms of rapture to shudder fiercely through her body, devastating her innocence for ever as she confronted, for the first time, her own sexuality, and his power to arouse it.

And as the first harsh glory of her climax softened into quiet ripples of satiation, there were tears on her face.

Alessio kissed the salt drops away, holding her close, soothing her, murmuring endearments in his own language.

At last she murmured huskily, 'You should have warned me.'

'Warned you of what, *carissima*?'

'How you were going to make me feel.'

She felt him quiver with laughter. 'You do not think, *mia bella*, that might have sounded both conceited and presumptuous?'

She buried her own smile in his shoulder. 'Well—maybe—a little.' She hesitated. 'But I don't expect you've had many failures,' she added with a touch of wistfulness.

There was a silence, then he said gently, 'Shall we agree, *mi amore*, to allow the past to remain where it belongs?' He paused, altering his position slightly but significantly, making her gasp soundlessly. 'The immediate future should concern us more.' He slid his hands under her, lifting her slightly towards him. 'Or I think so—don't you?'

His dark eyes were questioning, his faint smile almost quizzical as he looked down at her, and she felt the hardness of him between her thighs, pressing at the entrance to her newly receptive body.

Laura was suddenly aware of a pang of physical desire so strong—so incredible—that she nearly cried out. Suddenly, she knew that she could not allow herself time to think—to become afraid. To doubt her own capacity to absorb all that male size and strength, and return the pleasure he'd gifted to her only moments before.

Instead, she found herself reaching for him, forgetting her instinctive shyness as she caressed the powerfully rigid shaft with fingers that shook a little, making him groan softly, pleadingly. And then, with a total certainty she barely understood, guiding him into her. Surging almost wildly against the initial restraint of his first thrust to welcome him deeply—endlessly. To defy once and for always any discomfort that might still linger for her in this complete union of their bodies.

But this time there was no pain, only the heated, silken glide of him possessing her—filling her completely over and over again.

Making her realise, with shock, as she clung to his sweat-dampened shoulders, her slim hips echoing his own driving rhythm, that her body had not yet finished with its delight.

That his urgency had captured her too, lifting her, all unaware, to some other unguessed-at plane with heart-stopping speed, showing her that the pinnacle of rapture was there, waiting for her if only—if only she could reach...

Then the last remnants of reality splintered, leaving nothing but the primitive agony of pure sensation. And as she moaned aloud in the final extremity she heard Alessio's voice, hoarse and shaken, saying her name as his sated body crumpled against hers in sheer exhaustion.

The warm scented water was like balm on her sensitised skin, at the same time soothing the frank, unexpected ache of her muscles. Laura lay in Alessio's arms in the deep sunken bath, her head pillowed dreamily on his shoulder as his lips caressed the damp silk of her hair.

There was no point, she thought, in trying to rationalise what had just happened between them. It defied reason or coherent thought. It just—was.

And now nothing would ever be the same again. Or, at least, not for her.

For him, she thought with sudden unhappiness, it was probably just routine. Another eager girl to be taught the art of sexual fulfilment by a man who was undoubtedly ardent and generous— but also diabolically experienced.

He said, 'Where have you gone?'

She glanced up at him, startled. 'I don't know what you mean,' she parried.

'A moment ago you were here with me, and happy. But no longer. So what happened?'

'I'm fine.' She sent him a deliberately provocative look under her lashes. 'Perhaps you're better at reading bodies than minds, *signore*.'

But his glance was thoughtful rather than amused. 'And perhaps you do not always tell the whole truth, *signorina*.'

She turned, pressing her lips passionately against the smooth skin of his shoulder. 'Alessio, I am happy. I swear it. I—I never dreamed I could feel like this. Maybe I'm a little—overwhelmed.'

'And maybe you also need food.' He was smiling now as he reached forward to drain the water. 'I think we must forget dinner, *mia bella*, but maybe I can coax Emilia to provide us with a little supper, hmm?'

'Oh, God.' Laura groaned as he helped her out of the bath. 'What is she going to think?'

He grinned. 'That we have the rest of the night to enjoy, *carissima*, and need all our strength. She will feed us well.'

And so she did, although, to Laura's relief, Emilia allowed Alessio, who had gone on his quest wearing only a pair of jeans, to bring the basket of food from the kitchen himself.

Laura, having ruefully examined the ruin of her dress, had put on his discarded shirt. Now she pirouetted self-consciously for his inspection.

'What do you think?'

The dark eyes glinted. 'I think perhaps supper can wait.'

She laughed, and skipped out of range. 'But I'm starving, *signore*. You wouldn't want me to faint.'

He slanted a wicked grin at her. 'Well, not through hunger, certainly.'

The basket contained cold chicken, cheese, red wine and warm olive bread, which they ate and drank outside in the courtyard, while the goddess Diana stared over their heads with her cold, remote smile.

Laura said, 'I don't think she approves of us.'

'According to the old stories, she approved of very little,' Alessio said lazily as he refilled her glass. 'My grandfather originally commissioned the statue, but I think he was disappointed in the result, and I know my parents were planning to have it replaced at some point.'

'Yet they didn't?'

He was silent for a moment. 'They did not have time,' he said eventually, his voice expressionless. 'My mother was killed on the *autostrada* when I was sixteen. A lorry driver fell asleep at the wheel, and his vehicle crashed through the barrier. And my father never recovered from her death. Within the year, he had suffered a fatal heart attack, which his doctors always believed was triggered by his grief.'

'Oh, God.' Laura sat up, staring at him, shocked. 'Oh, I'm so sorry. I shouldn't have said anything...'

He touched her cheek gently. '*Carissima*, I have not been sixteen for a very long time. And I was looked after with infinite kindness by my godfather, the Marchese D'Agnaccio, and his wonderful wife, Arianna, so I was not left to mourn as a lonely orphan.'

Oh, but I think you were, she told him silently. However well you were looked after. And I think, too, that this explains some of the contradictions I sense in you. The way you seem to retreat to some remote fastness where no one can reach you. The emotional equivalent, perhaps, of this house.

He said, 'You have left me again.'

She bent her head. 'I was thinking of my own father. He died of a heart attack too. He'd liquidised all his assets, remortgaged the house to start up an engineering business with an old friend. He came back from a business trip with a full order book to find the place empty, and his partner gone, taking all the money with him. He must have been planning it for ages, because he'd covered his tracks completely. We were going to lose everything, and Dad collapsed on his way to the creditors' meeting.'

Alessio drew her into his arms, and sat with her, his lips resting gently against her hair.

After a while, he said, 'Would you like to sleep a little, *mia cara*?'

She found her eyes suddenly blurred. 'Yes,' she whispered shakily. 'Yes, Alessio, please. That would be good.'

He took her hand and led her back to the shadowed bedroom. Gently he unbuttoned the shirt, and slipped it from her shoulders, then put her into the bed and drew the sheet over her.

As he came to lie beside her Laura turned into his arms, and heard his voice murmuring to her softly, soothingly, in his own language until drowsiness prevailed, and she drifted away into oblivion.

It was very dark—some time in the small hours—when she awoke to his mouth moving gently, persuasively on hers, calling her senses back to life, and her body to renewed desire.

She yielded, sighing in sensuous acceptance as she fitted herself to him, waiting—eager once more to be overwhelmed—to be carried away on the force of his passion.

But he was, she soon discovered, in no hurry to enter her. No hurry at all.

Instead, she found herself shivering—burning in response as his fingertips stroked and tantalised every warm inch of her, awakening needs that, yesterday, she had not known existed.

His lips caressed her breasts, tugging gently on the hardening nipples until she moaned faintly, then kissed their way down her body, until he reached the joining of her thighs to demand a different kind of surrender.

She was beyond protest, unable to resist him as his mouth claimed her, and she experienced the intimate sorcery of his tongue working its dark magic upon her.

The breath sobbed in her throat as her body writhed helplessly beneath him, torn between shame and exaltation.

He was smiling against her skin, saying that she must speak— must tell him what she liked—what she wanted him to do to her. And was it this? And this? And—most of all—this? And as she was swept away into the maelstrom of anguished pleasure he had unleashed for her she heard her own drowning voice whispering an endless, 'Yes.'

It was almost dawn before they'd finally fallen asleep in each other's arms, and the next time Laura opened her eyes it was full morning, and sunlight was pouring through the slats of the shutters. For a moment, she lay still, savouring her memories, then she turned her head to look at the sleeping man beside her. Only the bed was empty.

She sat up bewilderedly in time to see Alessio emerge from the bathroom, pushing a white shirt into the waistband of his jeans.

She said, 'You're dressed,' and was ashamed of the open disappointment in her voice.

He was laughing as he knelt on the bed beside her, and kissed her mouth. 'I have to wear clothes sometimes, *carissima*. People expect it. Besides, I must go out. It seems that Fredo has recovered consciousness, and is asking for me.'

She stretched delicately, watching the sudden flare in the dark eyes as the sheet slipped down from her body. 'Shall I come with you?'

He glanced swiftly, regretfully at his watch. 'Next time, *carissima*. Now I really must go.' His hand tangled in her hair, drawing her head back for another kiss, longer, slower, deeper than the last, and she slid her arm round his neck, holding him to her.

'Stay here, and get some rest,' he told her softly, detaching himself with open reluctance. 'Because you will need it when I return.' He paused. 'I shall tell the servants you are not to be disturbed.'

Laura groaned. 'I don't think I shall ever be able to face them again.'

He grinned at her. 'Ah, but you will, *Madonna*. Now go back to sleep and dream about me, and I will return very soon.' At the door he turned. 'And then we must talk.' He blew her another kiss, and was gone.

She lay quietly for a while. She had never thought much about her body, except as something to be fed and clothed. Had found the physical facts of passion and consummation faintly ludicrous, and the prospect of actually finding herself in bed with a man—submitting to him—as both awkward and embarrassing.

And she'd never imagined herself as anyone's sex object either. She'd always supposed she was too thin, and her breasts were too small, to make her the focus of a man's desire.

And yet in one terrifying, rapturous night all her ideas had been overturned, and her principles swept aside.

She belonged body and soul to Alessio Ramontella. And every nerve ending she possessed, each muscle, and inch of skin, was providing her with a potent reminder of his total mastery. And of how much he had, indeed, desired her.

She realised she was blushing and pushed the sheet away, swinging her legs to the floor. Too late for blushes now—or even to remember her own careful taboos about casual sex. Although those hours of lovemaking could hardly be described as casual.

And, she thought, she didn't regret a thing. How could she?

She quickly straightened the bed, plumping the crumpled pillows and smoothing the covers flat, then wandered into the bathroom to take a long, luxurious shower. As she soaped herself she recalled other hands touching her, sometimes tantalising, sometimes almost reverent, and felt her heartbeat quicken uncontrollably.

I want him here, she thought, pressing a clenched fist against the tiled wall. I want him now.

As she emerged from the shower and reached for a towel she glimpsed herself in one of the many mirrors and paused, all her earlier doubts about her lack of glamour confirmed.

She turned away, sighing. She still had nothing to wear, and frankly she didn't fancy traversing the house to collect a change of clothing from her room, so she borrowed Alessio's black silk robe instead, rolling up the sleeves and tying the sash in a secure double bow round her slender waist.

The faint fragrance of the cologne he used still lingered in the fabric, she discovered with ridiculous pleasure as she stretched out on top of the bed to wait. She could almost pretend that he was here with her, his arms around her.

And the fantasy became even more real if she closed her eyes. She hadn't meant to doze, but the room was warm, the bed soft, and the shower had relaxed her, so the temptation was irresistible.

As she pillowed her cheek on her hand she remembered how Alessio had kissed her awake only a few hours before, and exactly what it had led to. And she wriggled further into the mattress, smiling a little as her eyelids drooped.

It was the sound of the dog barking excitedly that woke her.

Laura propped herself up on an elbow, and stared around her, momentarily disorientated. Caio, she thought, trying to clear her head. Caio in the courtyard outside her room, wanting her to come out and join him. Except he wasn't here—he was at Lake Trasimeno with the Signora. And—this wasn't her room either. It belonged to Alessio.

Just, she thought slowly, just as she did herself.

And, with that nosedive into reality, she suddenly became aware of something else. The sound of women's voices arguing, not far away. One of them was Emilia's. But the other...

Oh, God, Laura thought, transfixed with horror. It's the Signora. She's back. I have to get out of here.

But she was too late. The door was flung wide, and the Signora came stalking into the room, brushing away the volubly protesting Emilia as if she were a troublesome insect.

'So.' She stared at Laura, still huddled on the bed, and her smile was gloating. 'Just as I expected.' She turned. 'Paolo, my poor son, I grieve for you, but you must come and see this slut you brought here. This *puttana* you thought to honour with our name, and who has become yet another of your cousin's whores.'

Paolo followed her into the room, his expression sullen and

inimical. The look he sent Laura was enough to freeze the blood. 'Fool,' it said plainly.

'Sì, Mammina,' he said curtly. 'You were right about her and I was wrong. She has totally betrayed me, and now I cannot bear the sight of her.' He spat the words. 'So, get rid of her. Make her go.'

I'm still asleep, thought Laura. And this is a nightmare. A bad one. He couldn't still intend to keep up this ludicrous pretence, surely?

The situation was fast slipping out of control, and somehow she had to drag it back to reality. It was hard to be dignified when wearing nothing but a man's robe, several sizes too large, but she had to try, she thought, scrambling off the bed and facing them both, her head held high.

She said coldly and clearly, 'Paolo, I do not appreciate having my privacy invaded, or being insulted like this. So, please stop this nonsense, and tell your mother the truth.'

'And what truth is that, pray?' the Signora enquired.

Laura sent Paolo an equally fulminating glance. 'That your son and I are not involved with each other—and never have been.'

'And nor will we ever be,' he flung back at her. 'You faithless bitch. Do you think I would want my cousin's leavings?'

Laura felt as if she'd been punched in the midriff. She said, 'But that's insane—and you know it.'

'I know only that I want you thrown out of this house.' He turned to his mother. 'Arrange it, Mammina. I wish never to see her again.'

He stalked from the room, slamming the door behind him. Leaving Laura and the Signora looking at each other.

The older woman sent her a grim smile. 'You hear my son. Pack your things, and go. As the matter is urgent, my car will take you to the airport at Rome.'

Laura swallowed. 'This is not your house, signora. You do not give orders here. And I am going nowhere until Alessio returns.'

'You are over-familiar, signorina.' The Signora's tone was ice.

'Or do you imagine some sordid romp gives you the right—a
nobody from nowhere—to refer to the Count Ramontella by his
given name?'

She paused derisively. 'You mentioned the truth just now. So,
hear it. I arranged this little comedy, and I am now ending it.
Because I have achieved what I set out to do. I have separated
you from my son. With the assistance, of course, of my dear
nephew.'

There was a silence, then Laura said slowly, 'What—what are
you talking about?'

'I am talking about you—and your host.' She snorted. 'You
think my nephew would have laid a finger on you of his own
free will? No, and no. I simply made it necessary for him to—
oblige me. And he has done so.'

Laura was very still. 'I don't know what you mean.'

The Signora laughed. 'But of course not. You did not know—
how could you?—that my nephew has been conducting a disrep-
utable affair with a married woman—the worthless wife, unfortunately, of an old friend's son.' She sighed. 'So sad—and potentially so scandalous. But I agreed not to make this shameful
episode public if Alessio would, in his turn, use his powers of
seduction to win you away from my son.

'At first, he was reluctant. You are not the type to whom he
would naturally be drawn, and very much his social inferior. But
he decided that his mistress's dubious honour must be protected
at all costs.' She picked up Laura's torn dress from the floor, and
studied it. 'And it seems that, in the end, he—warmed to his
task.'

Her malicious smile raked like rusty nails over Laura's quivering senses. 'He promised me he would send you home with a
beautiful memory, *signorina*. I gather that his ability to do so is
almost legendary, so I hope he has kept his word.'

'You mean I was—set up?' Even to her own ears, Laura's
voice sounded husky—uncertain. 'You're lying.'

'Ask him,' said the Signora. 'If you are still here when he
returns.' She gave a delicate yawn. 'I advise you go quickly and

spare him the obvious recriminations. They will do no good. Alessio is, and will always be, a law unto himself.

'Besides,' she added, shrugging, 'it is clear he wishes to avoid a confrontation. As you see, when he learned I was returning, he immediately contrived to be absent. He may feel it is wiser to stay away until you have finally departed.'

'He—knew?' The words stuck in her throat.

'But of course. I telephoned earlier.' The older woman sounded mildly surprised. 'I needed him to make sure you would be found in his bed. That was our agreement.'

She nodded. 'Alessio has fulfilled his part of the bargain, and can now resume his liaison with that pretty idiot Vittoria Montecorvo in perfect safety, as long as he is discreet.' She smiled again. 'As you have found, *signorina*, he prefers fools. And variety.'

She added more brusquely, 'Your services are no longer required, *signorina*. You have amused my nephew for a short time, but anything else is only in your imagination.'

Did I imagine it? Laura asked herself numbly. Did I imagine the murmurs and laughter? The peace and sense of belonging? Was it really—just sex all along?

The Signora turned and opened the door. 'So, please go quietly without embarrassing scenes.'

Laura said quietly, 'Do you really think I'd want to stay?' She brushed past the older woman, and walked quickly away down the passage towards her room, stumbling a little on the hem of the robe.

In the courtyard, the goddess Diana still smiled with that chill serenity. But then, thought Laura as the first slash of pain cut into her, she was accustomed to having love torn to pieces in front of her. So this was the place where she truly belonged.

She ran the rest of the way, just making it into the bathroom before she was violently sick, retching into the toilet bowl until the muscles of her empty stomach were screaming at her, and the world was revolving dizzily round her aching head.

Eventually, she managed to drag herself back to her feet, to rinse her mouth and wash her face somehow. The light golden tan she'd acquired had turned sallow, she thought, wincing at her reflection, and her eyes looked like hollow pits.

While beating like a drum in her tired brain were the words, 'I have to get out of here. I have to go. Before he comes back. I have to go.'

Alessio parked the Jeep in front of the villa and sprang out, humming to himself. He had assured himself that Fredo was going to make a full recovery, then made his excuses and left, intent on returning as fast as possible to his warm, beautiful girl.

He had felt totally relaxed and serene on the homeward journey, but his mind was clear and sharp as crystal, visualising the whole shape of his future life laid out in front of him like a golden map.

He strode into the house and went straight to his room, but it was empty. He shrugged off his faint disappointment that Laura was not there, waiting for him, and went in search of her.

As he walked through the hallway Caio advanced out of the *salotto* barking aggressively, halting Alessio in his stride. His brows snapped together as he realised with sharp dismay the implications of the dog's presence, and, as if on cue, his aunt appeared in the doorway of the drawing room.

'*Caro*,' she purred. 'I did not expect you back so soon.'

'And I did not expect you at all, Zia Lucrezia.' His tone was guarded. 'The road has only just opened again.'

'So Guillermo informed me when I telephoned. He seemed to feel I should not take the risk, but my driver is a good, safe man.'

She paused. 'You will be pleased to hear that our little conspiracy was entirely successful. Paolo was cured of his foolish infatuation as soon as he saw the English girl sprawling half naked on your bed.' She added brightly, 'And soon, she will be on her way to the airport and out of our lives for ever. *Bravo*, nephew. You have done well.'

Alessio had a curious sensation that it was suddenly impossible to breathe.

He said hoarsely, 'What have you done? What have you said to my Laura?'

She shrugged a shoulder. 'I simply—enlightened her as to the real reason for her presence here—and for being honoured with your attentions. Did I do wrong?' She smiled maliciously, adding, 'She seemed to accept the situation quite well. No weeping or hysteria. I was—surprised.'

He said on a groan, *'Santa madonna,'* and began to run.

Laura had taken out the clothes to wear to the airport, and put them on the bed. She went back into the bedroom to fetch her toothbrush and wash-bag, and when she emerged Alessio was standing there.

She recoiled instantly, with a little incoherent cry, and saw him flinch.

He said with shaken urgency, 'Laura, *carissima*. You must let me talk to you. Explain.'

'There's really no need, *signore*.' There was a terrible brightness in her voice. 'Your aunt has already told me everything.'

'No,' he said. 'Not everything.'

'Then at least all I needed to know,' she flashed. 'Which is—I got screwed. Several times and in several different senses of the word.'

His head went back. He said icily, 'How dare you describe what happened between us in those terms?'

'Too vulgar for you, my lord?' She dropped a curtsy. 'I do apologise. Blame my social inferiority.'

He drew a deep breath. 'We shall get nowhere like this.'

'I shall get somewhere,' she said. 'Rome airport, to be precise. After which I shall never have to see anyone from your lying, treacherous family again. And that includes you—you utter bastard.'

There was a tingling silence, then Alessio said quietly, 'I do not blame you for being angry with me.'

'Thanks for the gracious admission,' she said. 'And now perhaps you'll go. I have to finish up here, and your aunt's driver is waiting.'

He said curtly, 'My aunt will need her driver herself. She and Paolo are leaving.'

She lifted her chin. 'Your aunt didn't mention it.'

'She does not yet know. If you wish to go to the airport, I will drive you.'

'No.' She almost shouted the word. 'No, you won't, damn you. Can't you understand? I wouldn't go five yards with you. In fact, I don't want to breathe the same air.'

He looked at her wearily. '*Dio*, Laura. You cannot believe what you are saying.'

'Oh, but I do,' she said. 'And I also believe your aunt. Or are you going to deny that you had me brought here so that you could seduce me?'

He bent his head, wretchedly. '*Mia cara*, it may have begun like that, but—'

'But that's how it ended as well,' she cut across him. 'If memory serves. Now, will you please get out of this room?'

'Not until we have talked. Until I can get you to understand...'

'But I do. It's all perfectly clear. You have a mistress who is married. Your aunt threatened to make the affair public. You took me to bed to keep her quiet.' Her glance dropped scorn. 'You really didn't have to go to those lengths, *signore*. If you thought I was dating your loathsome cousin, then you only had to ask me to stop.'

'Laura—listen to me. I—I wanted you.'

'Please don't expect me to be flattered. What was I—your practice round? Keeping you in shape for your married lady?'

'Your memory does not serve you very well,' he said. 'You know it was not like that.'

'My most recent recollection,' she said, 'is being found by that unholy pair in your bedroom, and having to listen to their insults. Because you set me up. Your aunt telephoned you and said she was on her way.'

'I received no such call,' he said. 'And if I had, then you would have left with me.' He paused. 'If you still insist on going to Rome, then Guillermo will take you. But stay with me, *bella mia*, I beg you. Let me try and make amends.'

'There is nothing you can say, or do.' Her throat ached uncontrollably. 'You tricked me, and I shall always hate you for it. I just want to leave—and never see you again.'

There was another dreadful silence, then he said, slowly and carefully, 'Unfortunately, it may not be that simple for either of us. Last night, I failed to protect you as I should have done, a piece of criminal stupidity for which I must ask your forgiveness. However, it is a fact that you could be carrying my child.'

'Well, don't worry too much, *signore*.' Her voice bit. 'If I am, I'll take appropriate action to deal with it—and it won't cost you a red cent. So you can return to your mistress without a backward glance.'

'Vittoria is not my mistress.' His voice rose in exasperation. 'She never was. It was wrong, and I admit that, but it was only a one-night stand—nothing more.'

'And so was I,' she hit back at him. 'They seem to be your speciality, *signore*.' She saw his head jerk back as if she had struck him, and took a steadying breath. 'Now, if you have nothing more to say—no more lame and meaningless excuses—then, perhaps, you'll finally get out of this room, and leave me alone.'

She could feel his anger like a force field, and braced herself for the explosion, but it did not come.

Instead, he looked her over. 'There is one thing.' His tone was almost conversational. 'My robe. I would like it back, if you please.'

'Of course. I'll leave it—'

He held out a hand. 'Now.'

There was a silence. At last she said quietly, 'Please—don't do this.'

His brows lifted. 'What is your objection, *signorina*?' His tone mocked her. 'I am asking for nothing but the return of my property. Or do you wish me to take it from you?'

Her lips silently formed the word 'no'. She undid the double bow, fumbling a little, then took off the robe, which she rolled into a ball and threw at him. It landed at his feet. She stood her ground, making no attempt to cover herself with her hands. Trying to tell herself that it did not matter. That he already knew everything there was to know about her.

And at the same time, desperately conscious that it mattered terribly. Because the lover who'd adored her the previous night was gone for ever, and in his place was a stranger who had no right to look at her.

But Alessio was not even glancing at her naked body. His impenetrable dark gaze was fixed on her eyes—on the anger and fierce contempt in their stormy depths.

He said softly, 'You know, do you not, that I would only have to touch you?'

Yes, she knew, and the shame of it was like an open wound in her flesh. Somehow, she had to retrieve the situation. Somehow...

She said in savage mimicry of his intonation, 'And you know, *do you not*, that I would rather die?' She paused. 'So will you please get out of my life? Now.'

'*Naturalmente.* And I will give Guillermo his instructions.' He gave a curt inclination of the head. '*Addio, signorina.* I wish you—happiness.'

Then he was gone, closing the door behind him, leaving the discarded robe still lying on the floor.

Laura reached down, and picked up the mass of crumpled silk, carrying it to her face and holding it there. Breathing the scent of his skin for the last time.

'It's over,' she whispered. 'Over. He's gone. And I shall never see him again.'

CHAPTER TWELVE

ALESSIO was in his study with the door shut, but he still heard the car drive away taking Laura to the airport, and he sat for a long moment, his head buried in his hands, fighting for self-command.

He had been blazing with anger as he'd walked out of her room earlier, furious at her refusal to listen to reason, and outraged at the way she had spoken to him. Dismissed him so summarily.

Never, he'd raged inwardly, had he been treated like that before by any woman. But, then, honesty compelled him to ask, when had he ever behaved as badly before to any woman?

And the acknowledgement that he'd deserved every contemptuous word she'd hurled at him did nothing to soothe his temper.

But now his anger was beginning to cool, leaving in its place a bleak and echoing emptiness. He was stunned by his own wretchedness. And by his total failure to win her round, or reach her in any way that mattered.

And now she was gone from him, he thought starkly. How could he have allowed it to happen?

More importantly, how could he have stopped her?

Well, there was no way. She had made that more than clear, her words lashing him like a whip. And at least he had not suffered the ultimate humiliation of falling on his knees, as he'd been desperately tempted to do, and begging her to stay. Or committed the folly of telling her he loved her—something he had never said to anyone before—and having that rejected too.

He pushed his chair back impatiently, and rose. There was no point in brooding, he told himself. He could not change what had just happened. She'd left—hating him. But he could and would deal with the fallout, as he'd sworn he would.

On his way to the *salotto*, he was waylaid by an unhappy Emilia. 'I am so sorry, *Excellenza*, but we tried to keep the *signora*, your aunt, away from your room—and the little one—but we could not stop her. Is this why the Signorina Laura has gone away?'

He said gently, 'The blame is mine alone, Emilia. And the *signorina* had her own reasons for wishing to return to England.'

'But she will come back?'

He found he was bracing himself. Avoiding her concerned glance. 'No,' he said. 'I do not think so.'

He found his aunt ensconced on a sofa, glancing through a fashion magazine and drinking coffee.

'Alessio, *caro*.' She barely glanced up. 'Now that our unwanted guest has departed, I thought I might invite Beatrice Manzone and her father here for a short stay.' She smiled smugly. 'She and Paolo seemed to enjoy each other's company at Trasimeno so much. Maybe, even without your intervention, he might have come round to my way of thinking. Yet it was probably better to be safe.'

'I am sure you would think so.' His voice was harsh. 'However, I must decline to entertain any more guests of yours, Zia Lucrezia. Nor do I wish you or your son to spend another night under my roof.'

There was a silence, then she said, 'If this is a joke, Alessio, it is a poor one.'

His gaze was unswerving. 'Believe me, I have never been more serious. I do not wish to have anything more to do with you. Ever.'

'But Paolo and I are your closest living relatives.' There was a shake in her voice. Uncertainty in the look she sent him. 'Your father was my brother.'

He said icily, 'As I am ashamed to acknowledge. And for most of his life, you and he were strangers—at his wish.' He shook his head. 'I should have ordered you to leave my apartment as soon as you mentioned Vittoria,' he added grimly.

'Yet you did not,' she reminded him swiftly. 'You agreed to

my terms, and you carried them out to the letter, because you did not wish your liaison with her to become known.'

'No,' he said, after a pause. 'I did not. But, on reflection, I think I agreed for Fabrizio's sake, rather than hers. He is a fool, but he is a fool in love, and I cannot blame him for that.' His mouth tightened, then he went on levelly, 'Nor does he deserve public humiliation because his wife does not return his affection.' He shrugged. 'One day he may discover the truth about her, but it will not be through me.'

He gave her a cool, hard glance. 'Guillermo is driving Signorina Mason to Rome, so your own driver is free to take you wherever you wish to go. I would be glad if you would leave as soon as possible.'

The controlled, controlling veneer was beginning to crumble. She said, 'I cannot believe you mean this. You are hardly a saint, Alessio, to trouble yourself over the bedding of one stupid English girl.'

'That is enough.' His voice rang harshly through the big room. 'Believe that the matter is closed, and my decision is final.' He made her a swift formal bow. '*Addio*, Zia Lucrezia.'

She called after him, panic in her tone, but he took no notice.

He was in the library, forcing himself to look through his emails in an attempt at normality, when the door opened and Paolo came in.

He said uneasily, '*Mammina* says you have ordered us from the villa. There must be some misunderstanding.'

'No.' Alessio rose and walked round the desk, leaning back against it, arms folded across his chest. 'This is simply a day for departures—for finally severing damaging connections.' He looked icily at Paolo. 'As you yourself have done, cousin.'

'You mean the little Laura?' Paolo shrugged. 'But consider— if I had pretended to forgive her for sleeping with you, *Mammina* would never have believed it. So what else could I do but get rid of her?'

Alessio considered him, his mouth set. 'You do not seem distraught at her loss,' he commented.

'On the contrary, it is damned inconvenient,' Paolo said sourly.

'Until your intervention, I had *Mammina* nicely fooled. Another few days, and she would have admitted defeat over the Manzone girl.'

'How little you know.' Alessio's eyes were coolly watchful. 'And how was Signorina Mason involved in this—foolery?'

Paolo shrugged. 'There's no point in keeping it secret, any longer. The truth is, I picked her up in London. *Mammina* was right about that. Offered her a free holiday, plus cash, if she pretended to be in love with me.'

He gave a lascivious grin. 'I must say she threw herself into the role. Under all that English cool, she was a hot little number—as you must have found out last night.

'But I'm surprised she didn't tell you herself—during pillow talk,' he went on. 'But perhaps you didn't give her time, eh? I've been there myself, cousin, and I'm sure you had much better things for that pretty mouth to do...'

There was a blur of movement, and the odd sensation that he'd collided head-on with a stone pillar.

He found he was lying on the floor, his jaw aching, with Alessio standing over him, flexing his right hand.

He said softly, dangerously, 'That is a filthy lie, and we both know it. You never touched Laura Mason, and you will never speak of her in those terms again.' He paused. 'When you return to London, it will be to clear your desk. You no longer work for the Arleschi Bank. Now get out.'

He strode from the room, leaving Paolo to scramble to his feet, unaided and cursing violently.

'You will be sorry for this, cousin,' he whispered silently, gingerly feeling his jaw as Alessio's tall figure disappeared. 'And so will your little bedmate. Oh, yes, I know how to make her very sorry.'

Laura sat down at her desk and switched on her computer. It was almost a relief to find herself back at work, she thought, sighing. At least it would mean she would have something else to think about—during daylight hours, anyway. At night, it was not so easy to control her thoughts or dreams.

The long drive to the airport had been conducted pretty much in silence, although she'd been aware of Guillermo sending anxious glances in her direction.

Once they'd arrived, he had asked her quietly if she was sure—quite sure—she wished to do this, and she had said yes—yes, she was. And he had taken her to the desk, and arranged to have her ticket transferred to the next available flight in four hours' time. The transaction had taken place in Italian, and she was sure she heard him mention the Count Ramontella's name, but it had seemed wiser not to ask or protest. She was getting out of there, wasn't she? And more easily than she could have hoped?

The actual means had no longer seemed important.

'You have no message for me to take to His Excellency?' His voice was sad as he bade her goodbye.

'No,' she said, past the agonising tightness in her throat. 'No, thank you. Everything necessary has been said.'

On the plane, she pretended to sleep while the events of the past twenty-four hours rolled like a film loop through her weary mind, tormenting her over and over again. Telling her how gullible she'd been. The worst kind of fool.

The time since her return had not been easy for her either. Gaynor had naturally wanted to know why she'd come back earlier than expected, and didn't seem wholly convinced by Laura saying evasively that things hadn't worked out exactly as expected.

Her friend was also astute enough to read the signs of deep trouble behind Laura's attempt at a brave face.

'Please don't tell me you ended up falling for this Paolo after all?' she asked, dismayed.

'God, no.' Laura's voice was vehement with disgust. She'd encountered him briefly just as she'd been leaving the villa, and he'd called her an ugly name and told her she wouldn't get a cent of the money he'd promised. And for a second she'd stared at him, almost dazedly, wondering what he was talking about. Because it had all been such a long time ago, their arrangement, and now everything had changed, so that nothing—nothing mattered any more, least of all money...

'Well, that's a relief.' Gaynor gave her a shrewd glance. 'But, all the same, I'm sure there was someone. And when you want to talk, I'll listen.'

But Laura knew she would never want to discuss Alessio. The pain of his betrayal—of the knowledge that she'd been cynically seduced for the worst of all possible reasons—was too raw and too deep. She simply had to endure, somehow, and wait for time and distance to do their work.

However, at least she knew she wasn't pregnant. She'd had incontrovertible proof of that only two days after her return, and, for a long, bewildered moment, she'd not known whether to be glad or sorry. Just as there'd been times when she'd found herself wondering if he would—come after her...

But that was just a stupid lapse into unforgivable sentimentality, she told herself strongly. And never to be repeated. She wasn't having his baby, and he hadn't followed her to England. So, she'd been fortunate to be spared even more regret—more heartbreak. Nothing else.

And now she had to concentrate on things that really mattered, like her work. Because this was a big day for her. Her trial period at Harman Grace was complete, and she was about to receive her final appraisal and, hopefully, a permanent job offer, which would give her tottering confidence a much-needed boost.

So, she went into Carl's office for her interview with her shoulders back, and a smile nailed on.

But she'd no sooner sat down than he said, 'Laura, I'm afraid I have some bad news.'

She looked at him, startled. 'My appraisal?'

'No, that was good, as always. But, things are a bit tight economically just now, and we're having to make cuts, so there's only one job on offer instead of two as we planned.' His face radiated discomfort. 'And it's been decided to offer it to Bevan instead.'

'Bevan?' Her voice was incredulous. 'But you can't. He's struggled from day one. We've all had to pick up the pieces from his mistakes. Everyone knows that. My God, you know it.'

He did not meet her gaze. 'Nevertheless, it's the decision that's been reached—and I'm personally very sorry to lose you.'

Laura looked down at her hands, clenched together in her lap. She said half to herself, 'This cannot be happening to me. It can't.'

There was a silence, then Carl leaned forward, speaking quietly. 'I should not be telling you this, and it's strictly non-attributable. But the decision came from the top. One of our big new clients has put in some kind of complaint about you. Alleged you were incompetent, and impossible to work with, and that they'd take their business elsewhere unless you were fired. Times are hard, Laura, and the directors decided they couldn't take the risk.'

Laura gasped. 'They didn't even ask me for an explanation? It could be some terrible mistake.'

Carl shook his head. 'I'm afraid not.' His glance was compassionate. 'Some way, and only God knows how, you've managed to make an enemy of the head of the Arleschi Bank, honey. Alessio Ramontella himself. I've actually seen his personal letter to the board. And that's about as bad as it gets. No further explanations necessary.' He paused, saying sharply, 'Laura—are you OK? You look like a ghost.'

She felt like one too, only she knew she couldn't be dead, because she was too hurt, and too angry. It wasn't enough for Alessio to destroy her emotionally, she thought. He'd deliberately set out to ruin her career as well. She supposed it had to be revenge for their last encounter. After all, his anger had been almost tangible. He must have acted at once, to punish her for the things she'd said.

She thought, 'But that's impossible. He doesn't even know I work here,' and only realised she'd spoken aloud when Carl stared at her in disbelief.

'You mean there's something behind all this. You really know this guy?'

She lifted her chin. 'No,' she said quietly and clearly. 'I don't know him, and I never have done. Thankfully, he's a total stranger to me, and that's how he'll remain.' She rose. 'Now, I'll go and clear my desk.'

Alessio glanced at his watch, wondering how soon he could make a discreet exit from the reception. Attendance had been unavoidable, but now his duty was done and he wanted to leave. Not least because the Montecorvos were there, and he had been aware all evening of Vittoria's eyes following him hungrily round the enormous room.

If I'd known, he thought, wild horses wouldn't have dragged me here.

Since his return to Rome, Vittoria's letters and phone calls had returned in full force, although he'd responded to none of them. But she was clearly not giving up without a struggle, he realised, caught between annoyance and resignation.

He was on his way to the door when a slender crimson-tipped hand descended on his arm, and he was assailed by a waft of perfume, expensive and unmistakable.

He halted, groaning silently. 'Vittoria,' he offered insincerely. 'What a pleasure.'

She pouted, standing close to him, offering him a spectacularly indiscreet view of her cleavage. 'How can you say that, *caro mio*, when you know you have been avoiding me? Is it because of your aunt?' She lowered her voice, shuddering. 'She made my visit to Trasimeno a nightmare, the old witch, dropping hints like poison. But now she is no longer in the city. She has moved to her house in Tuscany, and Fabrizio's mother says she has no plans to return. So, we are safe.'

He began, 'Vittoria—' but she interrupted.

'*Caro*, I have good news. A friend of mine has an apartment not far from the Via Veneto, only she has been sent to Paris on business.

'And I have the key. We can meet there, without danger, whenever we wish.'

She smiled up at him, showing him the tip of her tongue between her lips. 'And you do wish it, don't you, *carissimo*? Because you are not seeing anyone else. I know that. Since you came back from Umbria over a month ago, you have been living like a recluse. Everyone says so.'

'Then, I am obliged to everyone for their concern,' he said icily. 'Unlike most of them, I have work to do.'

'But you cannot work all the time, *mi amore*.' Her low voice was insinuating. 'Your body needs exercise as well as your mind. And you cannot have forgotten how good we were together, Alessio *mio*. I shall never forget, and your Vittoria needs you— so badly.'

He met her gleaming, greedy gaze, and, with a sudden jolt of renewed pain, found himself remembering other eyes. Grey eyes that had smiled up at him in trust, then turned smoky with desire, before shining with astonished rapture as her body had yielded up its last sweet secrets. And all for him alone.

All that warmth and joy—and the small wicked giggle that had entranced him—and which it almost broke his heart to remember.

Laura, he thought with yearning, and sudden passion. Ah, *Dio*, my Laura—my beloved.

And suddenly Alessio knew what he had to do, just as surely as he'd done when he'd driven back to the villa on that last morning, only to find his plans—his entire future—wrecked by the disaster that had been waiting for him.

He took the hand that was still clutching his sleeve, and kissed it briefly and formally.

'You flatter me,' he said with cold civility. 'But I fear it is impossible to accept your charming invitation. You see, I have fallen deeply in love, and I hope very soon to be married. I am sure you understand. Feel free to tell—everyone. So, goodnight, Vittoria—and goodbye.'

And he strode away, leaving her staring after him, with two ugly spots of colour burning in her face.

It had been raining all day, and the air felt cool, promising a hint of autumn to come as Laura arrived back at the house and went slowly upstairs to her room.

She had been suffering from stomach cramps for most of the

evening, and, as the wine bar was quiet, Hattie, the owner, had dosed her with paracetamol and sent her home early.

She didn't usually have painful periods, but supposed wearily that her symptoms could be caused by stress. Because she still hadn't found another agency to take her on. Carl had given her a good reference, but prospective employers always wanted to know why she'd left Harman Grace after only three months. And they did not like the answer they were given.

So she was fortunate that Hattie could offer her full-time waitressing. But the money wasn't good, and there was little to spare once the rent was paid.

Her room felt damp and cheerless as she let herself in, and she shivered a little. She decided a shower might be comforting, but soon discovered that the water was only lukewarm in the small chilly bathroom. She sighed to herself. It seemed she would have to settle for the comfort of a hot-water bottle instead. She put on her elderly flowered cotton pyjamas and her dressing gown, and trailed off to the kitchen, carrying the rubber bag with its Winnie the Pooh cover.

She found Gaynor there ahead of her, taking the coffee jar from the cupboard, the kettle already heating on the stove. She swung round, starting violently, as Laura came in.

'My God, what are you doing here?'

'I live here.' Laura stared at her. 'Is something wrong?'

'No, no. But you're usually so much later than this. I wondered.'

'It's that time of the month again.' Laura grimaced. 'Hattie let me finish the shift early.' She held up the hot-water bottle. 'I just came to fill this.'

'Oh, hell.' Gaynor looked dismayed. 'I mean—what—what a shame. Poor you.' She gave Laura a smile that on anyone else would have looked shifty. 'Well, you go ahead. Your need is greater than mine, so the coffee can wait,' she added, backing to the door. 'I mean it—really. I—I'll check on you later.'

Laura turned to the stove with a mental shrug. There were two beakers on the small counter, she noticed, so clearly her friend had company. But what was there in that to make her so jumpy?

She carefully filled her bottle, and carried it back to her room, pausing first to tap at Gaynor's closed door and call, 'The kitchen's all yours.'

She'd taken two steps into the room before she realised that she was not alone. Or saw who was waiting for her, tall in his elegant charcoal suit, his dark face watchful and unsmiling as he looked at her.

He said quietly, *'Buonasera.'*

She clutched her bottle in front of her as if it were a defensive weapon. 'Good evening be damned,' she said raggedly. 'How did you get in here?'

'Your friend, who took pity on me when she heard me knocking, told me you had returned, and the door was open. So I came in.' He paused. 'It is good to see you again.'

She ignored that. 'What—what the hell are you doing here?' she demanded shakily. 'How did you find me?'

'The postcards you wrote that day in Besavoro, and I mailed for you. They had addresses on them.'

'Of all the devious...' Laura began furiously, then stopped, and took a deep breath. 'What do you want?'

'I want you, Laura.' His voice was quiet. 'I wish you to return with me to Italy.'

She took a step backwards, glaring at him. 'Is that why you had me fired—to offer me alternative work as your mistress?' She lifted her chin. 'I don't regard sharing your bed as a good career move, *signore*. So I suggest you get out of here—and I mean now.'

Alessio's brows lifted. 'Is that what you mean?' he asked with a kind of polite interest. 'Or what you think you should say?'

'Don't play word games,' she hit back fiercely. 'And before you ask, by the way, there's no baby.'

'So I gather.' His tone was rueful. 'Your friend has already informed me I have chosen the wrong time of the month to visit you.'

The hot-water bottle fell to the floor as Laura said hoarsely, 'Gaynor—said that—and to you?' She shook her head. 'Oh, God, I don't believe it. I—I'll kill her.'

For the first time, he smiled faintly. 'Ah, no, I was grateful for the warning, believe me. My friends who are already husbands tell me that sometimes a back rub can help. Would you like me to try?'

She stared at him in outrage, then marched to the door and flung it open. 'I'd like you to go to hell.' Her voice shook. 'Just— leave.'

'Not without you, *carissima*.' Alessio took off his jacket, and tossed it over the back of her armchair, then began to unbutton his waistcoat.

'Stop,' Laura said furiously. 'Stop right there. What do you think you're doing?'

He smiled at her. 'It has been a long and interesting day, and it is not over yet. I thought I would make myself comfortable, *cara mia*.'

'Not,' she said, 'in my flat. And don't call me that.'

'Then what shall I say?' he asked softly. 'My angel, my beautiful one? *Mi adorata?* For you are all these things, Laura *mia*, and more.'

'No.' She wanted to stamp in vexation, but remembered just in time that she was barefoot. 'I hate you. I want you out of my life. I told you so.'

'*Sì,*' he agreed. 'I am not likely to forget.'

'Nor did you,' she threw at him. 'In fact you wrote a stinking letter to Harman Grace, telling them to sack me as a result.'

'A letter was certainly written,' he said. 'I saw it today. But it did not come from me.'

Her jaw dropped. 'You—went to the agency.'

'It was during working hours,' he explained. 'I expected you to be there. I hoped you might be more welcoming when others were present. Instead I spoke to your former boss, who eventually showed me this ridiculous forgery.'

'It was on your notepaper,' Laura said. 'Signed by you. He told me.'

'I replaced my letterheads a few months ago. Those at the villa, I only use as scrap now. Paolo of course would not know this. And his imitation of my signature was a poor one, also.'

She blinked. 'Paolo? Why should he do such a thing?'

'He was angry and wished to revenge himself on me—on us both. And, to an extent, he succeeded.'

'But—he didn't care about me—about what had happened.'

'Ah,' Alessio said softly. 'But he cared very much when I knocked him down.'

She gasped. 'You did that? Why?'

'It is not important,' he said in swift dismissal. 'And his own troubles are mounting rapidly. He now works for Signor Manzone, and I am told his wedding is imminent.'

He paused. 'And you would have had to give up your job in any case, *mi amore*,' he added almost casually. 'You cannot live in Italy and work in London. The commuting would be too difficult.'

She lifted her chin. 'I think you must have lost your mind, Count Ramontella. I have no intention of living in Italy.'

He sighed. 'That makes things difficult. I have already had the statue of Diana removed from the garden, and had drawings commissioned so that we can choose a replacement. Also work has begun on the swimming pool to provide a shallower end until you get more confidence.

'And Caio is inconsolable without you. He howls regularly outside your room. At times, I have considered joining him.'

'Caio?' Laura lifted a dazed hand to her forehead. 'How does he feature in all this? He's your aunt's dog. Is she still at the villa?'

'No,' he said with sudden grimness. 'She is not. She left shortly after you, and I have no wish ever to see her again.

'But Caio did not wish to go in the car when she departed, and bit Paolo, who tried to make him. Then my aunt unwisely intervened, and he bit her too. She announced she was going to have him put down immediately, so Emilia quite rightly rescued him and brought him to me.'

He smiled at her. 'But we all know the one he truly loves.'

She said passionately, 'Stop this—stop it, please. I don't understand. I don't know what's happening. Why you're talking like this.'

He said gently, 'If you closed the door, and sat down, I could explain more easily, I think.'

'I don't want you to explain.' Her voice rose almost to a wail. 'I want you to go. To leave me in peace. It's cruel of you to come here like this. Saying these things.'

'Cruel of me to love you, *carissima*? To wish to make you my wife?'

'Why should you wish to do that, *signore*?' She didn't look at him. 'To make it easier for you to go on with your secret affair with that—that woman?'

He came across to her, detached her unresisting fingers from the handle, and closed the door firmly, leaning against it as he looked down at her.

He said quietly, 'Laura, I did a bad thing, and I cannot defend myself. Nor do I wish to hurt you more than I have done, but I must be honest with you if there is to be any hope for us.

'I am not having an affair with Vittoria Montecorvo. I never was. But we had met several times, and she had let me see she was available. After that our paths seemed to cross many times. I think someone must have hinted to my aunt that this was so, and she decided to have me watched.'

Laura stared up at him. 'Your own aunt would do that?'

He said grimly, 'You have met her. My father told me once that since childhood she had enjoyed observing other people's misdemeanours, and discovering their secrets, so that she could use them to gain unpleasant advantages, like a spider keeping dead flies in a web to enjoy later. Oddly, I never thought she would do it to me.

'Unfortunately, her need for a favour coincided with Vittoria's brief incursion into my life, and as I did not wish to cause the breakdown of Vittoria's marriage, or even see her again after my one indiscretion, it seemed I had no choice but to do as I was required, however distasteful.'

He sighed. 'And then I saw you, Laura, and in that moment everything changed.' He tried to smile. 'Do you remember how Petrarch spoke of his Laura? Because you too went from my eyes straight to my heart, *mi adorata*, and I was lost for ever.

Although I did not realise that immediately,' he added candidly. 'Which is why my original intentions were not strictly honourable.'

'No,' she said in a low voice. 'I—realised that.' Lost for ever, she thought. I felt that too.

He took her hand. Held it.

'You see—I am trying to be truthful,' he said quietly. 'I thought that once you belonged to me that everything would be simple. That I would take you away where my aunt could not reach us, and you would never need to know about that devil's bargain I had made with her. I even told myself it no longer mattered, because I wanted you for myself—and myself alone. And that justified everything. Only, I soon found it did not.

'When I realised—that first time—that you were a virgin, it almost destroyed me. Because I knew that you did not deserve to surrender your innocence for such a reason. That I could not—would not do what my aunt demanded, and to hell with the consequences.'

'Yet you did—eventually.' Her voice was small and strained.

'*Mi amore*, as I told you, I took you only because I could not live without you any longer. And I thought you felt the same.' He looked deeply—questioningly—into her eyes. 'Was I so wrong?'

'No,' she admitted, with reluctance. 'You were—right.'

'I was also certain that news of the landslide would keep my aunt at bay for another twenty-four hours, at least,' he went on. 'And that would give me time.'

'Time for what?'

'To tell you everything, *mia bella*, as I knew I must, if there was to be complete honesty between us. So, I drove back from Besavoro to make my confession, and beg absolution before I asked you to become my wife. But, again, it was too late. Once more, I had underestimated my aunt.

'And when you looked at me—spoke to me as you did—I thought I had placed myself beyond your forgiveness for ever. That, hurting you as I had done, I could hope for nothing. That I had ruined both our lives.'

He took her other hand. Drew her gently towards him. 'Is it true, Laura *mia*? Is all hope gone? Or can you try to forgive me, and let me teach you to love me as I think you were beginning to? As I love you?' His voice sank to a whisper. 'Don't send me away, *carissima*, and make us both wretched. Try to forgive—and let me stay with you tonight.'

She said jerkily, 'But you can't—stay. You know that.'

He sighed, and kissed the top of her head. 'Do you think I am totally devoid of decency or patience, *mi amore*? And do you also intend to turn me out of our bed each month when we are married? I don't think so.' He paused. 'I want to sleep with you, Laura. To take care of you. Nothing more. Don't you want that too?'

'Yes, I suppose—I don't know,' she said with a sob. 'But I still can't let you stay. I just—can't.'

'Why not, my angel?' His voice was tender. 'When it is what we both want.'

There were so many sensible and excellent reasons for sending him away for ever, yet she couldn't think of one of them.

Instead, she heard herself say crossly, 'Because I'm wearing really horrible pyjamas.' And then she burst into tears.

When she calmed down, she found that they had somehow moved to the armchair, and she was sitting curled up on Alessio's lap.

'So,' he said, drying her face with his handkerchief. 'If I promise to buy you something prettier in the morning, may I stay?'

'I can hardly throw you out,' she mumbled into his shoulder.

'And will you marry me as soon as it can be arranged?'

She was silent for a moment. 'How can I?' she asked unhappily. 'We hardly know each other. And I don't belong in your world, Alessio. If I hadn't been forced on your attention, you'd never have given me a second glance.'

'You are my world, Laura,' he said softly. 'Without you, there is nothing. Don't you understand that, my dear one?

'I want yours to be the face I see when I wake each morning. I want to see you smile at me across our dining table. I want to teach you to swim so well that you will dive off the side of our boat with me. I want to be with you when our children are born, and to love you and protect you as long as we both live.'

She said with a little gasp, 'Oh, Alessio—I love you too, so very much. I wanted to stop—I tried hard to—and to hate you—but I—I couldn't. And I've been so lonely—and so terribly unhappy. And I'd marry you tomorrow, if it was possible. Only it isn't. I—I can't just disappear to Italy with you.' Her hands twisted together. 'There's my family to consider. That's why I needed a decent job, so that I could help my mother with my brother's education.'

She swallowed. 'I only agreed to help Paolo because he was going to pay me, but then he didn't.'

'Good,' he said. 'Because I have no wish for you to be obliged to such a creature.' He stroked her hair back from her face. '*Mia cara*, I am going to be your husband, and I shall look after your mother and brother as if they were my own. How could you doubt it?'

'But I don't know that she'll accept that.' Laura's face was troubled. 'She has her fair share of pride.'

'We will go and see her tomorrow,' he said. 'After all, I have to ask her permission to marry you. And I will talk to her—persuade her that it will be my pleasure to care for you all. I am sure she will see reason.'

Laura raised her head from his shoulder, and looked at him in quiet fascination. 'I bet she will at that,' she said, her lips twitching in sudden amusement. 'Are you always going to expect your own way, *signore*, once we're married?'

'Of course,' he said softly, and wickedly, drawing her close again. 'But I will always try to ensure that your way and mine are the same, my sweet one.'

He bent his head and kissed her, his mouth moving on hers with a gentle, almost reverent restraint that made her want to cry again. But she didn't. And they held each other, and kissed again, whispering the words that lovers used. And were happy.

Much later, Laura was sitting up in bed finishing the *tisana* he had made her from Gaynor's herb tea when Alessio came back from the bathroom, her refilled hot-water bottle dangling from his lean fingers.

She looked at him with real compunction. 'Darling, I'm sorry. It's all so—unromantic.'

'Then maybe we should put romance aside for a while,' he said gently. 'And think only about love.'

He undressed quickly, and slid into the narrow bed behind her, wrapping her warmly and closely in his arms. Making her feel relaxed and at peace for the first time in weeks.

She was almost asleep when a thought came to her. 'Alessio,' she whispered drowsily. 'Will you promise me one more thing?'

'Anything, *mia bella*.'

She smiled in the darkness. 'Will you still teach me to play strip poker?'

'It might be arranged,' he returned softly. 'On some winter night, when we are safely married, and the fire is warm and the candles are lit.' He paused. 'But I must warn you, *carissima*. I cheat.'

Laura turned her head and aimed a sleepy kiss at the corner of his mouth.

'So do I, my darling,' she murmured in deep contentment. 'So do I.'

THE FRENCH COUNT'S
PREGNANT BRIDE

BY
CATHERINE SPENCER

Catherine Spencer, once an English teacher, fell into writing through eavesdropping on a conversation about romances. Within two months she'd changed careers, and sold her first book to Mills and Boon in 1984. She moved to Canada from England thirty years ago, and lives in Vancouver. She is married to a Canadian and has four grown up children — two daughters and two sons — plus two dogs. In her spare time she plays the piano, collects antiques, and grows tropical shrubs.

PROLOGUE

8:00 p.m., November 4

FOR once, Harvey arrived at the restaurant ahead of her, already settled in their favorite corner. She left her satin-lined cashmere cape with the hat-check girl, smiled at the sweet-faced, very pregnant young woman perched on a bench near the front desk and threaded her way through the maze of other diners to where he sat. Twenty-eight red roses, one for each year of her life, and a small package professionally gift-wrapped in silver foil and ribbons, occupied one end of the linen-draped table; a bottle of Taitinger Brut Reserve chilling in a silver champagne bucket and two crystal flutes, the other.

"Am I late?" she asked, lifting her face for his kiss, when he rose to greet her.

"No, I'm early." Ever the perfect gentleman, he waited until she made herself comfortable on the plush velvet banquette, before reclaiming his own seat.

"What, no last minute emergencies?" She laughed, happy to be with him. Happy that he'd made the effort not to keep her waiting on her birthday. So often, he was delayed, or called away in the middle of whatever they'd planned, be it dinner, the theater, or making love. So often, he seemed preoccupied, distant, tense. Lately he'd even paced the floor some nights, then ended up sleeping in the guest room, worried he'd disturb her with his restlessness. She supposed that was the price a wife paid for being married to such a dedicated, sought-after cardio-thoracic surgeon.

"Not tonight," he said. "Ed Johnson's covering for me." He took the bottle of champagne, filled their flutes two-thirds full and raised his in a toast. "Happy birthday, Diana!"

"Thank you, sweetheart." The wine danced over her tongue, light and vivacious. Not too many years ago, the best they could afford when it came to celebrating special occasions was a bottle of cheap red wine and home-cooked spaghetti. Now, the only things red at the table were the long-stemmed roses, and there was nothing cheap about them.

Lifting the damp, sweet-smelling petals to her face, she eyed her husband mischievously. "These *are* for me, aren't they?"

"Those, and this, too." He pushed the foil-wrapped box toward her. "Open it before you order, Diana. I think you'll like it."

What was there not to like about a diamond and sapphire bracelet set in platinum? Speechless with pleasure, she fastened the lobster-claw clasp around her wrist, then tilted her hand this way and that, admiring the way the lamplight caught the fire and flash of the gems. "It's the most beautiful thing I've ever owned," she murmured, when she could speak. "Oh, Harvey, you've really gone overboard, this year. How am I supposed to compete with something like this, when *your* birthday comes around?"

"You won't have to." He smiled and gestured to the leather-bound menu in front of her. "What do you fancy for dinner?"

She studied the list of entrées. "I'm torn between the rack of lamb and the Maine lobster."

"Have the lobster," he urged. "You know it's your favorite."

"Then I will. With a small salad to start."

He nodded to the waiter hovering discreetly in the background. "My wife will have the mesclun salad with lemon vinaigrette, followed by the broiled lobster."

"And you, sir?" The waiter paused, eyebrows raised inquiringly.

Harvey lightly tapped the rim of his champagne flute. "I'm happy with the wine, thanks."

"You're not going to eat?" Perplexed, Diana stared at him. "Why not, sweetheart? Aren't you feeling well?"

"Never felt better," he assured her, reaching into his inside jacket pocket and pulling out a credit card. "The thing is, Diana, I'm leaving you."

Why a chill raced up her spine just then, she had no idea. But in less time than it took to blink, all her warm fuzzy pleasure in the moment, in the evening, evaporated. Striving to ignore it, she said, "You mean, you're going back to the hospital? But I thought you—?"

"No. I'm leaving you."

Still not understanding, she said, "Leaving me where? Here?"

"Leaving you, period. Leaving the marriage."

Heaven help her, she laughed. "Oh, honestly, Harvey! For a minute there, I almost believed you."

There was no answering smile on his face. Rather, pity laced with just a hint of contempt. "This is no joke. And before you ask why, I might as well tell you. I've met someone else."

"Another woman?" Her voice seemed to come from very far away.

"Well, hardly another man!"

"I suppose not." Very precisely, she set her champagne glass on the table, careful not to spill a drop. "And this woman…how long…?"

"Quite some time."

When she was six, she'd fallen into the deep end of her family's swimming pool and would have drowned if her father hadn't been close by and promptly hauled her to safety. Even so, she'd never forgotten the soundless, suffocating sensation that had briefly possessed her. Twenty-two years later, it gripped her again.

Floundering to find a lifeline in a world suddenly turned upside-down, she blurted, "But it won't last. These things never do. You'll get over it, over *her*…and I'll get past the hurt…I will, I promise! We'll pick up the pieces and go on, because that's what married people do. They honor their wedding vows."

He reached across the table, took both her hands firmly in his and gave them a shake. "Listen to me, Diana! This isn't a passing affair. Rita and I are deeply in love. I am committed to a future with her."

"No…!" She struggled to pull herself free of his hold. To shut out his words, and the cool, clinical dispassion with which he uttered them. As if he were wielding a scalpel on a comatose patient. As if she were incapable of feeling the pain. "You're in love with *me*. You've said so, a hundred times."

"Not for a very long time now. Not for months."

"Well, I don't care!" Distress and shock sent her own voice rising half an octave. "I won't let you throw us away. I deserve better than that…we both do."

He released her hands and sat very erect in his chair, as though to put as much physical distance between himself and her as possible in that intimate little corner of that intimate little restaurant. "Stop making a spectacle of yourself!" he hissed.

She clamped her mouth shut, but inside, every part of her was weeping—every part but her eyes. For some reason, they remained dry and hot and disbelieving. Still clutching at straws, she said, "Then what's all this about? The champagne and roses and bracelet?"

"It's your birthday." He shrugged. "I'm not completely without affection for you, you know. I wanted to give you something memorable to mark the occasion."

"And you thought telling me our marriage is over wouldn't do it?"

He regarded her pityingly. "Oh, come now, Diana! I can't believe you're entirely surprised. You must have realized things between us weren't the same anymore—that something vital had died."

"No. I sensed a change in you, but I put it down to stress at the hospital." She looked at the roses, at the gleaming sterling cutlery, at the platinum wedding ring on her left hand, and finally, at the man she'd married almost eight years ago. Then she laughed again, a thin, hollow, scraping sound that clawed its way up from the depths of her lungs. "But then, they do say the wife's always the last to know, don't they?"

"I can see that you're shocked, but in time you'll realize that it's better we make a clean break and end matters now, rather than wait until things deteriorate to the point that we can't speak a civil word to one another."

"Better for you, perhaps."

"And for you, too, in the long run." He drained his glass, and pushed back his chair. Again like the perfect gentleman he prided himself on being, he bent and kissed her cheek. "Enjoy your lobster, my dear. Dinner's on me."

Then he made his way across the restaurant to where the pregnant woman waited. She rose to meet him. He put his arms around her, gave her a lingering kiss full on the mouth, then ushered her out of the restaurant as carefully, as tenderly, as if she were made of blown glass.

Pregnant...

The woman he was leaving her for was having the baby he'd refused to give his wife. And at that, something really did die in Diana...

CHAPTER ONE

4:00 p.m., June 12

AIX-EN-PROVENCE was stirring from its afternoon siesta as Diana eased her ancient rental car onto the road that would take her to Bellevue-sur-Lac, fifty-three miles northeast of the town limits.

Aix-en-Provence: a beautiful city, rich in history, culture and art. The city where, twenty-nine years ago, a seventeen-year-old French girl allowed an American couple in their late forties to adopt her out-of-wedlock baby.

The city where Diana had been born...

Bellevue-sur-Lac, the village where she'd been conceived...

The names, the facts, the minute clues, were etched so clearly in her memory, she could recite verbatim the letter she'd found in her father's study, after her parents' death, two years previously.

Admittedly her husband's desertion had pushed them to the back of her mind for a while. A thousand times or more in the weeks after he left, she questioned where she'd gone wrong. Asked herself what she could have done differently that might have saved her marriage. But in the end, she'd been forced to accept that there was nothing. Harvey had fallen out of love with her, made up his mind he wanted to spend the rest of his life with someone else and that was that. She was alone, and he was not.

Seven months, though, was long enough to mourn a man who'd proven himself unworthy of her tears, and just over a week ago, she'd awoken to the realization that, little by little, her despair had melted away. Without her quite knowing when or how, her resentment toward Harvey had lost its bitter edge and sunk into indifference. If anything, she was grateful to him because, in deserting her, he'd also set her free. For the *first* time in her life, she could do exactly as she pleased without worrying that she might upset the people closest to her.

Which was why she now found herself in the south of France, heading toward a tiny lakeside village surrounded by lavender fields, olive groves and vineyards; and where, if the gods were on her side, she'd rediscover herself, now that she'd been legally stripped of her title and status as Dr Harvey Reeves's dutiful but dull little wife.

"You can't possibly be serious!" Carol Brenner, one of the few friends who'd stuck by her after she found herself single again, had exclaimed, when she learned what Diana had planned.

"Why ever not?" she'd asked calmly.

"Because it's crazy, that's why! For Pete's sake, haven't you gone through enough in the last seven months, without adding this?"

Shrugging, she said, "Well, they do say that what doesn't kill you, makes you stronger."

Carol shoved aside her latte and leaned across the coffee shop's marble tabletop, the better to make her point. "I'm not convinced you *are* stronger. Quite frankly, Diana, you look like hell."

"Oh, please!" she said ruefully. "Stop beating about the bush and feel free to tell me what you really think!"

"I'm sorry, but it's true. You've lost so much weight, you could pass for a refugee from some third world country."

Diana could hardly argue with that. Once she no longer had to prepare elegant dinners for her husband, she sometimes hadn't bothered preparing any dinner at all. As for breakfast, she'd skipped it more often than not, too. Which left lunch—a sandwich if she had any appetite, otherwise a piece of fruit and a slice of cheese.

"You've been like a ship without an anchor, the way you've drifted through this last winter and spring, not seeming to know what day it was, half the time," Carol went on, really hitting her stride. "And now, out of the blue, you announce you're off to France on some wild-goose chase to find your biological mother?" She rolled her eyes. "You'll be telling me next, you're joining a nunnery!"

"It's not out of the blue," Diana said softly. "This is something I've wanted to do for years."

"Diana, the point I'm trying to make is that I'm one of your closest friends, and I didn't even know you were adopted."

"Because it's always been a closely guarded secret. I didn't know myself until I was eight, and even then, I found out by accident."

Obviously taken aback, Carol said, "Good God, who decided it should be kept secret?"

"My mother."

"Why? Adopting a child's nothing to be ashamed of."

"It wasn't shame, it was fear. Apparently mine was a private adoption, and although my father made sure the legalities were looked after, the arrangement wasn't exactly…conventional. Once my mother realized the secret was a secret no longer, things at our house were never the same again."

"How so?" Carol asked.

Diana had rested her elbow on the table and cupped her chin in her hand, the events of that long-ago day sufficiently softened by time that she'd been able to relate them quite composedly….

She'd raced home from school and gone straight to the sunroom where her mother always took afternoon tea. "Mommy," she burst out breathlessly, "what does 'adopted' mean?"

Even before then, she'd understood that her mother was, as their cleaning lady once put it, "fragile and given to spells," and she realized at once that in mentioning the word "adopted," she'd inadvertently trodden on forbidden territory. The Lapsang Souchong tea her mother favored slopped over the rim of its translucent porcelain cup and into the saucer. "Good heavens, Diana," she said faintly, pressing a pale hand to her heart, "whatever makes you ask such a question?"

Horrified at having brought on one of the dreaded "spells," Diana rushed to explain. "Well, today Merrilee Hampton was mad at me because I won the spelling bee, so at recess she threw my snack on the ground, so I told her she was stupid, so then she told me I'm adopted. And I told her it's not true, and she said it is, because her mother said so, and her mother doesn't tell lies."

"Dear God, someone should staple that woman's mouth shut!"

Happening to come into the sunroom at that precise moment, Diana's father had flung himself into a wicker chair across from her mother's and said cheerfully, "Who are you talking about, my dear, and why are you ready to string her up by the thumbs?"

"Mrs. Hampton," Diana had informed him, since her mother seemed bereft of words. "She told Merrilee that I'm adopted, but I'm not, am I, Daddy?"

She'd never forgotten the look her parents exchanged then, or the way her father had taken her on his lap and said gently, "Yes, you are, sweet pea."

"Oh!" Terribly afraid she'd contracted some kind of disease, she whispered, "Am I going to die?"

"Good heavens, no! All being adopted means is—"

"David, please!" her mother had interrupted, her voice sounding all funny and trembly. "We decided we'd never—"

"*You* decided, Bethany," he'd replied firmly. "If I'd had my way, we'd have dealt with this a long time ago, and our child would have learned the truth from us, instead of hearing it from someone else. But the cat's out of the bag now, and nothing you or I can do is going to stuff it back in again. And after all this time, it can hardly matter anyway."

Then he'd turned back to Diana, tugged playfully on her ponytail and smiled. "Being adopted means that although another lady gave birth to you, we were the lucky people who got to keep you."

Trying to fit together all the pieces of this strange and sudden puzzle, Diana said, "Does that mean I have two mommies?"

"In a way, yes."

"David!"

"But you're our daughter in every way that counts," he went on, ignoring her mother's moan of distress.

Still unable to grasp so foreign a concept, Diana said, "But who's my other mommy, and why doesn't she live with us?"

At that, her mother mewed pitifully.

"No one you know," her father said steadily. "She was too young to look after a baby, and so, because she knew we would love you just as much as she did, and take very good care of you, she gave you to us. After that, she went back to her home, and we brought you here to ours."

"Well, I can see why you'd want to learn more about this woman," Carol said, when Diana finished her story. "I guess it's natural enough to be curious about your roots, especially when they're shrouded in so much mystery. What I don't understand is why you waited this long to do something about it."

"Simple. Every time I brought up the subject, my mother took to her bed and stayed there for days. 'Why aren't we enough for you?' she'd cry. 'Haven't we loved you enough? Given you a lovely home, the best education, everything your heart desires? Why do you want to hurt us like this?'"

"Uh-oh!" Carol rolled her eyes again. "I realized she was a bit over the top temperamentally, but I'd no idea she stooped to that kind of emotional blackmail."

"She couldn't help herself," Diana said, old loyalties coming to the fore. "She was insecure—very unsure of herself. I don't know why, but she never seemed to believe she deserved to be loved for herself, and nothing I said could convince her that, as far as I was concerned, she and my father were my true parents and that I adored both of them. In her view, my wanting to know about my birth mother meant that she and my father had failed. So eventually I stopped asking questions, and we all went back to pretending the subject had never arisen. But I never stopped wanting to find answers."

"Then tell me this. If it was that important to you, why didn't you pursue the matter after she and your father died, instead of waiting until now?"

"Harvey didn't think it was a good idea."

"Why ever not?"

"I think he was…embarrassed."

"Because you were adopted?"

"Pretty much, yes."

Carol made no effort to disguise her scorn for the man. "What was his problem? That you might not be blue-blooded enough for him?"

"You guessed it! 'You're better off not knowing,' he used to say, whenever I brought up the subject of my biological mother. 'She was probably sleeping around and didn't even know for sure who the father was. You could be anybody's brat.'"

"And you let him get away with that kind of crap?" Carol gave an unladylike snort. "You should be ashamed, Diana, that you let him walk all over you like that!"

"At the time, what mattered most was my marriage. I wanted it to succeed, and Harvey was under enough stress at the hospital, without my bringing more into our private life, as well."

"A fat lot of good it did you, in the end! He walked out anyway, and left you an emotional wreck."

"For a while, perhaps, but I'm better now. Stronger, in some ways, than I've ever been."

"Enough to stand the disappointment, if you don't find what you're looking for?"

"Absolutely," Diana said, and at the time, it had been true.

The car coughed alarmingly and clunked to a halt at the foot of a hill. *It serves you right,* Carol would have said. *If you'd taken the time to book ahead, you wouldn't have been stuck with an old beater of a car no right-minded tourist would look at.*

With some coaxing, she got the poor old thing running again, but as she approached a fork in the road, and found a sign pointing to the left, showing Bellevue-sur-Lac 31 kms, panic overwhelmed her and, for a moment, she considered turning to the right and heading for Monaco and a week of reckless betting on the roulette wheel, rather than pursuing the gamble she'd undertaken.

What if Carol was right, and she was inviting nothing but heartache for everyone by chasing her dream?

"The chances of your finding this woman are slim to non-existent, you know," her friend had warned. "People move around a lot, in this day and age. And even if you *do* find her, what then? You can't just explode onto the scene and announce yourself as her long-lost daughter. You could blow her entire life apart if she's married and hasn't confided in her husband."

"I realize that. But what's to stop me talking to her, or even to people who know her, and trying to learn a little bit about her? I might have half brothers or sisters, aunts and uncles. Grandparents, even. She was seventeen when she had me, which means she's only forty-five now. I could have a whole slew of relatives waiting to be discovered."

"And how will that help you, if they don't know who *you* are?" Carol asked gently.

It had taken all her courage to admit, "At least I'll know I'm connected to someone in the world."

"You have me, Diana. We might not share the same blood, but you're like a sister to me."

"You're my dearest friend, and I'd trust you with my life, which is why I'm confiding in you now," she replied. "But first and foremost, you're Tim's wife and Annie's mother." She opened her hands, pleadingly. "Can you understand what I'm saying?"

"Yes," Carol said, and her eyes were full of tears suddenly. "But I care too much about you to want to see you suffer another disappointment. You give your heart so willingly, Diana, and sometimes people see that as an invitation to trample all over it. Hotshot Harvey's done enough damage. Please don't leave yourself open to more. Don't let anyone take advantage of your generosity. Just once, think of yourself first, and others second."

The advice came back to her now as the car rattled around another bend in the road, and crossed a little stone bridge above a wide stream that burbled over brown rocks. Bellevue-sur-Lac 25 kms, a sign said.

What if she found her birth mother destitute? Abandoned by her family for her adolescent indiscretion? How could any decent person not lift a finger to help?

"I'll find a way," Diana promised herself, thumping the steering wheel with her fist. "I'll buy her a house, clothes, food—whatever she needs—and donate them anonymously, if I must."

It was the least she could do, if she was to live with herself, and heaven knew, she could afford it. Within reason, she could afford just about anything money could buy. In his eagerness to be rid of her and married to his mistress before the birth of their child, Harvey had been generous. Added to what she'd inherited from her parents, it added up to a very tidy sum. But would it be enough?

Probably not, she thought. When all was said and done, money never could buy the things that really mattered.

The car wheezed around another bend in the road. In the distance, she saw tidy rows of grapevines climbing a steep hillside. In the valley below, a subdued purple touched the earth. Lavender fields just bursting into bloom.

Another sign post, painted blue with white lettering. Bellevue-sur-Lac 11 kms.

Hand suddenly clammy with sweat, Diana eased the car over to the side of the road and rolled down the window. Wild-flowers grew in the ditch, filling the air with their scent.

"Let me come with you," Carol had begged. "At least you'll have me in your corner if things don't go well."

Why hadn't she taken her up on the offer?

Because this was something she had to do by herself, that's why.

Reaching into her travel bag, she pulled out the single sheet of stationery she'd hoarded for so long. Spreading it over her lap, she smoothed out the creases, searching as she had so often in the past for any clues she might have missed that would help her now. The ink was faded, the script elegant and distinctly European.

Aix-en-Provence
December 10

Dear Professor Christie,
I write to inform you that Mlle. Molyneux has returned to her native village of Bellevue-sur-Lac. From all accounts, she appears to have put behind her the unhappy events of this past year, the nature of which she has kept a closely guarded secret from all who know her. I hope this will ease any concern you have that she might change her mind about placing her baby with you and your wife, or in any other way jeopardize the adoption.

I trust you are well settled in your home in the United States again. Once more, I thank you for the contributions you made to our university program during your exchange year with us.

With very best wishes to you, your wife and your new
daughter for a most happy Christmas,
Alexandre Castongués, Dean
Faculty of Law
University Aix-Marseille

Did Mlle. Molyneux ever regret giving up her baby? Wonder
if her little girl was happy, healthy? Or was she so relieved to be
rid of her that she never wanted to be reminded of her, ever again?

There was only one way to find out.

Refolding the letter and stuffing it back in the side pocket
of her travel bag, Diana coaxed the car to sputtering life again,
shifted into gear and resumed her journey. Seven minutes later,
the silhouette of a château perched on a cliff loomed dark
against the evening sky. Immediately ahead, clustered along the
shores of a long, narrow lake, buildings emerged from the dusk
of early evening, their reflected pinpricks of light glowing
yellow in the calm surface of the water.

Passing under an ancient stone arch, she drove into the center
of the little village.

Bellevue-sur-Lac, the end of her journey.

Or, if she was lucky, perhaps just the beginning?

CHAPTER TWO

CROSSING the square en route to his car, which he'd left in the inn's rear courtyard as usual when he'd spent the day with the supervisor of his lavender operation, Anton noticed the woman immediately. Strangers who lingered in Bellevue-sur-Lac after sunset were a rarity, even during the summer months when travelers flocked to Provence. Usually they came for the day only, arriving early by the busload to tour the château, winery, lavender distillery and olive mills.

By now—it was almost half-past five o'clock—they were gone, not only because accommodation in the village was limited to what L'Auberge d'Olivier had to offer, but because they preferred the livelier nightlife in Nice or Marseille or Monaco.

This woman, though, sat at a table under the shade of the plane trees, sipping a glass of wine, and what captured his attention was not so much her delicate features and exquisite clothing, but her watchfulness. Her gaze scanned the passing scene repeatedly, taking note of every person who crossed her line of vision. At this moment, it was focused on him.

"Who's the visitor, Henri?" he asked, leaning casually against the outdoor bar where the innkeeper was busy polishing glasses in preparation for the locals, who'd gather later to drink cassis and play dominoes.

Henri paused in his task long enough to shoot an appreciative glance her way. "An American. She arrived last night."

"She'd reserved a room here?"

"No, she just showed up unannounced and asked if I could accommodate her. She's lucky the man you were expecting canceled at the last minute, or I'd have had to turn her away. Too bad he broke his leg, eh?"

"For him, and me both. I'm going to have to find someone to replace him pretty quickly." Again, Anton looked at the woman, observing her from the corner of his eye. Not just watchful, he decided, but nervous, too. Drumming her fingers lightly on the tabletop as if she were playing the piano. Keeping time by tapping her foot on the dusty paving stones. "What do you know about *her*, Henri?"

The innkeeper shrugged. "Not much. She speaks very good French, the high society kind. And she's in no hurry to leave here. She's taken the room for a month."

"A *month*?"

"That's what she said."

"Did she happen to mention why?"

"She did not."

When Marie-Louise died, reporters had descended on the area within hours, posing as innocent tourists to disguise the fact they were sniffing out scandal, real or imagined, with which to titillate their readers. In less than a week, Anton had been front-page news throughout France and most of Europe. *COMTE'S WIFE'S MYSTERIOUS DEATH*, the tabloid headlines screamed. *MURDER OR SUICIDE? POLICE QUESTION HUSBAND.*

Although public appetite for sensationalism eventually found other victims on which to feed, having his private life exposed to malicious speculation had been a nightmare while it lasted, not just for him and his immediate family, but for everyone in Bellevue-sur-Lac. Since then, he'd been mistrustful of strangers who chose to linger in such a backwater village, content to live in a small inn where they'd be sharing a common bathroom with other guests. And with the third anniversary of his wife's death coming up, he was especially wary. Like those which had gone before, it promised a burst of renewed interest in the whole tragic mess.

"One has to wonder how she plans to occupy her time," he remarked.

"Perhaps she's an artist."

She, and a hundred thousand others—would-be Cézannes, Van Goghs, Picassos, sure if they breathed the golden light of Provence, genius would ooze from their pores. They came looking suitably tormented by their muse, right down to their disheveled appearance and the paint under their fingernails.

Not this woman, though. She wouldn't allow a speck of dust to settle on her shoe.

Anton did not, as a rule, patronize the inn. Tonight, though, he was inclined to make an exception. He couldn't put his finger on exactly what it was, but something about the woman—the set of her slender shoulders, perhaps, or the tilt of her head—seemed vaguely familiar. That alone was enough to increase his suspicions. Had he seen her before? Was she one of the rabid reporters, come back for another helping of empty speculation?

"Pour two glasses of whatever the lady is drinking, Henri," he said, arriving at a decision.

Although Henri knew better than to say so, his face betrayed his surprise. Much might have changed since feudal times, but the people of Bellevue-sur-Lac and the surrounding area had been under the protection of the de Valois family for centuries. Whether or not he liked it, Anton reigned as their present-day *seigneur*.

They came to him to arbitrate their differences, to seek his advice, to request his help. That Monsieur le Comte would choose to sit among them at the L'Auberge d'Olivier, drinking the same wine they drank, would do more for Henri's reputation than if he'd been awarded the Legion of Honor.

As far as Anton was concerned, being the object of such reverence was nothing short of ludicrous. When all was said and done, he was just a man, no more able than any other to control fate. His wife's death and the reason behind it was proof enough of that. But tragedy and scandal hadn't been enough to topple him from his pedestal, any more than his disdain for his title relieved him of the obligations inherent in it.

"I should serve it immediately, Anton?" Henri wanted to know, still flushed with pleasure.

"No," he said, turning away. "I'll signal when we're ready."

The square was deserted now. No faces for the stranger to scrutinize. Instead she stared at her hands where they rested on the table.

"A beautiful woman should not sit alone on such a night, with only an empty glass for company," he said, approaching her. "May I join you?"

Startled, she looked up. Her face was a pale oval in the gloom, and he couldn't tell the color of her eyes, only that they were large. He'd addressed her in English, and she replied in kind. "Oh, no…thank you, but no."

It was his turn to be taken aback. Her slightly panicked rejection smacked more of propriety than guile. Hardly the response of a seasoned scandal-hunter, he thought. Or else, she was very good at hiding her true identity.

Covering his surprise with a smile, he said, "Because we haven't been formally introduced?"

She spared him the barest smile in return. "Well, since you put it that way, yes."

"Then allow me to rectify the matter. My name is Anton de Valois, and I am well-known in these parts. Ask anyone. They will vouch for me."

He thought she blushed then—another surprise—though it was hard to be sure, with night closing in. "I didn't mean to insult you," she said. She had a low, musical voice, refined and quite charming.

"Nor did you. It pays to be cautious these days, especially for a woman traveling by herself." Then, even though he already knew the answer, he paused just long enough to give his question the ring of authenticity before suggesting, "Or perhaps I'm mistaken and you're not alone after all, but waiting for someone else. Your husband, perhaps?"

"No," she replied, far too quickly, and lowered her eyes to stare at her left hand which was bare of rings. The lights in the square came on at that moment, glimmering through the branches of the plane tree to cast the shadow of her lashes in perfect dusky crescents across her cheeks. "No husband. Not anymore."

Again, not quite the attitude or the response he expected. Rather, she seemed lost, and very unsure of herself. On the other hand, he knew well enough that appearances could be deceiving. That being so, he led into the subject she'd surely latch on to with a vengeance, if she was indeed, as he suspected, a brash journalist with a hidden agenda.

"Then we share something of significance in common," he remarked, sliding into the chair across from hers without asking permission this time. "I also lost my spouse several years ago."

"Oh, I'm not a widow!" she exclaimed, meeting his gaze again. "I'm…divorced."

She uttered the word as if it were something of which she was deeply ashamed. A clever ploy, perhaps, designed to deflect attention from her true motives.

"What kind of man would be fool enough to let you go?" he inquired, sickened by the taste of false sympathy on his tongue. He was normally a straightforward man with little use for subterfuge.

"Actually…" She gave a tiny shrug and bit down briefly on

her lower lip. She had a very lovely mouth, he noticed. Soft, sensitive, defenseless. "He's the one who left me."

Afraid that the longer he engaged in a game of cat and mouse with such a woman, the duller the sharp edge of his suspicions might grow, Anton observed her closely, willing himself to uncover artifice, but finding only sincerity. Was he overreacting? At the mercy of his own paranoia—and she its innocent victim?

Suddenly despising himself for toying with memories she clearly found painful, he murmured with honest compassion, "In that case, he is a double fool and a cad. I can see that he's caused you much unhappiness."

"At the time, yes, but I'm over it now."

"And over him?"

She managed another smile, and if it was a trifle hesitant, it was also unmistakably genuine. "Oh, yes. Most definitely over him."

Choosing not to examine the real cause of the relief flooding through him, he nodded to Henri, who scooped up a tray bearing the two glasses of wine and a lighted candle, and brought it to the table. "Then we shall celebrate your freedom with a toast."

"No," she began. "It's very kind of you, but I meant what I said before. I really—"

Sweeping aside her objection, Anton said, "Henri, your lovely guest isn't certain it's safe to get to know me. Reassure her, will you, that I'm quite respectable?"

He'd switched to French, aware that Henri's English was minimal, at best. Without waiting for Henri to reply, she spoke, also in French, and it was, as the man had said, flawless. "I'm sure you're respectable enough. I'm just not accustomed to being approached by strange men."

"Strange men?" Henri set down the tray with a distinct thump. "Madame, you speak of the Comte de Valois!"

"A real live Comte?" She tipped her head to one side and this time managed a slight laugh. "In this day and age?"

Henri drew himself up to his full one hundred and seventy-five centimeters—about five feet eight inches in her part of the world. "A gentleman remains a gentleman, regardless of the times, Madame, and you may rest assured Monsieur le Comte fits the description in every way."

"Thanks, Henri," Anton intervened, knowing he scarcely deserved the accolade in the present circumstances. "That'll be all, for now."

She watched the innkeeper march back to the bar, his spine stiff with outrage, then switched her gaze to Anton again. "He wasn't joking, was he? You really are you a Count."

"I'm afraid so."

"Oh, dear! Then I owe you an apology. You must think me incredibly rude, not to mention gauche."

"I find you quite delightful," he said, and with the sense of floundering ever deeper into dangerous waters, realized he spoke the truth.

She clasped both hands to her cheeks. "I don't quite know how to behave or what to say. I've never had drinks with royalty before."

"I don't consider myself royalty. As for how you should behave, simply be yourself and speak your mind freely. Isn't that always the best way?"

"I'm not sure," she said. "It hasn't done me a lot of good, in the past."

He touched the rim of his glass to hers. "Then let us drink to the future. *À votre santé.*"

"À votre santé aussi, Monsieur le Comte."

Continuing in French, he said, "To my friends, I am Anton."

"I hardly think I qualify as a friend on such short acquaintance."

The candle flame illuminated the classic oval of her face, the dimples beside her cupid's bow mouth and the delicate winged brows showcasing her eyes which, he saw now, were the same deep, intense blue as a Provencal sky in high summer. Her shoulder-length hair, worn simply, shone with the luster of a newly polished, old gold coin.

Was she beautiful?

Not in the conventional sense, no, he decided. Hers was a more subtle appeal, one he found quite irresistible. "Sometimes," he said earnestly, "friendship, like love, can strike instantly, as I believe it has between you and me."

"How can that be? You don't even know my name."

Returning her smile, he said, "You think I haven't noticed? I've been trying to learn it from the moment I saw you, but you've evaded me at every turn."

"It's no secret. I'm Diana. Diana...Reeves."

He noticed her slight hesitation, but decided not to push the point. She was skittish enough as it was. Instead, taking her hand, he raised it to his lips. "I'm very pleased to meet you, Diana Reeves. What did you have for dinner, last night?"

"Beef stew with potato dumplings."

"Then we'll order something different, tonight."

"I don't recall saying I'd have dinner with you. Not that that seems to mean much," she added ruefully. "I didn't agree to have a drink with you, either, but I'm doing it anyway. Do you always get your own way?"

"If I want something badly enough, I do. It's one of the perks of being a Count."

She regarded him soberly. "You're being very charming, Anton, and I'm sure most women would be flattered by your attention, but I think it's only fair to tell you that I'm not very good at flirting."

"I know," he said. "It's one of the qualities about you that I find most attractive."

"My ex-husband said I took things far too seriously and didn't know how to have fun."

"I thought we already established that your ex-husband is a fool."

Her dimples deepened as another smile lit up her face. "You're right, we did."

"Then forget about him and concentrate on us and friendship at first sight. When did you arrive in France?"

"Just yesterday."

"And you came straight here, to Bellevue-sur-Lac?"

At his question, tension emanated from her, so fierce that he half expected to see blue sparks crackling from the ends of her hair. "As a matter of fact, I did. What's wrong with that?"

Why so defensive, all of a sudden? he wondered, his suspicions on high alert again. "I didn't say there was anything wrong, Diana," he replied mildly.

Color swept into her cheeks. "Well, you *sounded* as if you did."

"Perhaps you interpreted surprise as disapproval."

"Why should you be surprised?"

He shrugged. "Bellevue-sur-Lac is barely a dot on the map of Provence, and has little to offer a tourist, yet you chose it over the many other, more interesting villages in the region."

Avoiding his glance, she said, "You might not think it interesting, but I find it thoroughly delightful."

"And on behalf of everyone living here, I thank you. But how did you discover it?"

She took a moment to consider her answer. "By chance," she said finally. "I'd fallen into a rut after my marriage ended, and decided I was ready for a little adventure. I knew I wanted to visit the south of France, so I stuck a pin on the map, promised myself I'd explore the spot I found, no matter what, and here I am. I consider myself lucky that I ended up in a place that offers food and lodging, and not on top of a mountain with nothing but the stars for company."

"Yet you're wasting the opportunity to see the best Provence has to offer. Why else do you think we make no real effort to accommodate tourists here?"

"I'm not exactly your average tourist. I don't care about seeing the sights. I just want a place where I can find a little peace."

A plausible enough story on the surface, and one he might

have accepted were it not that she still couldn't quite meet his gaze. "Not nearly as lucky as I consider myself, that you chose here," he returned smoothly. "Fate brought us together, no question about it, which means we definitely must dine together. I highly recommend Henri's bouillabaisse."

But she'd already gathered up her straw handbag and was preparing to leave. "Some other time, perhaps, but not tonight, thank you. After my earlier faux-pas, I'm afraid Henri might poison me. I even wonder if he'll still allow me to stay here."

A pity he couldn't keep her a little longer and discover the reason for her sudden uneasiness, Anton thought, but he had a whole month in which to uncover her secrets, and could afford to bide his time. "I don't think you need to concern yourself about that," he said, coming around the table to pull out her chair. "Henri Molyneux is one of the most equable fellows you'll ever meet."

In her eagerness to escape him, she must have risen too quickly because she staggered, and if he hadn't steadied her with a hand at her shoulder, he thought she might have fallen. As it was, her bag slipped from her grasp and fell on the table, knocking over her wineglass and sending it rolling to the dusty paving stones where it shattered.

Concerned, he said, "Diana? Are you okay?"

"No," she muttered distractedly, as breathless as if she'd run five kilometers in under five minutes. "I spilled my wine and broke the glass."

"*Alors,* don't worry about that. It happens all the time. See, Henri's already coming to clean it up."

"No," she insisted. "It's my mess. I'll clean it up."

Pressing her down onto the chair again, he said firmly, "You'll do no such thing. You're shaking, and white as a sheet. What's the matter?"

"*Nothing!*" she cried. Then, as if she realized she was behaving oddly, she made a concerted effort to pull herself together. "I'm sorry, I didn't mean to shout. It's just that I haven't eaten all day, and two glasses of wine on an empty stomach…"

"That settles it, then. We're having dinner." He nodded to Henri who, having shoveled up the broken glass, was wiping down the table. "How's the bouillabaisse coming along, my friend?"

"Not ready for another fifteen minutes, I regret to say," he replied, and cast an anxious glance at Diana. "You did not cut yourself, *madame*? You are not hurt?"

Diana stared at him wordlessly, her eyes huge. Two bright spots of color bloomed in her cheeks, making the rest of her face that much paler by comparison. Although the evening was pleasantly warm, she shivered as if it was winter and the mistral blew.

Baffled, Henri swung his glance to Anton. "Perhaps a little cognac might help?"

Equally mystified, Anton shook his head. There was more going on here than a missed meal. He was no doctor, but he recognized shock when he saw it. What he couldn't determine was its cause. In fact, nothing about this woman quite added up. "No alcohol," he said, laying his hand against her forehead and finding it clammy. "She's cold. Bring her a *tisane* and some bread instead."

She flinched at his touch, as if she'd been startled from sleep. "I don't need tea," she mumbled, struggling to her feet. "I'll get a sweater from my room."

"Send someone else for it. Those stairs—"

"No. I felt a little faint for a moment, but I'm fine now, and I'll be even better after I've freshened up a little."

"Very well," he conceded. "But don't think for a minute I'll allow you to miss dinner. If you're not back down here by the time the bouillabaisse is ready, I'm coming up to get you."

She managed a smile, as if the very idea of trying to avoid him would never cross her mind, and turned to Henri. "Fifteen minutes, you said?"

"At the very most, *madame*."

"Okay. I'll be ready and waiting."

* * *

Yesterday, when the chambermaid had shown her to her room, Diana had considered it barely acceptable. At little more than twelve feet square, with its old, mismatched furnishings, it was, without question, the least sophisticated space she'd ever occupied, and certainly not one in which she planned to spend much time. Now, leaning against the closed door, she surveyed the narrow, iron-framed bed, hand-painted night table, carved armoire and three-drawer chest, with fond gratitude for the haven they represented.

Even the age-spotted mirror hanging above the old-fashioned washstand held a certain charm. Its most grievous sin lay in distorting her reflection on its wavy surface so that one half of her face looked as if it didn't quite belong to the other. Unlike Comte Anton de Valois, who possessed an unnerving talent for seeing clear through to her brain and detecting every nuance of hesitation, every carefully phrased falsehood.

She doubted he'd swallowed her excuse that hunger had left her light-headed, but it had been the best she could come up with on short notice, most especially since she really had been thrown for a loop at learning that Henri was a Molyneux.

"You are alone?" he'd inquired, when she'd shown up last night and requested a room.

She'd nodded and murmured assent, so captivated by everything she saw that it simply hadn't occurred to her to ask his full name. It had been enough that everyone called him Henri.

Bathing her in a welcoming smile, he'd pushed an old-fashioned ledger across the counter for her to sign. "Then you're in luck. It so happens a single room just became available."

L'Auberge d'Olivier was a picturesque building with the date, 1712, stamped above the open front door. Its thick plaster walls were painted a soft creamy-yellow. Flowers tumbled from baskets perched on the sills of its sparkling, deep-set windows. Outside, under a huge plane tree, candles flickered on wrought-iron tables where old men hunched over glasses of dark wine and smoked pungent cigarettes.

Charmed, she'd seen it as a fortuitous start to her search. Because Bellevue-sur-Lac was so small, she'd thought it would be easy to unearth clues that would lead her to her birth mother. Had spent this entire day combing the narrow streets, convinced success was around the next corner. Behind the protection of her sunglasses, she'd scrutinized every woman she came across, searching for a physical resemblance, a visceral intuition, that would tell her she'd found the right one. But the very smallness of the village turned out to be a serious drawback.

"How do you plan to tackle this harebrained scheme of yours?" Carol had asked, just before she'd dropped her off at SeaTac airport.

"Very discreetly," Diana had replied smugly. "I'll be so smooth and subtle, no one will even notice me, let alone guess what I'm after."

In fact, she'd been an object of suspicious curiosity everywhere she went. Although they'd been polite enough, people had closed ranks against her, not trusting a lone American wandering the area, and she'd come back to the inn that evening, no farther ahead than she had been when she'd left there that morning.

Was she really so naive that she'd expected all she had to do was show up, and her mother would instinctively know her? So foolish as to think that, in the unlikely event such a miracle occurred, a woman who'd kept her baby's birth a secret for over twenty-eight years would willingly reveal it now?

"You're rushing into this, Diana," Carol had warned. "You need to take a step back and consider the pitfalls, the most obvious being that you're the world's worst liar. What makes you think you can pull off such a monumental deception?"

She should have listened to her friend. Perhaps then, she wouldn't have made a spectacle of herself with a man smart enough to recognize something fishy when it was staring him in the face.

And so accustomed to having his own way that he wouldn't take "no" for an answer.

What had he threatened, before she fled to the sanctuary of her room? *Be down here by the time the bouillabaisse is ready, or I'm coming up to get you,* or words to that effect?

That he meant it was enough to have her changed into fresh clothes and on her way downstairs again in record time. If there was to be a confrontation, better it take place in public, than here in a room that was barely large enough for one. He was too pushy, too sure of himself—and, she admitted reluctantly, altogether too attractive for her to deal with him at close quarters.

She needed to keep her wits about her because, just when she'd been ready to concede defeat and admit Carol had been right all along, the one lead she'd hoped to find had fallen almost literally into her lap. Henri Molyneux, her host, might very well be the key to the mystery of who her birth mother was, and whether or not he knew it, Anton de Valois was going to help Diana unlock it.

Falling under his charming spell would undermine her resolve and might very well turn out to be a fatal mistake, because he struck her as a man of many layers; a classic example of the old saying that still waters run deep.

She must resist him at all costs.

CHAPTER THREE

A MAN likes to be seen with a woman who knows how to dress,
Harvey used to say. *That she cares enough about his opinion
to want to make him proud when he takes her out in public, tells
him he made the right choice in marrying her.*

A belittling definition of a wife's worth, Diana thought now,
although she hadn't said so at the time, and she was pretty sure
Anton de Valois would see past such superficiality. Even so, she
dressed with care, and from the way his glance swept over her
in frank approval when she joined him again, knew she'd
chosen well. Her sleeveless navy dress, deceptively simple but
superbly cut, was enhanced only by a silver bracelet, lending
just the right touch of low-key elegance for what, to all apparent
intents and purposes, was supposed to be a low-key dinner.

"You took rather longer to return than you were supposed
to, but it was well worth the wait," he remarked, pulling out her
chair. "You look quite lovely, Diana, and very much better than
you did half an hour ago."

"Thank you. I'm feeling better." She took her seat, out-
wardly poised, but when his hand brushed against her bare
skin, a shock of sensual heat flashed through her, and briefly—
very briefly indeed!—she longed to lean into his touch and soak
in his warmth.

This was a man put on earth to tempt a woman to stray from

her intended course. He turned her thoughts to such nonsense as love at first sight, to happy-ever-after, when any person with a grain of sense knew there was no such thing. Yet for all that she tried to distance herself from him, his magnetism tugged at her, drawing her ever deeper into its aura.

Simply put, she found him both irresistible and intriguing. The cast of his mouth, the slow-burning fire in his eyes, spoke of a passion which, once aroused, be it from anger, pride or sexual desire, would not easily be quenched. The lean strength of his body betrayed a working familiarity with manual labor, yet cashmere, silk and fine leather were created with his particular brand of natural elegance in mind.

Why hadn't she met him sooner, before she'd learned to be so wary, so disillusioned? she lamented. Before she'd married the wrong man and had all her womanly dreams turned to ashes?

Annoyed by her wandering thoughts, she stiffened her spine, both physically and mentally. She was here on a mission, and the handsome French Count resuming his seat across from her, merely the means to an end.

Blithely ignorant of her thoughts, the handsome French Count smiled winningly and said, "Enough to tolerate a glass of wine before we eat?"

"Perhaps not quite that much," she said, deciding she needed to keep a clear head. So what if his voice was dark as midnight, his smile enough to melt the polar ice cap, and his face the envy of angels? She'd learned the hard way how easily sexual awareness could cloud other important issues between a man and a woman, and she wasn't about to let it lead her astray again. "At least, not until I have some food in my stomach."

He indicated a basket containing a sliced baguette, and a shallow dish of black olives mashed to a paste with roasted garlic. "Try some of this, then. Henri bakes his own bread, and the olives are home grown on de Valois soil."

"Ah! So you own olive groves. I was wondering how Counts earn their keep these days."

She spoke lightly, hoping he wouldn't discern such a nakedly transparent attempt to discover more about him. But knowledge was power, and the more she learned about Anton de Valois, the better prepared she'd be to withstand his appeal and deal with whatever it was that really motivated his interest in her. Because all his smooth Continental charm notwithstanding, the alert calculation in his gaze whenever it settled on her, betrayed him. For some reason she couldn't begin to fathom, he didn't trust her. And *that,* she reminded herself sternly, was ample reason for her not to trust him.

"Olives keep me busy enough," he replied, bathing her in a singularly breathtaking smile, "but they're by no means my chief obsession."

She spread a little of the paste on a piece of bread and sampled it. "They should be. This is outstanding."

"Then I insist you try at least a mouthful of the wine. My vineyards produced the grapes which my vintner blended to create this very fine Château de Valois Rouge."

"Thanks anyway, but I'll take your word for it. As I mentioned not five minutes ago, I don't care for any wine right now."

She might as well have saved her breath. "*Mon dieu,* Diana, relax and live a little!" he scoffed, pouring a small amount into her glass. "A sip or two won't send you to hell in a hand cart, but I promise you, it will enhance your meal. In this part of Provence, a well-chilled red wine is, to bouillabaisse, what American beer is to pretzels."

It was a pretty wine, she had to give him that. It glowed in her glass with all the fire of a ruby. Still, if getting her drunk was his aim, he was in for a disappointment. She found him intoxicating enough, without falling victim to his *vin rouge.* She'd wet her lips with the stuff, and that was all.

"Very pleasant," she said, allowing a mere trickle to roll

down her throat, and changed the subject before he decided she hadn't tasted enough to know if it was wine or water. "So what else keeps you busy, apart from overseeing your vineyards and olive groves?"

"Doing the same for my lavender farm and distillery. I'm a hands-on kind of man and, given a choice, I'd prefer to be more actively involved in the actual operation of all three enterprises, but the administrative end of things is so time consuming that I frequently put in ten-hour days without once setting foot outside my office."

"My goodness, you really *are* a working model of a Count! What do you do for relaxation?"

She realized at once her mistake. Without missing a beat, he lowered his long lashes in seductive slow motion, a move that aroused a disturbing response in the pit of her stomach. "Coerce beautiful Americans into having dinner with me. Speaking of which, here comes our bouillabaisse. Prepare to be impressed."

Oh, she was already impressed, pathetically so, but not by Henri's culinary skills! Anton de Valois, however, was a different matter altogether. She should be ashamed for falling victim to the practiced moves of the French equivalent of Don Juan!

Henri arrived at their table, wheeling a cart holding a thick pottery tureen on a matching platter, as well as bowls, plates and cutlery. With great pomp and ceremony, he removed the tureen lid and wafted his hand over the escaping steam, sending a mouthwatering aroma of slow-simmered tomatoes, garlic, saffron and herbs drifting her way.

Chunks of red mullet, monkfish, John Dory and conger eel, as well as mussels and various other shellfish, floated in the rich broth. *"Bon appetit, mes amis!"* he pronounced with a smile, and left them to it.

Anton ladled a generous helping of the stew into a bowl and passed it to Diana. "Try this and tell me what you think," he coaxed.

What she privately thought was that simply feasting her eyes on him and drinking in his charm was sustenance enough. But since that route surely led to nothing but trouble, she wrenched her runaway emotions under control, obediently took a spoonful of the fish stew, savored it slowly, then closed her eyes and sighed with genuine pleasure. "Pure heaven!" she sighed.

"That's pretty much the reaction Henri Molyneux always gets when his bouillabaisse is on the menu."

She couldn't have asked for a better reminder of the *real* reason she was supposed to be sharing a meal with him. Swallowing her food along with the lie she was about to fabricate, she said, "I don't think I've come across that name before."

Another mistake she quickly came to regret! "A woman with your fluency in French has never heard the name *Henri?*" Anton inquired with blatant disbelief. "Come now, Diana! You surely don't expect me to swallow that!"

"Oh, not his *first* name," she amended hastily, a telltale blush warming her face. "I was referring to Molyneux. Is it…very unusual?"

"Not in these parts," he said, continuing to eye her suspiciously. "There are Molyneux's everywhere."

Her pulse gave an erratic leap. Struggling to sound as if she was merely making trivial dinner conversation when, in reality, her entire world hung on his reply, she asked lightly, "Don't tell me they're all related."

"Not necessarily all, but quite a few, certainly. So many families are linked, either directly, or through marriage. As I said, it's a very common name. Henri, for instance, is the eldest of seven children, and has three of his own, as well as two grandchildren."

"He doesn't look old enough to be a grandfather."

Anton rolled his rather magnificent eyes. "Tell him that, and he'll be your slave for life! He turns sixty next month. I know, because a big birthday bash is in the works, to which everyone within a fifty-mile radius is invited."

Filing away that gem of information, Diana continued her inquisition with a casual, "What about his siblings? Are they married, as well?"

"Yes, and all but one with children and grandchildren of their own. At last count, there were thirty-eight Molyneux's in his branch of the family alone. Multiply that a few times, and you'll understand why I say the name is as thick on the ground in these parts, as plane tree leaves in autumn."

Little pieces of her personal jigsaw puzzle were beginning to fall into place almost too neatly. Trying hard to contain her growing excitement, Diana said, "And Henri's six siblings, are they all brothers?"

"The youngest is a sister, and just as well, according to Henri's father. Gérard always said that if the seventh baby had been another boy, he'd have been kicked out of the house and made to spend the rest of his days with the cows in the barn. Not that anyone believed the story. He and his wife were devoted to each other, and to their sons. But from what I understand, there's no doubt that Jeanne was special. Their whole family adored her."

"Does she have children, too?"

"No," he said coolly. "Tell me, Diana, why are we talking about people who can't possibly be of interest to you, when we could be spending the time getting to know one another better?"

Back off! the voice of caution advised. *You're betraying too much interest in the Molyneux family and arousing his suspicion!* But increasingly convinced she was finally onto something, Diana ignored the warning and leaned forward urgently. "I don't agree. Even the lives of strangers are interesting, so please go on."

"Go on?" The chill in his voice was more pronounced than ever. "Go on with what, exactly?"

She needed to stop. To dismiss the subject with a laugh, and turn the conversation to something light and inconsequential.

And she would have, if it hadn't been that so much of what he told her fit the profile of her birth mother. Henri was almost sixty and the eldest of seven. He had only one sister, the baby of the family, and the woman Diana had traveled halfway around the world to find was forty-five. Mental arithmetic might never have been her strong point, but even she could do the math on this one.

"With what you were telling me about Henri's family," she said, hard-pressed not to reach across the table and literally shake the words out of him. "The whole idea of seven children in one family fascinates me."

"Really," he said, with marked skepticism.

"Yes, really!"

He regarded her steadfastly over the rim of his glass, and took a slow sip of his wine. "Then I'm sorry to disappoint you but there's nothing else to tell. The Molyneux's are good people, and that's about it."

He was wrong. One ambiguity remained, and terrified though she was of what she might learn if she questioned it, the prospect of remaining in ignorance terrified her even more. She'd lived with enough uncertainty to last her a lifetime. She wouldn't allow it to derail her now. So, clearing her throat, she plunged ahead. "But I notice you speak of Henri's sister in the past tense. Is that because she died?"

Oh, how horribly blunt the words sounded, and Anton must have thought so, too, because he almost choked on his bouillabaisse. *"Mon dieu, non!"* he exclaimed. "Why would you think such a thing?"

"I'm not sure," she said, fumbling for a plausible reply. "It was just the way you spoke of her, that's all. It made me feel…sad."

"But why? You don't even know these people. Why do you care about them?"

"I don't," she whispered, blinking furiously to stem the sudden rush of tears welling in her eyes.

But he was too observant to be so easily fooled. "That simply isn't true. Clearly you care very much—indeed, far more than the occasion warrants. Did my speaking of the Molyneux's somehow revive unhappy memories of your own family?"

The candle flame bloomed into a multihued disc, perforated at its rim with pinpricks of brilliance. She blinked to clear her vision and a tear rolled down her face. "In a way. Hearing you talk about families and marriage brought home to me that I don't have either anymore."

"Your parents—?"

"Died within six months of each other, two years ago."

"And you were an only child?"

I don't know for sure, she cried inwardly. *That's what I'm trying to find out.* "Yes."

"Then we have even more in common than I first supposed," he said, with more kindness and compassion than Harvey had ever shown, "because I, too, was an only child. My parents died in a train derailment when I was seven, and I was left in the care of my two aunts who live with me still."

"Oh, Anton!" she cried, mortified. "You must think I'm incredibly self-absorbed, to be wailing on about my own woes, when you had a much tougher time of it."

"Not at all. My aunts are exceptional people and came as close as anyone could to taking the place of my mother and father. Of course, I grieved, but I never felt alone or abandoned, because those two women, who never married or bore children of their own, stepped into the role of parents as naturally and wholeheartedly as if they'd been preparing for it their entire lives. They loved me unconditionally, gave me the gift of laughter, instilled in me a respect for others, taught me the meaning of integrity and never once lied to me."

He paused a moment, seeming lost in thought, then suddenly lifted his gaze and stared at Diana. The absolute candor in his eyes, the utter integrity shining through, struck her with such force that, with a sudden sense of shock, she found herself wishing *he'd* been the man she'd married.

Yes, he was a stranger, and yes, he made her uneasy with his probing gaze, but she knew instinctively that he'd never have cheated on her. Never have lied so cruelly.

"At the end of the day, they're the qualities that define us as human beings. Without them, we're not worth very much at all," he finished soberly. "Don't you agree?"

Shame flooded through her. How was she supposed to reply, knowing as she did that she was deliberately misleading him about herself and her reason for being there? Yet he was too astute not to notice if she tried to evade his question.

"In principle, yes," she finally allowed, steering as clear of outright deceit as possible. "Unfortunately no one's perfect, and even the best of us sometimes fall short."

He continued his close observation a few unnerving seconds longer, then dropped his gaze to her hands, playing nervously with the stem of her wineglass. "I appear to have a talent for making you uncomfortable, *ma chère.*"

"Whatever makes you think that?"

"You keep fidgeting with your glass."

"Well, if you must know," she said, somehow managing to meet his unwavering gaze without flinching, "I think I might like a little more wine, after all."

"As you wish." He poured an inch into the bowl of her glass. "This is a Syrah and something of an experiment for us. Take a decent taste, this time, and save your dainty sipping for afternoon tea with English royalty."

Add "insufferably arrogant" to his list of qualities, she told herself, bristling at his tone, and just to let him know she wasn't a complete ignoramus, she took her time going through the ritual of sniffing, swirling and tasting the wine.

"Well?" he demanded imperiously. "Will it do?"

Still playing for time, she let the mouthful she'd taken linger on her tongue a moment longer, swallowed, then closed her eyes and did that weird little trick of exhaling down the back of her throat to catch a final bouquet—the mark of a true oenophile, according to Harvey, who'd always made an exorbitantly big deal of conferring approval on the wine, when they entertained or dined out.

"Delightfully complex, with a remarkable nose," she conceded.

Harvey would have been tickled pink by her performance. Anton, on the other hand, didn't seem at all impressed. He simply poured more wine into both their glasses and returned to a subject she'd hoped he'd forgotten about. "You mentioned earlier that you came here looking for a little peace."

"That's right."

"I've always seen peace as a state of mind, not a place on the map."

"Normally I'd agree with you, but I needed a change of scene, as well."

"Why is that?"

"Because running into my ex-husband all the time wasn't helping me recover from the breakup of my marriage."

"You live in a small town where that sort of thing happened often, do you?"

"No. I live in Seattle."

"Ah, the Space Needle city." He raised his elegant eyebrows derisively. "Large enough, I'd have thought, that you could easily avoid one another, unless, of course, you work together."

"Hardly! He's a surgeon."

"And what are you, Diana?" he inquired, imbuing the question with unspoken skepticism.

"Nothing," she said, rattled as much by his questions as the cool disbelief with which he received her answers. "I was his wife, and now I'm nothing. Why are you giving me the third degree like this?"

"Is that what I'm doing?"

"Well, what would *you* call it?"

"Getting to know you." He permitted himself a satisfied little smile and lifted his shoulders in a perfectly executed Continental shrug. "You surely can't blame me for that?"

He was playing with her the way a cat plays with a mouse before closing in for the kill. And she was helpless to put a stop to it.

Oh, he was too suave, too sure of himself, too…*everything,* with his chiseled features, and sexy, heavily lashed eyes, and tall, elegant frame! "How am I supposed to answer that, Anton?"

"You can start by relaxing, and not judging every man you meet by your former husband. As for your remark about being nothing, that's absurd. You're intelligent and beautiful and sensitive, three good reasons for any man with half a brain to find you interesting. How long do you plan to stay here?"

The man had the unnerving habit of infiltrating a woman's defenses then, before she could regroup, firing a sudden question in her face. "A few weeks," she admitted, bracing herself for further interrogation.

"Good. That means we can see more of each other."

"I'm not sure I'm ready to start dating again."

"I'm not casting myself in the role of suitor," he informed her dauntingly. "I'm extending the hand of friendship to a stranger, in an effort to ensure she leaves here satisfied that it was worth the time and effort it took her to make the journey in the first place."

Good grief, was the man *never* at a loss for just the right words? "I already feel that way."

"Excellent!" He added more wine to her glass. "So tell me, Diana, what were you, before you became a wife?"

"A university student, majoring in modern languages. I'd hoped to become a teacher after I graduated."

"But you changed your mind?"

"Yes."

"Because you decided you didn't like children enough to want to spend six or more hours a day with them, ten months of the year?"

"Not at all! I love children. If it had been up to me—" She stopped, Harvey's ultimate betrayal flaring up like a nagging toothache that never quite went away. "But it wasn't."

"You couldn't have children?" Anton asked, his voice hypnotizing in its sudden deep sympathy.

"I don't know, because I never tried. Harvey thought we should wait until he was established before we started a family, so I quit university and went to work as a translator for a law firm whose major clients were European."

"What you're saying, in a very nice way, is that you put your own career and wishes on hold, in order to promote your husband's."

"Something like that, yes."

"I wonder how long it will be before this foolish man realizes what a treasure he cast aside—which is, of course, exactly what will happen, in time."

"I rather doubt that."

Reaching across the table, he wrapped her fingers warmly in his in a way that gave her palpitations. "But if it did, and he asked, would you take him back?"

"Never," she managed breathlessly, and wondered what it was about him that left her feeling as if she'd never held hands with a man before.

Whatever the reason, she steeled herself to resist him. Because, of course, he *was* coming on to her, whether or not he admitted it, and given half a chance, he'd probably be quite happy to take her to bed and make love to her.

The problem was, although he'd probably dismiss such a happening as a pleasant summer interlude, she was an all-or-nothing kind of woman, no better at casual sex than she was at flirting. Emotionally vulnerable and needy as she knew herself to be, she couldn't afford to lay her heart on the line again, just to have him trample all over it when he decided he'd had enough of her. She'd already gone through that with Harvey, and once was enough.

"That's what I was hoping to hear," Anton said, bathing her in a slow, seductive smile that threatened to reduce her rational judgment to a blob of molten hormones. "I'd hate to have to challenge him to a duel at dawn."

She untangled her fingers from his while she still retained a smidgeon of common sense. "There's no danger of that. My ex-husband is no more interested in me than I am in him."

"What does interest you, then?"

"Catching up on my sleep." She faked a yawn behind her hand. "It's past my bedtime."

He made a big production of looking at his watch. "You're surely not serious?"

"I surely am."

"But the night is still young, *ma belle ange.*"

Withstanding his flattery was definitely more than she could handle. "Not for me, it isn't," she insisted, forcing herself to her feet and clutching her purse to her breasts like a shield. "I'm fading fast, and your wine, excellent though it was, isn't helping any. Good night, Anton. Thank you for a lovely evening."

Before she could make the speedy exit she'd planned, he was on his feet and blocking her escape. "The pleasure was all mine," he murmured, brushing his lips over the back of her hand.

That she could deal with. He was French, after all, and a Count, to boot. But then, instead of releasing it, he turned her hand over and pressed a soft, warm kiss in the center of her palm. And for reasons that completely eluded her, she felt the effect all the way to the soles of her feet. She wasn't absolutely certain, but she thought she might even have let out a tiny whimper of pleasure, too.

Accurately guessing exactly the effect he'd had on her, he

folded her fingers over the spot, and fixed her in a gaze veiled by his fringe of dense black lashes drooping at half-mast. "Until tomorrow, Diana," he murmured.

Not if she had any say in the matter! Vividly aware of his gaze measuring her every step, she resisted the urge to bolt, and schooled herself to walk with a reasonable facsimile of decorum through the inn's front door. Then, when she was quite sure she was out of his sight, she *did* bolt, scuttling up the stairs and down the narrow corridor to the sanctuary of her little room as if the devil himself were in pursuit.

The woman was a mass of contradictions, he decided, watching as the light came on in her room. Educated, refined and with a certain sophistication, on the one hand; on the other, curiously naive and unsure of herself.

She blushed like a teenager, and looked out on the world with the eyes of an innocent. But she'd pursued her interest in Henri and his family with the sharp-minded tenacity of a terrier on a rat. If, as Anton had first suspected, she was really a tabloid reporter hiding behind a false identity, she was either very good at what she did, or hopelessly inept.

Instinct told him that she had a hidden agenda, and he'd learned long ago to trust his instincts. Yet despite his doubts and suspicions, he found himself drawn to her like no other woman he'd ever met. All of which made her doubly dangerous to his peace of mind.

Absorbed in his thoughts, he didn't notice his general manager had joined him until the man dropped into her recently vacated chair. Julien Laporte looked after the publicity end of things, and was very good at it. But from the discouraged slump of his shoulders now, he clearly brought bad news.

"I'm glad I caught you, Anton," he began. "That university student who was supposed to replace the other who broke his leg, has changed his mind and won't be coming to work for us this summer, after all. I've called in all my markers, trying to find a suitable substitute, and come up empty-handed. The kind of seasonal employee with the qualifications we're looking for was snapped up long ago. The way things look right now, we might be forced to cancel tours of the château and gardens this summer. A pity, I know, but better that than to bring in someone unable to do the job well. We have a reputation to maintain."

Up in her room, Diana showed no sign of her professed exhaustion as she paced back and forth in front of the window. Even from a distance, it was obvious she was either very agitated, very excited, or both.

"Courage, *mon ami!*" Anton replied thoughtfully, pushing himself to his feet. "We haven't exhausted all our options quite yet. Order us a cognac, Julien, and I'll be right back."

He could have made no secret of where he was going, and simply entered the inn through the main entrance and made his way upstairs in full view of the other patrons. But not even he would have been able to silence the gossip such a move would provoke, so in the interest of discretion, he went around the back of the building to where an iron fire escape connected the upper floor to the rear courtyard.

As usual at this time of year, the door at the top stood open, giving him easy access to the interior. What struck him as somewhat less usual was that her bedroom door also was slightly ajar. Not only that, her voice floated clearly into the quiet corridor, and given the frequent pauses in the conversation, it became immediately clear that she was on the phone.

"I was all ready to give up," he heard her say. "Honestly, Carol, it just seemed as if the entire village closed ranks against me…. Oh, no one actually *said* anything, but I could tell they were wondering what I was doing there…I know you said it wouldn't be easy, but I really thought I'd pick up some sort of lead that would point me in the right direction, since I could hardly just come straight out and ask… Oh, stop saying 'I told you so.' I can lie along with the best, when I have to, and do it without swallowing my tongue!

"…Okay, that's why I called you, because the day turned out not to be a total loss after all. I met the local Count…yes, *that* kind, although I haven't noticed anyone tugging on a forelock when they address him. They're respectful enough, without going overboard…. How do I know? Because I ended up having dinner with him, that's how… In his mid-thirties, I'd guess…

"Well, now that you mention it, yes, he is. Rather too gorgeous, for my peace of mind. Reminds me a bit of George Clooney and I don't mind telling you, when I'm with him, I have a hard time focusing on why I'm here. Look, the point is, he's the one who gave me the opening I've been looking for, so first thing tomorrow, I'll follow up on it. Just think, Carol, the next time I call, I might have real news…

"I *am* being careful. I can see the square from my window. He's already left, and some other guy's at our table…. I know, I'm losing you, too. It's because I'm using my cell phone, instead of the public phone downstairs, and the reception's not the best…. Of *course* I'll keep you posted. Say hi to Tim, and sorry I disturbed you so early in the day, but I knew you'd be anxious to find out how things are going…."

So she was a fraud, just as he'd suspected! Stealthily Anton retraced his steps, fueled by a flame of anger that reduced his attraction to ashes. In its place rose a grim determination to best her at her own game.

Given a choice, he'd have her run out of town before she could put into action whatever plans had brought her here, but even the Comte de Valois couldn't resort to such extreme measures on the strength of eavesdropping. However, he'd learned at his father's knee the value of an iron fist disguised in a velvet glove when necessity called for one, and he'd have no compunction about using it in this instance.

Whatever she was up to, he'd uncover it, and the easiest way to accomplish that was by keeping her firmly in his sights. And from her unguarded comments to whoever Carol was, he knew exactly how to go about it.

Whether or not she was ready to admit it, Diana Reeves was starving for male attention, and ripe for the plucking. And he was more than man enough for the job.

Nobody made a fool of Anton de Valois with impunity, least of all a slip of a woman like her.

CHAPTER FOUR

"*WORK* for you*?*" Diana almost blew coffee in his face.

It was seven-thirty, only. Early enough, she'd thought, that she could sit undisturbed in the morning sun, sipping café au lait from the huge bowl-shaped cup Henri had brought out to her. Then, before he became too busy with his regular customers, she'd hoped to engage him in casual conversation, to help her ferret out enough information about his sister to deduce whether or not she might indeed be Diana's mother. But within five minutes, Anton de Valois had shown up, plunked himself down at her table as if he owned it, and made the outrageous suggestion that she spend her time here acting as tour guide at his château.

"Don't think of it as work," he chided affably, looking disgracefully wide-awake and sexy in a narrow-striped, green and white shirt, and superbly tailored black pants. "Think of it as helping out a friend in need."

"We're not friends."

He regarded her from soulful, incredibly beautiful gray eyes. "You wound me. I thought we established, last night, that we are. What changed your mind?"

My good friend, Carol, she could have told him. *She quite rightly warned me to watch my step around you.* "Last night, the wine was talking. I'm seeing things in a different light, this morning."

"I dispute that. You drank almost nothing. But even if you're right, that's still no reason to turn me down without at least considering my proposal. I really am in a bind, *ma chère* Diana. I wouldn't have come to you, if I wasn't."

At the best of times, she'd never been much good at saying "no" to people, least of all someone as persistent and persuasive as the inestimable Count. Given the way she'd tossed restlessly most of the night, mostly because of him, this morning found her at an even greater disadvantage. "Why me?" she asked resentfully. "Corral one of the locals to help you out."

"I would, if I could, but for this particular job, it's simply not an option. To begin with, it's seasonal work only, and those living here who choose to work are already fully employed. That's why I usually hire university students, since they're always eager to make money over the summer. But just as important, I need someone completely fluent in English and French, and preferably with a working knowledge of Italian and Spanish, also." He sent her one of his winning smiles. "All of which, in the absence of a language arts student, makes you the ideal candidate. So, what do you say, Diana? Will you do it?"

"No."

"I'm prepared to pay you well for your time."

"I don't care about the money."

"Then what's the problem?"

"You are," she said bluntly. "Last night, you inflicted yourself on me, even though I made it clear I preferred to be alone, and you're doing it again now, before I've finished my first cup of coffee. Stop badgering me, Anton. I'm barely awake yet."

"You're not a morning person," he purred soothingly. "I understand. But that's the nice thing about this job. You don't have to be up at the crack of dawn. The tours don't start until eleven. You can sleep in as late as you like."

"In case I didn't make myself clear last night, I'm here on holiday."

"But, Diana," he said, trying hard to look guileless, and succeeding about as well as the wolf, right before it jumped out of bed and attacked Red Riding Hood, "how are you going to fill your days when there's nothing to do here but soak up the sun and watch the hours drift by?"

"After the year I've just had, the prospect of doing nothing but soak up the sun and watch the hours drift by, holds more appeal than you can possibly begin to appreciate." *And it's a whole lot safer than being around you all day!*

"For a little while, perhaps, but it'll lose its charm soon enough, and you'll wish you had something more stimulating to occupy your mind."

The problem, Anton, is that I find you altogether too stimulating—and not just in my mind!

Dousing the thought before it transposed itself into a betraying blush, she said staidly, "If that indeed happens, I'll be sure to let you know. Meanwhile, I plan to wade through the stack of books I brought with me, write letters to friends I haven't contacted in months, take lots of photographs as souvenirs of my travels, and soak up local color as well as sunshine. Trust me, that's stimulation enough."

"If you come to work for me, you'll still be able to do all those things," he cajoled.

"No," she said again, quickly, before her determination wavered. "Go away, and leave me alone. You might be able to bend everyone else in these parts to your will, but you're not going to railroad me."

As though realizing looking bereft and helpless wasn't helping his cause, Anton changed tactics. "It would seem I'm wasting my time," he declared loftily, lifting his shoulders in one of his trademark shrugs. "If your idea of saturating yourself in local custom extends to sharing a bathroom with strangers, *ma chère madame,* perhaps I've misjudged you, and you're not as bright as I took you to be."

He made it sound as if she planned to indulge in a group back-scrubbing session with her fellow guests, but she knew when she was being baited, and refused to be drawn in. "Perhaps you have," she said. "And just for the record, I'm not your *chère* anything. Now run off and torment someone else."

"All in good time," he replied, unfazed by her rejection and instead flashing her a smile that made her heart turn over. She'd thought him handsome enough last night, but now, in the sun-splashed light of morning, the full extent of his male beauty became apparent. "First, tell me what you have planned for today."

Involuntarily her gaze swung to Henri, busy wiping down the other outdoor tables. "Nothing special."

Following her gaze, he drawled with unmistakable innuendo, "Indeed? If I didn't know better, I'd say, from the hungry glance you just cast at your host, that you have something very specific in mind."

For heaven's sake, the man could very well turn out to be her uncle! "Are you implying I plan to seduce a man old enough to be my father?" she asked, unable to stifle a burst of incredulous laughter.

"Not at all. I don't think he's quite your type, and even if he was, his wife would take a cast iron skillet to your skull before you so much as laid a hand on him. But there are other ways of taking advantage of someone, particularly if a person has a hidden agenda." He leaned closer, a sudden coating of steel overlaying his deep velvet voice. "But that couldn't possibly be the case with you, could it, Diana? You wouldn't try to exploit a man as harmless as Henri for your personal gain, would you?"

He knows what you're up to, her inner voice whispered, even as her common sense questioned how that could possibly be so. She'd confided only in Carol, and Carol would never betray her secret.

Bolstered by the realization, she said with a commendable

veneer of scorn, "Dear me, are you this protective of everyone in the village, or just a select few?"

"Every last one, Diana," he declared flatly. "These people have stood shoulder to shoulder with my family for centuries, and in more recent times, proved their loyalty to me in ways I'll never forget. So you may be assured I'll come down with a very heavy hand on anyone looking to take advantage of them."

"I'll bear that in mind," she said. "Now, if that's all…?"

He stood up, all lithe, elegant six feet plus of him blocking out the sun and leaving her chilled in his shade. "That's all—unless you decide to take me up on my proposition, that is, in which case, by all means feel free to get in touch." He dropped a business card on the table. "You can reach me at this number, anytime."

Hell will freeze over first, Monsieur le Comte! she thought, watching as he stalked away. *I'll go home empty-handed before I turn to you for anything.*

She was still simmering with resentment when Henri emerged from the kitchen, carrying a basket of hot rolls, a flat dish of butter curls and a little pot of preserves. "For your *petit déjeuner,*" he announced, setting them before her, and spreading a red linen napkin over her lap. "Would you like more coffee to go with them?"

The little square was deserted, and the inn only just stirring to life. Not about to squander such a heaven-sent opportunity, she said, "Thank you, I would, Henri, and I'd like it even better if you poured a cup for yourself and kept me company a while."

He agreed willingly enough, settling his bulk on the hard metal chair, a thick cup of black coffee cradled between his big hands. "My wife made the *confitures* from berries my granddaughter picked last week," he told her, watching as she buttered a roll, "and the brioches I baked myself, just this morning."

"You take care of all the meals, do you?"

"*Oui, madame!* Cooking is what I do best."

"Don't you get tired, working such long hours?"

"I'm used to it," he said, cheerfully. "It is my life, and I have five brothers I can count on for extra help, should I need it."

She could have pretended this was the first she'd heard about his large family, but she was already knee-deep enough in lies she'd have preferred to avoid and saw no point in compounding them unnecessarily. "So Monsieur de Valois told me, last night." She paused, filled with trepidation, now that the moment she'd anticipated was finally at hand. In the next few minutes, he could breathe new life into her hopes, or dash them to pieces.

Her heart thudded so violently, she was sure Henri must be able to hear it; could surely see how its fluttering agitation made the front of her blouse quiver. "Five brothers...but also a sister as well, right?"

His face lit up. "*Mais certainement, madame!* My sister, Jeanne."

"Does she help you out here, too?"

"She would, if she had the time," he said. "But she is kept too busy running the château for le Comte."

"*She works for the...him?*"

Her question exploded in shock before she could contain it, but Henri didn't appear to notice anything amiss. "*Oui.* She is his..." He tugged at his earlobe, searching without success to find the right word. "In French, we call her his *gouvernante.*"

"His housekeeper?"

"Exactly so, *madame.* She and her husband have been employed at the château for many years. Since they were newlyweds, some twenty-five years ago, in fact. Gregoire is in charge of the vineyards, and—"

"She got married when she was nineteen?"

Too late, she realized her slip. "How did you know that, *madame?*" Henri inquired, narrow-eyed suddenly.

Floundering, she stammered, "Well, I didn't, not really. It was a wild guess, based on the fact that Monsieur de Valois said she was fifteen years...younger than...you...."

"And why would he tell you my age?"

She closed her eyes, and wished she'd done the same with her mouth, before she managed to put both feet in it.

You'll never carry this off, Carol had predicted. *You're just not the undercover type. Sooner or later, you'll trip yourself up—and knowing you, it'll probably be sooner.*

How right she'd been!

"Because I said you seem much too young to be a grandfather," she babbled, desperately trying to patch the holes she'd inadvertently poked in the fabric of her cover-up. "You know how we Americans are, Henri—obsessed with our weight and age, to the exclusion of just about everything else. For a man of your years to look so youthful…well, you'd be the envy of people half your age, in my country."

She was stretching the truth considerably, but she'd learned well, during her marriage, the need to stroke a man's ego when necessary, and could only hope Henri was as susceptible to flattery as her ex-husband had been.

It appeared that he was. "It is the diet," he proclaimed mollified. "The olive oil is good for the skin, the garlic good for the health and the tomatoes good for the manliness."

She wasn't sure quite what he meant by his last remark, nor did she care to find out. His masculine prowess was none of her business. His sister, however, very well might be. "Something must be working in the women's favor, too," she suggested lightly. "Imagine having seven children, and six of them boys! Your mother deserves a medal. Were you all born here?"

"*Oui, madame.* All seven of us in the same house, on Rue Sainte Agathe, where my youngest brother now stays with his wife and three children, and to this day we all live within a few miles of each other. It is the way to keep families close."

Diana couldn't have asked for a better lead-in. "I suppose it is, but did none of you ever want to go farther afield, and see a bit more of the world?"

"Never the boys," he said, little realizing what a loaded question she'd asked. "We were working men from the day we finished our schooling."

"What about your sister?"

He grimaced. "Ah, Jeanne was different—a rebel, if you like, with her head full of unrealistic dreams."

Sensing she was on the brink of vital discovery, Diana struggled to keep a lid on her excitement. "Unrealistic how?"

"She wanted too much, more than she had a right to expect, and when she decided she wouldn't find it here, she ran away from home when she was only sixteen, leaving behind nothing but a note saying she had gone to Marseille. The shame almost killed our mother and father."

"Shame?"

"*Oui, madame.* Society sees things differently now, but in those days, good girls did not risk their reputations by acting so recklessly. My little sister darkened our family name with her actions."

Good girls? Diana almost choked on her anger. How about *frightened* girls? *Desperate* girls? Girls who made a mistake and had no one to turn to in their trouble? Or didn't they count? Was it only the sons who mattered? "Didn't you at least try to find her?"

"*Bien sûr!* My brothers and I searched the streets of Marseille for many days. But it is a large city, and unless you have tried to locate someone who doesn't wish to be found, you cannot know how impossible a task you set yourself."

Not impossible, Henri, Diana thought, her heart bleeding for the young woman who increasingly fit the mold of her lost mother. *You just have to want it badly enough not to be fooled by false leads.* "So what are you saying? That you gave up on her?"

"Never that! But we were not miracle workers, and by then had wives and babies of our own waiting for us here, at home. Jeanne had chosen to follow a wild path, and in the end, she had to live with that."

Containing herself with difficulty, Diana said, "How would you ever have forgiven yourselves, if something bad had happened to her?"

"Ah, but we knew she was alive and well, because every once in a while, she would phone here, to the inn, and tell us so."

At that, Diana's rage spilled over. For grown men to be so willfully naive struck her as unforgivable. *"And you believed her?"*

"What other choice did we have?" Henri raised his hands, palms up, and rolled his eyes. "We learned to be content with what she gave us, and to hear her voice was better than silence. She had made her choice, and there was nothing we could do but accept it, and hope she would eventually come back to us. Which, after several months, she did." A beatific smile split his face. "What is it they say, that there's no place like home?"

"How did she explain her absence?"

"She didn't," he admitted. "She never spoke a word of how she made enough money to live on."

"And it never occurred to you to ask?"

He flung her a dark glance. "A pretty girl, with no means of supporting herself, alone in a city like Marseille? We were better off not knowing! It was enough that she'd learned her lesson. As she most surely had. Even though my parents forgave her and welcomed her with open arms, she wasn't the same girl who'd left us, almost seven months earlier. There was a pensiveness to her, an air of that sorrow that clung to her like a mist which never disperses, no matter how hot the sun might shine. She has it still, to this day."

You'd have it, too, if your firstborn was taken from your arms and given to strangers! "Poor girl. She was so young—too young, to bear so much alone."

"She was not alone for very long," Henri said, misunderstanding. "Within a very short time, she fell in love with Gregoire Delancie. They became engaged a year later, and married a year after that. She was fortunate that such a good man wanted her. To many, she would have been considered soiled goods. As it was, she had a husband, and the Mesdames de Valois, who were by then living at the château, were so kind as to offer her respectable work."

Doing what? Catering to the boy who was to become Count? Cooking his meals, laundering his clothes, picking up after him and generally being at his beck and call, twenty-four hours a day? Again, Diana had to swallow her indignation.

"She is a very lucky woman," Henri stated, heaving himself to his feet. "And I will be one very sorry man if my wife discovers me gossiping with you, when I should be preparing the ratatouille for tonight's meal." He gave her a quaint little bow. "*À toute à l'heure, madame!* It was a pleasure talking to you."

"Yes," Diana replied with a smile, though her next move already taking shape in her mind. "See you later, Henri."

Anton's card remained where he'd dropped it on the table. Half an hour earlier, she'd have said nothing would induce her to touch it. Now, though, she reached for it gingerly, wishing there was some other way, one that wouldn't involve such a complete loss of face. But pride had no place in her dilemma. As the old saying went, she couldn't afford to look a gift horse in the mouth, not even one as disturbingly attractive as the incomparable Count, not when he presented the means for her to get to know the woman she was now convinced was her birth mother.

He picked up his phone on the first ring.

"I've given the matter some thought and changed my mind," she informed him, plunging into what she had to say without preamble, before she gagged on the humiliation of having to retract her previously scornful dismissal of his proposition. "If your offer from this morning still stands, I'm prepared to accept it."

So help her, she thought, holding her breath, if he gloated, she'd slam down the phone so hard, he'd rupture an eardrum.

But, "The offer still stands, Diana," he said neutrally. "How soon can you start?"

"How soon would you like me to start?"

"This afternoon. Get your stuff together, and I'll pick you up."

"There's no need for that. I have my own car."

"If it's that pitiful piece of junk parked behind the inn, it's leaking oil and has a flat tire."

"Then I'll rent something else."

"I'm afraid not. The nearest leasing outfit is fifty kilometers east of here, so stop arguing and start packing. I'll be there in half an hour."

Who did he think he was talking to? Grinding her teeth in fury, she fought the impulse to tell him to take his job and stuff it down his throat, and instead replied meekly, "That doesn't give me much time, Anton."

"Half an hour, Diana," he repeated implacably, and broke the connection.

He drove a dark green Range Rover that smelled of leather and money. "Are you going to tell me what brought about such a sudden change of heart?" he asked, sparing her a fleeting glance before returning his attention to the road winding through shady olive groves and neat vineyards, to the château on the hill.

"I decided the positives of helping you outweighed the negatives," she said blandly, having prepared herself to answer just such a question. "I enjoy meeting people, and I've never lived in a castle before."

His mouth curved in amusement. "Come now, Diana! It was having to share a bathroom at the inn that persuaded you."

"That, too," she said, reminding herself she couldn't afford to like this man too much. But that did nothing to diminish the impact of his smile.

Harvey seldom smiled at all, unless he was trying to impress someone, she recalled, and even then, his mouth remained pinched, as if the effort pained him. "Medicine is serious business," he used to say. "The things I see on the operating table don't leave much room for levity."

Why did it take Anton de Valois for her to recognize such a statement for the pretentious nonsense it was?

"I asked my housekeeper to prepare a suite for you," Anton continued, steering around the last bend in the road. "Although the original château was built over six hundred years ago, much has been done to bring it into the twenty-first century, and I think you'll find it very comfortable. Once you're settled in, we'll have lunch, and talk about what your work entails."

Up close, the château and its surroundings were even more breathtaking than from a distance. Immediately ahead, a long, straight avenue bordered by Lombardy poplars ended at what was once a fortified gateway.

The house itself sat on a small rise, with sweeping views of the vineyards and more distant lavender fields. Dark blue slate covered the steep mansard roof, but the walls were of stone, dappled in shades varying from palest lemon to deep honey-gold by the angle of the sun. Flowers bracketed the doorways and spilled exuberantly from windowsills rising three stories from the ground. Above them, graceful turrets and parapets gleamed against a background of intense blue sky.

Diana stared, awestruck. The closest she'd ever come to such a spectacular scene was in the books of fairy tales she'd devoured as a child. "Anton, your home is magnificent!"

"It has its drawbacks," he said, "but for the most part, it'll do."

"You must need an army of staff to look after it."

"A small army to tend the grounds and take care of general maintenance, certainly, but not that many to look after the running of the house. Except for special occasions, when I bring in outside help, we get by with a housekeeper, cook and four maids."

"That seems like a lot, for just three people."

"I like to spread the load. It might have been acceptable in the old days for household staff to work fourteen-hour days, seven days a week, but it's not my idea of fair treatment."

Well, she could hardly take issue with that sentiment. "I'm sure your employees appreciate your consideration."

Another smile touched his mouth. "It cuts both ways, Diana. Treat people well, and they generally give back in kind."

They'd reached the top of the avenue by then. The Range Rover cruised under the gateway and into a forecourt where another vehicle, an old Mercedes convertible covered in dust, was parked haphazardly to one side of the steps leading to the château's massive front door.

At the sight of it, Anton's expression darkened forbiddingly. "I hope that doesn't mean what I think it does," he growled.

As if she'd been waiting for her cue to appear, a woman stepped out from the château's dim interior. "Surprise, Anton!" she trilled in a throaty contralto, slinking down the steps with the stealthy grace of some exotic, overbred cat.

Heaving a sigh, he stepped out of the car, submitted to her embrace and replied with markedly less enthusiasm, "Hello, Sophie. Surprise, indeed. I wasn't expecting you."

Not the least put out by his cool reception, she laughed and, with the kind of confidence Diana envied, cooed, "But now that I'm here, you're glad to see me, *oui?*"

"As long as you don't mind keeping yourself entertained. I can't spare much time to play host."

"With you, *mon cher,*" she replied, winding her arm through his and leaning against him suggestively, "a little goes a very long way!"

Feeling very much like a third wheel, Diana slid out of the Range Rover and tried to blend into the background, but she'd have done better to remain out of sight in the car. Belatedly realizing that he'd not arrived alone, Sophie unglued herself from Anton's side, and fixed Diana in a stare that stripped her to the bone. "And who, may I ask, is this?"

"Diana Reeves," he said, starting to unload Diana's luggage from the back of the Range Rover.

"And she's moving in with you?" Sophie's formerly purring tones soared dramatically.

"Oui. She has very kindly agreed to conduct tours of the château and gardens, until such time as I can find someone else to take on the job."

"Oh, just an *employee!*" Sophie flipped her elegant hand dismissively. "You had me worried, *mon cher* Anton! For a moment, I thought she was *someone.*"

"Stop behaving badly, Sophie, or I'll send you packing," he warned her severely. "Diana, this is Sophie Beauvais, a distant cousin on my mother's side of the family, and I apologize for her appalling manners, since it's unlikely that she'll see fit to do so."

"Hi," Diana said, and left it at that, since it was obvious the woman wasn't the least bit interested in being introduced to anyone who wasn't *someone.*

But that one word was enough to send Sophie's eyebrows shooting skyward. "You're American?"

"Yes."

"Well, unless you have a permit, you're not allowed to work while you're here."

"Technically she's not working, because she's not accepting payment for services," Anton intervened. "She's simply a houseguest who's offered to help out a friend, and that, I believe, is perfectly legitimate, no matter where she's from."

"I'm not sure the authorities would agree, Anton."

She had to be the most unpleasant creature in the whole of France, and the thought of having to placate her, enough to turn a person's stomach. But it was either that, or risk having her entire plan of operation derailed, and Diana had come too far to allow that to happen. "Look at it this way," she said, gagging inwardly at the conciliatory tone she was forced to adopt. "My being here frees Anton to spend more time with you."

Sophie regarded her a moment, eyes narrowed appraisingly. "I hadn't thought of it in that light. Perhaps keeping you around isn't such a bad idea, after all."

"Of course it's not." Taking perverse pleasure in the killing glare Anton directed at her behind his cousin's back, Diana continued, "Just enjoy your visit, and forget I'm even here."

The truce, if indeed it could be called that, soon ended. "You're forgotten already, *mademoiselle,*" the revolting creature declared, turning away. "Anton, *mon cher,* let one of the hired help lug those suitcases inside, and pour me a glass of wine before lunch, won't you?"

"I'll pour us all a glass. Come with me, Diana." He cupped her elbow, and under cover of ushering her up the steps, muttered grimly, "*Mon dieu,* you're turning out to be more trouble than you're worth!"

"I have no idea what you're talking about," she said, his warm breath arousing such unmentionable sensations in her ear that she went weak at the knees.

"Certainly you do, trying to land me in the hot seat with that woman! Obviously I'm going to have to set out a few ground rules, but it'll have to wait because, right now, my housekeeper is waiting to greet you."

She looked up then, and at the sight of the woman standing in the shadow of the great doorway, everything to do with him and his obnoxious cousin fled Diana's mind. Her breath froze, her palms grew damp, her throat closed and her senses swam to the point that she was afraid she might pass out.

"Diana," Anton said, his words seeming to float toward her from very far away, "may I introduce my housekeeper, Jeanne Delancie. Jeanne, this is Diana Reeves, our house guest."

"*Bonjour, madame,*" the housekeeper said, the singsong accent of Provence gentle in her voice. "*Bienvenue au Château de Valois.*"

Of course, it was her mother. Her eyes were not blue, as

she'd expected, but one glance into their clear brown depths, and that visceral instinct Diana had relied on to guide her, told her with utter certainty that she'd come face-to-face, at last, with her birth mother.

It was all she could do not to fling herself into the woman's arms and burst out crying. Fortunately Anton retained a firm enough grip on her elbow to make such a move impossible.

CHAPTER FIVE

"SHE'S never going to be able to handle the job, Anton. For pity's sake, she could hardly bring herself to speak to that housekeeper of yours. How do you suppose she's going to cope with a mob of tourists plying her with questions?"

"I'm sure she'll be perfectly fine," he said, which was an outright lie. Although not about to admit it to Sophie, he'd been completely taken aback by Diana's tongue-tied response to Jeanne.

His cousin held out her glass for a refill. "That's easy to say, but how much do you really know about her?"

Not nearly enough, obviously. Just when he thought he had a handle on what she was all about, she challenged his perceptions yet again. How she could have dealt so skillfully with Sophie, who had to be the most volatile and contrary individual he ever hoped to meet, yet not be able to string two words together with soft-spoken, softhearted Jeanne, added one more layer to the enigma calling herself Diana Reeves. "Perhaps she's shy."

"She's socially inept, *mon amour!* Wherever did you find her?"

"She was staying at the inn. I ran into her by accident, last night."

Sophie let fly with a squawk of laughter. "Staying at the inn? That should have been enough to tell you she's not the sharpest knife in the drawer! No one, least of all an American used to the very latest in modern conveniences, would willingly subject herself to the primitive conditions *that* place has to offer."

In his view, the unpretentious simplicity of the inn was its most appealing characteristic, but Sophie's conclusions regarding American women's tastes in hotel accommodation coincided exactly with his own. Again not disposed to share the fact with Sophie, he shrugged and said idly, "Why else do you think I invited her to stay here?"

"Because you're much too gallant for your own good—although turning over the Ivory Suite to her wasn't very kind when you know it's my favorite place to stay when I'm visiting." She eyed him coyly over the rim of her glass. "On the other hand, the suite I've been assigned is much closer to yours."

God preserve me! he thought, making a mental note to lock his door every night. "Exactly why *did* you decide on this sudden visit, Sophie? The last I heard, you were playing house with some man in Paris."

"He bored me to tears. All he cared about was his work. We'd never have made a go of it together, so I moved out."

In other words, he wasn't prepared to be your next meal ticket and kicked you out! "I'm sorry."

"Don't be," she said, tucking one leg under her and managing to display several inches of sleek thigh in the process. "I'm not interested in another divorce. My next husband is going to be my last."

"After three failed marriages, I'm surprised you'd even consider a fourth."

"It'll be different, the next time. Before, I've made do with second best, because the man I really wanted wasn't available, but that's no longer the case." She dipped her finger in her wine. "Marie-Louise has been gone almost three years. Don't you miss having a wife, Anton? A sympathetic ear to listen to your troubles, after a hard day? A warm, willing body in your bed at night?"

He didn't care for the hungry gleam in her eye, or the suggestive way she slipped her finger in her mouth, then drew it slowly out again. He had nothing against marriage, or sex, but he'd gladly swear off both before he got involved in either with his cousin, Sophie. He wasn't fond of black widow spiders.

Just then, Diana came out to the terrace. "Hope I haven't kept you waiting," she said, appearing more herself again. "I decided to unpack my suitcases before I came down for lunch."

"Your timing's perfect," he assured her, more grateful for her interruption than she could begin to realize. "How do you like your rooms?"

"Oh, they're…luxurious! My goodness, I feel like a princess!"

And if it weren't for the fact that you're the most duplicitous woman I've ever met, you could well pass for one, he thought, taking note of her elegant carriage. "I'm glad you're pleased. If there's anything you need, you have only to ask Jeanne."

"I know. She told me the same thing." She ducked her head diffidently, once again adopting the role of a naif suddenly unsure of herself in sophisticated company. "She was very kind, very helpful."

"Why wouldn't she be, Diana?" he asked silkily. "Unless you're presenting yourself as something you're not, I'm sure she'll take great pleasure in making you feel right at home."

Her blush told him his comment had found its mark, and part of him took savage satisfaction in knowing he was one step ahead of her and whatever scheme she was cooking up. But another part—a weaker part he despised—experienced a stab of disappointment that she couldn't be as sweetly innocent as she so often seemed.

"That's more than can be said for the way your housekeeper treats me," Sophie pouted. "Frankly, Anton, I don't find her very welcoming at all."

Switching personalities yet again, Diana spoke up in spirited defense of the woman whom, at first sight, she'd appeared to find intimidating. "Perhaps because she has enough to do running such a large household, without the aggravation of having guests drop in unexpectedly."

"If you feel that strongly, perhaps *you* should lend her a hand—when you're not fulfilling your other duties around here, that is," Sophie retaliated.

In no mood to referee a catfight, Anton seated Diana on his left, put Sophie on his right and heaved an audible sigh of relief as the maids showed up to serve lunch.

The best part of the meal, Diana decided, was not the cold cucumber soup, or prawns in aspic, wonderful though they were, but the fact that the inimical Sophie pretty much drank herself into a stupor and staggered off to take a siesta before dessert and coffee were served.

"I don't think she approves of me," she told Anton ruefully, still smarting from some of his cousin's more barbed remarks.

"Don't take it personally," he said. "Sophie doesn't like too many women, especially not those she perceives to be a threat."

A startled laugh escaped her. "Oh, please! I can hardly be considered a threat!"

His mouth tightened ominously. "False modesty ill becomes you, Diana. You've looked in the mirror. You know very well that most men find you attractive. Even Henri has fallen under your spell."

But not you, she thought, wondering what had brought about his black mood. He'd been unusually curt throughout lunch, and at first she'd put it down to his irritation with Sophie's constant need to be the center of attention. Now, though, with his cousin removed from the scene, he seemed more annoyed than ever.

"Are you upset with me, Anton?" she ventured. "Have I done something to offend you?"

He flung her a glance simmering with pent-up emotion.

Passion…or anger? She couldn't tell. Knew only that the air between them crackled with tension.

"If I didn't know better," he said, wrestling himself under control, "I'd say you had a guilty conscience. Of course, I'd be mistaken…wouldn't I?"

"Not entirely," she admitted, running her tongue over lips suddenly gone dry. "I feel I'm imposing on your hospitality. All this…" She indicated the china and heavy sterling cutlery, both embossed with the de Valois family crest, the cut crystal water goblets. "Well, it's rather more opulent than what I expected when I agreed to work for you. I'd feel a lot more comfortable if we could get down to business and you told me exactly what my duties entail. If I'm going to take on the job, I'd like to do it well."

"It's really quite simple. If you're done with your meal—"

"I'm done."

He rose abruptly from the table. "Then rather than tell you what's involved, I'll show you. Come with me."

She followed him to the grand entrance hall. "Since the tour groups assemble here, we'll start on this level, and work our way up," he began. "Notice that the floors and stairs are made of carrara marble, imported from Italy. The château itself is over six hundred years old and has seen a number of changes over the centuries, not all of them desirable, but my grandfather embarked on a complete restoration to preserve the integrity of the original design, while implementing modern innovations that make it not just a historical treasure, but a comfortable home for me and my heirs."

"That's a lot of information to digest, and you've barely begun," she said, desperate to ease the tension still arcing between them. "Should I be making notes on the palm of my hand?"

"No." He fixed her in an unsmiling glance. "You should stop interrupting and pay attention."

"I'm trying to, but—"

"Try harder," he snapped, and manacling her wrist in an iron grip, drew her behind him as he marched across the hall. "Certain areas only are open to the public. The family's apartments are private, as you'd expect. Here on the main floor, we have the chapel, the ballroom, the formal banquet hall and the entrance to the wine cellar. One floor up, you'll find the library, the formal drawing room and the ladies' parlor. And among other things on the top floor, the bedroom where a seventeenth-century Pope, Clement the Eighth, is reputed to have slept."

She nodded as if she was obediently drinking in everything he told her when, if truth be known, she was so vividly conscious of his fingers wrapped around her wrist, so powerfully entrapped in his magnetic field, that he might as well have been speaking in ancient tongues.

At such close quarters, she could detect his aftershave and just the faintest shadow of new beard darkening his lean jaw. Every time he glanced at her, his lashes swept down, dense and black above the dramatic silver-gray of his irises. His dark hair lay thick and glossy against his well-shaped head.

Unaware that her mind was straying, he continued to pepper her with information. "The family quarters are roped off, although you'll have to keep an eye out for the odd tourist who tries to sneak away from the group and go poking around in places he doesn't belong, but once you're familiar with the layout of the place, you won't have any trouble."

I'm already knee-deep in trouble, she thought, wishing he was revoltingly obese, or effeminate, or had chronically bad breath, instead of being so thoroughly masculine and utterly, perfectly beautiful that all she could do was fixate on his mouth and wonder how it would taste against hers. How it would feel, sliding over the heated skin of her body. "And the grounds?" she inquired faintly.

Still oblivious to his detrimental effect on her faculties, he steered her up the stairs to a large leaded window on the first landing, which overlooked a sweeping view of the south side gardens. "Again, fairly straightforward," he practically barked. "You conduct a walking tour of the area immediately below the balustraded terrace down there, pointing out the ornamental fountain, the parterre, the orange grove and the hundred-year-old oak trees on the island in the middle of the man-made lake. If you like, you may stop by the crypt—you can see its roof just beyond that stand of pines to your right—where generations of de Valoises lay entombed, but not everyone's into burial sites, so you have to use your judgment on that one."

But I don't trust my judgment anymore, she thought helplessly. *If I did, I wouldn't be allowing my thoughts to stray to matters totally inappropriate both to the present situation, and my personal circumstances. I've just come out of a marriage I thought would last forever. To be entertaining sexual fantasies about any man, least of all this proud, autocratic Frenchman, is emotional suicide.*

"This area usually arouses a lot of interest, so you might need to brush up on your art history," he went on, turning down a long gallery on the third floor, whose walls were lined with paintings. "For example, this is a Renoir, and there's a Caravaggio over there, with a Rubens hanging next to it."

"Don't you worry someone might try to steal them?"

"Not in the least. They're wired to an alarm system. Anyone so much as touches a frame, and all hell breaks loose at the central switchboard."

The gallery was fairly dim, probably because the only lighting came from concealed floods designed to showcase the art, but one painting, a portrait of a couple, done in oils, drew her attention. "I don't recognize this artist or the subject. Is it very well-known?"

"No," Anton said. "It's of my great-grandparents, and was painted by a friend of theirs, in the late 1930s."

Unlike most stiffly-posed, husband-wife portraits of that era, this couple had been depicted in the château gardens. She half-reclined at his feet, all dreamy elegance in a flowing, blush-pink dress, with a Japanese parasol at her side. He smiled down at her from his high-backed wicker chair, his hand resting on her shoulder. "They look as if they were very much in love."

"I'm told they were," he said briefly, turning away.

But Diana lingered, cast them one last glance, then, to her horror, heard herself ask, "Did you love your wife?"

He stopped dead in his tracks, his spine so rigid, he might have been turned to stone. "Of course I did."

She should let the matter drop there. Be satisfied that he hadn't told her in no uncertain terms that his relationship with his late wife was none of her business. But she couldn't help herself. She had to know more. "Do you still mourn her death?"

"Not the way I once did. Why is this of interest to you?"

"I'm wondering how long it takes to get over losing someone."

"I'd say that depends on the individual, and the reason the connection was broken."

"I thought I'd never stop loving Harvey, but now I find myself wondering what it was I ever saw in him. Is it wrong, do you think, that I'm already forgetting what he looks like?"

"Not wrong at all. It's a sign that you're ready to put the past to rest, and move on."

Ironically they'd reached the end of the gallery and could go no farther because a heavy door blocked access to the remainder of that part of the house. Although he no longer held her by the wrist, Anton stood close enough for his body to brush hers as he swung back to face her. She had to crane her neck to look at him. To look into those remarkable eyes, which could change in an instant from dusky moonlight to stormy gray. And at that moment, the storm reigned supreme, filling them with anguish.

"Move on to what?" she asked.

Their glances held. His breath caught. He lifted his hand. Let it ghost over her hair and down her cheek. "This," he ground out, and brought his mouth down on hers.

She thought it would end there; that he'd quickly pull away and swipe the back of his hand over his mouth to rid himself of the taste of her. Instead he lifted his head just long enough to cradle her face between his palms, then kissed her again.

She'd been kissed before, and not only by Harvey, but never in quite the way that Anton de Valois went about it. His mouth was an instrument of sublime torture beside which all other men's faded into insignificance, not because he used his tongue or teeth to seduce her, but because he teamed raging passion with circumspection, and turned them into an art that left her aching. Rather than tightening in rejection, her lips softened beneath his in total submission. Instead of shoving him away, as any woman with a grain of concern for self-preservation would have, she sank against him and clutched a fistful of his shirt.

It wasn't right. She wasn't ready for such an experience. But telling herself so didn't prevent the taut suspense in her body from finding release in a sudden damp explosion between her thighs. Most humiliating of all, it didn't silence the pitiful little moan that escaped her throat when he at last ended the kiss and she sagged, weak-kneed, against the door at her back. *Dear heaven!*

"I shouldn't have done that," he muttered harshly, his chest heaving and torment etched in every line of his face, "but I'd be lying if I didn't say I'd like to do it again."

"Why don't you, then?" she whispered.

Disgust darkened his expression. "Because we're both past the age to be making out in dark corners like a couple of hormone-driven teenagers."

Quickly, before she passed beyond all shame and begged him to take her somewhere more private where they could behave like consenting adults, she said shakily, "Yes, we certainly are. So to get back to business, what else is there to see up here?"

He held her gaze for a moment before replying. "The bedchamber where the Pope supposedly slept. It's the first room on the left as you come into the gallery. During the tours, the door is left open, with a small viewing area just inside. Of the remaining two suites, one is a baby's nursery, furnished as it would have been in the seventeenth century, with nanny quarters attached, and the other a governess's apartment, complete with small classroom. We'll take a look at them before we leave."

"And this door, here?" Unlike the rest, which were heavily carved, with wide, ornate casings, the one blocking off the end of the gallery consisted of a solid oak slab of more recent vintage, although the keyhole was large and elaborate to complement the antiquity of those on the remaining doors.

"Leads to the east wing and is kept locked at all times."

"Why?"

"Because that part of the château is no longer in use."

That she'd said the wrong thing again was immediately apparent. His tone was glacial, his expression remote, his eyes the color of flint. "I'm sorry I asked," she said.

"Forget it. You had no way of knowing."

Forget it? How was that possible, when, after a cursory glance into the aforementioned rooms, he swept her through the rest of the château, so clearly anxious to complete the tour and be rid of her that she could barely keep up with him?

"…coffered ceiling in the library…rare first editions…family bible on table…recorded births and deaths going back four hundred years…seating for a hundred in the banquet hall…still used on occasion…same with ballroom…frescoed dome there merits extra attention…floor highly polished…make sure no one steps off the runners…don't need any lawsuits…."

He rattled off facts, spitting them out like bullets as he fairly raced her through the remaining rooms. Then, returning to the great hall just as the long case clock struck three, he informed her that he had other matters requiring his attention, that cocktails were at seven, that they dressed for dinner at eight, but not black tie except on special occasions, that she'd do well to review what she'd learned, and prepare herself to start conducting visitors on Tuesday of the following week.

"That allows you plenty of time to settle in, find your way around and learn what you need to know," he finished.

"You've got to be kidding!" she exclaimed, but might as well have saved her breath because, lord of the manor to the core, he'd already stalked away down the hall to what she presumed must be the west wing, leaving her, lowly hand-maiden that she was, standing there dumbfounded and wondering what the devil she'd gotten herself into.

"It's a lot to take in all at once, isn't it?" another, kinder voice observed, and looking up, Diana found Jeanne observing her from the same corridor down which Anton had disappeared.

"A lot?" She blew out a frustrated breath. "It's impossible!" *He* was impossible!

"Try not to worry. It'll all fall into place, you'll see."

"I'm not so sure of that." She pressed her fingers to her throbbing temples. "Everything's so jumbled up in my head, it feels as if it's about to burst."

Her mother touched her arm sympathetically. "Let me make you a cup of tea, *madame*. It'll help you relax."

A rush of tears barely held in check caught Diana by surprise. I'm not Madame, I'm your daughter! she ached to say, but knew she couldn't, not yet, and perhaps never. Perhaps she'd eventually leave this place with her mother none the wiser of the bond they shared.

"Madame? You would like tea?"

"Thank you, I'd love some, but only if you'll join me." Then, sensing her mother's hesitation, she rushed to add, "Please, Jeanne! You'd be doing me an enormous favor. As I understand it, you've worked here for so long, you must know the place like the back of your hand, and I desperately need some help sorting out my information."

"Well, if you don't mind coming to my office…?"

"I don't mind."

In truth, she'd have walked over fire for the chance to spend more time alone with her mother. The few minutes they'd shared when Jeanne had shown her to her suite of rooms had been all too brief.

Under any other circumstances, Diana would have been totally entranced by the restful ivory and sage-green decor of her little sitting room, with its silk upholstered love seat and lady's *escritoire;* by the four-poster bed in the large sleeping chamber, and the elegant appointments of the marble bathroom. But her attention had been focused mainly on Anton's housekeeper. She'd found no evidence, in Jeanne's steady gaze and gentle smile, of the young rebel who'd run away to bear a child alone. Rather, under that calm and kindly demeanor, she'd detected a woman tamed by grief. A woman designed all through to be a mother, but robbed of the opportunity.

Accompanying her now down the corridor to her office, Diana wasn't sure what to expect. Something low-ceilinged, cramped and distinctly "below stairs," probably. But the light, airy room into which she stepped was spacious, functional and charming.

Two large computer desks filled one wall, each with a window at eye level offering views of the stables and a hillside filled with ruler-straight rows of grapevines. Bookcases and filing cabinets took up space on another wall. A table filled the middle of the floor, piled with neat stacks of mail and brochures.

Next to where she stood, just inside the door, a calendar, the week's menus and a list of household supplies needing to be purchased were pinned to a cork board. On the fourth wall were mullioned doors, similar to those in her own suite, but where hers gave access to a narrow balcony, these opened to a walled courtyard large enough to accommodate a wrought-iron table shaded by an umbrella, two comfortable chairs, a ceramic planter overflowing with scarlet geraniums and a small stone fountain.

This was no corner of a damp, miserable basement, Diana had to admit, and nor was Jeanne its Cinderella. Her pale gray shirtdress was smart and fashionable, her shoes, though built for comfort, stylish. She wore lipstick, a trace of eye shadow, a hint of perfume. Pearl stud earrings peeked out beneath her short, curly hair, and an old-fashioned diamond engagement ring nested beside her wedding band.

"I'd like tea for two, please, Odette," she instructed, speaking into an intercom on the desk. "And a plate of shortbread, please."

At first, they sat in the courtyard, sipped fragrant Earl Grey tea and sampled little coins of lavender-studded shortbread so light they melted on the tongue. Then her mother pushed aside the tray and produced a floor plan of the château, the kind sold to tourists from the gift shop at the lavender distillery. With her help, Diana marked the route she'd follow when she conducted her tours and made notes of the facts she needed to memorize.

"You see?" Jeanne said, when they were done. "It's really not so complicated, after all. Basically the west wing is off-limits to the public. The family has exclusive use of the upper two floors. The Count's office, the administration office, central switchboard and staff quarters occupy the ground floor."

Diana knew she shouldn't, but she couldn't help herself. Still smarting from the way Anton had kissed her as if he couldn't get enough of her one minute, and shut her out completely, the next, she said, "Why is the upper east wing closed off?"

Her mother hesitated briefly, then lifted her shoulders in a faint, regretful shrug. "Maintaining a house as large as this is labor intensive and cost prohibitive. It makes no sense to waste time and money on rooms that stand empty all year and are of little historical interest to tourists."

"Has it never been used?"

"It was, once." Again, Jeanne hesitated. "But...not recently."

She seemed uncomfortable talking about it which, added to the way Anton had shut down on her when she'd questioned him on the same subject, served only to sharpen Diana's curiosity. But she could hardly remark on that to her mother, whose loyalty to her employer was evident.

Instead she turned the conversation to something that mattered to her a great deal more than a moldy set of empty rooms. "Do you enjoy your work here, Jeanne?"

"Very much. My husband and I are given free rein in our separate endeavors, treated with kindness and respect, and rewarded well for our labors. What more could we ask for?"

What, indeed? Yet for all that she seemed in cheerful command of her world, Henri had put it well when he said there was a stillness to Jeanne, a hint of sorrow that never went away. It showed in the sometimes faraway look in her big brown eyes, as if, no matter how pleasing the present might be, or how rosy the future, she couldn't quite let go of the past.

Or was that wishful thinking on her part, Diana wondered.

"So this is where you are, *mon ange,* whiling away the afternoon in idle gossip when you should be preparing my dinner!" The man stepping out of the château to lean over Jeanne's chair and drop a kiss on her head was tall and slender, with the nut-brown skin of one who'd spent a lifetime working long hours in the sun.

"Gregoire!" Jeanne sprang up from her seat, the lilt in her voice, the smile on her face, that of a young girl in love. "I didn't expect you back so soon. Madame Reeves, this is my dear husband, Gregoire."

"I am delighted to meet you, *madame,*" he said. "And I apologize if I was overly familiar with my remarks just now. I didn't realize you're a guest of the Count."

"I'm very happy to meet you, too," Diana said. "And I'm actually a working guest, which isn't quite the same thing. So will you both please forget the Madame Reeves business, and call me Diana?"

Gregoire Delancie's inscrutable blue eyes subjected her to

a thorough inspection. "If you wish. Jeanne, my love, you're needed in the kitchen. Something to do with the pear sauce for tonight's dessert, I'm told."

"Then I'd better see what's it's about." She turned to Diana with a smile. "You will excuse me, Diana?"

"Of course. I should be leaving anyway. Thank you, Jeanne. You've been a great help. Goodbye, Gregoire."

"Goodbye," he returned, stiffly enough that she knew without his having to say so that he hoped she wouldn't make a habit of invading their quarters. Nor, she noticed, did he use her given name.

Why doesn't he like me? she wondered, making her way back to the main part of the house and up the marble staircase.

Then she forgot about him completely because, as she reached the third-floor landing and turned into the west wing, she ran smack into Anton. And one look at his face was enough to tell her his mood was no sweeter now than it had been two hours ago.

Oh, for heaven's sake! What had she done, or not done, to find herself the object of *his* displeasure, as well? Why couldn't he turn back into that charming man from last night who seemed so thoroughly in charge of his world? Better yet, why couldn't he just take her in his arms, tell her how glad he was they'd met and kiss her again?

She found out soon enough.

CHAPTER SIX

"WHERE the devil have you been?" he demanded, taking refuge in anger, because pride wouldn't let him admit he'd been frantic at her disappearance. "I've spent the last hour and a half looking everywhere for you."

"Well, now you've found me," she said, wincing, "so please let go of my arm. You're hurting me."

He released her, shocked as much by the surge of relief that had swept over him at the sight of her, as he was by the red imprint of his fingers on her skin. "I was beginning to wonder if you'd run out on me."

"Don't think the idea didn't cross my mind."

"If I was abrupt with you earlier—"

"*Abrupt?* You were downright unpleasant!"

"It won't happen again."

"It had better not! If this afternoon was an example of what I've got to look forward to in the days ahead, you can find someone else to lead your benighted tour groups. You acted as if you'd caught me stealing the family silver, when all I did was ask a perfectly harmless question."

Harmless, Diana? he wondered, torn by conflicting emotions. *Maybe…or then again, maybe not.* "If that's the impression I gave, then I apologize. I didn't mean to offend you. The truth is, I was annoyed with myself, not you. I had no business kissing you."

"Oh." A flush tinted her face. "If it's all the same to you, I'd rather not talk about that. Can't we just forget it ever happened?"

You might be able to, he thought, the taste and feel of her so vivid in his mind that it was all he could do to keep his hands to himself, *but it'll be a long time before I can.*

In fact, it had been a long time since any woman had moved him so deeply, and *that,* if he was honest with himself, was the real root of the problem. He'd recovered from his wife's death—at least, as much as any man could, given the circumstances—and was ready to explore another relationship, but not with this enigmatic foreigner who played by rules different from the women he knew.

He'd lured her under his roof with one aim only: to uncover the real reason she'd chosen Bellevue-sur-Lac as her "holiday" destination. The phone call he'd overheard, her sudden about-face in accepting his job offer, and most especially, her frequent uneasiness around him, all pointed to an ulterior motive. Even now, with no logical reason to be nervous, she was worrying the sheet of paper she held, repeatedly rolling and unrolling it.

He'd be a fool to complicate matters further by allowing sex to enter the equation. No man was at his sharpest when he was between the sheets with a woman as beautiful as Diana Reeves.

"Well?" She tapped her dainty foot impatiently.

"Certainly we can forget it," he said. "We'll wipe the slate clean and start afresh, as of now."

"Thank you." Clearly braced for yet another confrontation, she continued to eye him warily. "So, why were you looking for me?"

"My aunts arrived home from their weekly jaunt to Aix and were anxious to meet you."

Her expression underwent a change. Grew open and filled with unfeigned warmth and interest. "So much has happened today, I'd forgotten they live with you. I'd love to meet them."

"Well, I'm afraid you'll have to postpone the pleasure until you join us for cocktails. They're dressing for dinner, now."

"Good heavens, is it that time, already? Then I should be getting dressed, too."

"Not until you answer my question," he said.

"What question is that?"

"Where did you go this afternoon, after I left you?"

"Nowhere. I was here the entire time."

"Then how is it that I couldn't find you?"

She shrugged insolently. "What can I say? You must have been looking in the wrong place. Now, if you don't mind…?"

She went to slip past him, but anticipating her move, he threw out his arm and blocked her escape. "I mind," he said flatly.

"That's your problem, Anton."

She tried to elbow him aside, and in doing so, dropped the rolled-up sheet of paper. It fluttered to the floor and landed at his feet. Smothering an exclamation of annoyance, she bent to retrieve it, but he was quicker, scooping it up before she could lay hands on it.

Recognizing it at once as part of a tourist information brochure showing the floor plan of the château, he said, "You were at the gift shop?"

"No."

"Then where did you get this?"

Another, deeper flush stained her cheeks. "Well, I didn't steal it, if that's what you're thinking."

"Don't be ridiculous! I'm thinking no such thing."

"If you must know, Jeanne gave it to me."

Puzzled, he said, "My housekeeper? Why didn't you say so in the first place?"

"I didn't want to land her in trouble. She was only trying to help me get a better fix on the layout of the château."

"Why would she be in trouble for that?"

"Because we had tea together. In her office." She flung the confession at him defiantly.

"So? Jeanne's free to entertain whomever she pleases—in her office, and just about anywhere else in this house, for that matter. She's practically a member of the family."

"Tell that to her husband. When he showed up, he couldn't get me out of there fast enough."

"Gregoire tends to be overprotective of his wife at times."

"'Unnaturally possessive' are the words I'd use to describe him. Where I come from, men don't treat their wives like chattels."

"This isn't America, Diana," he was quick to point out, "and from what you've told me about your own marriage, you're in no position to be criticizing any man for treating his wife with a good deal more respect and affection than your husband ever showed you. I'm sorry if Gregoire seemed distant, but things aren't always as they seem, and it so happens that he learned from bitter experience that it pays to be cautious with strangers."

"Well, he's got nothing to fear from me. I like Jeanne very much and certainly wish her no harm. We were having a lovely visit, until he came on the scene."

"If you say so."

"I do. Now, if you're done with the third-degree, I'd like to go to my room."

"By all means."

She gestured imperiously at the floor plan. "And I'd like to take that with me. I've marked the tour route on it, and made a few notes—all perfectly innocent, in case you're wondering!— that I need to study."

"Of course." Carefully he smoothed the curled edges of the paper flat before handing it over, then stepped aside. "I'll expect you for cocktails at seven, in the family drawing room. As I mentioned earlier, we dress for dinner here. I hope that doesn't present a problem for you?"

"Relax, Anton! I'll be there, appropriately clad. Despite

the impression I might have given, not all Americans are Neanderthals." Color still high with indignation, she swept past him.

"And I'm not a complete fool," he murmured under his breath, watching as she disappeared into her suite, and wondering what her reaction would be if she'd realized he'd taken a good look at her notes before returning them to her. "I made it clear the east wing's off-limits, so why, if you're the innocent you claim to be, did you see fit to circle a big question mark over it?"

Troubled on a number of fronts, he ran his fingers over his jaw. By her account, she and Gregoire had taken an instant dislike to one another. But Anton had known Gregoire Delancie nearly all his life, worked closely with him for more than eleven years, and in all that time the man had made only one error in judgment. That had been right after Marie-Louise's death, when he'd inadvertently said more than he should to the tabloid hunters swarming around the place.

If he'd picked up on something about the lovely Diana that didn't ring true, it bore investigation. He wasn't a man to take an irrational dislike to someone without cause.

The ping of fine crystal and murmur of voices led Diana to the family drawing room. Arriving unnoticed, she paused a moment on the threshold to survey the scene, and her immediate reaction was one of relief that she'd packed a couple of semiformal dresses among her outfits.

For a start, the sheer magnificence of the room itself merited nothing less than the best from its occupants. All graceful curving walls, tall mullioned windows swagged in silk, and sparkling chandelier sconces, it filled the entire circumference of the west wing's second floor.

Anton stood at a carved library table, pouring champagne into wafer thin flutes. Sophie, glamorous in a clinging scarlet dress whose plunging neckline revealed an enviable amount of cleavage, perched on the arm of a nearby chair, swinging one long leg negligently and practically devouring him with her eyes. Not that Diana could blame her. In a black pin-striped suit, white shirt and burgundy tie, he looked good enough to eat.

The people who captured most of Diana's attention, however, were the two ladies she assumed to be Anton's aunts. In their late sixties or early seventies, they sat close together on a lushly upholstered sofa, not far from where she stood. One wore classic black silk, the other green moire taffeta.

"We both know she's after his money," the green taffeta declared audibly, flinging a scornful glare across the room at Sophie.

"She's after his body, as well, but she won't be getting either if I have any say in the matter," the other one countered. "Anton went through enough with Marie-Louise. I'm not about to stand idly by and let this brazen trollop sink her hooks into him, just when he's ready to resume a normal life again."

The green taffeta nodded grimly. "Nor I, *ma sœur*."

Realizing the conversation wasn't intended for an outsider's ears, Diana was on the point of making her presence known when Anton happened to catch sight of her. "Diana! How long have you been standing there?"

"Hardly any time at all," she said, flustered by his welcoming smile.

It wasn't fair. No man given to bouts of irrational bad temper had any business being blessed with such an abundance of charm. It undermined her ability to arm herself against him and made her regret having snapped at him when he'd accosted her before dinner.

"Well, don't stand there waiting for an invitation. Come on in and let me introduce you to my aunts. They've been hopping with impatience to meet you." Leaving Sophie to her own devices, he drew Diana to where the two women turned to observe her with bright-eyed curiosity. "Aunt Hortense, Aunt Josette, this is Diana."

"Good evening, Diana, and welcome to the Château de Valois," Hortense, in the green taffeta, declared regally.

"Yes, welcome!" Josette echoed. "Anton told us about you, but he neglected to mention how young and pretty you are."

Too unfamiliar with titled aristocracy to know if she should address them individually as Madame la Comtesse, or even if they were Countesses to begin with, Diana opted for a safe, "Thank you, Mesdames de Valois. I'm very pleased to meet you."

"You have lovely manners, Diana. Such a rare thing among many young people, these days." Hortense shot a disapproving glance at Sophie. "But Mesdames de Valois is such a mouthful, let's dispense with the formalities. Just call us Aunt Hortense and Josette."

"And tell us about yourself." Josette patted the sofa's middle cushion. "All we know from Anton is that you're an American and you've volunteered to help out around here as tour guide this summer. What else about you is interesting and unusual?"

Anton rolled his eyes. "I'll serve the champagne," he said dryly. "I have a feeling you're going to need it, Diana."

"There's really not much else to tell," she confessed, accepting a seat between the aunts. "I'm here on holiday, speak French and can spare the time to lend a hand. That's about it."

"That's not it, at all!" Hortense shook a reproving finger. "We want to know about *you, cherie.* About your family, and where you live in America and where you went to school, and what kind of career you have."

Sophie drifted over and arranged herself in an armchair. "I'd like to hear what you've got to say about that, too. Everyone has a past, *mademoiselle.* Tell us about yours. For example, are your parents French?"

"My parents are dead," she replied, wondering what prompted such a question. "And they were American."

"So who taught you to speak such excellent French?"

"*They* did."

"Then they must have lived in France at some point. No American I've ever come across has that fine an ear for our language, unless they've spent a lot of time here."

Suppressing a twinge of uneasiness at the covert hostility in Sophie's manner, Diana said, "If they did, it was before I was born. This is the first time I've visited France."

Not the exact truth, perhaps, but close enough to pass for a little white lie.

"The first time?" Sophie regarded her skeptically. "Then why on earth would you choose to come here?"

Diana flicked a glance at Anton, remembering he'd asked her pretty much the same thing, and found him watching her now, waiting to hear her answer. "Why not? From everything I've read, Provence is a popular destination for overseas visitors."

Sophie wrinkled her nose. "But why settle for a backwater place like Bellevue-sur-Lac, when St. Tropez, Cannes and Antibes are only a stone's throw away, and have so much more to offer?"

"Because it's a beautiful, tranquil area, and the complete opposite of what I'm used to," she replied, increasingly ticked off with the woman's unrelenting stream of questions. "Why do *you* come here?"

"Because I'm family."

"Barely," Hortense intervened. "And only when it suits your convenience. Stop harassing our guest, Sophie, and let her speak without interruption. Go on, *ma chère.*"

"I really don't have anything else to say," Diana replied, so rattled by Sophie's pitbull tenacity that she was afraid she'd trip herself up and let slip something incriminating.

Until then, Anton had stationed himself by the fireplace, content to remain an observer, but at that point he broke his silence. "What Diana isn't saying is that she's been through a difficult time lately, and finds talking about it still very painful.

She came looking for a place to heal her bruised spirit, and found it here, and that's all there is to it. Isn't that right, Diana?"

The gaze he settled on her was filled with such straightforward commiseration that she had to look away. "Yes," she said, and wished it was the truth, because lying to him was becoming too painful to bear.

There was more to this man than his good looks and irresistible charm. He possessed what she now realized Harvey had never owned: an integrity, a strength, a nobility of character that had nothing to do with his aristocratic birthright.

Never mind that she'd met him only yesterday and would be gone from his life within a month. She knew she'd remember him the rest of her days. Knew, too, with an unwavering instinct, that if circumstances had been different, if she could have shed the subterfuge which had brought her here, she might have learned to love him more completely, more passionately, than she'd ever loved before.

Josette touched her hand. "Your heart is sore," she said softly, "but you've come to the right place. You will heal here, *cherie*. We will see to that."

Just as well the dinner gong sounded then. One more second, one more sympathetic word, and Diana would have burst into tears.

The weekend passed uneventfully. She didn't see much of Anton, except in the evenings, but the aunts more than made up for it and kept her entertained.

"You must see the estate and meet everyone," Josette decided on the Saturday, and off they went, with Hortense behind the wheel of a station wagon almost as decrepit as Diana's rental car.

"I love it," Hortense said, jolting the poor thing merrily over the dusty, rutted roads. "We've grown old together and understand one another."

During the next hour or so, Diana was introduced to the people who ran the olive mill, lavender distillery, gift shop and perfumery, all of which remained open to the public, seven days a week. Finally they drove to the winery. Gregoire wasn't there, which Diana didn't see as any great loss, but his second-in-command showed her the gleaming equipment in the sheds and took her on a private tour of the cellars, or *caves,* although the aunts declined to accompany them because "it's too cool down there for our old bones."

In between each stop, they regaled her with details of how they'd come to live at the château, a story Anton had touched on only briefly.

"Our brother had run this entire estate," Hortense explained. "At the time of his and his wife's death, I was studying anthropology in Ecuador."

"And I was in Sweden on an extended visit with an old school friend," Josette continued. "Of course, when we heard of the tragedy, we came home immediately. Anton needed us, and not for a moment did we hesitate about devoting ourselves to him. In time, we sent him away to school and eventually to university, in order for him to learn how to take over for his father. But how to safeguard his inheritance in the meantime?" She shrugged eloquently.

Again, Hortense picked up the thread of the story. "The thing is, you see, we knew nothing about running an estate this size. We muddled along as best we could, at the mercy of unscrupulous outsiders who almost ruined us. The château was in disrepair, the grapevines diseased, the lavender fields and olive groves untended.

"If we hadn't persuaded Gregoire and Jeanne to come and help us, I do believe we'd have lost everything. Jeanne brought some sort of order to the running of the household, and Gregoire took over as chief vintner—he has 'the nose' required to run a successful winery. But willing though they were, they were but two people, and couldn't work miracles."

"Then, one day, Anton came home again, a man, and everything changed. He took charge," Josette declared, all puffed up with pride. "The village was dying, with more people in the church graveyard than walking the streets. To men and women alike, he gave life and hope and employment. Every day, from dawn to dusk, he worked beside them wherever he was needed—in the vineyards, the fields, at the château. He directed them in repairing the machinery, the buildings, the house."

"In short," Hortense concluded, "*Château de Valois et Cie* became the engine that drives the economy of Bellevue-sur-Lac. It's no wonder people here credit Anton with saving their lives and will go to any lengths to protect him."

Protect? The word struck an odd note to Diana's ears. Why would a man so highly esteemed need protection? She could hardly put the question to his aunts, though. He was clearly their hero.

Sunday was so warm and pleasant that, after dinner, they all took coffee on the terrace. The moon swam high, throwing dense shadows across the landscape. Romantic songs from the 1950s filtered from the drawing room, where Josette had loaded a stack of old vinyl LPs on the stereo turntable.

"They take me back to my youth," she said, swaying dreamily in the arms of an imaginary partner, the handkerchief hem of her purple chiffon dress whispering around her ankles. "Oh, to be in love again!"

"Oh, to be spared such maudlin rubbish," Sophie muttered.

"Do you like to dance, Diana?" Josette called, still twirling with her invisible partner to the soulful accompaniment of Edith Piaf singing *Je ne Regrette Rien*.

"Of course she does," Hortense scoffed. "You've only to look at her to know she was the most popular girl in her crowd."

"No, I wasn't," Diana had to admit. "I was shy, too smart in class and not particularly good at sports. As a teenager, I'd be the girl no boy asked to dance. I'd sit by myself and smile and pretend I was having a good time but inside I was bleeding."

"But you'll dance with me now, Diana," Anton said, and without waiting for an answer, took her hand and drew her to her feet.

The paving stones were uneven beneath her feet, but he held her so securely, she might have been floating on polished marble.

"Do you know why none of those boys asked you dance?" he murmured against her hair. "Because you were too beautiful, too fine, too unattainable. But in their hearts, you were the belle of the ball. The prize they all longed to win."

Don't talk like that, she begged silently, dazzled by a rush of pleasure that left her blood singing. *You make it too easy for me to fall in love with you.*

"That was lovely to see," Hortense sighed, when the song ended and Anton led Diana back to her chair. "So romantic, just the way it used to be, before we all forgot there *is* such a thing as romance. Don't you agree, Anton?"

"I do," he said. "What about you, Diana?"

She looked up to find him watching her intently, and her flesh burned under his gaze; burned in places that had lain cool and untouched for far too long. How was it that, with a single glance, he could bring her alive again? Remind her that she was a woman with a woman's needs, a woman's hunger?

Embarrassed by her body's responses, hidden, thank heaven, from his all-too-observant gaze, she cleared her throat and managed a noncommittal shrug.

Making no secret of her contempt for such unsophisticated entertainment, Sophie helped herself to more cognac. "All this harking back to the good old days is enough to drive a person to drink."

"Well, we won't have to worry about driving you," Josette

informed her sharply. "From the amount of alcohol you manage to put away every night, I'd say you're already there."

You took the words right out of my mouth, Diana thought. Sophie was so spiteful at times, she wanted to pinch her.

It wasn't until the next night, though, that she realized just how thoroughly hateful Anton's cousin could be.

The evening started out much as usual with the usual beautifully prepared five-course meal. The difference was that Jeanne came to supervise serving it, and witnessing her mother in the role of domestic, while she herself was treated like royalty, cut Diana to the quick. Not that Anton or his aunts were in the least overbearing toward Jeanne. Rather, they were warm and relaxed and very appreciative of her contribution to the evening, as well as that of the young maid working with her.

"Thanks for helping out tonight, Jeanne," Anton said, as she wheeled in the main course. "You put in enough hours during the day, without having to give up your evenings as well."

"Don't give it a second thought," she told him cheerfully. "I'm happy to lend a hand. Corinne's still nursing a migraine, and Odette's too new at the job to manage on her own."

"Well, please give Corinne our best, and tell her we hope she'll feel better soon."

"I will," she promised, and moved on to give quiet encouragement to the nervous young maid trying to fill up the water goblets without spilling a drop.

Sophie, on the other hand, appeared completely unfamiliar with the words "thank you," and seemed to think it was beneath her dignity to acknowledge the presence of anyone not actually seated at the table. When the subject of Henri's birthday party came up, she didn't even bother to wait until Jeanne had left the room before saying, "I hope we're not expected to take part in this bucolic celebration."

"You're more than welcome to stay away," Hortense replied,

"but we will certainly put in an appearance, and I hope that you, Diana, will join us."

"I wouldn't miss it," she said, miserably aware from her heightened color that Jeanne had heard Sophie's disparaging comment. "Henri treated me very kindly during the short time I stayed at the inn."

"I'm not surprised." Hortense smiled knowingly. "He's a very good-hearted man."

But Sophie, oblivious to Anton's black glare, was determined to have the last word. "I don't see what that's got to do with it. The fact is, he's a working-class individual and has nothing in common with people like us."

"*I* work for a living, Sophie," Anton pointed out, as Jeanne ushered the maid from the room. "Does that put me beyond your social pale, too?"

"Don't be silly, *cher,*" she cooed. "You're merely managing your assets, which is a different thing entirely."

"No doubt you see your exhaustive search for another rich husband in the same redeeming light," Hortense remarked, which set Josette's long dangling earrings to taking on a life of their own as she tried to stifle a laugh.

Even Anton was hard-pressed not to smile. "All right, no more wine for you, Hortense," he scolded, the severity he tried to inject into his voice belied by the amusement dancing in his eyes.

"At my age, my dear nephew, a woman does what she must to survive the moment, and if that means getting plastered once in a while, well so be it," she retorted blithely, which practically put her sister under the table.

"The other event coming up, of course, is the Lavender Ball," Josette sputtered, when she managed to control herself. "I do so look forward to that. You'll enjoy it very much, Diana. We hold it here at the château, on the third Saturday in August. It's one of the few times the ballroom's used anymore, although when I was a young girl, there always seemed to be some grand occasion taking place."

"I'm not sure I'll still be here then," Diana said.

"Of course you will," Hortense decreed. "Three years is long enough to observe mourning, and it's past time Anton had a pretty woman on his arm again. If you don't have an evening gown, Josette and I will take you shopping in Nice."

And that was when the evening turned into a complete disaster. Jeanne and Odette had come back to the dining room to clear away the main course. Still smarting from having been put in her place by Hortense, Sophie vented her annoyance on poor Odette who had the misfortune to let the fork slide off Sophie's plate and into her lap.

If the hapless maid had deliberately emptied a glass of water over her head, Sophie couldn't have been more outraged. "What the *hell* kind of people do you have working for you, Anton?" she exploded.

"Calm down, Sophie. It was an accident," he said quietly.

Hurrying to the rescue with a clean linen napkin, Jeanne murmured, "I'm very sorry, *madame*. I'll take care of your dress and have it dry-cleaned in the morning."

"If you take care of it the way you train your maids," she snapped, slapping aside Jeanne's efforts with the back of her hand, "I don't want you within a mile of it, or me."

Diana saw the flash of anger in her mother's eyes. Saw how she opened her mouth to defend herself, then closed it again and averted her gaze. And she couldn't stand it.

"Don't speak to Jeanne like that," she said sharply.

Sophie sent her a poisonous glare. "It's none of your business how I choose to speak to the servants, Mademoiselle Reeves."

"I'm making it my business, Mademoiselle Beauvais," she shot back. "And unlike those you so carelessly dismiss as 'servants,' I'm free to tell you exactly what I think of your appalling lack of sensitivity. I don't know who taught you your manners, but they made a lousy job of it."

"Well said, Diana," Hortense murmured approvingly. "I couldn't have put it better myself."

Ignoring her, Sophie directed another blast at Diana. "Just who do you think you're speaking to?"

"Someone not fit to clean—!" *My mother's shoes, you unfeeling bitch!*

She stopped short, appalled at how close she'd come to letting slip a truth not hers to reveal. Sophie, though, wasn't inclined to let the matter drop.

"What?" she taunted. "Don't stop now. Speak your mind and have done with."

Chest heaving, Diana took a deep, shuddering breath. It managed to dampen her fury, but couldn't stem the tears that filled her eyes. Throwing down her napkin, she pushed herself away from the table. "Never mind! You're not worth spit, let alone the energy it takes to reason with you," she choked, and knew she had to leave before she said something she'd really live to regret.

The dining room was long, a mile or more it seemed, as she stumbled to the door at the far end, leaving behind a babble of voices. Josette's, sharp and critical, directed at Sophie. Hortense's joining in, blistering with anger. Anton's deep and forbidding, commanding order out of chaos. Odette weeping, and Jeanne's gentle tones dispensing comfort to the girl.

Dear God! Diana thought, fleeing up the stairs to her suite. What have I started with my insatiable need to find my mother? Why didn't I listen to Carol when she warned me nothing good could come of this? How will I ever face Anton again?

She didn't have to wait long to find out. Hadn't even made it as far as her door, in fact, before she heard his footsteps racing to catch up with her. "Diana, wait!" he said, his hands closing over her shoulders and putting an end to her blind dash to escape him.

"Go away," she cried, knowing how she must look, with her face all blotchy, and streaked with mascara, and squinched up like a wrinkled old apple. She'd humiliated herself enough for one night, without him seeing her like this.

"No," he said. "Not until you tell me what set you off back there."

"Isn't it obvious? Your benighted cousin is about as pleasant as a blood clot, and since you didn't see fit to tell her so, I did it for you."

"That's not what I'm talking about. I was watching your face, long before you opened fire on her. There's something else going on here, something that troubles you deeply, and I want to know what it is."

"I can't…" She was sobbing openly now. "I can't talk about it, not tonight."

"All right," he said quietly, after a lengthy pause. "All right."

Then guiding her through her door and closing it firmly behind him, he took her in his arms and let her cry. She sank against him, borrowing his strength. Wishing it was hers to keep forever. He smoothed her hair. Ran his hands up and down her back; long, soothing strokes meant to comfort.

At what point did it all change? When did she lift her face to his, knowing that he couldn't mistake the naked need in her eyes? When did his lips stop murmuring words of reassurance and, instead, settle softly on hers? Most of all, how did a kiss that started out as a fleeting benediction evolve into a hot, greedy, openmouthed confession of desire?

She had no answers. Knew no truths but the one her body had recognized practically from the first. Her hands stole up around his neck. Closing her eyes, she let her head fall back in tacit surrender as his mouth traveled a path from her jaw to her throat.

His fingers slid up her rib cage and rested cool against her bare skin as he pushed aside the broad straps of her dress. He kissed her shoulder, her collarbone. Delicately. With restrained finesse. Flirting with her breasts, but never quite touching them. Until she was so hungry for him that she whimpered and begged him not to stop.

"Are you sure?" he asked, his voice rough with passion.

"Oh, yes," she gasped.

There was no restraint, after that. Sweeping her off her feet as if she weighed next to nothing, he strode through her little sitting room to her bedroom and set her on her feet again.

With nothing but a Provence moon glimmering through the window to guide him, he found the zipper at the back of her dress, the clasp holding closed her bra. Dropping to his knees, he peeled away her silk stockings, and then, as if he couldn't deny himself a moment longer a taste of what was to come, he put his mouth on the satin triangle of her panties.

She felt his tongue swirling against her, his hands reaching up to caress her breasts, and a lightning bolt flashed the length of her. Her thighs trembled. Her knees buckled.

He caught her before she fell, and eased her onto the bed. Looked down at her. Shaped with his hands the curve of her hip, the dip of her waist, the slope of her breast. Touched her between her legs, lightly, deliberately. And when she arched off the mattress with a sharp cry, he stripped off his own clothes, yanking impatiently at the knot in his tie, ripping open the buttons on his shirt. His shoes landed with a thud on the floor, his cuff links flew through the air, shooting streaks of silver in the night.

She caught a brief, moon-washed glimpse of his naked body. The planes of his chest, the width of his shoulders. His flat stomach, his long, strong legs…and *it,* jutting big and hard and powerful from the dark nest of his pubic hair. The breath caught in her throat. He was magnificent.

She opened her arms and he came to her, burying her under his weight and entered her in one long, smooth thrust that rocked her soul. Effortlessly he swept her with him on a mounting wave of passion that turned the familiar into something far, far beyond the range of her previous experience. No hurried, pedestrian exercise this, with him spent and satisfied in minutes, and her straining to find a release which always eluded her. This, she thought dazedly, as the distant ripples of orgasm intensified in the deepest part of her, was not sex, it was ecstasy. It was sharing and caring and joy.

And when, with a moan that ripped her in two, she climaxed at the same time that he did, it was much more than that. It was love.

After, when he rolled to his side and cradled her in his arms, may God forgive her, she thought, just for a second, of Harvey. "It's got nothing to do with size," he used to bluster. "It's knowing what to do with it that counts."

She smiled into the warm curve of Anton's neck. Poor Harvey. He really didn't have a clue—on either point!

CHAPTER SEVEN

OF COURSE, the euphoria didn't last. Like a man waking from a very bad dream, Anton eventually stirred and, with a great sigh, swung his legs over the side of the bed. "*Mon dieu!* What have I done?" he muttered, burying his head in his hands.

A chill crept over Diana as all the lovely warmth seeped from her body. She ached to touch him; to lay her hand against the smooth skin of his back, and say, "You just taught me what making love is all about."

But he'd cloaked himself in distance. Was already rooting around in the dark for his clothes and climbing into them with insulting haste. She'd have been crushed, if she hadn't been too numb with shock to feel much of anything.

Not about to let him know how humiliated she was, she reached out and flicked on the bedside lamp. By then, he had on his trousers and was buttoning his shirt, although he'd not yet tucked in the latter. "There," she said. "That should help. If you hurry, you might still make it back to the dining room in time for dessert."

He stared at her as if he thought she'd lost her mind. "Are you all right, Diana?"

No, she wanted to scream at him. *I ache in places I didn't know existed. I'm still throbbing inside from the explosion of an orgasm the likes of which, until tonight, I've only ever read about. Thanks to you, I'll never be the same again.* "What do you want me to say, Anton?"

"Something other than a glib remark about a missed course at dinner, certainly! What just happened between us…shouldn't have. I'm not in the habit of jumping into bed with someone I've known little more than a week, and nor, I think, are you."

"True. But we can't turn back the clock. What's done, is done."

"*Pour l'amour de dieu,* woman, you could be pregnant!"

Oh, if only! To have not just a child, but *his* child! To hold his son to her breast, to touch his baby-soft skin, and smell his baby-sweet scent…! Her heart clenched at the thought. "It's a bit late in the day to think about that, wouldn't you say?"

He groaned and tunneled his fingers through his hair. "Damn you, anyway! You bewitched me."

"It took two, Anton. Don't lay all the blame on me. You're the one who followed me upstairs. You're the one who decided you had the right to come inside my suite. I didn't invite you in."

"You didn't kick me out, either."

She fell back against the pillows, all the fight going out of her. "No, I didn't," she said, hollow with pain. "What kind of a fool does that make me?"

He scooped up his tie, retrieved one of his cuff links and gave up on finding the other. "This is pointless. As you say, what's done is done. We have no choice now but to deal with the consequences."

"Well, if you're worried I'm going to try to rope you into a shotgun wedding, don't be," she said. "That's more your cousin Sophie's style than mine. Even if I did find myself pregnant, I wouldn't ask you for anything. I have the resources to look after myself *and* a child, if I have to."

"And if you think for one moment that a child of mine is going to grow up not knowing his father, you're sadly mistaken!"

"Oh, go away, and stop trying to intimidate me," she sighed wearily. "Quite apart from the fact that you don't want me in your life, and I wouldn't let you take my baby out of mine, we're anticipating problems that might never arise. Go back to your dinner party and tell your aunts I have a headache. It won't be a complete lie."

"I have no more appetite for a dinner party than you have," he replied stonily. "But you're right. There's nothing to be gained by our continuing this conversation now. We will talk later, when cooler heads prevail."

Like hell we will! she almost said. *I'm out of here, first thing tomorrow, and nothing you can say or do is going to stop me.*

But that wasn't true, she realized, even as the thought took shape in her mind. She'd come to the château for one reason only: to substantiate her belief that Jeanne was her mother and establish some sort of permanent connection with her, no matter how tenuous it might be. Until she'd achieved that goal, nothing and no one was going to chase her away.

Quite how she'd face Anton during that time was another matter entirely. But she'd find a way. She had to.

She was late coming down the next morning. When she finally appeared, she seemed composed, but the smudges under her eyes attested to how poorly she'd slept.

"How are you feeling, *ma petite?*" Josette wanted to know.

"I've been better," she admitted.

"We're so sorry about last night."

Her glance flickered to him, and shied away again. "I'm the one who should apologize. I'm afraid I created quite a scene."

"No, Diana," Hortense said. "You put an end to a scene not of your making, and you did it in fine fashion. Help yourself to some breakfast, *ma chère.* You'll feel better after you've eaten."

Anton watched as, avoiding his gaze, she went to the sideboard where the usual selection of fresh fruit, rolls and coffee was laid out. Last night, she'd worn silk that had whispered under his hands, beguiling him to slide it down her body. Today, she'd chosen a navy skirt and white cotton blouse.

So proper, he thought, watching her moodily as she buttered a roll. *So restrained. Who'd guess her capable of the fire burning under that prim, nunlike outfit?*

He wished he could forget. Had paced the floor most of the night, trying to erase the memory of the taste and scent and feel of her. But more than that, he'd struggled to empty his mind of the way she'd responded to him. Wild with passion. Uttering desperate little cries. Shattering around him. The polar opposite of poor, driven Marie-Louise whose sole reason for intercourse had nothing to do with desire.

Setting down his coffee cup, he rose abruptly from the table. "I need to go over a few things with you when you're done here, Diana," he said tersely. "I'll be in my office. By now, you know where to find it. Please don't keep me waiting any longer than necessary."

He felt his aunts' astonished stares following him as he strode from the room, and knew they were taken aback by the brusque arrogance of his tone. How much more horrified they'd be, if they learned that the reason for it sprang from his sense of deep personal shame. *Droit du seigneur* had not been part of their teaching when they'd instructed him on his role as the most recent Comte de Valois, and never mind that Diana wasn't a virgin. That he'd taken advantage of her when she was at her most vulnerable was almost as bad.

She showed up at his office twenty minutes later. Time enough for him to rehearse what he knew he had to say. "Thank you for coming," he began, closing the door.

"I wasn't aware I'd been given any choice in the matter," she said stonily.

He pulled forward a chair. "Please, Diana, sit down and hear me out."

Mouth set in a stubborn line, she perched on the edge of her seat, ready to take flight at the slightest provocation. Resuming his place behind his desk, he watched her a moment, trying to determine what thoughts lay hidden behind her pale, lovely face. Finally he said, "First of all, I need to ask—have I made it impossible for you to remain here?"

She looked down at her fingers which lay knotted in her lap. "I don't know. I'm still trying to decide."

Encouraged that she hadn't handed him a flat, *Yes, you unfeeling bastard!* he nodded. "Then before you do, let me say this. I assume full responsibility for what took place between us last night. I was wrong and can offer no excuse for the way I behaved."

"The whole incident could have been avoided, if you'd spoken up at the dinner table, instead of leaving it to me."

"You hardly gave me the chance."

"That cousin of yours needs to be taught a lesson."

"And I'll deal with her in a way she won't forget, never fear that. But right now, I'm more concerned about you—and us."

"There isn't any 'us.'"

"There might be, and that's the other reason I needed to speak to you in private as soon as possible. Diana, I want your solemn promise that if you find yourself pregnant, you'll tell me immediately. I say this not to threaten or coerce you in any way, but because I have an obligation to the mother of my child that I cannot and will not ignore."

"If, by that, you're suggesting we get married—"

"I'm suggesting nothing. I'm asking for your promise to keep me informed. How we proceed from there, should the situation in fact arise, is something we'll decide together, but it would be premature on both our parts to assume that marriage is the only course open to us. We are strangers."

"Who've been intimate with one another." She shook her head, whether in disgust or despair, he couldn't tell.

"Yes." He let a beat of silence pass before phrasing the

question he felt compelled to ask. "Is it likely, do you think, that you could have conceived?"

"I don't know the answer to that. My ex-husband was so against our having children that he was very careful not to risk producing any—at least, not with me. How easily I could conceive…" She shrugged. "I guess that remains to be seen."

"Then let me put it this way. Are you at that stage of your monthly cycle when a woman is most likely to conceive?"

She blushed. "That's a very personal question, don't you think?"

"It's a very *relevant* question, given the circumstances."

"And where exactly is it written that, just because you're the Comte de Valois, you're entitled to access the private details of my life?"

"Answer the question, Diana."

The hunted glance she cast around the room confirmed his worst fears even before she opened her mouth to deliver a stark, "Yes."

"Then if you *are* pregnant, we'll know within a week or two."

"I suppose." She slapped the arms of her chair and glared at him. "Is that it? May I leave now?"

"Not until you tell me what prompted your outburst to my cousin, last night, and don't bother passing it off as a spur-of-the-moment impulse. You'd been biting your tongue from the moment we sat down at the table."

"I'm American," she said. "We don't 'do' class systems in our society. Household staff aren't treated as if they're a lower form of life. Poor Odette was so terrified, she was shaking."

"Yet you seemed more upset at the way my cousin responded to Jeanne."

"I was. I've told you before, I like Jeanne very much, and it made me sick to see a woman her age having to take such shabby treatment from someone young enough to be her daughter."

"Well, not quite that young, Diana, unless Jeanne gave birth when she was still a child herself!" he said, and wondered why the color rode up her face a second time. "But I see your point. What *you* perhaps don't see, though, is that Jeanne was more disturbed by your behavior than she was by Sophie's. However well meant, your reaction put the spotlight on her and made a bad situation worse. I suggest that the next time you decide to take my cousin to task, you do so privately."

"There won't be a next time," she informed him. "I'll be eating my meals with the rest of the *hired help*, in future."

"Do that, and you'll be making exactly the kind of class distinction you accuse me of tolerating. And that, I promise you, will make Jeanne far more uncomfortable than anything my ill-mannered cousin metes out."

"Oh, that's the last thing I want! She might be just the housekeeper to you, but I'd be proud to call her my…friend."

"She's a lot more than just a housekeeper to me, Diana. She's been my friend since I was a boy. A second mother, even. We just play by slightly different rules here from what you're used to in America, that's all."

He saw how she struggled to come to terms with what he'd said. The way she pressed her lips together, the sigh she couldn't suppress, the very real distress in her eyes were impossible to miss. At last, on yet another sigh, she muttered, "All right, you've made your point. As long as I'm living under your roof, I suppose I must do things your way. When in Provence, and all that…"

If only I could be sure you mean it, Diana, he thought, *how much easier it would be for me to trust you—and how much more difficult I'd find it to stay out of your bed!*

Wrenching his outrageous thoughts under control with difficulty, he said, "Then let's put the matter to rest and get down to business. The tours start tomorrow and include the wine cellar, which you've yet to learn about, so I've arranged for Gregoire to show you around and explain what you need to know."

Her face fell. "Why him?"

"Because he's the wine expert around here and the best person for the job." *And I don't trust myself to be alone with you, most especially not in a dimly lit and cloistered space.*

"Well, if I must…"

"It'll be painless, Diana, I promise."

She tilted one shoulder dismissively, and he wished she hadn't. The soft rise and fall of her breasts were more than his libido could handle with equanimity. "If you say so. Is there anything else?"

"Non," he said, doing his damnedest to ignore the blood surging in his groin. *"C'est tout—pour le moment."*

"C'est tout." Gregoire Delancie brushed one hand against the other. "That's all, *madame*. Do you have any questions?"

"None that I can think of," she said, heading for the cellar's massive oak door, as anxious to be rid of his company as he undoubtedly was of hers. "You've been very helpful. I'll study your notes, and if I run across any problems, I'll let you know."

"Then just one more thing before you leave, *s'il vous plaît*."

"Yes?" She turned back and caught the oddest look on his face.

"What's your interest in my wife?"

Goose bumps that had nothing to do with the cellar's chill raced over her skin. Why would he put such a question to her? What did he think he knew? "I'm not sure I understand the question."

"You seem to be making a point of singling her out for your attention. I'm wondering why."

"If you're referring to us having tea together—"

"That, and the incident at dinner, last night."

"Jeanne told you about it?"

"Certainly. I am her husband. Of course she confided in me. Why would you, a stranger, feel compelled to interfere in a situation that in no way involved you?"

"She's a very nice woman and I didn't like the way she was being treated. Isn't that reason enough?"

"Why don't you tell me, Madame Reeves?" he said.

"I don't owe you any explanations, Monsieur Delancie."

"That is true. But in the interest of fair play, allow me to offer a warning to you. Jeanne is a kind and trusting soul who takes people at face value until they give her reason not to. I, however, am less inclined to be so charitable, and instinct tells me that you, young lady, are not quite as you'd like us all to believe. I don't pretend to understand why this is so, but let me make it very clear that if, for whatever the reason, you hurt my wife in any way, you'll answer to me."

Flabbergasted, she said, "You seem to be confusing me with the other guest in the house, Monsieur Delancie. I'm not the one who treated your wife like dirt, and I have absolutely no interest in causing her any kind of grief at all, *ever!*"

"I'd like to think you're telling me the truth."

"I am," she said shortly. "And if you choose not to believe me, that's your problem, not mine."

For a moment, he almost smiled, and she thought she saw a grudging respect in his eyes before he schooled his features into their usual grim impassivity. "You're a spirited woman, Madame Reeves," he remarked ambiguously, and held open the door for her.

And you're a jerk! she thought, stalking past him. *Why in the world would my mother marry a man like you?*

The week following passed, for the most part, in a blur of tourists peppering her with questions, her fielding answers and hoping she had her facts straight, and parents letting their children dart under the ropes barring entry to the different rooms, or, worse yet, losing track of them altogether in the gardens. By the Friday, though, as her familiarity with the château and its history increased, she'd grown more comfortable in her role and more confident in her dealings with the public.

The remaining days of the month formed a pattern in which

her intensive hours of work were offset by interludes of utter relaxation. Each morning before breakfast, she swam in the pool. After the last tour of the day, she lounged on the terrace, reading or visiting with the aunts. They showered her with affection, made her laugh with their witty observations and generally went out of their way to treat her as if she were one of their own.

Even Sophie made a grudging effort to be pleasant, largely, Diana suspected, because Hortense and Josette wouldn't give her the time of day, and she had no one else to talk to until the evening, when Anton usually put in an appearance.

Diana's skin turned honey-colored from the sun, and the sharp protrusion of her hips and collarbone, legacy of her marriage breakdown, softened into curves as a result of the wonderful menus her mother organized. Without being too obvious about it, she reinforced their budding friendship whenever the opportunity arose, sometimes with a compliment on a particular dish, sometimes just in passing the time of day when they happened to run into one another about the house. As far as Diana was concerned, no occasion was too brief or insignificant to be wasted, and seeing her mother's face light up at the sight of her gave her spirits a lift that nothing could dampen.

Well, almost nothing. Counting the hours until her next period was due, and trying to bury the ache in her heart whenever she let her thoughts stray to Anton, cast a cloud on even the sunniest day. Try though she might, she couldn't forget his touch, his kisses, or the way he'd filled her with his passion and vigor.

Of course, it wasn't love. How could it be when, as he'd so succinctly put it, "We are strangers"? But whatever it was she felt for him neither went away nor diminished, but raged in her blood with inexhaustible appetite.

It was just as well that she saw him only in the evenings, and always with other people present. At least that way, she had to keep her emotions in check. Even so, she found her glance repeatedly settling on his face, so compelling in its spare, aristocratic beauty. Caught herself committing to memory how his mouth moved when he spoke, how he used his hands to illustrate a point in conversation.

He watched her, too. But not for the same infatuated reason. *Well?* his eyes would ask, his gaze locking with hers.

It's too soon to tell, she'd radio back.

And his aunts, missing nothing and misinterpreting everything, would nod to one another and exchange satisfied smiles that said, *They're falling for each other! Let's start planning the wedding!*

It isn't what you think, she wanted to tell them.

And it wasn't. It was worse because, as the second week in July dragged to a close, Diana was forced to recognize that she could no longer pretend time was on her side. Even though it frequently felt imminent, her period did not happen. Instead other changes took its place. Her breasts grew tender and felt fuller. She was unusually tired all the time and experiencing the need to urinate frequently. Certain smells made her queasy—coffee, for instance, which she loved.

Meanwhile, the countdown to Henri's birthday party, scheduled for the following Saturday, clicked into high gear. As she understood it, friends and relatives were preparing trays of ratatouille and other vegetable dishes. His youngest brother, who was also the village butcher, had ordered a suckling pig for roasting on a spit over a bed of coals on the beach.

The baker had hauled out his molding machine and made dozens of *Caissons d'Aix,* little boat-shaped pastries which he filled with almond paste and topped with sugar icing. Anton was donating the wine. Jeanne and her staff were baking a cake large enough to feed a hundred guests.

Just hearing about it all was enough to give Diana the heaves and send her to bed for a long nap. When the Saturday dawned hot and sunny, she debated pleading a headache and begging off attending, but since everyone, from the latest newborn to Anton and the aunts, would be there, this was one occasion when no one would think it strange to see the Count's American visitor socializing freely with his housekeeper, and that wasn't an opportunity to be passed up lightly.

"Anton's filled the Range Rover with wine and folding chairs, and doesn't have room for a passenger, so you'll drive to the lake with us," Hortense decreed, after breakfast. "Gregoire will bring the car around at eleven."

Oh, yes, her mother's ever-vigilant, obsessively possessive husband! Diana had done her best to forget about him although, to be fair, he'd been civil enough, the few times she'd seen him since the day he'd shown her around the wine cellar. So, wearing a loose-fitting dress of gauzy white Indian cotton, and red, flat-heeled sandals, she dutifully showed up at five minutes to the hour, a camera tucked in her bag. She intended taking as many photographs of Jeanne as possible, just in case they were all she had to remember her mother by, after she left France.

Hortense and Josette were already ensconced in the back seat of a vintage Pierce Arrow convertible sedan, the likes of which would have stopped traffic had it rolled down any street in the U.S., but which seemed perfectly at home in the timeless serenity of rural Provence.

The party was well underway by the time they arrived. Henri, wearing a smile that wouldn't go away, sat in the place of honor, surrounded by some of his extended family. Others clustered around the fire pit while their wives kept an eye on long, cloth-covered tables that groaned under a mountain of food. Young mothers sat in the shade with babies on their laps, watching their male counterparts kick around a soccer ball. Children splashed in the warm waters of the lake.

Her uncles, her cousins, her aunts—and her mother, coming

to where Diana, fighting off a wave of nausea, stood apart from the crowd.

"You're looking pale, Diana. Is the heat too much for you? May I bring you something cold to drink?"

"Water," she managed to say, swallowing the saliva pooling in her mouth.

Alert as always to his wife's whereabouts and doings, Gregoire joined them. "This is your brother's day, *mon amour.* Be with him and leave me to take care of Madame Reeves."

"Actually I think I'm going to take a walk, so I really don't need either of you to take care of me," Diana insisted faintly.

Gregoire eyed her critically, then took her arm in a surprisingly gentle grip. "Jeanne's right. You don't look well, *madame.* Perhaps you need to eat something."

Her stomach lurched. "Oh, no…!"

But he ushered her to the tables anyway. Trays of sliced tomatoes sprinkled with oregano and swimming in oil gazed up at her…fat green olives and purple aubergine and anchovies and pickled eel. Gagging, she turned aside, and came face-to-face with the suckling pig rotating on the spit, fat hissing and spitting and running down its carcass.

"Madame, I am concerned. I think you should sit down."

"No! Please, Gregoire…!" Desperate to escape his watchful gaze, she pulled free and stumbled toward a stand of trees some distance away.

"Diana," she heard him call, but she kept going, her hand clamped across her mouth, until she could go no farther.

Bent double, she retched time and time again, her mouth filled with the sour, acidic taste of bile.

Anton ran her to earth not long after, and took one look at her as she leaned weakly against the trunk of a young pine tree, with her face bathed in sweat and her hair sticking to her scalp.

"Since we both know the reason, I won't insult my intelligence or yours by asking the cause of your sudden *maladie,*

Diana," he said, mopping her forehead with his handkerchief. "The only relevant questions are, how long have you known, and when were you planning to share the news with me?"

CHAPTER EIGHT

"DON'T start on me, Anton," she moaned, clutching at her midriff. "I'm not in the mood."

That much was obvious. She looked half-dead. "Is there anything I can do for you?"

She spared him an evil glare. "You've already done enough, thanks."

Well, he thought, he'd walked right into that one. "Look, Diana," he said patiently, "in your present condition, you're not helping anyone, least of all yourself, by trying to pick a fight you don't have a hope of winning, especially not with me."

"Oh, that's right! Nobody challenges the almighty Count de Valois, who ranks second only to God as far as everyone in these parts is concerned. Forgive me for having forgotten."

Foolish, stubborn creature! Her attempt to cut him to ribbons with sarcasm might have stood a better chance of finding its mark if she'd been able to deliver it without her chin quivering uncontrollably, and she hadn't been hanging on to the tree trunk for dear life because it was the only thing keeping her upright.

Recognizing it was pointless trying to reason with her, he left her alone with her misery and made his way back to the party. Apart from Gregoire, no one appeared to have missed him.

"You found her, Anton?"

"Yes. Thanks for the heads-up, Gregoire. You're right. She isn't well."

"What seems to be the trouble?"

"An upset stomach. Must be something she ate."

"I'm sorry. Is there anything I can do?"

"Yes." Anton handed him the keys to the Range Rover. "My car's in the public parking area, with everyone else's. Do me a favor, will you? Drive it down to this end and park it off the road, under the trees. That way, we can make a quiet exit and not spoil the party for others. And, Gregoire, if anyone asks, you haven't seen us."

"I understand. You can count on my discretion."

"I know it." He clapped the man on the back, took a bottle of mineral water from a nearby picnic hamper, and headed back into the wooded area again.

She was where he'd left her, except she was sitting at the base of the tree with her eyes closed, and her head resting against its trunk. Squatting down beside her, he uncapped the water. "Try a little of this. It might help."

Wordlessly she accepted the bottle, and took a few lethargic sips.

"Better?" he asked, when she was done.

"A little." She set down the bottle and expelled a weary sigh. "I'll be okay now. You can go back to the party."

"And leave you here? Don't be absurd. I'm taking you back to the château."

"I don't need you to take me anywhere," she said irritably. "Stop fussing, Anton! I can look after myself."

He took her hands firmly in his. "And I need you to understand that I'm not the enemy, Diana. You don't have to look after yourself. I'm here and I want to help you. We're in this together."

"No, we're not," she whispered, tears sparkling in her eyes again. "We had sex once, that's all."

"It would seem that once was enough."

She bit her lip and looked away in such despair that he wanted nothing more than to take her in his arms and comfort her. But the longer they lingered here, the greater the chance that they'd be discovered, and he wasn't ready to share with anyone else news he'd not yet had time to come to grips with, himself.

The familiar sound of his Range Rover slowing to a stop beyond the trees spurred him to action. *"Viens!"* he said, hoisting her to her feet and slipping an arm around her waist. "Lean on me, and let's get out of here."

Five minutes later, they were speeding back to the château and by the time they arrived, her color had improved. "Would you like to lie down and rest for a while?" he asked, guiding her inside the house.

"No." She shot him a weak smile. "The nausea's passed, and I'm feeling almost human again."

Maybe so, but she still looked as if a good wind would blow her over. "You'd feel better still if you ate something. The staff have been given the day off so there's no one in the kitchen, but the refrigerator will be well stocked and I can boil an egg and make a pot of coffee, if you like."

She shuddered delicately. "No egg, thanks, and no coffee. But I could probably manage some toast and tea."

"Go put your feet up then, and I'll get to it."

"For heaven's sake, Anton," she objected, shying away from him as if she thought he might toss her over his shoulder and force her into submission, "I'm pregnant, not paralyzed! I can make my own toast."

Willing to let her have her way, at least for now, he raised his hands in surrender. "Okay, then we'll both raid the kitchen. Toast and tea for you, and something a bit more substantial for me, since I'm missing out on all that good food down at the lake."

"There's no reason you have to miss out on anything. Go back to the party and have a good time."

"And how do I do that, Diana?" he asked wryly. "By pretending the last half hour didn't happen?"

"You might as well. Staying here isn't going to change anything."

"That is true, but there's a lot we need to talk about, and now's as good a time as any to get started."

"We can do that later."

"Non, ma chère," he contradicted her flatly, steering her down the corridor to the kitchen end of the house. "We do it now."

In the wake of her marriage breakdown, one thing Diana decided she'd never again tolerate was having her opinions dismissed as if they weren't worth the breath it took to utter them. But when Anton high-handedly ordered her to leave the preparation of their impromptu meal to him, she was glad enough to let him get on with it. She hadn't seen the kitchen before and, wandering to the far end of the room, she flopped down on a wide padded window seat, curious to learn more about her mother's domain.

The room was vast, with rough-hewn beams and white plaster walls that had been there since the château was first built. Essentially split into two areas, the working half contained streamlined luxury appliances and gleaming countertops that offered the ultimate in convenience and efficiency. But where she sat, the charm of French country furniture served as a reminder that even in a house this grand, the kitchen was more than just a place to cook meals. In many ways, it still represented the heart of the home.

A bouquet of roses and lavender, arranged in a yellow pitcher, graced the middle of an old farmhouse table, which was surrounded by rush-bottomed ladder-back chairs of the same vintage. A beautiful carved dresser stood against one wall, its open plate racks filled with colorful Provençal pottery.

Braids of garlic hung from the ceiling. Pots of herbs grew

on the windowsills. A black iron pot was suspended over the hearth in the big, brick fireplace. Ripe red tomatoes in a dark blue bowl made a splash of color against the white marble work surface of a center island.

If things had been different, she could have grown up here, playing with her dolls by the fire in winter, or sprawled on the window seat, reading, in the summer. She could have learned to walk on the tiled floor, stood on a chair and licked the spoon when her mother baked a cake. Sent letters to Santa Claus up the big open chimney. Opened gifts piled under a Christmas tree in the corner, and—

"Wake up, dreamer! Your toast and tea are ready."

Anton's voice put an end to her fantasy of a past that never was, and brought her back to a present altogether real and riddled with uncertainty. Joining him at the table, she nibbled at her toast while he dug into the cheese omelet he'd prepared for himself.

When the first pangs of hunger were satisfied, he put down his fork and said, "You're quite sure you're expecting a baby, are you, Diana?"

"Well, I can't give you proof positive, if that's what you mean," she conceded. "Pregnancy test kits aren't exactly thick on the ground around here, and since I'm presently without a car, I haven't been able to visit a pharmacy. But yes, I know enough about the early symptoms to be pretty certain that I am."

"Then we must see a doctor. We'll take care of it, first thing on Monday."

"We?"

"Of course, we! You don't suppose I'm leaving you to handle this on your own, do you?"

"I don't know," she said, afraid to let him see how badly she wanted to believe him. "Even though you've known all along that this might happen, it still must have come as a shock. It's hardly what you had planned, after all."

"Life's like that, sometimes. I've learned to cope with the

unexpected. And not to put too fine a point on it, but who else do you have to turn to?"

My mother, she thought, the pain of not being able to reveal herself to Jeanne more acute than usual. If ever there was a time when a woman needed her mother, it had to be when she was expecting her own first baby. Who better understood the fears, the doubts, the hopes? Who better able to offer reassurance and advice? But in this instance, Jeanne was relegated to the role of observer, with no idea that she was about to become a grandmother.

"You knew that before you met her," Carol had said the night before, when Diana had phoned and tearfully confided in her friend. "For now, let friendship be enough. At least then, you can keep your hopes alive that something better might evolve in the future. But spill the truth, and you could lose what little you have."

"What you're trying to say," she'd countered, "is that I still have no solid proof that Jeanne's really my mother."

"I know you want her to be, Diana, but wanting doesn't make it so, and it seems to me that you've got complications enough in your life enough right now, without adding more. The Diana I know would show more sense than to let herself be seduced by a man she barely knows, even if he is handsome as sin and an honest-to-goodness Count, as well. What in the world were you thinking?"

"Obviously I wasn't, or I wouldn't be in this mess, now. But that doesn't change how I feel about my mother."

"But what if you're wrong, and she isn't your mother? Think of the fall-out, if you start making allegations that aren't true about a woman your lover values so highly."

But Diana knew in her bones that she wasn't wrong. With every passing day, she grew more convinced of the blood tie between her and Jeanne. How else to account for the inexplicable emotional connection, the gut-level certainty, that tugged at her every time their eyes met?

"What the devil…?" Again, Anton interrupted her stream of thought, and startled by his tone, she looked up to find him poised to leap out of his chair, his head cocked attentively. Then she heard it, too: the sound of the outside service door quietly opening and footsteps approaching.

A moment later, Jeanne and Gregoire came into the kitchen, but stopped short at the sight confronting them.

"So sorry, Anton," Gregoire said, his glance taking in the eggshells, block of cheese and loaf of bread on the counter, and the frying pan on the stove. "We had no idea you'd be down here, and didn't mean to intrude."

"Why are you here at all?" he responded brusquely. "You're not due back until five o'clock."

"When Jeanne heard Madame Reeves wasn't feeling well and had returned to the château, she insisted on coming back too, in case she was needed."

So I'm Madame Reeves again, am I? Diana thought, remembering he'd called her by her first name, down by the lake.

Visibly annoyed, Anton said, "I thought I asked you to keep your mouth shut on the subject, Gregoire?"

"I did my best," he replied miserably, "but Jeanne had already spoken with Madame Reeves and knew something was amiss."

"That's true, Anton," Diana said, feeling almost sorry for the man. "Don't blame him, or Jeanne, for that matter. If anyone's at fault, I am. I knew I wasn't feeling up to par, and should have stayed home in the first place." She aimed a sympathetic smile at the worried couple. "But as you can see, I'm much better now, so the two of you should hurry back to your party before you, too, are missed."

"I'm afraid it's too late for that, Diana," Jeanne confessed. "When I realized you had disappeared, and I couldn't find my husband, I told Mesdames Hortense and Josette. They were worried enough that they didn't want to stay at the party, either."

Annoyed all over again, Anton blurted, "Are you saying you brought them back here, as well?"

"We had no choice," Gregoire replied. "They wouldn't have it any other way. Of course, when we dropped them off at the front door—"

"They spotted my car, and are probably prowling the halls, looking for us, even as we speak." He rolled his eyes in exasperation. "So much for keeping a low profile!"

Pushing back her chair, Diana urged him toward the door. "It can't be helped, Anton, and there's no real harm done. Let's just go find them and put their minds at rest. Jeanne, Gregoire, thank you for being so kind. I'm sorry I've spoiled the day for you, and for the mess we've made of your kitchen."

"Think nothing of it," her mother exclaimed. "We're just very relieved that you're feeling better. You looked so ill before, I was quite frightened for you."

Oh, Mother, if only I could explain that I'm not sick at all, how quickly your fear might turn to joy! Biting her lip, Diana paused in passing and squeezed Jeanne's hand. "Don't worry about me, Jeanne," she murmured huskily. "I'm really quite fine."

They met Hortense and Josette at the foot of the stairs in the grand hall. Less easily convinced that there was no need for worry, the aunts bombarded them with questions.

"Where were you? We've looked everywhere."

"Why didn't you let us know Diana wasn't well, instead of sneaking away without a word?"

"Have you called Dr. Savard, Anton?"

"Do you have a fever, Diana?"

"Are you in pain?"

"Shouldn't you be in bed?"

Finally Anton put a stop to the hullabaloo. "Enough, both of you! If Diana was unwell before, she has to be feeling a lot worse now, with all the fuss you're creating."

"That's easy for you to say," Josette scolded, "because, like most men, you see only what's under your nose, but we've noticed for several days now that Diana has looked peaked, and we have every right to make a fuss about it, if we choose. Someone has to look out for the poor child."

"*I'm* looking out for her!"

"I can look out for myself," Diana began, tired of being treated as if she wasn't able to speak for herself, when the front door suddenly flew open and Sophie burst onto the scene.

"Will someone kindly explain why the four of you saw fit to abandon me to a bunch of yokels whose idea of entertainment is to see who can spit the farthest?" she inquired indignantly.

"Diana wasn't well, and had to leave," Anton said.

"Oh, well, that explains everything!" she sneered. "What's the matter, Diana? Nothing as fatal as a hangnail, I hope?"

Weary of the whole conversation, Diana retorted, "No, Sophie. Sorry to disappoint you, but I think I'm going to survive."

"And you'll do it much faster without us hovering over you," Hortense decided. "Come along, Josette, and you, too, Sophie. We're not needed here. Diana's in good hands with Anton."

But Sophie, noticing that Anton had slipped his arm around Diana's waist, eyed them suspiciously. "There's something else going on here, if you ask me. Just what are the two of you up to?"

"Whatever it is," Anton informed her coldly, "it's our business, not yours."

"Not for long," Diana muttered, as the women went their separate ways. "At this rate, they'll soon be putting two and two together and coming up with four."

"With three, at any rate," he agreed. "Which is all the more reason we waste no time taking control of the situation."

"Taking control," she discovered, meant Anton calling in favors and securing an appointment with the best obstetrician in Aix, for ten o'clock on the Monday morning. The irony was not lost on Diana. Like mother, like daughter, she thought, the difference being that unlike Jeanne, she was not alone and desperate. At the very worst, she could afford to keep her baby and give it a good life.

And at the best? She slid a quick glance at Anton as the specialist joined them in the consulting room after examining her. Was he really as composed as he appeared?

The doctor didn't even bother to open the patient chart lying on his desk. "Congratulations, both of you. Today's advanced technology means we're able to confirm pregnancy much earlier than was once the case, and after running the necessary tests, I can say with certainty that you have a baby on the way."

Diana wilted in her seat, not sure whether to laugh or cry, but Anton leaned forward, focused, intense. "What about the nausea she's experiencing?"

"Perfectly normal, Monsieur de Valois. Desirable, even, since it indicates successful implantation of the embryo. Madame is in excellent health and I anticipate a healthy, full-term baby."

Anton heaved a great sigh, smiled and gripped her hand tightly in his. "And the due date?"

The specialist spared the patient chart a quick glance. "March 17, give or take a week."

"What about special instructions—level of activity, diet, that sort of thing?"

"Pregnancy is not an illness, *monsieur*," the doctor said, smiling. "It's a natural condition caused by—"

"Trust me, Doctor," Anton interrupted, "I know what caused it. Now I'd like to be sure I do nothing to jeopardize it."

"No doubt!" The doctor permitted himself another small smile. "Harmony, lack of stress, support—these you can provide. For the expectant mother, at this stage my only recommendations are prenatal vitamins, a healthy diet, plenty of rest and regular exercise. Beyond that, she's free to lead a perfectly normal life as her energy allows."

"And you'll see her again when?"

"In one month, barring any unforeseen complications." He rose, dismissing them. "Relax, *monsieur.* You have nothing to worry about. Your lady is in fine shape. Good day, and remember to book an appointment with my receptionist before you leave."

As he escorted her across the street from the obstetrician's office to where he'd left the car—not the Range Rover she'd expected, but a sleek BMW he handled with the same sure expertise he brought to everything he did, Anton made no reference to the news they'd received. Instead he said quietly, "You had nothing but tea and toast at breakfast, and must be hungry. We'll have lunch somewhere on the Cours Mirabeau."

Diana nodded absently, staring unseeingly out of the window during the short drive there, lost in her own thoughts. Had her mother been overwhelmed by the bustle of activity, when she came here, alone and pregnant? Did she find it too much, after the slow pace of life in her native village? Was she afraid? Lonely? Or just glad to have escaped the probing scrutiny of all eyes, every time she set foot outside the house?

Anton parked the car in a square close to the Cours Mirabeau, a beautiful avenue lined with sidewalk cafés and bookshops, and alive with the sound of water. Large and small, simple and ornate, fountains splashed and bubbled and shot in clear green jets at every turn, casting shifting shadows over the facades of the buildings and lending texture to the deep shade of the plane trees.

"This will do," he decided, shepherding her into *Le Grillon,* an elegant terrace restaurant where a waiter showed them to a quiet corner table for two.

She ordered sole, lightly poached and mineral water with lime. Anton chose smoked salmon and spinach baked in a flaky pastry crust, and a glass of white wine which he sipped meditatively while they waited for their meal to arrive.

It was early yet, not quite noon, and there were few other patrons ordering lunch, which made his silence that much more oppressive. She thought he must be in shock; that even though she'd told him she was pretty sure she knew what the doctor's verdict would be, he hadn't really believed her.

Finally she could stand it no longer and, clearing her throat, spoke her mind. "You've been very quiet since we left the doctor's office, Anton, but sooner or later, we're going to have to talk about the elephant we're both pretending isn't sharing this table with us."

"The pregnancy, you mean?"

"What else!"

He responded by taking another mouthful of wine.

Did he think getting potted was going to change anything? "Look," she said, trying not to sound desperate, "I can see that you're shocked, but—"

"I'm not shocked at all," he cut in calmly. "I'm figuring things out and thinking how lucky we are that we have at least a little time on our side."

"Time?" she repeated, unsure where this was leading. "Time for what?"

"To plan our future and let people get used to the idea that we're a couple."

Confused, she stared at him. "What on earth are you talking about?"

"I'd have thought it was obvious," he said, lifting his clear gray gaze to her face. "If you're having my baby, Diana, we're getting married. As soon as possible and most definitely before summer's end. And don't even think about opposing me on this, because the matter is *not* up for discussion."

CHAPTER NINE

"YOU can't possibly be serious!" she stammered, when she finally found her voice. "We already agreed, when we first discussed it, that in the event I should be pregnant, marriage wasn't an option."

"No. We agreed not to jump to any premature conclusions until we knew for sure if you had conceived. Now that it's been confirmed that you have, marriage is the logical next step."

"In your antiquated world, maybe," she said, rendered almost speechless with indignation at his cold-blooded assessment of the situation, "but not in mine."

"You're carrying my baby, Diana," he reminded her loftily.

As if she was likely to forget! "That doesn't make me your chattel."

"That word again?" He laughed scornfully, as if such an outdated concept was beyond his understanding. "Stop over-reacting! I'm merely stating the obvious, which is that a man honors his obligation to take care of his own, and I can't think of a better way to do that than by making you my wife."

"Absolutely not," she said, firmly shutting out the insidious little voice whispering inside her head that she shouldn't be so quick to turn him down. Hadn't she dreamed about him almost every night for a month or more? Woken to find her body throbbing with hunger for him? Didn't she melt when she remembered his kisses, his touch?

"Why not? Does the prospect of taking me for your husband fill you with such distaste?"

"It's not that," she mumbled, refusing to meet his gaze.

"Then what's the problem?"

How could he be so blind? So obtuse? "*We* are!" she said emphatically. "For heaven's sake, we're strangers in all the ways that matter, and I'm not talking about something as trivial as not knowing each other's favorite foods or colors. Culturally and socially, we're poles apart. You're an aristocrat, and I'm…" *The illegitimate child of your housekeeper!*

Beset by the truth as she saw it, she wilted with despair. "I'm a commoner. An American, with no more understanding of what your heritage means to you, than you have of what baseball and hot dogs mean to people like me. Face it, Anton. With such barriers separating us, how can we even contemplate marriage, and expect it to work?"

Completely unfazed by her emotional outburst, he said calmly, "The only barriers are those you've erected in your mind. I've seen how smoothly you've adapted to a way of life different from what you're used to. I've seen how readily my aunts have accepted you—and trust me, Diana, they do not confer their approval lightly. You handle mobs of tourists with grace and intelligence. Treat people with respect and kindness. Quite frankly, these qualities alone are enough to convince me you're exactly the right woman to become my wife."

He lowered his voice to the seductive softness of midnight velvet. "But there's also my personal, very private experience, the memory of which still stirs me to desire. We made love only once, but it was enough for me to recognize a passion in your soul equal to that in mine. Together we were magnificent, and that alone is more than many couples ever achieve."

"Be reasonable!" she implored, even as that traitorous little voice urged her to forget reason and follow her heart. "I know nothing about your work, your ambitions—"

"That's where time is on our side. You can learn. Before our child is born, you will be as familiar with his inheritance as you are with your own name."

He was entangling her in a web of logic; hypnotizing her with his fatal magnetism. In a last desperate bid to escape, she said, "You seem to have forgotten that I have a job to do."

"Nonsense!" he scoffed, sweeping aside such a feeble excuse with the contempt it no doubt deserved. "To begin with, how do you expect to conduct tours when you're nauseated all the time? And even if that wasn't a problem, do you seriously think that I will allow my future wife to work for her keep? No, Diana. Until I find someone else to fill the position, my assistant manager will take over the job. As of this minute, your health, your well-being, come before all else."

Armed with such confidence, he could have turned the tide, had he wished. Stopped the clock and spun time backward, if it had pleased him to do so. Instead he made her the focus of his unswerving determination, and the resolve she fought so hard to preserve collapsed into a faint, bewildered, "Do you really think we can make it work?"

He folded her hand in his. Mesmerized her with his unblinking gaze. "I don't *think* we can, Diana. I *know* it."

Why was she opposing him? What were the alternatives if she persisted in refusing him? To give their child a life with only one parent, when he or she could easily have both? Anton would never allow it. To subject their child to a split existence and torn loyalties: summer with father and great-aunts; winter with mother? She herself wouldn't allow that.

To agree to his terms, and inherit the best of all worlds: a family of her own, not just with Anton and his aunts, but with her mother—and the hope that, one day, her connection to Jeanne would be a secret no longer? What greater gift could she offer, than to give Jeanne the chance to enjoy with her grandchild all the things she was denied with her own baby?

"Are you absolutely sure, Anton?"

"I am absolutely sure, Diana, believe me."

Oh, she wanted to! With all her heart, she wanted to fall in with his plans, and let her reservations evaporate in the heat of his conviction. But not once since their night together had he approached her as a man toward his lover. Not once had he tried to kiss her or be alone with her. Only now, when he knew for certain that she carried his child, did he profess to care.

On the other hand, how could she not believe him? His beautiful eyes couldn't lie. There was nowhere in their clear gray depths for the truth to hide.

"All right, then."

"You'll do it? You'll marry me?"

A tremor of nervous anticipation quivered through her heart. "I will."

"You won't regret this decision," he said. "Together, we'll be invincible, you'll see."

Diana hadn't expected their absence would go unnoticed, nor did it. They arrived back at the château with barely enough time to change before dinner, mostly because Anton, overriding her objections, insisted on spending the afternoon shopping for an engagement ring and having it sized to fit.

"Nice of you to ask if I felt like a jaunt into town." The last to come down for the cocktail hour, Sophie sidled up to him, all pouty lips and bedroom eyes. "I was bored silly, here by myself all day. What was so urgent that you had to race off without a word to anyone?"

"You'd have been even more bored if you'd come with us, Sophie," he replied smoothly. "Diana and I had business to attend to in Aix that concerned just the two of us."

"Oh, really?" Josette looked up eagerly and nudged Hortense. "Are you going to let us in on it?"

"Certainly." He came to where Diana sat sipping sparkling

water and furtively keeping her left hand hidden in the folds of her cocktail gown. "It's too soon for this," she'd protested, when he'd slipped the diamond solitaire on her finger. "We've known each other less than a month. No one's going to believe we're engaged."

"Then we'll have to convince them they're wrong, won't we?" he'd said, with his usual imperturbable certainty that he had the world by the tail.

Taking her hand now, he pulled her up to stand next to him and slipped his arm around her waist. "You're looking at a very happy man, *mesdames*. This afternoon, I asked Diana to marry me and I'm both honored and pleased to tell you that she accepted my proposal."

Given the aunts' uninhibited exclamations of delight and exuberant hugs, Sophie's reaction to the news might have passed undetected by the others, but Diana saw the color leach from her face and the sudden narrowing of her eyes.

Oblivious to any undercurrents, Hortense raised her glass. "We must have a toast! To you, my dear, dear nephew, and to your beautiful—!"

"This is a joke!" Sophie cut in, with a laugh so harsh, it ripped through the atmosphere like a saw. "Anton's pulling your leg. Tell her, Anton!"

Spearing his cousin with a quelling glare, Anton lifted Diana's left hand to reveal the diamond flashing blue fire in the light from the crystal wall sconces. "Does this look like a joke to you, Sophie?"

Her jaw dropped briefly. Then, with a superhuman effort, she wrestled herself under control. "No, it doesn't," she managed, pasting a grim smile on her face. "But am I the only one who finds this...*engagement* very sudden?"

"It's not sudden at all, as you'd know if you paid attention to anyone but yourself," Josette snapped. "Hortense and I guessed days ago that something like this was in the offing, and we couldn't be more delighted. When is the wedding to be, *mes chers enfants?*"

Anton bathed Diana in a victorious smile. "No later than the end of August, and sooner if I have any say in the matter. I want to take my wife away on our honeymoon before the grape harvest begins."

"That doesn't allow much time to make arrangements."

"Diana and I have discussed it, and decided on a small, discreet affair, *ma tante,*" he said. "Just family and a few close friends. It is, after all, a second marriage for both of us."

Sophie fixed Diana in a gimlet-eyed stare. "How many of your family will be attending?"

"None," Diana said.

"Why not?"

"I believe I already told you that my parents are dead and I was an only child."

"But you must have other relatives?"

"Not as far as I know," she said, the cost of having to deny her mother blinding her to just how much she'd revealed with her answer.

But Sophie leaped on it with avid hunger of a starving woman suddenly presented with a ten-course feast. "What kind of person doesn't *know* if she has relatives? Were you a foundling, or something?"

Broken only by a muffled gasp of outrage from one of the aunts, a drop of silence fell into the room and, like the ripples from a stone cast carelessly onto the calm surface of a pond, spread until Diana felt herself smothering in it. *So here it comes,* she thought, flinging an anguished glance at Anton. *The moment of truth, and the price one pays for keeping it hidden.*

Lifting her chin, she looked her enemy straight in the eye. "I was adopted at birth, if that's what you mean."

Sophie opened her eyes very wide, and shaped her lip-sticked mouth into a silent and protracted *Oh!* At length, she breathed "I see! No wonder you're so anxious to join this family, then."

"Sophie," Anton interposed, his voice coated with steely displeasure, "you're testing my patience sorely. Please stop. And if that's asking too much, then perhaps it's time you went back to Paris."

"And miss the wedding of the year?" She shot Diana a malicious smile. "I wouldn't dream of it!"

Dinner was a nightmare. Although Anton and the aunts made a valiant effort to behave as if nothing untoward had occurred, Diana felt their covert glances. Sick as much from emotional stress as pregnancy, she forced down most of the chestnut-flavored pumpkin soup which started the meal, but her stomach rebelled at the main course, a small guinea hen stuffed with foie gras, and bathed in mushroom sauce.

Of course, Sophie noticed, just as she noticed that Diana refused wine with the meal, and frequently dabbed at the little beads of perspiration dotting her upper lip. And being Sophie, she commented, cloaking her nasty little remarks in a veneer of concern as transparent as glass.

Finally Anton put an end to it. "Be silent, woman!" he exploded, rising from his chair so violently that he knocked over his wineglass and sent a stain red as blood soaking into the fine damask tablecloth. "We've all heard enough from you for one night!"

Then, without so much as a glance at Diana, he threw down his napkin and strode from the room.

The aunts stared at Sophie as if she was something they'd had to scrape off the bottom of their shoes. "Don't look at me like that," she snapped.

"We'd greatly prefer not to have to look at you at all," Hortense replied severely. "You're an offense to civilized society, Sophie Beauvais, and I thank God you're no relation of mine."

At that, Sophie, too, slammed out of her chair, though not with the same dramatic effect Anton had managed. "Like it or not, Hortense, I am a member of this family, and I refuse to sit here and be spoken to as if I were nothing but a glorified employee like someone else at this table."

Hortense lazily swirled the wine in her glass. "Then do us all a favor and leave."

Sophie did. In high dudgeon, and with a last malevolent glare at Diana.

"We're going to have to watch that one," Josette murmured, as the door banged closed. "Left to her own devices, she's capable of causing no end of trouble, and I'm afraid she has you in her sights, Diana."

"She thinks I'm not good enough for Anton, and she's probably right." *Because my falling in love with him doesn't change the fact that I'm here under false pretenses.*

Hortense patted her hand bracingly. "If, by that, you're referring to the circumstances concerning your birth, there's no shame attached to being adopted."

"Of course there isn't!" Josette crowded her on her other side and gave her a warm hug. "You do Anton an injustice to think he cares about that."

They were so kind, so willing to believe in her, that to her chagrin, Diana burst into tears. "I'm sorry," she wept. "I don't know what's wrong with me. I don't usually cry at the drop of a hat, but Anton was so furious—"

"Not with you, *ma chère,*" Hortense pointed out. "This was a very special day for the two of you, and that witch of a cousin is the one who spoiled it. You'd both be less than human if you weren't affected by such uncalled-for spite."

"Hortense is right," Josette said gently. "You worry about important things, such as choosing a wedding dress, and leave Sophie Beauvais to us. We'll make sure she doesn't cause any further trouble."

They meant well, but Diana had seen the hostility in Sophie's eyes and knew it would take more than these two well-meaning women to put an end to her machinations. She'd earmarked Anton for herself, and if she couldn't have him, she'd stop at nothing to make sure no one else did.

And if, in the process, she ruined a few lives? Diana could well imagine her answer. *That's what happens in war. There are bound to be casualties.*

But Diana herself was the one most at fault. If she'd been honest with Anton from the start, Sophie might still be full of resentment toward someone she considered an interloper, but she'd be powerless to make innocent bystanders the target of her rage.

Too ashamed to sit there a moment longer, the undeserving recipient of the aunts' generous outpouring of sympathy, Diana begged to be excused. She had to find Anton. The time had come to tell him everything.

She'd no sooner left the room and started down the hall than she ran into Jeanne. "I was just coming to get you," her mother said. "You have a phone call. It came through to the central switchboard, as all calls do after nine o'clock in the evening, but I'll transfer it to the west wing library, where you'll have privacy." Then, her eyes full of concern, she added, "You appear very upset, Diana. Is there anything I can do?"

Oh, if only she could pour out her heart to this kind and gentle soul! If only she dared say, *I think I'm your daughter, and I need so badly for you to be my mother because, in trying to find you, I've made such a mess of things and I don't have anyone to turn to for advice.*

But even if she had the right to unburden herself to Jeanne, now was not the time. Not until she'd spoken to Anton. So, "No, thank you, Jeanne," she choked. "It's just been a very long day, that's all, and I'm very tired."

"Then while you take your call, I'll fix you a cup of herbal tea to help you sleep, and bring it to your room."

Puzzled as to who'd be phoning her at this hour, Diana shut herself in the library, a large, dimly lit room she'd visited only once before. Bookshelves lined the walls. A brass table holding cognac and a selection of liqueurs stood to one side of a big stone fireplace. Flanking the hearth were four comfortable, high-backed leather reading chairs with side tables, on one of which was an empty brandy snifter. But these details she noticed only peripherally as she crossed to where the phone sat on a desk at the far end of the room.

Lifting the handset, she waited until she heard the click of the call being connected, before uttering a guarded, "Hello? This is Diana Reeves."

Carol's voice blasted across the miles. "Finally! I've been trying to get through to you for the last two hours."

"Sorry," she said. "I've had my cell phone turned off all day."

"No kidding, Sherlock! Why else do you think I jumped through hoops to get the château listing from the international directory? For crying out loud, Diana, you said you'd let me know what the doctor said. I walked the floor half the night, frantic with worry when I didn't hear from you—much to my husband's annoyance, I might add!"

"I forgot," she said contritely. "I'm really sorry, Carol, but so much happened today that it slipped my mind completely."

"Well?" Carol's impatience hummed over the line. "Now that I've tracked you down, don't keep me hanging. What's the verdict?"

"I'm pregnant all right."

Her voice softened. "Ah, Diana, I was hoping for a different answer. Does Anton know?"

"Yes. He was there when the obstetrician gave us the news."

"How did he take it?"

"He wants to marry me," she said bleakly. "He even bought me an engagement ring."

"Did you accept it?"

She looked down at the diamond solitaire adorning her finger. "I suppose so. I'm wearing it."

"And you sound about as thrilled as if he'd asked you to get all your teeth pulled. What's the problem?"

"Oh, Carol, that you even have to ask! You know very well what the problem is."

"If I did, I wouldn't have put the question to you, so spit it out. Are you saying you don't care for him as much as you thought you did?"

"Hardly! I once read that when it comes to falling in love, ten minutes is all it takes, but I never believed it until I met him. He's everything I ever hoped to find in a man."

"How does he feel about you?"

"He acts as if he cares. He says he does."

"Then, I repeat—what's the problem?"

"His cousin, Sophie. She's still here, and sniffing around looking for trouble."

"So let her look. It's not as if you've done anything wrong."

"Yes, I have. It's wrong to agree to marry a man, and not tell him everything he has a right to know."

"What are you getting at?" Carol asked sharply.

"I have to come clean with him. I have to tell him what brought me here in the first place. I can't risk having his mean-spirited cousin stumble on the truth and blindside him with it. He deserves to hear it from me."

"You're forgetting one thing, Diana," Carol reminded her soberly. "This isn't your secret to tell. It's Jeanne's—if she is, indeed, your mother. And she might not want it spread abroad. At the very least, you have to speak to her first, and only if she agrees, do you have the right to mention it to Anton."

Much though she'd have liked to argue the point, Diana had to acknowledge her friend was right. "I know," she said. "At bottom, I've known it all along. Thanks for the straight talk, Carol."

"Hey, what else are friends for?" she said. "Listen, you sound beat, so I'll hang up now, but keep me posted, okay?"

"I will. Love to you and Annie, and my apologies to Tim."

She replaced the handset and stood a moment, slumped against the edge of the desk. She'd do what she had to do, but not tonight. She didn't have the energy.

Rubbing her temples wearily, she turned to leave the room and let out a strangled gasp of horror as a reading lamp flicked on at the other end of the room, to reveal Sophie curled up in the big leather chair beside the fireplace.

"I haven't figured out what your big, dark secret is, and I really don't care," she said conversationally, "but I can tell you this—whatever you think you know, there's a whole lot more you *don't* know. And if you've convinced yourself that Anton's marrying you because he gives a damn about you, you're delusional, and I can prove it."

CHAPTER TEN

DON'T listen.... This woman is not to be trusted.... She's a negative, embittered force bent on destroying you because she believes you've come between her and Anton.... Walk away before she succeeds.... Walk away now...!

The words hammered at Diana, appealing to her common sense, her self-respect, her belief in her fiancé, and every other instinct geared toward her own survival and preservation of the status quo. But her body refused to obey. Try though she might to propel herself toward the door, her feet sank into a morass of uncertainty provoked by Sophie's amusement and the utter conviction in her tone.

Recognizing her dilemma, Sophie unfolded her long legs from the chair, wove her way to the liquor table and poured a hefty two inches of cognac into the empty brandy snifter now cradled between her fingers. "So Anton's knocked you up," she drawled insolently. "I was wondering why you weren't swilling back the champagne to celebrate your sudden engagement—which, by the way, suddenly makes *oh*-so-much sense."

"How much have you had to drink, Sophie?"

She sauntered over to where Diana stood with the desk at her back. "Not nearly enough to prevent me from figuring you're about as gullible as a chicken trying to stare down a fox, *petite imbecile!*" she replied gleefully.

Diana couldn't remember seeing her smile quite so broadly before, and wished she hadn't bothered now. It was not a pleasant sight. "Get out of my way, Sophie. I've got better things to do than stand here listening to your drunken ramblings."

"Well, of course, little mother!" she cooed. But instead she stepped closer, enough to infuse the air with the overpowering scent of her perfume. "Just satisfy my curiosity on one point, before you go. Has Anton told you how his first wife died?"

She endowed the question with such ungodly delight that a quiver of dread prickled over Diana. Trying hard to dismiss it, she said flatly, "No. And I wasn't insensitive enough to ask. I assumed she'd died of some terminal illness, or else been killed in an accident."

"Why assume? Why not simply ask?"

"I didn't feel it was my place to probe into something I know must have caused him great pain. What matters is that it's in the past. Anton's over it."

"You think?" Sophie let out a squawk of scornful laughter. "You'd better deliver a healthy son, or you'll find out fast enough just how 'over' it he is! Oh, Diana, you poor, foolish creature! You have no idea of what's really going on. No idea, at all!"

How long are you going to let this woman taunt you like this? Diana's pride demanded. *If you can't bring yourself to walk away, then call her bluff, and have done with, but don't give her the satisfaction of knowing she has you twisting in the wind.*

Ashamed, she grabbed her dwindling gumption and forced it to assert itself. "Spare me more riddles, Sophie," she said curtly. "Either say what's on your mind, or save your breath."

"Well…if you insist." Sophie ran the tip of her tongue over her lips as if she were about to sample a deliciously forbidden morsel. "But you might want to sit down to hear this."

"I'll stand, thanks."

She shrugged. "Suit yourself," she crooned, and took another sip of brandy.

"I'm losing patience, Sophie. Let's hear it."

"Well…all right…I'll tell you—because really, you have the right to know." She made a big production of staring at the ceiling, her forefinger pressed melodramatically to her chin. "Let's see now, how do I begin? I guess, since it has all the trappings of a fairy tale, at least at the start, there's only one way.

"Once upon a time, a gently reared young French woman called Marie-Louise fell in love with, and married a handsome French Count named Anton. It was quite the ideal match, you understand, both of them being of aristocratic birth. For a while—several years, in fact—theirs was a match apparently made in heaven. But, as with most fairy tales, there had to be a wicked something or other to spoil the couple's bliss, except, in this case, it wasn't a stepmother, or a witch, it was a fatal flaw within the bride herself."

How Sophie was enjoying this, Diana realized, sickened by the relish with which the woman wallowed in her tale. Yet she continued to listen anyway, a captive audience to a story whose shades of tragedy grew darker with every word.

"In the end, it became more than the poor creature could bear. Oops!" Sophie stopped and let loose with another cackle of unholy mirth. "Unfortunate choice of words, that! Let me rephrase it. Unable to face the disappointment in her husband's eyes, or the travesty her marriage had become, the unhappy wife threw herself off the roof of the château one morning. One of the gardeners found her body on the terrace."

"Oh, God!" Recoiling in cold horror, Diana pressed both hands to her mouth.

"She made quite a mess, let me tell you. Of course, the police became involved, which by itself was bad enough because never a breath of scandal had ever touched the de Valois name before, but imagine, if you can, how much worse it became when suspicion arose that perhaps she had not committed suicide at all, but had been murdered. By her husband."

"You're lying!" Diana cried, her heart fluttering madly in her throat.

"Well, I admit he was eventually cleared. The faithful came forward in droves to provide proof he was nowhere near the château when the incident occurred. But rest assured that he drove her to her death, and has her blood on his hands as surely as if he'd pushed her off that parapet. And why, you ask? Because she couldn't give him an heir, though, God knows, it wasn't for lack of trying."

"I don't believe you! You're making this up because Anton wants me, not you."

"Don't believe me, then," Sophie said calmly. "But ask yourself this. When did he suddenly become so enamored of you that he wanted you for his wife—before he found out you were pregnant—or after? More to the point, has he ever actually come out and said those three magic little words, *I love you?*"

The questions flew like missiles, scoring a direct hit where Diana was most vulnerable. In response, the doubts she'd tried so hard to subdue rose up in protest again, crying out to be heard.

Why, if he found her so desirable, had he never attempted to come back to her bed? Never stolen a kiss in the hall, or nudged her knee with his under the table at dinner, or reassured her with a loving touch, a whispered endearment? Why, as he'd slipped his ring on her finger, had he kissed her with lips as devoid of warmth as the mistral in January?

Dear heaven, was it possible that his urgent insistence on their marrying owed nothing to his unimpeachable sense of honor, and everything to expedience? If Sophie was to be believed, the answer seemed plain enough.

And to think she'd felt guilty about not telling him she was adopted! Numb with shock, Diana sagged against the desk.

"Just as I suspected!" her tormentor crowed, accurately inter-preting the dismay she couldn't hide. "Face it, Diana, you're merely a convenient brood mare. As long as you're carrying his child, he'll cosset you and lead you to believe he has only your best interests at heart, but once you've produced the requisite heir, you'll have served your purpose. So forget any ideas you have of assuming the role of chatelaine, or of being a part of your baby's life. You'll become redundant as soon as the brat's weaned."

Like hell she would! Harvey had denied her a child, and she'd be damned if she'd let another man rob her, too. "You forget, Sophie, that I'm the mother of this child, and no one is going to deprive me of my rights—always assuming, of course, that this story you've spun for me tonight is the truth."

"You think I made it up?"

"I think you're capable of such a stunt, yes."

Sophie shook her head pityingly. "Then get Anton to show you the upper floor of the east wing—oh, but I forgot. He keeps it locked all the time, doesn't he, and refuses to discuss the reason for it? Aren't you the least bit curious as to why?"

"I know why. It's to cut down on maintenance. Jeanne told me so."

Another hoot of merriment split the air. "Jeanne would swear the earth is flat, if Anton instructed her to say so. But don't take my word for it. Do yourself a favor, get hold of that key, and go see for yourself what's hidden behind that locked door." She drained her brandy snifter and set it down on the desk. "And then, if you've any sense at all, you'll hotfoot it back to America before you find yourself legally bound to Anton in marriage…and long before your child is born!"

He paced the terrace, unease sitting in the pit of his stomach like badly digested food. Not that he cared that Diana had been adopted, or that she'd not seen fit to mention it to him sooner. After all, they both carried a lot of history yet to be revealed. But her guilty reaction to what was, on the surface, an innocent enough admission, her hunted inability to meet his gaze, the way her face had drained of color, brought back with vivid clarity the events of that night at the inn—how long ago it now seemed!—when they'd met.

His first and most abiding impression, that she wasn't all she pretended to be and couldn't be trusted, had been confirmed by the telephone conversation he'd overheard outside her room. Yet somewhere between then and now, he'd pushed to the back of his mind that the reason he'd brought her into his household was to monitor the possible enemy in their midst and, if necessary, neutralize her actions. Instead he'd lowered his guard enough to let her insinuate herself into his arms and his heart.

Damn her anyway, with her big, innocent blue eyes and sweet vulnerable mouth! Damn her gentle charm, her spirit and fire, her soft, womanly curves, and everything else about her that made him forget to be careful! That made him, even now, hot and hard and aching for her!

Increasingly restless, he spun on his heel and paced the length of the terrace again. Where the devil was she? Dinner had to be over, by now. Why hadn't she come looking for him, to chase away his doubts with a smile, a touch, a straightforward explanation? He was willing to listen, even willing to understand if, having deceived him in the beginning, she'd now had a change of heart. People made mistakes—he certainly had!—but acknowledging them, trying to put them right, made them forgivable. Most of the time, at least.

But not always. Not with Marie-Louise. She'd made certain of that. Good God, was he about to take another wife who refused to trust him enough to confide her deepest fears, her most closely guarded secrets?

Turning again, he glanced up and saw that the light had come on in Diana's room, the one place he'd avoided, except for the night she'd conceived, because he hadn't been willing to risk compromising her reputation in his household. Well, reputation be damned! There was more at stake here than his misplaced sense of honor.

* * *

She had no idea she wasn't alone in the suite until, having changed into a short cotton nightgown and washed her face, she came back to her little sitting room and picked up the cup of herbal tea Jeanne had left on the low table in front of the love seat. Even then, she didn't notice him right away. Not until his shadow, elongated and sinister, reached across the floor to block the light from the lamp on the *escritoire.*

The tea splashed down the front of her nightgown, then, stinging where it touched her skin. "Good *grief,* Anton, you scared me!" she uttered, on a choking cry.

"Did I?" he said softly.

No word of apology, she noticed. No expression of concern that such a sudden shock might jeopardize her pregnancy. Nothing at all, in fact, but an icy, unnatural calm.

She had a pretty good idea what prompted it. He was hurt and angry that she hadn't told him about her adoption—maybe even alarmed because her being unable to supply any medical history of her biological parents could possibly pose a threat to the health of her unborn child. "I suppose," she murmured, "you're here because of what came out at dinner tonight, about my being adopted."

He rocked back on his heels. "You suppose right. Why didn't you tell me sooner, Diana?"

He was giving her the opening to confess everything, and an hour ago, she'd have seized it with both hands. But that was before her mind had been poisoned with ugly suspicions. Much though she wished it was otherwise, there'd been a ring of truth to Sophie's revelations that couldn't be dismissed. Suddenly everything to do with Anton was suspect, and until her doubts could be put to rest, Diana was determined to keep her secrets to herself.

No longer trembling with fright, she set the cup back on its saucer, took the small linen napkin from the tray and mopped at the stains on her nightgown. "It didn't occur to me. It's not something I dwell on, any more than I do that I'm five feet six, and a natural blonde. It's part of who I am, that's all." She glanced up and met his gaze unflinchingly. "But it seems to disturb *you,* Anton. Why is that? Does it make me less worthy in your eyes?"

Outrage sparked in his eyes. "I'm insulted you'd even ask such a question, Diana! What kind of man do you take me for?"

"I'm not sure," she said. "Perhaps the kind who values lineage, more than most. You are, after all, *le Comte de Valois,* and I'm probably illegitimate. In other words, a bastard, in the true sense of the word."

"Unlike me, you mean, who's a prime example of the corrupted version of the word, and acts like a perfect fool on occasion?"

"I didn't say that."

"But you thought it." His mouth curled in faint amusement. "Come on, Diana," he challenged. "Admit it."

I'm admitting nothing! she determined, steeling herself against his insidious charm. Apart from anything else, the nausea that had been building for the last hour was suddenly imminent, leaving her in no shape to prolong the discussion, even if she'd wanted to. "It's been a very long day, and I'd like to go to bed—get some sleep, I mean. Can we please continue this another time?"

She'd have done better to say nothing. Closing the distance between them, he tilted up her chin, the better to examine her face. "You're feeling sick again, aren't you?"

"No," she said, closing her eyes against his probing stare, and willing her dinner to stay put long enough for her to get rid of him. Throwing up in front of him was more than she could handle; the ultimate indignity in an evening beset by one affront after another. "I just need to lie down."

"You need to change your nightgown, first." He plucked the damp garment away from her body. "Did you burn yourself with the tea?"

"No. I'm fine." She swatted feebly at his hands. "Please just go, Anton, and…"

It was no good. She couldn't keep up the pretense. Consigning dignity to hell, she lurched away from him, staggered from the sitting room, through the bedroom, and made it to the bathroom in the nick of time. Dropping to her knees, she hung her head over the toilet bowl and let go, too immersed in misery to care that he'd followed her, or that his hand smoothed the hair away from her face.

"Oh, that was fun," she panted, collapsing against the side of the bathtub when the retching finally subsided. "How long did the doctor say it would last?"

He took a washcloth from the stack piled on the vanity, rinsed it in cold water and knelt before her to wipe her face. "Usually just for the first three months, and you're already halfway there. Another six weeks, and you'll be through it."

She shuddered. "This is all your fault!"

"I daresay you're right, and I'm sorry…for everything. I had no business coming here and bullying you."

"It doesn't matter," she said wearily. "It's over now."

"It might be over, but it matters a very great deal. Your health and well-being are my responsibility, Diana, and the last thing I want is to distress you in any way. I'd never forgive myself if something happened to you or my baby."

My baby, he said. Not *her* baby, or at the very least, *their* baby.

As long as you're carrying his child, he'll cosset you and lead you to believe he has only your best interests at heart, but once you've produced the requisite heir, you'll have served your purpose….

Sophie's word floated back to haunt her, a cruel reminder of a past he seemed loath to mention. But for the knowledge that tipping her hand would give him the advantage she presently had, Diana would have challenged him to tell her how his first wife had died—and why.

"I'm perfectly fine now," she said, struggling to her feet and wanting only to be rid of him before temptation got the better of discretion. "You can leave with an easy mind."

"Not until you've changed this for a clean one, and I've seen you safely into bed," he told her, and to her horror, grabbed the hem of her nightgown and lifted it past her hips, and past her waist.

"Stop that!" she moaned, feebly trying to yank it down again.

Too little, and much too late! He'd already seen everything she had to show, and was staring at it with bemused fascination.

"Why, look at you!" he whispered.

"I'd just as soon not, and I'd definitely prefer that you don't," she spat.

He circled her nipple with a gentle fingertip, cupped the weight of her breast in the warm palm of his hand. "But you're beautiful, Diana. Beautiful in a different way from how you were before."

"No surprise there," she said, willing her traitorous flesh to ignore the seduction of his touch. "Pregnancy does that to a woman, so I'm told."

He brought his other hand to rest against her abdomen, splaying his fingers to encompass the width of her pelvis. "To think you carry a tiny life in here—my son or daughter…!" He lifted his gaze to hers, and she saw his eyes were bright with unshed tears. "It's a miracle. *You* are a miracle!"

Heat coiled within her. Left her nipples taut and aching. Left her wet and swollen at her core. Should he slide his hand lower, slip his finger between her thighs and the folds of her flesh, and touch her, she'd climax.

In outlining what she might expect in the coming months, the doctor had warned her this kind of thing could happen. "As for sex, it's been my experience that women either want no part of it, or they can't get enough of it," he'd advised her bluntly, as he drew blood from her arm. "Listen to your body. It will tell you what it needs."

It was telling her in no uncertain terms. Another second, and she'd be tearing at Anton's clothes, begging him to make love to her, there on the cool marble bathroom floor.

"Right now, I don't feel beautiful," she said shakily, "and the only miracle will be if I make it to bed without throwing up again. So if you must help, please look in the right of the top dresser drawer in my bedroom, and bring me the fresh night-gown you'll find there."

"Yes," he murmured, his gaze lingering one last time on her naked body, and drinking in the sight. "Certainly. Right away."

The second his back was turned, she grabbed the terry robe hanging on the bathroom door, thrust her arms into the sleeves, and secured the belt very firmly around her waist.

"I don't see any nightgowns in this drawer," she heard him say.

Of course he didn't. Moving swiftly to the bedroom, she joined him at the dresser and pulled open the next drawer down. "I just remembered, I put them in here," she said, with a con-vincing display of apology. "Sorry for the mix-up."

"That's okay, *ma chère*. No harm done."

Not much there wasn't! She tossed the gown on the bed and regarded him expectantly. "Yes...well, good night then."

She needed to get him out of her suite, out of her blood. Needed to sit calmly and consider her next move. To trust, or not to trust? To search for answers that would either condemn or exonerate him—or to dismiss everything Sophie had told her as the unfounded ravings of a woman driven to desperate lengths by jealousy?

"Just one more thing before I go, Diana." He tucked a strand of hair behind her ear, and dipped his head lower, bringing his face close to hers.

Don't let him kiss you! You'll be lost, if you do...!

Stepping quickly out of range, she faked a yawn behind her hand. "Oh, please, Anton! Can't it wait until morning?"

If he noticed how she shied away from him, he hid it well.

"That's just it," he said, his eyes mapping her face, feature by feature. "I'm leaving early in the morning for business meetings in Toulouse and won't be back until the day after tomorrow. I'd invite you come with me, but given the shape you're in—"

"Not a good idea. Not right now. But thank you for the thought." Her movements as jerky and uncoordinated as her speech, she scuttled to the little foyer and opened the door.

"You're welcome." He paused with his hand on the doorknob and searched her face again. "Take care of yourself while I'm gone. I'll miss you."

"I'll miss you, too," she lied.

His glance slid from her eyes to her mouth. Drifted lower, and lingered at the vee formed by the terry robe where it crossed over her breasts. "Will you?"

Her fist shot up and clutched the fabric tightly. Dear heaven, of all the times to grow a cleavage! "Of course."

A shadow crossed his face. "Diana, are we…okay?"

"What do you mean?"

"Is everything okay between us? Because if there's something not right, if you're troubled about something, you can talk to me, you know."

May God forgive her, she looked him straight in the eye and lied again. "Everything's fine."

He hesitated a moment longer, then lifted his shoulders in a faint shrug. "I guess that's it, then. See you in a couple of days."

"Yes," she said. "Drive safely."

"Will do." He dropped a dry, impersonal kiss on her cheek, and a moment later was gone.

She locked the door then, went to the bathroom, took off the terry-cloth robe and stared at herself in the full-length mirror. His voice all husky and deep, he'd looked at her and said, *You're beautiful in a different way.* To her critical eye, though, the only noticeable change was the tracery of blue veins on her breasts that left them looking a bit like a pair of bulbous road maps, marked in the middle with nipples gone from pale pink to dark rose. Hardly the kind of thing to inspire poets to wax lyrical, or artists to create masterpieces.

But if Sophie was to be believed, he hadn't been concerned with Diana's outward appearance. The place he'd found beauty was in her womb where his child lay.

And if Sophie had fabricated her story...?

Diana pulled on the clean nightgown, brushed her teeth and took a last look in the mirror, her mind made up. "All that stands between you and the answer is the key to the east wing," she told her image. "Fortunately you have all day tomorrow to find it."

CHAPTER ELEVEN

IT DIDN'T take all day, it took all of five minutes, although waiting for the right opportunity to get started seemed interminable. By half past ten, though, the aunts had left for their weekly shopping spree in Aix, and Sophie, seeming anxious to avoid contact with her at all costs, lay stretched out beside the swimming pool, slathered in tanning oil.

Deciding the two most logical places to look were Anton's office and his private apartment, Diana chose the latter first. Apart from the distant hum of a vacuum cleaner in the vicinity of the dining room, the house was quiet and the upstairs area deserted.

Like hers, his suite consisted of a small foyer, and two rooms, but where her sitting room was furnished in silks and delicate pastels, his was all burgundy leather, stark-white walls and rich, dark wood. A man's room, with a pedestal writing desk, small bar, television and stereo unit, and bookshelves.

Heart thumping, she went first to the desk, which had three deep drawers down either side, separated by a shallow center drawer above the knee-hole. Beginning with the center drawer, she carefully eased it open, and stared in stunned disbelief at what she saw. There, tossed in among a collection of pens and pencils in a divided tray, lay a large, ornate key she recognized immediately as the mate of the large, ornate lock on the east wing door.

"Why," she murmured to herself, "if he is so obsessed with

keeping people out of that part of the château, would he not keep this better hidden—inside a hollowed-out book, for instance, or behind a picture, in a wall safe?"

Her conscience promptly supplied the answer. *Because, Diana, he has no reason to think anyone in his loyal household would deliberately go against his wishes and force entry into an area he's deemed off-limits, or be sneaky enough to search his suite behind his back. And doesn't that leave you blushing with shame?*

Yes, it did—but not enough to stop her from slipping the key into the side pocket of her skirt. She might have thought twice about violating his trust if her sole intent had been to determine the wisdom of going ahead with the marriage. But this concerned the future of their child, and she'd go to whatever lengths she must to secure that.

The drive to Toulouse went well the next morning, despite his having had a lousy sleep. He was on the road by five, and with little traffic to contend with, arrived in plenty of time for his first appointment at ten. Yet for all that the meeting was of vital interest and importance to him, he found his mind frequently straying to Diana.

There'd been something "off" about her, last night. Even after they'd smoothed over their little contretemps, she'd remained distant, and so damned eager to be rid of him, she'd practically pushed him out the door. He wasn't a man prone to unwarranted anxiety, but as the morning dragged on, he couldn't shake off the vague sense that they'd reached a crisis point in their relationship.

A week ago, he'd have taken that as a sign to step back and weigh carefully the pros and cons of their relationship before taking it to the next level. Measured his pervasive doubts about her trustworthiness against his growing emotional attachment to her, and let the result dictate his next move. But that was before he'd seen her naked for the first time since they'd had sex. Before he'd found himself so deeply moved by the faint flush of pregnancy touching her body, that he'd wanted nothing more than to drop to his knees at her feet and adore her.

Until then, he'd have said, had he been asked, that he'd come to terms with her condition well enough. But he'd realized at that moment that he'd accepted it at a cerebral level only. Suddenly the emotional half of the equation hit home, and its impact had almost felled him.

This slender, delicate, beautiful woman would grow big with his child. Because of what he'd done, a few months from now she'd bleed and she'd sweat and she'd cry out with pain. And instead of punishing him for being the cause, she'd reward him with a son or daughter.

Where the hell did he get off, then, continuing to harbor doubts about her? To look for hidden motives? What did it matter that they'd started out on separate routes, with different ends in mind? The simple fact was, everything had changed not, as he'd once supposed, when they learned she was pregnant, but at the very moment of conception, when he'd lost himself in her silken heat, and she'd called out his name on a tremulous sigh of passion, and somehow taken hold of his heart and never given it back again.

Was this love—the kind that bound a man and woman together for life? He didn't know. Wasn't even sure he'd ever known. But of one thing he was certain. The time had come to let go of the suspicion. To stop wondering what she might try to take away from him, and focus instead on the hope and the joy and the promise she brought to his life.

"Certainement," he concurred, realizing his colleagues were proposing to adjourn the meeting for lunch in the old part of the city. "Whatever you decide is fine with me."

But she stayed in his mind, and later, on his way back to his car after oysters at a café in the Vieux Quartier, a display of estate jewelry in an antique shop window caught his eye. Pushing open the door, he went inside the shop and cast around for something special to take home to her.

As a peace offering? A bribe?

No. As a symbol of a new beginning, and better times to come. Not diamonds, he decided. They were too cold, too hard, for her tender heart. Not the heavy gold necklace studded with five carat rubies, either. It was too massive for her slender neck.

"If price is not a factor, perhaps these might be what you're looking for," the wizened old man behind the counter said, taking a rope of pearls from a case behind him and laying it tenderly on a black velvet pad. "They are round South Sea pearls, between nine and nine-and-a-half millimeters, and as you see, *monsieur,* are perfectly matched. Because they are old, the body color, which is normally white, has a creamy overtone, but the luster is extraordinary because of the thickness of the nacre."

Heat curled low in Anton's belly. Both body color and luster, he thought, reminded him exactly of the bloom on Diana's skin. Warm, glowing, and utterly perfect. It would have given him the greatest pleasure to drape her from head to foot in a dozen such strings, had they been available.

"I'll take them," he said, the need to see her, to touch her urgent in his blood. But he had business to conduct first, and made it to his afternoon meeting with seconds to spare.

Tired from their trip, the aunts retired earlier than usual after dinner, and since Anton wasn't there to bait, Sophie saw no need to hang around, either. Even so, before taking a flashlight and creeping along the gallery to the east wing, Diana waited an extra half hour after the château sank into that deep silence indicative of a house at peace for the night.

The key turned smoothly in the lock. The heavy oak door swung open on oiled hinges. Leaving it slightly ajar so that she could make a fast escape if necessary, she passed through, and with the aid of her flashlight's beam, found the switch that turned on the sconces set in the walls of a long hall that was, in effect, an extension of the gallery itself.

She hadn't been sure what to expect as she came to the end of the corridor and opened a second door that led into a large, predominantly square room with a sitting nook set in the rounded section that followed the curve of the east tower. Dilapidation and decay, reminiscent of something out of a ghost story, perhaps, complete with the scurrying of tiny mice feet? But apart from a few cobwebs and a little dust, the handsomely furnished former master suite might have been occupied as recently as that morning. And *that* proved more horrifying than anything her imagination had been able to devise, as she realized when she ventured farther into forbidden territory and discovered twin en suite dressing rooms and bathrooms.

Those she presumed to have been Anton's had been stripped bare, but Marie-Louise's full-length formal gowns, cocktail dresses and chic daytime outfits still hung behind mirrored doors in her dressing room. Cashmere sweaters arranged by color lay neatly folded in glass-fronted drawers. Footwear for every conceivable occasion, from spindle-heeled, sequined evening shoes to riding boots, stood cheek by jowl on sloping shelves. Crystal perfume bottles and body lotions remained on the dressing table, as well as her chased silver hand mirror and hairbrush, the latter even with a few long, dark hairs caught in its bristles.

In the main room, a lace-trimmed peignoir had been tossed over the bed. A pair of satin mules lay in crooked disarray on the rug next to it, as if they'd been cast off in a hurry. A gold locket on a chain, and a plain gold wedding band had been abandoned at the base of a table lamp.

On top of a carved dresser were two photographs. The first, a wedding picture in a heavy silver frame, showed a younger, more carefree Anton smiling into the camera, and beside him, his dark-haired beauty of a bride. Sunlight glanced off the diamonds at her throat. A summer breeze tugged playfully at her gossamer-fine silk illusion veil. She looked happy, radiant, full of vitality; a young wife deeply in love with her husband.

But the second, a candid shot of Marie-Louise sitting alone in the gardens, told a different story. Here, the photographer had captured a woman whose spirit was locked in torment and whose body had grown thin and gaunt with sorrow. Although still beautiful, her dark eyes had lost their light, her mouth its laughter. Her skin was stretched taut over bones that looked too brittle to bear her weight. And why?

Scattered over the top of the bedside table, fertility charts, ovulation monitors and digital thermometers spelled out the yearning of a woman desperate to conceive. Sophie, it appeared, had told the truth on one score, at least.

Driven by growing dismay and morbid curiosity, Diana opened the mullioned door set to one side of the curved tower wall and, stepping out, found herself on a narrow walkway that ran parallel to the east-facing facade of the château. Above her, the mansard roof rose steeply toward the star-speckled sky. Below lay the quiet gardens and peaceful Provencal countryside, washed with moonlight and painted with shadows. And the only thing between her and them? A wall topped with broad coping stones, low enough that even a child could have scaled it.

As the likelihood hit home that Sophie had told the truth in every respect, and that Marie-Louise had indeed fallen to her death from there, a wave of nausea that had nothing to do with her pregnancy swept over Diana. With a broken cry, she sank to her knees and hugged her arms over her stomach.

It was almost midnight when he eased the BMW into the fore-court, and killed the engine. No point in waking up the entire household at that hour, especially not Diana who needed her sleep, he decided, keying the remote entry code to let himself inside the château. But the minute he stepped through the front door and went to rearm the security system, he saw at once that something was wrong. The signal light beside Zone 5 was flashing.

Someone was in the upper gallery, and whoever it was didn't know that, in addition to the building's perimeter alarms, unused sections of the house were protected every night by infrared security beams which, when broken, tripped their relays. Could be the kitchen cat had escaped and found her way up to the third floor, he rationalized, but he'd check it out anyway.

The gallery lay in darkness and it wasn't until he turned on the lights that he noticed the door to the east wing was open. He knew then not only that he couldn't blame the cat, but that whoever was trespassing in an area well-known to be off-limits, had also snooped through his private suite to find the key that would give her access.

And that he was dealing with a woman was as much a foregone conclusion, as her identity.

Fury boiling in his blood, he strode the length of the gallery, passed into the hall beyond and covered the remaining distance to the bedroom. "Damn you, Sophie!" he roared, slamming its door back on its hinges. "How dare you intrude in here, and what the devil are you after?"

Although at first glance the suite appeared deserted, a soft whimper of distress drew his attention to the open door leading to the walkway. At that, his rage died, chased away by a chilling sense of déjà vu. *Not again,* he prayed, his mind assailed by blood-soaked memories of a tragedy he should have foreseen and been able to prevent. *Dear God, not again!*

But his dread persisted. As surely as he knew Sophie had come to Provence a sad, embittered woman hoping for another shot at marriage with a man who could afford her, he also knew he was not, nor ever could be, that man. He'd thought she knew it, too.

But if his announcing he planned to marry Diana had driven her over the edge of reason…if she'd decided she'd couldn't face being cast aside again by a man who didn't want her…?

Galvanized by fear, he raced to the open door, only to stumble to a halt on the threshold, his vision impaired by the sudden change from light to dark. "Sophie?" he called softly, peering blindly into the night. "Where are you?"

After a second or so, a figure rose from the shadow of the parapet, a pale blur in the gloom, too slight to be his cousin. "Here. And I'm not Sophie," Diana replied.

Supporting herself with one hand against the wall, she stumbled past him into the room, her face ashen, her expression frozen. Shocked almost speechless, he followed her, and only when he realized she was making her unsteady way to the door that would take her out of the east wing, did he find his voice again and say sharply, "Hold on a minute, Diana. Where do you think you're going?"

"Anywhere, as long as it's away from you," she said hoarsely.

"Not quite yet," he ruled, closing his fingers around the soft skin of her upper arm. "Not until you explain what you're doing here in the first place."

"I came looking for the truth, and I found it."

"And what truth is that?"

"You're a smart man," she replied with unvarnished scorn. "Figure it out for yourself."

A different kind of anger gripped him then, one directed entirely at himself. *This,* he raged silently, *is what happens when a man breaks his own rules, ignores the instincts that have guided him all his adult life and lets his hormones rule his mind. He loses perspective, along with his self-respect and damn near everything else he ever valued! You bloody fool, you've got exactly what you deserve!*

"I figured you out a long time ago, Diana," he replied bitterly. "I admit, you've got more class than most, but I got it right the first time when I realized that, at bottom, you're nothing but an underhanded opportunist."

Yanking her arm free, she rounded on him, spitting fire and fury. "Well, that makes two of us, then, doesn't it, because what kind of man keeps a shrine to his poor, barren dead wife, at the same time that he actively pursues a replacement who can give him what *she* could not?"

"What the hell are you talking about?"

"The fact that I'm nothing to you but a…a *womb!*"

So that was it! She'd snooped around and found out about Marie-Louise's inability to bear a child; the deep, dark motive the police had tried to pin on him, when they'd put him under suspicion for her death! "If a womb was all I wanted, I could take my pick from any number of women willing to lend me theirs—without my having to offer to marry them first," he informed her coldly. "You're sadly behind the times, Diana. Not only are the days of noblesse oblige long past, but there are recognized medical facilities offering everything a man needs to produce an heir, from in vitro fertilization of donor eggs to genetic surrogacy. I didn't ask you to become my wife because you happen to be pregnant with my child, although I'll admit that lent a certain urgency to my proposal. I asked because, foolishly, I thought we'd found something special and could make a good life together."

"Sure you did!" she shot back scathingly. "That's why, except for the night we had sex, you've never tried to be alone with me again, and why you never touch me or kiss me as if you mean it."

"You think I stayed away from you because I didn't want you?" He slapped the flat of his hand to his forehead. "For pity's sake, Diana, I'm a man, not a eunuch, and you're a beautiful, desirable woman. Even though you're woefully lacking in moral scruples, I've kept my distance because I want you so badly, I don't trust myself to be near you."

"You could have fooled me!"

"Apparently I fooled myself more. I refused to listen to my head, and followed my heart instead, even though I've suspected from day one that you've been lying to me and everyone else in this house. You didn't come here to recover from a broken marriage. You came to poke around in people's lives and dig up painful history, without any thought for the damage you might cause."

Her eyes bright with sudden tears, she cried, "Of course I thought about it! I never wanted to hurt anybody. I just wanted to get to the truth."

"Don't make me laugh," he said, disgust thick in his throat. "Sensationalism is the only truth people like you understand. But you picked on the wrong victim, this time. I had my fill of third-rate reporters when my wife died, and I'll be damned if I'll put up with one again."

She looked at him as if she thought he'd lost his mind. "What in the world are you raving about?"

"Tabloid journalism, what else? *Mon dieu,* you have the nerve to accuse me of not being able to let go of my dead wife, but it's you and your kind who won't let her rest in peace."

"You think that's why I'm here—to try to dig up dirt on your poor wife's death?"

He had to applaud her. Her voice fell to a shocked whisper of disbelief, and she gave an excellent imitation of a woman who'd had the wind knocked out of her. But hadn't he recognized from the first that she was very good at projecting just the right reaction to whatever situation she happened to find herself in? Suitably modest, when necessary? Swamped in misery, if the occasion called for it? Sweet as sugar, when it suited her to be?

"That's exactly why you're here, so spare me the wide-eyed innocent act, because it's not working any longer," he said harshly. "I might have lost my head long enough to sleep with you, but the damage to my brain was only temporary. It's functioning on all cylinders now."

She leaped at him then, and only his quick reflexes fended her off before her fingernails raked down his face. "You arrogant, ego-maniacal…*jerk!*" she wailed. "This isn't about you or your tragic past. It's about me, and my future."

"Meaning what, exactly? That you're willing to forfeit your career, if it means snagging me for a husband?"

She lifted her gaze to his, and the way she looked at him, as if seeing him clearly for the first time, filled him with self-loathing. Finally, in a small, defeated voice, she said, "I didn't come here to trap you in marriage, or harm you or your family in any way, Anton. I came looking for my birth mother. And I think I've found her."

"Here?" He wished he could reject her claim as the last-ditch attempt of a woman forced to resort to the outlandish in order to justify her actions, but the fight had gone out of her. Tears again filled her big blue eyes and rolled down her face. And he knew with sudden, blinding certainty, that she spoke the truth. "*Here,* Diana?" he repeated, more gently this time.

She nodded. "Don't ask me to name her," she sobbed. "I don't have the proof, or the right."

A flood of guilt washed over him at that. He, who prided himself on being a man of reason, had rushed home full of magnanimous forgiveness for sins she'd never committed. Yet, like the *imbecil* he undoubtedly was, it had taken him no time at all to leap to erroneous conclusions and condemn her accordingly.

Overcome with remorse, he caught her in his arms and drew her to his chest. Her heart fluttered against his, desperate as a bird trapped in a net. "Ah, Diana," he murmured, "don't you know you can tell me anything?"

"No," she sobbed. "You won't believe me. You don't trust me. You think I'm—"

He hushed her with his mouth, bringing it down on hers in

a desperate attempt to absorb her pain and absolve his guilt and let her know how sorry he was. She tasted of tears and despair, and all he intended was to let her know he was sorry for having misjudged her, not just tonight but from the very start.

What made him think he was above the weakness of other men, and that, once unleashed, the hunger he'd fought so hard to control would be satisfied with just a simple touch, a fleeting taste?

Heat roared through his blood, savage and unstoppable, reducing penitence to ashes. Driven past all sense of decency, he kissed her more deeply, persuaded his tongue between her lips and thrust it repeatedly into the sweet, dark recesses of her mouth.

She gave a little murmur. Her hands crept up around his neck. She leaned into him, aligning her soft curves to accommodate his hard angles. Flattening her breasts against the wall of his chest. Tilting her hips to cradle his erection against her belly.

It was too much, and not nearly enough. Almost immediately, he was throbbing, pulsing, embarrassingly close to ejaculating.

He lifted his mouth from hers. "Diana…?" he groaned urgently.

She opened her eyes, saw the agony in his, and knew what he was asking. "Yes," she breathed, on a soft sigh of surrender. "Yes. But please, Anton, not here."

"Of course not here," he said, and hoisting her in his arms, he carried her away from that haunted place to the sanctuary of his suite in the west wing.

CHAPTER TWELVE

HE KICKED his door closed, and with the blood thundering through his veins, took her, there in the foyer. Propping her up against the wall, he raised her nightgown with one hand, opened his fly with the other, and pushed himself between her thighs.

She parted them willingly, so wet and eager to receive him that, before he was fully inside her, the plump folds of her flesh were already rippling around him in anticipation of her climax. Helpless to stop them, she gasped aloud, buried her face at his throat and clutched the lapels of his jacket to keep herself upright.

This was madness. A man his age knew better than to be fumbling in a dark corner like a randy teenager at the mercy of his hormones. The bedroom lay no more than seven meters away, the study closer yet. But his body…hers…they weren't concerned with decorum or finesse. They cared only about banishing the ghosts that had come so close to dividing them.

He couldn't get enough of her. Wanted to lose himself completely in her tight, hot core. Sliding both hands under her buttocks, he lifted her up, the better to fill her. As instinctively as if she'd done it a thousand times before with him, and knew exactly his shape and texture and just what was needed to drive him wild, she locked her ankles in the small of his back, and widened her thighs further.

He sank deeper and again, he almost came. To prolong the

exquisite agony, he withdrew until just his tip rested inside her. At that, she wrapped her arms tightly around his neck. "Don't leave me, Anton," she begged.

He drove into her again. And again. Rocking wildly. Deeper, faster, his chest heaving, his heart hammering. "Never, *mon ange,*" he promised hoarsely, teetering on the edge of sanity. "Not for as long as I have breath in my body."

Then his words were swallowed up by a mighty groan as the control he'd fought so hard to retain broke free in a shattering burst of passion, filling her with everything he had to give: his semen, his heart, his life.

He felt her shudder as the climax rolled over her. Held her tight as the spasms wrenched her body unmercifully. Whispered words of love in her ear as she screamed his name softly, over and over again, on a long-drawn out sigh, until at last she sank against him, spent and shivering.

Concerned, he said, "You're chilled, *mon amoureuse.*"

"No," she insisted drowsily. "I'm warm right through to my soul."

But the goose bumps pebbling her skin said otherwise, and sliding out of her, he carried her to his bathroom, flicking on lamps as he passed. He filled the tub, helped her in, then stripping off his clothes, climbed in behind her and drew her back to lean against his chest.

"Do you feel up to talking, Diana?" he asked, smoothing his hands down her arms.

"Yes," she said, her voice soft as the murmur of a dove. "Talking is something that's long overdue between us."

"Will you tell me, then, why you went into the east wing?"

"To find out if what Sophie had told me was true."

"Ah, Sophie!" He expelled an irate sigh. "I should have guessed she had something to do with it. What did she say?"

"To begin with, she found out I'm pregnant by listening in on a private phone conversation I had with my best friend in the States. Afterward, she confronted me and said your wife had killed herself by jumping off the balcony outside your room, and that, at first, the police suspected you'd actually pushed her over the edge, because she couldn't give you children."

The malicious, interfering bitch! He'd have her out of his house at daybreak, if not sooner! "Was that all she said?"

"No...."

He heard the little catch in her breath that spoke of hesitation. "Tell me the rest, sweetheart," he urged. "Trust me to understand."

"She said that the only reason you were marrying me was that I was pregnant, and that once I'd given you an heir, you'd have no further use for me." Her voice dropped lower. "And that you'd never let me be part of our baby's life because I'm not upper-class enough." She turned so that her profile faced him. "I had to find out how much of what she told me was the truth."

"Yes, you did," he said. "But what a pity you didn't just come to me and ask."

"I didn't dare. The one time I questioned you about why you kept the east wing locked, you shut down on me completely."

"With good reason—or at least, it seemed so, at the time. When Marie-Louise died, the story made the front page of every tabloid in Europe. My ancient family name, which had never been tainted by scandal, was suddenly linked to a murder investigation, and the hyenas of every newspaper rag in Europe showed up in droves to feast on the carcass."

She linked her fingers with his and uttered a soft purr of sympathy. "Coping with that, on top of your wife's death, must have been unbearable."

"It was harder on my employees. At least I could lock the gates and keep the Press out. But they were waylaid as they left their homes, followed to work and hounded with questions. Anything they said was dissected for whatever scrap of juicy gossip it might contain, and you've been here long enough to know by now that the people of this village aren't used to dealing with journalists and don't realise how their words could be twisted and taken out of context. Gregoire, who is as loyal to me and my family as if he were my brother, felt the sting of that, more than most."

"Why? What did he do?"

"He made a statement to the effect that the news crews might as well pack up and move on to their next target, because there wasn't a man, woman or child in this area who would betray me or any member of my household, and whatever secrets might lie behind these walls would remain hidden forever."

"Oh dear! A well-intentioned, but misguided response, I'm sure, since everything there was to know had already made headlines."

"That's just the point. The biggest secret of all never did come out, but only because the entire village closed ranks around me until the scandal-seekers finally grew tired of being stone-walled and went away. But you have a right to hear it, and after you do, you might decide I'm not the man you want to marry, after all."

He saw how the stillness crept over her, how she tensed as if preparing herself for a blow, and wished it weren't so. But secrets had a way of coming out, no matter how deeply buried they might be, and if he hadn't known it before, he knew now that the past was never over until it was fully put to rest.

"The thing is, Diana, despite what Sophie led you to believe, Marie-Louise was driven by her own demons, not mine. Emotionally fragile, insecure and possessive, she saw a baby as a means to keep me by her side, even though she hated intimacy and shrank from my touch except for those times when she might conceive. Even then, the most she did was tolerate me."

Diana reached over her shoulder for his hand, and when he covered it with his, pressed a kiss to his fingers. "You don't have to go on, Anton," she said, her voice low. "I can hear how much it pains you to talk about this."

"I want you to know everything, *mon amoureuse,* and I want you to hear it from me."

She inclined her head in consent. "All right."

"I felt like one of my Arabian stallions, expected to perform when the time was right. For a man, that's not easy. We can't pretend, the way a woman can. Either we're aroused, and it shows, or we're not—and that shows, too. What began as love on my part, eventually turned to pity. For her, if she ever loved me at all, it turned to hatred. Her rages became more frequent and could be heard all over this house. The maids, especially the young ones, were afraid of her, and left to work elsewhere. I suggested we seek medical help and marriage counseling, both of which she refused. To put it bluntly, Diana, things got to the point where I'd had enough and told her I wanted a divorce. And the next morning, she…" He bowed his head and fought to keep the tremor out of his voice. "She threw herself off the parapet. I had gone riding in the hills on the other side of the village. When I returned, I found one of my gardeners covering her body with his shirt."

Diana maneuvered herself around until she was kneeling before him. "Oh, my poor Anton, I'm so very, very sorry! For both of you," she murmured, stroking his face tenderly, even as tears poured down her own.

He caught her hands and brought them to his mouth. When he could look at her again, he said, "I couldn't bear to go near the east wing, after that. The memories were too painful. If it had been possible, I'd have had it burned to the ground. Instead I locked it up and pretended it didn't exist."

"Until I came along and forced you to confront it again." She leaned her forehead against his. "Forgive me, Anton. I was wrong to go against your wishes."

"You were right," he said, drawing her to her feet. "You've made me face the past, and I can let it go now—the unhappiness, the guilt, the tragedy, the terrible, terrible waste of life and time. You've made me whole again, my lovely Diana."

She smiled shakily, and with a pang he saw how pale she was, how weary she looked. Lifting her out of the tub, he took a bath sheet from the heated towel rack and dried her still-slender, supple body. "I've kept you up too long," he said contritely. "It's past your bedtime."

She wilted against the vanity. "I am rather tired."

Quickly toweling himself off, he took her hand and led her to the big wide bed in his room. "Will you sleep with me tonight, my love?"

"Yes," she said simply. "Please."

He lifted her onto the mattress, lay down beside her, pulled the covers over the two of them and took her in his arms again. She curled up against him, warm, soft and content. "Keeping your poor wife's secret was such a decent thing to do," she said, on a stifled yawn. "A lot of men would have capitalized on it to earn public sympathy and clear themselves of criminal investigation."

"I had to keep quiet. If the story of her mental instability had ever leaked out, it would have killed her parents. She was their only child, and everything in the world to them."

She smothered another yawn. "Did they blame you for her death?"

"Yes, at first. What parents wouldn't? They wanted so badly to see her happy and thought I was the person who could make that happen. In the end, when her death was ruled accidental, they softened toward me, and it was kinder to leave them in ignorance of what really happened. They'd suffered enough. And more than enough had been said—as Gregoire learned to his cost. He discovered the hard way the wisdom of keeping his mouth shut."

Another yawn, more long drawn-out than the others, preceded her next question. "Is that why he's treated me with such cool reserve?"

"Quite possibly. Ever since that time, he's been uneasy around strangers who show up for no apparent reason. In fact, he was so shaken by the fall-out from his off-the-cuff remarks after the tragedy that he tendered his resignation and offered to leave the area completely. Of course, I refused to accept it."

"Oh, I'm so glad you did," she murmured drowsily. "Otherwise, I might never have found my mother."

The next moment, she was asleep. Her lashes rested thick and dark against her cheeks, her breathing grew deep and regular, and the hand she'd stroked up and down his chest lay limp against his skin.

But for him, what she'd let slip, in those last moments before she drifted off, hit Anton with the impact of a thunderbolt booming through the quiet night.

So that's it! he thought, all the disparate pieces of her story suddenly coming together in his mind and making perfect sense. *How the devil did I miss seeing it before?*

She awoke to sunshine, a rosemary and lavender scented breeze fluttering through the open windows, and the uncanny sense that she was being watched. Opening her eyes, she found Anton stretched out on his side next to her, with his head propped up on his hand. "Good morning," he said. "Remember me?"

"Mmm-hmm." She blinked groggily, and wondered why she was naked, but he was freshly shaved and fully dressed in tailored gray trousers and a cream shirt. "What time is it?"

"Almost ten."

"Ten?" Clutching the sheet to her breasts, she went to sit up, then wished she hadn't as nausea swept over her. Swallowing, she said, "But it's Wednesday. The first tour group will be here in an hour. I need to get moving."

"Uh-uh. I fired you, remember, and we have other business to take care of today." He eased her back against the pillows. "Right now, though, you're looking a little green, *ma belle.* Will the tea and dry toast I ordered help settle your stomach?"

"I hope so," she groaned, then, as the import of his remark

struck home, started up from the pillows again. "You ordered tea and toast to be brought *here,* to your room? For me? Good grief, Anton, you'll have your entire household buzzing!"

He swung off the bed and went to the breakfast tray waiting on his dresser. "Jeanne is the only one I spoke to, and I can rely on her discretion," he said, pouring tea into a cup and bringing it to her. "And what does it matter, anyway? Everyone's going to know you're pregnant before much longer, and as far as I'm concerned, the sooner the better. I'm done with secrets."

"Me, too," she said evasively, knowing she still harbored a big one of her own. But how best to share it—and with whom? Jeanne, or Anton?

He dropped a kiss on her nose. "Good," he said, and glanced at his watch. "How long will it take, do you think, before you feel well enough to get dressed and meet me in my office?"

"Half an hour, or so. Why?"

"I want to take care of that business I just mentioned," he said easily, a mysterious half smile touching his mouth. "Shall we say eleven o'clock?"

She searched his face, looking for a hint of what he meant, but he was giving nothing away. Probably he'd arranged for her to meet his lawyer, maybe to sign a prenuptial agreement or the like. It was a common enough occurrence these days. He was, after all, a very wealthy man, and although she was hardly a pauper, her assets didn't begin to compare to his.

"Okay," she said equably. "I'll be there."

CHAPTER THIRTEEN

WEARING nothing but a badly wrinkled nightgown, and scooting down the hall to her own suite undetected, took some doing, but Diana managed it without being seen. By eleven, she'd showered, shampooed and dried her hair, and showed up outside Anton's office shortly after, wearing a cool blue cotton dress loose-fitting enough to disguise her ever-so-slightly thickened waistline.

He opened the door immediately when she knocked and ushered her inside. To her utter shock, she found Jeanne and Gregoire seated in club chairs around a low table at the far end of the room, and a ripple of apprehension skimmed over her.

Swinging her gaze to Anton, she said, "What's this all about? What's going on here, Anton?"

He put his arm around her shoulders. "Forgive me, my love, but I'm afraid you've been set up."

"So it would appear," she said. "The question is, why?"

He shrugged. "I could think of no other way to introduce you to your biological parents."

Parents? Not mother, but *parents?*

The room swam dizzily. The floor rose up to meet her. Staggering, she groped blindly for the nearest solid object, and would have fallen had he not caught her securely and steered her safely to one of the remaining club chairs.

"That was clumsy of me," he whispered, pushing her head down between her knees. "Forgive me again, *ma trés chère Dianne*."

She drew in deep, reviving breaths, dimly aware that Jeanne and Gregoire had sprung up from their seats. Opening her eyes, she saw their feet close to hers and felt another hand against her back, small and feminine. "Bring her a glass of water, Gregoire," she heard her mother say.

At length, the room stopped spinning and she was able to lift her head. Gregoire knelt before her, his eyes filled with concern. Blue eyes, just like hers. No wonder she hadn't recognized them sooner. She'd been looking at the wrong face.

"Here, *ma fille,*" he said, offering the glass.

She had to hold it in both hands because she was shaking so badly, but the ice cold water helped restore her. "I don't understand," she said, when she could speak.

Anton dropped into the chair next to hers, while Jeanne and Gregoire resumed theirs. "That's why I asked you to come here. So that we could explain."

She slewed a resentful glare his way. "You mean to say, you knew all along, and you didn't say a word to me?"

"I knew only part of the story, and it wasn't mine to tell," he said. "Where you fit into it was something I learned only last night."

"Last night?" She frowned. He'd been with her, last night. "How?"

"Because you told me."

"I did no such thing!"

He made a pitiful effort not to smile, and failed miserably. "You don't remember, do you?"

"No, I can't say I do."

"We were talking about the publicity after Marie-Louise died, and I mentioned that Gregoire had wanted to resign his position here and move away, but I'd talked him out of it. The last thing you said before you fell asleep was you were glad he didn't because—"

"Because, if he had, I'd never have found my mother." The memory came back hazily, but too real to be a dream. "I remember it now."

She looked at Jeanne and Gregoire. They were holding hands, and Jeanne was crying. Swinging her attention back to Anton, she said, "But I still don't understand why you say you already knew part of the story."

He threw a questioning glance at Gregoire. "It's up to you to tell her, my friend."

Briefly Gregoire lowered his eyes. When he looked up again, they were dull with pain. "I am fifty-one," he began. "Six years older than Jeanne. But she was only sixteen when we fell in love, and so although we promised ourselves to one another, we kept our affair secret because, in those days, a man my age would have been horse-whipped for seducing so young a girl.

"Then, one day, I received a letter from her, telling me it was over between us, and she'd left Bellevue-sur-Lac for a better life somewhere more exciting. Angry, heartbroken, at a loss to know what to do next, I buried myself in my work and learned as much as I could about viniculture, but deep in my bones I never accepted that a love such as ours had died for no apparent reason."

"But there *was* a reason," Jeanne said, taking over the story. "I had discovered I was pregnant. My Gregoire was admired, well respected, building a successful career for himself and he would have lost everything if it had become known that he was my lover—perhaps even his life, because my brothers were fiercely protective of me. I loved him too much to let that happen, and so…"

She stopped and began to cry again, helplessly, bitterly. "And so," she sobbed, when she was able to continue, "I didn't tell him I was pregnant. Instead I ran away to Aix, to a convent for unmarried mothers, and although it broke my heart, when my baby was born, I gave her up for adoption, and then I came home again."

"What happened next?" Diana asked, not even realizing she was crying, too, until Anton plucked a tissue from a box on the table, mopped at her tears and draped a comforting arm around her shoulders. "Did you tell him what you'd done?"

"Not for a long time. I was afraid, and so I avoided him whenever I could. Of course, we ran into one another often. It's impossible to hide from anyone in a village as small as ours. But one day, we met by accident down by the lake. It was my baby's first birthday, and I had gone there because I was so sad and didn't want to be with other people.

"He had been fishing, and saw me when he brought in his boat. There was no one else there, just the cold winter wind and the gray sky, and suddenly all those feelings we'd both repressed just rushed up to the surface. The next moment, we were in each other's arms, and I was telling him why I had left him, and begging him to forgive me."

She lifted her tear-stained gaze to Diana, haggard heartbreak shadowing her eyes. "And now, I must beg for yours, Diana. Because, as you have suspected for so long, you are the child I gave away, although I didn't know it until this morning when Anton came to us and told us what he'd learned."

"If you must blame someone," Gregoire put in, a terrible emptiness in his eyes also, "then blame me. I am the one who made your mother pregnant, and it was because of me that she placed you for adoption. What it has cost her in silent sorrow and private tears over the years, only I know. I can tell you that she has paid dearly. We both have."

"Not you, surely," Diana said doubtfully. "You don't even like me."

"I saw the interest you took in my wife, and at first, it's true, I didn't trust you," he admitted. "But then I became suspicious for a different reason. Sometimes, a certain look about you, the way you laughed, the expression on your face, even the way you walked, they struck a familiar note."

"I thought the same thing, when I first met you," Anton interrupted, "but I was looking elsewhere for the reason and didn't make the connection."

Gregoire nodded. "For myself, I began to wonder, could it be? Had a miracle occurred? It didn't seem possible. Our child was born in France, and you were American."

"My adoptive father was a professor of law and spent a year on an exchange program, teaching at the university in Aix," she told him. "He and my mother—my other mother," she amended, "adopted me shortly before they returned to America."

"That explains it, then." Her father shook his head, as though he couldn't believe how all the pieces of the puzzle suddenly made sense. "I waited for you to declare yourself, but you never did, and my Jeanne had suffered enough, wondering if every young woman your age might be her daughter. She denied herself more children because of what she had done to you. I couldn't raise her hopes by sharing my suspicions with her, only to have them proved groundless. So I said nothing—not because I didn't like you, Diana, but because I was afraid I'd grow to like you too much."

"I don't know what to say." She stared at them all, helplessly. "Two months ago, I was alone in the world. Now I've found not only my biological mother, but my father, too. I have a fiancé, and I'm expecting a baby in—oh!" She stopped and flung a nervous glance at Anton.

"They know," he said, clasping her hand. "I've confessed, and your father's promised not to shoot me. And, sweetheart, we all understand it's a lot for you to take in."

"But I still don't understand where you fit into it, Anton."

"I've known Jeanne and Gregoire's side of the story ever since I took over the running of the estate, and my aunts have known it even longer."

"We couldn't allow the de Valoises to place such trust in us, without their knowing what we'd done," her father said. "Even the best-kept secrets sometimes have a way of coming out and hurting people. We respect this family too much to risk having such a thing happen to them."

"You see?" Anton stroked the back of his hand up her cheek. "Your parents are smarter than we are, Diana. They realized a long time ago something we've only just learned. You have to trust the people you care about."

She glanced from him to her parents. They sat tensely, their hands clinging together, their faces full of hope and full of fear, and she wondered why she was holding back, when all she wanted was to let them know how glad she was to have found them.

"I've been looking for you for so long," she said, her voice quavering helplessly, "and by some miracle, I've found you. As far as I'm concerned, from this day on, you're my mom and dad."

She felt it then, the unconditional love she'd always longed for. It showered over her, in the feel of the arms around her, in the tears they shed and the words they murmured.

They celebrated that night, with a formal, eight-course dinner and champagne for everyone, including the nonalcoholic kind for her. Even Sophie was invited because, when he heard she'd made arrangements to fly to Lisbon the next day, Anton relented and allowed her to stay at the château one more night.

Diana took pains to look her best, pinning up her hair and putting on the one evening gown she'd brought with her, a strapless number of softly draped silk chiffon that might have been designed for a woman in early pregnancy.

"Radiantly beautiful and needing only one more thing to make you perfect," Anton murmured huskily, when he stopped by her room to accompany her downstairs. Then, turning her around, he slipped something cool and smooth around her neck, and urged her toward the mirror. "These belonged to my mother, and I know she'd want you to wear them tonight. What do you think?"

"That you're going to make me cry again," she said, stunned by the beauty of the delicate layered diamond necklace glinting against her skin in the lamplight.

"Then prepare to cry often, because this is just the first of more good things to come."

"You don't have to buy me expensive baubles," she whispered, loving him with her eyes. If ever a man was made to wear black tie, it was her handsome fiancé. "I have you, and that's enough to make me happy."

Everyone else had gathered in the drawing room when they arrived, including her parents. Despite their reservations, Anton insisted they join the party.

"But I'm your housekeeper!" her mother had objected.

"You're also my future mother-in-law, Jeanne," he'd reminded her. "And that means some things are going to change around here, so you'd better get used to the idea."

"Well, of course, Josette and I knew you were pregnant," Hortense confided gleefully, taking Diana aside as they all trooped into the dining room. "You have that luminous look about you. And my darling, we're delighted. I've never seen Anton happier."

Not surprisingly, when she heard of Diana's connection to her cousin's housekeeper and head vintner, Sophie had to get in one last malicious dig. "Poor Marie-Louise wasn't up to much," she muttered behind her hand, "but at least she came with the right pedigree."

"Sophie, why don't you do us all a favor and stick a fork in your eye?" Josette suggested sweetly, a remark that promptly reduced Hortense to quivering hysterics.

Well, one thing was certain, Diana decided, unable to keep her own face straight. Life would never be dull, as long the aunts were around to keep things entertaining.

* * *

Later, when the excitement had died down and the château had settled into silence, he'd drawn her along the upper hall to his suite and locked the door behind him. "Tomorrow," he promised, "you'll decide which rooms are to be ours after we're married, and how you want them furnished. But you're spending tonight here, with me."

All through dinner, he'd watched her, impatient to be alone with her, yet enjoying seeing her glow in the affection of her parents and his aunts. Now, as she lay naked on his bed, with him sitting beside her, naked also, he watched her again, hungry and desperate to make love to her. But he was determined that, tonight, he would do so at leisure, with none of the frantic haste that had marked their previous encounters.

Flushing, she said, "You're staring," and went to turn off the bedside lamp.

"Don't," he said, forcing the word past the thickness in his throat. "Let me look at you. I want to see you when you come, when I touch you here…and here."

With slow reverence he skimmed her shoulders, her breasts, her hips, her thighs. Her skin was warm, and smooth as cream. And with every brush of his hand, encroaching passion flooded her until she was stained the color of rosé wine, and begging him with inarticulate little cries to fill her with his powerful strength.

"Easy, *mon trésor,* the night is long and all ours," he murmured, eluding her when she reached out to cradle his throbbing flesh, and dipped his head to press a kiss to the side of her mouth, to take the tip of one rosy nipple between his teeth and nip gently. "I have something to give you, first. I saw these in a shop in Toulouse, and knew they were meant for you."

Without taking his eyes from her face, he reached into the bedside table drawer and withdrew a black velvet sack. Loosening its drawstring with his teeth, he pulled out the long rope of pearls and let it fall softly at her throat. It rolled over her breasts, coiled sweetly in the hollow of her navel, slipped lower to her belly, then slithered to the mattress and nested against the side of her thigh. And everywhere it went, his tongue followed, dancing lightly over her skin until she was thrashing her head back and forth with need and clawing at his shoulders.

"What is it you want me to do?" he asked, adoring her with his eyes. "Tell me how to please you, Diana."

She groped wildly for his hand, and drew it between her legs. "Touch me here," she begged. "Please, Anton, I need to feel you here."

"Oui," he said, and with a single deft caress of his finger, brought her to the brink of orgasm. Then he lowered his head and stroked her with his tongue, and she arched off the bed with a strangled cry.

"Oui," he said again, lifting his head. "Just so, *mon cherie.*" And he brought to the brink a third time, feathering his tongue over the sensitized nub of flesh at her center until she splintered like crystal into a thousand prisms of sparkling ecstasy. Then, with the aftershocks still rippling over her, he buried himself in her sleek folds, and loved her with everything he had to give.

When it was over, and she lay panting and glistening beside him, he cradled her to his heart, and the words he'd been too proud to say before came easily to him because, after all was said and done, they were the only truth that counted. "I love you, Diana," he whispered.

She looked up at him, the rise and fall of her breasts, the sultry droop of her eyelashes, a promise in themselves that, this time, he had chosen well. Theirs would be a marriage made in heaven, and in bed, as well.

"I'm so glad," she replied softly. "Because I love you, too. With all my heart."

EPILOGUE

2:00 p.m., March 21

THEY came to the hospital in Aix to visit her and the baby, a steady stream of people, and every one related in one way or another. Aunts, uncles, cousins, they brought flowers and candy and fruit, and little hand-made gifts for her son.

They shook Anton by the hand, and hugged her. "We're so glad you found your way home," they whispered. "Look at your mother and father! You've made them smile again."

Stirring in his bassinet, the baby let out a squeak. "Stay put!" Hortense cried, pressing Diana back against the pillows when she reached for him. "I'll hand him over. You had a rough time of it, last night, and need to take it easy."

Seated on her other side, Anton leaned close. Touched her hair, her face, his gaze hungry. "I want to be alone with you and our son."

"Me, too," she murmured, "but we have the rest of our lives together."

"Even so, tell me if this rush of visitors gets to be too much, and I'll send everyone packing. You've been through enough in the last twenty-four hours…" He cleared his throat. Blinked his gorgeous gray eyes rapidly. "*I've* put you through enough."

She smiled and cupped his jaw. This proud, indomitable

husband of hers, who'd never backed down from a challenge in his life, had had a hard time of it, seeing her in the throes of childbirth. "*Mon dieu,* how much more can she stand?" he'd asked wretchedly, when at last she reached the final stages of delivery and was struggling to push their baby out into the world.

"Courage, *mon ami,*" the doctor had urged. "Your wife is magnificent!"

She hadn't felt magnificent, not then, with the sweat dripping from her hair and rolling down her face. Giving birth wasn't glamorous, but oh, it was beautiful and exhilarating! And now, bathed and perfumed, with the green hospital gown exchanged for a fine cotton nightgown embroidered in silk, her eight-and-a-half-pound baby safe in her arms, and her husband gazing at her as if she were the most extraordinary woman ever to walk the earth, she felt like a goddess.

"We made this baby together, my darling man," she reminded him, "and he's worth every minute of hard labor it took to bring him here."

At that moment, a nurse appeared at the door of her private room, which was just as well. The look on Anton's face, the hunger in his gaze as it slid over Diana…well, it had been a week or more since they'd last made love, and the strain was beginning to tell!

"Too many visitors in here," the nurse declared, shooing away everyone but Anton, his aunts and her parents, before ushering in Henri. "Immediate family only from now on, please, although I will allow this man a few minutes. He's been waiting patiently for the last half hour for his turn to indulge in a little baby worship."

"I was wondering where you were," Diana said, holding out her hand in welcome. "Come here and say hello to your great-nephew. He looks a little like you, don't you think?"

"Not from everything I've heard," her uncle said, dropping a slow wink Anton's way. "This one's a de Valois to the core—

with a bit of his mother's beauty thrown in for good measure, so I'm told."

She laughed. "Oh, very diplomatic, *mon oncle,* but then, you always did know just the right thing to say! What's in that basket you're carrying?"

"Bouillabaisse and bread still warm from the oven. Better than that abominable stuff they try to pass off as food in this place. I've brought enough for all of you, and your Tante Solange baked lemon tarts for dessert." He looked over his shoulder furtively. "I even smuggled in a bottle of champagne to celebrate the little one's safe arrival."

Very much the protective new grandfather, Gregoire said, "I'm not sure that's such a good idea. Diana's nursing, and champagne might not agree with the baby."

"What do you know about babies?" Henri scoffed good-naturedly. "*I* am the expert here, and I tell you, *mon ami,* a Frenchman is never too young to appreciate good champagne, and we now know that this young fellow is French through and through."

Diana shared a smiling glance with Anton.

I love you, he mouthed silently.

I love you, too, she telegraphed back, filled with a wonderful sense of peace and contentment. "It's okay, Dad," she said. "I don't need champagne to celebrate. I have my family. It's all I ever wanted, and more than enough for me."

THE ITALIAN
COUNT'S BABY

BY
AMY ANDREWS

Amy Andrews has always loved writing and still can't quite believe that she gets to do it for a living. Creating wonderful heroines and gorgeous heroes, and telling their stories is an amazing way to pass the day. Sometimes they don't always act as she'd like them to, but then, neither do her kids, so she's kind of used to it. Amy lives in the very beautiful Samford Valley with her husband and aforementioned children, along with 6 brown chooks and two black dogs. She loves to hear from her readers. Drop her a line at www.amyandrews.com.au

To Anna. A fabulous neighbour.
Thank you for Hotel Pasitea.

CHAPTER ONE

KATYA PETROVA clutched her stomach as the plane hit a small air pocket. Her insides lurched and she felt a flutter down low as the plane continued its smooth journey.

The baby? She kept her hand in place and waited, every cell in her body straining to detect a tiny foetal movement. *Come on, baby*. The seconds ticked by. Nothing. A few more. Still nothing.

Well, duh! She removed her hand impatiently. As if there would be. She was just twelve weeks. The baby was only about ten centimetres long! She had a good few weeks yet, maybe even up to ten according to some books, before she'd feel his or her first movements.

She made a mental note to stop reading books. She needed to stop this fantasy land she kept drifting into. There was absolutely no point getting more attached than she was because there was no way she could be a mother to this baby. No way.

It was bad enough that she already loved the baby more than her own life. She had to toughen up. Stop thinking of it as 'the baby' or 'he' or 'she'. 'It' was so much more removed. And that's what she needed to be—removed. Because she was doing the right thing here. When you loved somebody you wanted the best for them, right? And she was *so* not the best thing for this baby.

And that was why she was here on this plane flying to meet a man she barely knew. To find out if the best thing for the baby was its father.

By the time she disembarked an hour later and had gone through passport control and customs, Katya was feeling so tired and nauseated she wanted to scream. Now she was nearly in her second trimester the vomiting was settling but her extreme state of nervousness was a volatile mix for her delicate constitution.

It had been three months since she'd seen him, three months since she'd done the single most irresponsible thing she had ever done. And they had parted badly. And she was carrying his baby.

Being greeted by flowers did not improve her mood.

'I said strictly business.'

She glared at him, hands on her hips, staring at the massive bouquet of red roses. She could smell their delicate fragrance wafting towards her and pressed her hands harder into the bone and flesh of her hips to stop herself reaching for them.

People jostled past and around them at the busy arrivals gate of Leonardo Da Vinci Airport, eager to greet loved ones. The two of them stood out in the crush, the only two people keeping their distance despite the press of bodies around them. They did not embrace. They did not cry.

Count Benedetto Medici chuckled and feigned a wounded look. Just like he remembered her. Blunt. To the point. Her accented English making the words even more clipped. Someone who didn't know her might even describe her as unemotional. But he knew intimately that under the surface Katya Petrova was an intensely passionate woman. '*Cara*,' he cajoled.

'Do not *darling* me,' Katya said briskly, ignoring the way his voice stroked heat across her skin. That's what had got her into this mess in the first place. Memories of their last night together played like a film in her head. Unfortunately time, distance and weeks of throwing up had not immunised her against his charms or dulled her reaction to the sexy purring quality of his very deep, very male voice.

'But I bought them for you…as a welcome-to-my-country gift.'

Katya sniffed as his beguiling smile did funny things to her equilibrium. 'I am here to work, Ben. There is no need for gifts.'

'They are too beautiful to throw away,' he said softly, thrusting them towards her again.

Katya could smell the crimson blooms and she was, oh, so tempted. But there was a principle here. Flowers were for lovers and they weren't. Once did not count. Ben was a rich, attractive man—aristocracy for heaven's sake—used to getting his own way. But she wasn't here to be a rich man's darling. That was her mother's specialty.

She was here on a fact-finding mission. Just because she couldn't look after this baby, it didn't mean she was just going to let anybody do it. Ben may be the father but she knew so little about him. Yes, he could obviously provide for it. But could he give it the other things?

The intangibles. His love. His time. His devotion. His stories. His commitment. Katya knew too well what it was like, growing up without any of those things. She also knew what it was like growing up without a father. Maybe things would have been different if she had. Maybe not. But she wanted the very best for this baby and next to a mother, surely that had to be the father? And that was what she was there to find out.

She looked around her at the now thinning crowd and

spotted a young man rocking on his feet, anxiously scanning the arrivals corridor. 'Ask him who he's waiting for,' she said, turning back to Ben.

Ben chuckled again. But he did as she asked. There was a brief exchange between the two men. 'His fiancée,' Ben relayed.

Katya smiled. 'Perfect. She'll love them,' she said, and then strode forward, dragging her single suitcase behind her on its wheels, following the exit signs.

Ben threw Katya's medium-sized bag, which looked like it had seen better days, into the boot of his Alfa.

'This is all you brought?' he asked.

'Yes. Why?'

Ben shrugged. 'Most women I know need a bag this size just for their make-up.'

Katya found herself strangely irritated by his apparent knowledge of women and their luggage. 'I am not most women.'

Amen to that. Ben shut the lid down and gave the metal an affectionate tap. He glanced up to see her staring at the vehicle. 'What?' he asked warily.

She shrugged. 'I thought you'd drive a Ferrari or a Lamborghini.'

He smiled. 'Disappointed?'

'No. Surprised.'

Of course. Katya was truly the only woman he'd ever known who had been completely unimpressed with his title or his status. In fact, it had been obvious right from the start that she had resented his wealth. Had judged him harshly on the playboy image he projected through her jaded working-class eyes.

And the truth was, he *had* owned his share of status symbols, including a very sleek red Ferrari, but that had been in another life. Back when an indulgent, lavish lifestyle had been all he had known. But a lot of water had flowed under the bridge since then. And it bothered him that she found him wanting because of his bank account.

'Maybe you don't know me as well as you think,' he said, walking towards her and opening her door.

Katya raised an eyebrow. His entire time at MedSurg he'd been the epitome of a rich, spoiled playboy. The only time she had seen anything different had been the night they had made love. The night he'd received word of his brother's death.

That night she had seen a vulnerability, a glimpse of the man beneath the façade. All his layers had been stripped away by the shocking news and he'd been raw, totally open. The playboy had gone and the man had emerged. And she'd given him her virginity without a second thought. And that was the man she needed to be the father of her child.

'Maybe I don't,' she conceded.

Ben felt her warm breath on his cheek and was surprised by her concession. This was not the Katya he remembered. The sassy Katya. The Katya who gave him a hard time. The Katya who didn't give him an inch. But he had seen this Katya once before. The night she had offered him comfort and solace.

They were close now and visions of that night swamped him. He could smell her familiar scent. Cinnamon, just as he remembered, and he had a sudden urge to see if she would taste as he remembered, too. Her open-necked shirt afforded him a view of pale skin and prominent collar-bone and he suddenly wanted to lean in and nuzzle along the hard ridge and the hollow above.

Katya looked into his slumberous brown eyes and could see the passion flaring to life in their smouldering depths. Read exactly what he was thinking. God knew, she was thinking it herself. She could feel herself sway, hear her breath roughen, hear his follow suit.

A horn blared behind them, echoing around the cold cement corners of the car park, and they both froze. Katya's heart hammered as she pulled herself back from the brink. She was not here to pick up where they left off! She remembered how offhand he'd been the morning after, how confused she'd been by his casual job offer, like he'd just thrown money on her bedside table, and her determination to act like it hadn't been a big deal. She struggled to find that miraculous act again now.

'How long will it take to get to Ravello?' she asked as she slipped into the passenger seat on shaky legs.

'We are staying in Positano tonight,' he said when he joined her, 'in my mother's villa.'

He buckled up, noticing her body, which she'd been holding quite erect anyway, as if the luxury of the leather seats would taint her working-class skin, stiffen further.

'This was not part of the plan,' she said.

'My mother wishes to welcome you to Italy. She is preparing a feast in your honour. Relax,' he teased, and reached across to squeeze her denim-clad knee.

Katya glared at him and then at his hand, picked it up off her knee and put it back on the gear lever. 'That is not necessary.'

'My mother insists.' He shrugged. 'She will be very disappointed if we don't stop. We will go to Ravello in the morning. It is only half an hour, depending on traffic.'

He saw the grim set to her mouth and knew from experience she was itching to say more. He'd seen that glitter in her eyes before and had been the recipient of the caustic dialogue that usually followed. But he could also tell that she didn't want to offend his mother.

'Your mother knows we are work colleagues only, *da*? I trust we will have separate rooms?'

Ben couldn't help himself, he roared with laughter. His

mother was an old-fashioned woman, had raised them with traditional values. She thought premarital sex was a sin. 'You have nothing to fear there, Katya.'

'Good,' said Katya, and turned to gaze out of her window.

Ben concentrated on his driving, navigating his way out of Rome easily. He had spent a lot of his years in the capital and knew it well. The Medici family had residences in Rome and Florence and he had split his formative years between the two.

He took the *autostrada* exit to Naples. His family had always wintered on the Amalfi coast, his mother preferring the gentler climate of southern Italy, and the Positano villa had been her permanent home for five years now. For many years it had been his favourite place in all of Italy but too much had happened there and when he had left a decade ago he had sworn to never return. But the Lucia Clinic was there. His duty was there.

He glanced at Katya's profile. She appeared to be engrossed in the scenery and he took the opportunity to study her. She was dressed casually in hipster jeans. They were snug-fitting rather than tight, emphasising her slender thighs. Her white, short-sleeved shirt looked cool, the top few buttons undone, revealing a hint of cleavage.

Funny…he'd seen her almost every day for a year and yet had rarely seen her in civvies. In his mind, when he pictured her, which he did a little too often for his own sanity, it was as she'd been that last night. Gloriously naked, her body slick with sweat, her blue eyes wide and dazed with passion. He remembered the bite of her nails into his buttocks, the nip of her teeth into his shoulder, the gasps of pleasure from her mouth.

He dragged himself back from the fantasy with difficulty. Despite the evidence of his eyes, he couldn't quite believe that she was actually sitting here beside him.

To say he'd been surprised to take her call a few weeks ago was an understatement. After the way they'd parted, the way he'd acted after such an amazing night, it had hardly been his brightest moment.

Is that job offer still open? she had asked. And he had been so delighted to hear her accented English, so relieved that she was still talking to him after his morning-after bungle, that he'd forgotten what a shrew she could be and had said, *Of course*. In honesty, he'd missed her. Missed her frankness. Her cute accent. Her aloofness. She was the only woman he'd ever met who could turn him on through pure indifference.

In typical Katya fashion, she hadn't gone into detail about her reasons on the phone. She hadn't explained why she was now doing the very thing she'd told him she wouldn't. *I'd rather drink bad vodka*, that's what she'd told him that last morning. She had just lectured him about what her coming to Italy did and didn't mean. A work thing, she had said. No taking up where they had left off.

So why had she changed her mind? He had to admit to being a little more than curious. Perhaps she needed the money for some reason? The Lucia Clinic certainly paid its staff well. MedSurg, on the other hand, the charitable organisation they had both been employed by, while incredible to work for, did not.

But, then, no one joined its ranks to get rich. MedSurg involved a higher ideal. And Katya had been committed to staying on with them—for ever, she had said that awful morning. So something had come up to change her mind.

Wanting to change direction, she had told him on the phone. But he knew that was a lie. What were the words she had used when she'd first realised his family owned the world-renowned Clinic? *A place where rich vain people desper-*

ately trying to hold onto their youth were pandered to. Or words to that effect anyway. He smiled to himself. Would she tell him if he asked?

'Shouldn't you be watching the road?' Katya said, turning away from the window to pierce him with a disapproving glare.

Hmm. Maybe not.

Not even as the dense housing of Rome fell away and Italian countryside surrounded them could Katya ignore the weight of his stare. She'd been hyper-aware of him the minute she had spotted him, half-hidden behind the largest bouquet she had ever seen. She had hoped that their time apart would have put her attraction into perspective but, if anything, it seemed to be stronger.

It was the clothes, she decided. Although he filled out a pair of scrubs magnificently, it was nothing to how he looked dressed as Italian nobility. Everything about him screamed money. The cut of his trousers. The way the fabric of his shirt draped across the breadth of his shoulders and moulded to his chest, emphasising his six-foot-plus frame. The soft leather of his expensive shoes.

Who had said clothes maketh the man? Whoever it had been—they'd been right. In scrubs she'd been able to make believe he was just Ben. Gorgeous, flirtatious, persistent, annoying Ben. Ben the surgeon. That Ben had been relatively easy to ignore.

But in his civvies he looked…regal. Aristocratic. Like Count Benedetto Medici. Rich as sin. Hotshot plastic surgeon. And…the father of her baby. Katya knew she would find this Ben far from easy to dismiss.

Knew she couldn't afford to. Knew she had to get to know him. Get behind the façade, behind the clothes. Find the man she'd made love to three months ago, if indeed he actually existed, or whether he'd just been a temporary aberration in an extraordinary set of circumstances.

A car cut in front of them and then surged forward, swaying all over the *autostrada*, the white lines completely ignored.

Katya swore in Russian, clutching the dashboard, her heart racing at their near miss. 'Idiot,' she repeated in English at the car disappearing fast into the distance. 'Did you see that?' she asked, turning to him.

Ben chuckled. 'You will have a hoarse voice by the end of the day if you yell at everyone who does that. We Italians drive as we live. Passionately.'

'Bloody dangerously,' Katya muttered, trying not to think about the passionate Italian in Ben.

Ben had been right and the next two hours Katya clung to the edge of her seat as his powerful Alfa ate up the miles. 'Do you need to go so fast?' she asked him as she glanced at his speedometer and noticed he was going 140.

He smiled at her. 'This is not fast,' he said. As if to emphasise his point, three cars swerved around them and sprinted ahead, leaving the sporty car eating their fumes.

'Mad,' she said, shaking her head.

'This is nothing.' He winked. 'Wait till we get to the coast road.'

Katya wouldn't have believed that the experience could get any more terrifying, but she was wrong. The coast road was exactly as Ben had warned. A sheer white-knuckled adrenaline rush. The scenery was breathtaking on a sunny autumn afternoon—the craggy cliffs towering above them on one side and the sparkling blue Mediterranean on the other—but it was impossible to properly admire the majesty from behind her hands.

Speed was no longer an issue, too many cars made it impossible to get above forty. Now it was just sheer bloody-minded insanity. Cars and mopeds and trucks and tourist buses all vied for room on the narrow twisting roads that clung to the cliff face and even tunnelled through in places.

Cars were parked crazily on either side and sometimes both sides of the road, crammed into any remotely accessible space, narrowing the available room considerably. Katya covered her eyes as Ben manoeuvred his car through and around the general mayhem.

'It's a beautiful sunny Sunday. Italians always head for the beach,' he told her as he skilfully worked the gear lever.

She marvelled at how unruffled he appeared when her pulse was hammering madly in her neck. Mopeds darted around him like schools of fish, vehicles overtook them on blind corners and horns blared constantly. Some drivers even decided to pull up in the middle of the road and chat with pedestrians they apparently knew.

She had never seen such chaos in all her life. They traversed the narrow streets of villages, stopping for wandering dogs and groups of chatting locals. They passed dozens and dozens of restaurants and hotels lining the route, all decorated with gorgeous splashes of vibrant bougainvillea.

They passed several roadside vendors selling fruit from small trucks and even passed one with a raised metal frame upon which dozens and dozens of red chillies had been strung up, hanging in colourful plump bunches.

'Ben!' she yelled, pointing at an oncoming bus directly in their path as she clutched his thigh and shut her eyes.

Ben laughed and took the necessary evasive action. 'It's OK now, you can open your eyes,' he teased.

'Oh, God, how much longer?' she asked, still holding his

leg, the bulk strangely reassuring. It had taken them an hour to travel a handful of kilometres.

'Not long.' He grinned down at her.

Katya found his smile contagious and the confidence in his brown eyes soothing. She had seen that look, the calm, quietly confident look, many times in his operating theatre. And she needed that right now because the terrifying ride had wider implications. There were three people in this car and the thought of having an accident—the baby getting hurt—was too much to bear.

She smiled back at him, pleased that on a scenic cliff road on the Amalfi coast she was with someone who could handle the perils of the journey. She became aware of her hand resting on his thigh and felt heat creep into her face.

'Sorry,' she said, withdrawing her hand.

'Don't be,' he said, returning his attention to the road. 'It felt good.'

Katya swallowed, her hand still warm from the bulky muscle. Yes, it had. *Precisely why she shouldn't have done it*.

'Here it is,' he said a few minutes later, and turned off the coast road onto the Via Pasitea, the main thoroughfare that meandered down through the maze of cliff-face villas of Positano.

Katya breathed easier now the crazy pace and chaos had settled. They were still being overtaken by the odd moped but she didn't feel as if she was about to die. She even got to appreciate the scenery. It was late afternoon by now and the fading sunlight reflected off the colourful façades of the buildings that lined the road and the cliff faces in every direction.

Yellow, pink, white, terracotta. Flowering bougainvillea crept over walls and hung off trellises everywhere. Every home, restaurant and hotel was decorated with flower boxes ablaze with beautiful colourful blooms. The Mediterranean sparkled in the distance. Positano dazzled the eye and Katya was instantly charmed.

Ben waved at people as he passed. They called out to him and he smiled and greeted them by name. He seemed to know everyone.

'A popular man,' she mused.

'My family has had a home here for many generations.' He shrugged.

Katya turned back to the window, keeping her eyes firmly trained on the scenery. How would that be? To have grown up here? For the baby to grow up here? She thought back to her dreary upbringing in Moscow. State housing, sketchy services, going hungry on too many nights, going cold even more and a pervading climate of fear that even as a child she had been aware of. No neighbours greeting you as a long-lost friend—just keep your head down and stay the hell out of trouble. She wanted more than that for this baby.

'Here we are,' he said, slowing the vehicle.

Katya could just make out a whitewashed villa through the mesh wire of a very high fence. Ben removed a remote control from the centre console and a heavy-duty security gate swung open. He drove into the narrow space, just big enough for two small cars, and turned the engine off.

'Welcome to Positano.'

Katya looked over at the imposing villa. Inside the fence it looked even grander, dominating the cliff face perched over the sea below. Its grandeur scared the hell out of her. She suddenly felt like Cinderella at the ball and hoped she didn't trip or say something stupid or eat with the wrong utensil.

She pictured Ben's mother, a plump old lady with a mole on her chin and a twinkle in her eye, slaving over a hot oven for her. For her. Cooking a feast, Ben had said. The last thing she wanted to do was show how very little breeding she had. Not because she cared necessarily but, hey, a girl had her pride.

She climbed out of the car and allowed Ben to get her case for her then lead her to the front door. The side wall that faced them was stark white, two rows of arched windows breaking up the line of the house. Terracotta window boxes overflowed with red geraniums.

They walked up a short flight of stone steps. Pretty tiles inlaid along the tread of each stair were beautifully decorative. A large wooden door was an impressive barrier to the outside world.

Ben inserted his key into the lock and pushed the heavy door open, gesturing for Katya to precede him. She stepped in nervously, the white walls, towering ceilings and large blue floor tiles, the exact tone of the sea, dazzling to the eye.

'Mamma,' he called.

He strode through the house and Katya followed close behind, awed by the expensive-looking furniture, rugs and artwork that decorated the Medici villa. She had the urge to huddle into the broad strength of his back, feeling a bit like Alice in Wonderland. It was only her pride that kept her frame erect and her hands firmly by her sides.

They entered the kitchen, which smelt amazing. A blend of garlic, basil and onions tickled Katya's nose and emphasised how long it had been since she had eaten.

'Benedetto? Benedetto?'

One of the most elegant-looking women Katya had ever seen entered the room from stairs to their right. She was tall and regal, her silver hair swept back into a glamorous chignon. So much for round and soft with a mole on her chin! She threw her arms in the air and broke into enthusiastic Italian as she embraced her son.

Katya stood back and watched their easy affection. She felt a pang of envy as his mother grabbed his cheeks and planted an enthusiastic kiss on each. Their closeness was a stark contrast to the strained relationship she shared with her own mother and Katya felt even more out of her depth.

The similarities between the two were striking. He had his mother's high cheekbones and her strong patrician nose. And as the older woman opened her eyes and smiled at her, Katya realised that this would be her baby's grandmother. There was so much love in this room, in this homey Italian kitchen, that Katya felt tears well in her eyes. She blinked them away quickly but not before she saw a faint narrowing of the older woman's eyes. Ben's mother had seen her tears.

'Mamma, this is Katya Petrova,' Ben said, pulling out of his mother's embrace. 'Katya, this is my mother, Contessa Lucia Medici.'

Katya held out her hand tentatively, not sure how to greet a contessa. 'It's a pleasure to meet you, Contessa,' Katya said.

The contessa smiled and came forward, her arm outstretched, too, firing rapid Italian.

'English, Mamma,' Ben broke in, reminding her gently.

'Of course, I'm sorry.' The contessa smiled at Katya, slipping easily into near perfect English. 'Forgive my manners. Please, call me Lucia.'

The contessa swept Katya into a hug as enthusiastic as the one she'd given to her own flesh and blood. Katya felt awkward in her embrace, completely unused to displays of motherly affection. But the contessa's eyes were kind and again she felt absurdly close to tears.

'Shall we adjourn outdoors?' Lucia suggested as she pulled away. 'Benedetto.' She turned to her son. 'Bring the wine,' she commanded.

Katya followed Lucia down the stairs from where she'd entered the kitchen earlier. It led to a magnificent terrace with one-hundred-and-eighty-degree uninterrupted views of the Mediterranean below and the majestic craggy coastline in both directions.

There was a round outdoor table with a striking ceramic top. It had been hand-painted with a typical Mediterranean lemon-grove scene. A bowl of the bright yellow fruit sat in the middle of the table and Katya could smell their magnificent tartness.

Ben joined them, glasses clinking. He placed them on the table and poured them each a generous measure. Katya placed a hand over her glass. Ben raised his eyebrows.

'Wine gives me a headache,' she said, saying the first thing that popped in to her head.

Ben gave her a disbelieving look. *Since when?* 'This from a girl who could drink vodka for Russia.'

'Benedetto,' his mother scolded, 'don't be rude. Run up and get some water.'

'Yes, Benedetto,' Katya teased, unable to resist. 'Run along.'

Too late Katya realised that Lucia might disapprove of her informality. What if she thought that Ben should be addressed as befitting a man of his stature? But the contessa clapped her hands gleefully and her eyes twinkled with delight. Katya breathed a sigh of relief.

Calling him by his title would be plain weird, given the things they had been through. The times they had stood side by side, their hands inside some stranger's body, locked in a battle for their life. Or the time they had sought solace in each other's bodies. Some relationships transcended titles and if their work relationship hadn't cut it then their intimate joining certainly had.

Ben chuckled and left to do his mother's bidding. He returned quickly with a bottle of sparkling water and poured some into Katya's glass. He sat in the chair beside her and she was instantly conscious of his potent male heat.

'To bossy Russian nurses,' Ben said, raising his glass.

'Benedetto!' Lucia gasped.

Katya saw the twinkle in his eye and the perfect upward curve of his beautiful full lips. 'To flashy Italian counts,' she parried.

Lucia laughed and raised her glass. 'Touché.'

They drank their drinks and ate bruschetta as the sun set and the lights of Positano, spread below them, gradually twinkled on one by one. Katya found herself relaxing in the pleasant company, with the stunning scenery a luxurious backdrop. Ben made her laugh and it was the most relaxed she'd been since she'd discovered her indiscretion had had consequences over a month ago.

Katya slipped easily into the banter she and Ben were known for in MedSurg circles. They entertained the contessa with stories from their travels and Lucia seemed to enjoy Katya's irreverent attitude towards her son.

After it was dark Lucia served up a delicious seafood pasta with a delicate creamy sauce. It was so good Katya even had a second helping. Sitting there, enjoying a balmy evening, under a canopy of stars, perched above the Med, Katya felt a real sense of family. It certainly wasn't something she was used to and…she liked it. Wanted the baby to grow up surrounded with the same sense of family.

Thinking about the baby brought her mission squarely back into focus. The evening had been a lovely distraction but she couldn't afford to lose sight of why she was here. Would Ben be a suitable father?

She watched him regaling his mother with a story and he was the charming playboy from MedSurg. And sitting amongst the trappings of his wealth, she knew that he could give their baby everything. But where was the Ben she'd seen that special night? The real man? The father-material man. Did he exist or was he just a figment of her overactive imagination?

Ben laughed and her skin broke out in goose bumps. It would be so easy to be distracted. Like she had been tonight. Seduced by the warmth and promise of a real family for her baby. She could even fool herself for a fleeting second that she could be part of it also.

Stop this! Katya stood abruptly. Ben and his mother looked at her enquiringly. 'I'm sorry, it's been a lovely night but would you mind if I went to bed, I'm very tired.'

'Of course not,' Lucia said. 'Come, I'll show you to your suite.'

Katya had to brush past Ben to join Lucia and she was super-aware of his heat and his scent as their bodies made the barest of contact. She bade him a brief goodnight, with a husky voice and trembling legs.

'Goodnight, *cara*,' Ben called after her.

She could see him in her peripheral vision, leaning lazily back against the chair, his long frame stretched out as graceful as a giant slumbering cat. She remembered vividly how great his length had felt pressed against her.

'This way,' Lucia said.

Katya didn't need any further encouragement. His wicked chuckle followed her all the way up the stairs.

'Here you are. Please, let me know if you need anything else,' Ben's mother said, opening the door to Katya's suite.

'Thank you, Lucia. You are most kind.'

The contessa shook her head. 'No. Thank you. I haven't

heard Benedetto laugh that much in many years. He is too serious these days.'

Katya watched Lucia withdraw and sat on the bed, staring after her. Ben? Serious? She'd only ever known Ben as he had been tonight. The life of the party. Flirty. Teasing. Except for that once when he'd been blindsided by grief and she'd seen an incredibly passionate side to him. Yet Lucia had hinted at another very different person again.

So who was the real Ben? The playboy? The serious son? Or the lover? That was her puzzle.

And would any of these Bens also be a good father?

CHAPTER TWO

KATYA slept fitfully despite the luxury of her suite. She drew her knees up into her chest and hugged them to her. She was doing the right thing. She was. If nothing else, spending an evening with Ben and Lucia had proven that. The contessa was a warm, loving and supportive mother. She was affectionate. And also obviously worried about Ben. As far as motherly role models went, Katya figured you couldn't get any more exemplary.

But her? What role model did she have? What examples did she have to draw on, even subconsciously, to raise this baby right? None. From the age of eight she'd been the mother in their house. Had raised four siblings while her mother 'went out'. She knew enough about psychology to know that such cycles were too often repeated, and she was scared she'd fail. And she couldn't risk a child's life on it. And, frankly, she was twenty-seven and all mothered out.

Katya was grateful for daylight and pleased to hear movement downstairs. She showered and dressed quickly, zipping up her bag and carrying it with her, leaving it at the front door as she headed towards the kitchen.

Ben looked up from his coffee as she entered and gave her one of his killer smiles. '*Buongiorno*, Katya.'

Katya faltered a little. He looked very sexy this morning, sitting at the table like he was king of the castle. His hair was damp and his shirt was open at the throat, giving her a peek of the tanned column of his neck and a hint of chest hair. His brown eyes glowed warm and rich and tempting.

'You don't look like you slept very well.'

This man was too damn perceptive by half. 'Well, that's because I kept expecting to turn back into a pumpkin.'

Ben threw his head back and laughed. 'You think this is a fairytale?' He pushed a plate of sweet pastries her way and poured her a shot of espresso.

No. Fairytales had happy endings and Katya knew that for her there would be no happily-ever-after. But if she could secure one for her baby then she could rest easy knowing she had given it the best chance in life.

'I think you live a pretty charmed life,' said Katya, sitting and biting gratefully into a fruit-filled croissant with a sticky glaze.

Ben paused, his cup halfway to his mouth. He bit his lip to prevent a derisive snort from escaping his throat. He'd stopped feeling charmed a long time ago. About the time his older brother had stolen his fiancé. Katya's assumptions about his life goaded him to respond. If that was the way she still thought of him after their night together then so be it.

'Is there something wrong with that, Katya?'

Ben's voice was soft and silky, the hint of flint in it scraping seductively over her skin. Katya paused in mid-chew. Her breath caught in her chest at the intensity of his gaze. He seemed to be searching her soul, looking for the answer he wanted. She felt her nipples bead against the lacy fabric of her bra at the frank hunger in his eyes.

She shrugged. 'If you consider living in the lap of luxury

and pandering to the hedonistic lifestyle of the rich and famous at your clinic a worthwhile way to spend your time then who am I to say?'

Ben bit back the urge to set her straight. She could judge him at her own peril. 'Oh, come, now, Katya, don't tell me you could turn your back on all this? In fact, I could show you a really good time while you're here. Are you sure you don't want to pick up where we left off?'

Katya wasn't sure where this conversation was heading or even what it was really about any more. There was a dangerous glitter to his eyes. Gone was the teasing, flirty Ben. He looked every inch the aristocrat. A little ruthless and very virile. She didn't know this man at all.

She swallowed, his words seductive despite their cold edge. 'Strictly business, Ben. I meant what I said.' She forced her voice to be firm despite the quaking inside.

'Are you sure, *cara*?' he purred. 'We were good.'

Ben's soft, deep voice held her captivated. It had been good. Very, very good. 'It was a mistake,' she said, dismayed to hear the words coming out all husky.

Ben was surprised that her barb stung. It had been the only thing that had meant anything to him in the last decade. He held her gaze. 'It could be fun, Katya Petrova.'

She could feel her eyes widen at the promise in his words. She believed him. Now, that would be a first. Since when had life been just pure fun?

Stop this, Katya. Only the baby mattered now. 'I'm not the fun type,' she said emphatically, brushing the flaky crumbs of pastry from her hand, swallowing her espresso in one hit and standing. 'Shouldn't we be going?'

Ben chuckled, shrugging off the darkness she had aroused in him. She was right—no one who knew her would describe

Katya as fun. Blunt. Efficient. Sharp-witted. Quick-tongued. A sense of humour that bordered on the sarcastic. But fun? No.

'Come on, then. If we leave now, we should be in Ravello in plenty of time to show you around before the first case.'

She followed him to the front door. 'Shouldn't we say goodbye to your mother?'

'Mamma doesn't rise before ten,' he said, picking up Katya's case.

Katya stared after him, the denim of his jeans clinging to the contours of his bottom perfectly. *It could be fun*, whispered insidiously through her head as she pulled the door closed behind her.

Ben smiled to himself as he glanced down and noticed Katya's hands gripping the edge of her seat, her knuckles white. 'Relax,' he teased.

'Easy for you to say.'

'This is nothing,' he said, changing gear as the traffic slowed a little on the outskirts of Amalfi. 'Wait till we start to climb higher.'

'Goody, goody gumdrops,' Katya said, quoting a favoured expression of Dr Guillaume Remy, a colleague they had worked with at MedSurg.

Ben laughed at the slang pronounced in sexily accented English. 'How are Guillaume and Harriet?' he asked. 'Are they pregnant yet?'

Katya nodded, feeling her spirits lift. 'Their second cycle of IVF worked. Their baby is due in the New Year,' she said, remembering how close Harriet and Gill had come to divorcing over the baby issue. And now here she was—also with a baby quandary.

At least she'd be able to return to MedSurg after the baby.

Her colleagues there were the closest thing she'd ever had to a real family and it would be good to get straight back into the all-consuming work. To forget that she'd left her baby with Ben.

'That's great,' said Ben. He remembered how much he had enjoyed his time with the aid organisation and how good Gill had been with him. Performing surgery in the middle of a war zone had been a steep learning curve but he had flourished and learnt a lot.

Leaving had been hard, especially with the tempting presence of one Katya Petrova, and had his hand not been forced by his brother's death, Ben would still be working for them. But he'd returned home, despite his decade-old vow not to, to a job he despised and a life he hadn't wanted. He could feel the familiar tension creep into his neck muscles and along his jaw and he tightened his grip on the steering wheel.

The road came back down to sea level and he glanced over to the harbour on his right and saw his gleaming white boat, *The Mermaid*, bobbing in the calm water. He looked at her clean sleek lines and felt himself relax again.

'My boat,' he said to Katya and pointed. 'I'll take you out in it this weekend.'

'Don't bother. I get seasick,' she said bluntly.

Ben found her determination to keep things 'strictly business' amusing and laughed as he changed gear. He looked at her face, her cute button nose, her beautiful blue eyes, her soft mouth with its tempting full lips, high cheekbones and blonde pixie cut that feathered around her face. She was sassy and sexy and had the mouth of a shrew and, God help him, he wanted her!

He remembered what else her mouth could do when it wasn't busy putting him in his place. He remembered how she had kissed him with an intensity and reckless abandon that had stunned him and knew behind her no-nonsense façade lurked a very passionate woman.

He thought back to past relationships. How easy they'd been. How meaningless. He'd filled his life with pretty women since Bianca's betrayal, trying to exorcise his demons. Women who had been eager and willing. Who'd enjoyed the favours of a rich, generous playboy. But not one of them had got beneath his skin like this unimpressed, practical Russian nurse. What the hell would it take to impress her? And why the hell did it matter so much?

Katya shut her eyes as the mountain road narrowed even further than the coast road. It seemed like nothing more than a goat track in places. But every time her lids closed all she saw was his damn boat. Big and white and expensive. The type of boat she saw in magazines where royalty lounged on sundecks. She had half expected to see a movie star emerging from one of the galleys of the rows and rows of luxurious vessels.

She should be happy. Yet another confirmation that he could provide for their baby so much better than her. But strangely his wealth, which had always bothered her, seemed to bother her twice as much. His boat was a big flashy status symbol—like an aquatic Ferrari. And he'd asked her to join him. How many other women had he had on that boat? How many women would he parade in front of their child?

She'd grown up seeing a procession of partners through her mother's life. And how screwed up was she today? Her mother had been seduced into neglecting her children and Katya had been wise in the ways of the world way before her time. Is that what Ben would do? Neglect their child in favour of his lifestyle? He was a thirty-five-year-old playboy bachelor. An Italian count. Aristocracy, for God's sake. Was it even possible to give that lifestyle away?

They made it to Ravello by quarter past eight and Ben drove the Alfa through an arch in a vine-covered wall. They entered a large cobblestoned courtyard dominated in the centre by a spectacular fountain. There was ample room for several cars and Ben angled his into a reserved space.

'Welcome to the Lucia Clinic,' he said. 'Otherwise known as the palace for hedonistic rich people.'

Katya turned and gave him a withering smile. 'If you can't stand the heat, Count, get out of the kitchen.' And she opened the door and climbed out, his laughter following her.

The building was impressive. It was a U-shaped structure built around the courtyard. The wall they had just driven through towered behind her as high as the other buildings and gave the courtyard and the clinic a private feel, protecting it from view. The rendered walls were painted a pale orange, their aged, weather-beaten appearance giving the clinic a timeless quality.

Ben opened the boot and removed their bags. 'The main wing, in front of you,' he said, indicating the longest section of the clinic, 'is the patients' suites. We have twenty beds. Twelve suites and four twin share rooms. The west wing holds the operating theatres and X-ray facilities, the east wing is the kitchens and staff accommodation.'

'You have a lot of staff that live on site?' she asked following him as he moved towards the entrance.

'There are twenty rooms, but only half are used permanently as most of our staff live locally and commute. The others are used casually. I bunk down here during the week and, of course, one of these rooms will be yours.'

Katya could feel his gaze on her and refused to look at him. The mere thought of him sleeping nearby did funny things to her breathing. It had been the same during their time at

MedSurg. Communal staff facilities had seen to it that too often he had been the last person she had seen before going to bed and the first one she'd seen on waking.

'Come on, I'll introduce you around. Everyone is very friendly here and most speak English.'

Katya followed him through the magnificent arched entrance and almost gasped at the cool elegance of the reception area. It was luxurious. No expense had been spared, from the artwork on the walls to the marble on the floor to the crystal chandelier hanging above the sweeping stone staircase dominating the entrance hall.

Ben showed her to her quarters first. Katya put her bag on the bed as Ben stood in the hallway. She looked around at cool decorative tiles underfoot and the mirror edged with pretty ceramic tiles inlaid into an arched recess in the wall. It was beautiful but she was more conscious of him breathing and his bulky presence against the doorjamb and what had happened last time he had stood in her doorway. She wondered where he slept and then halted her thoughts. His quarters were of no concern to her.

'Come,' Ben said, 'meet some of the staff.'

Katya didn't have to be asked twice.

Ben introduced her to so many people her head spun and she knew it would take her a few days to remember everyone. He gave her a tour of all the medical facilities, including the two operating rooms.

'Is this the theatre list?' she asked, looking at the typed list stuck to Theatre Two's main door.

He nodded. 'For this theatre, yes.'

Katya scanned the scheduled operations, thankful to find it was written in Italian and English. Abdominoplasty. Rhinoplasty. Augmentation mamoplasty. She felt her heart sink. Tummy tuck. Nose job. Boob job.

She had known the Lucia Clinic was an exclusive plastic surgery clinic but seeing it in reality hammered it home. It was hard to believe that someone who had worked in war zones could ever consider pandering to such vanity worthwhile.

Ben could easily read the distaste on her face. He remembered his first day at the clinic, shaking his head in disbelief, too. 'Would you like to see the gardens?' he asked.

'Sure,' Katya said vaguely.

They wandered back through the building, Katya dazed from the opulence all around her. No expense had been spared anywhere. From the fittings to the surgical equipment, everything was high quality, top notch, the best that money could buy. It was a little sickening, actually. How many people could MedSurg and aid organisations like it help if they had this sort of money at their disposal?

Ben took her through one of the private suites that was empty and pushed open the doors onto a small balcony. Katya's breath caught in her throat as the magnificence of the view hit her. The grounds below had been terraced down the side of the hill and beautiful gardens adorned the rocky slope. Fountains and water features and lush greenery punctuated by colourful blooms, dazzled the eye.

And beyond the grounds was the endless blue of the Mediterranean. It sparkled in the mid-September sunshine like a beautiful priceless sapphire. The craggy cliffs dominating the coastline were breathtaking in their enormity, towering high into the sky and tumbling in weathered splendour to plunge to the sea.

Katya looked either side of her. Each suite had its own balcony and she was hard pressed to think of a more beautiful place to recover from surgery. It was a stark contrast to her

MedSurg job where patients too often recovered in cramped, less than ideal conditions.

'This villa is centuries old, as are many of the buildings around here,' said Ben. 'Ravello is famous for its villas and their beautiful gardens. Many Hollywood films were filmed here back in the early nineteen hundreds and there are regular chamber music concerts held throughout the village during the year.'

'It's amazing,' she said, the sheer beauty holding her in awe, the decadence overwhelming.

Ben heard a hesitant note in her voice. 'You don't sound so sure,' he said.

'No, it's…it's…wow.'

'Sounds like there's a "but" there.' He smiled. He knew exactly what she was thinking.

Katya shrugged. Her poor-as-dirt background and some of the horrors she had seen working with MedSurg made it difficult to reconcile the indulgences of the affluent. 'I was just thinking how different it is from some of the places I've been with MedSurg.'

He nodded. 'That it is.'

Katya blinked at his understatement. It seemed so flippant when she knew, as did he, there were people out there who couldn't get proper health care at all.

'Don't you think all this is a little obscene?' She felt nauseated suddenly by it all and wondered if she could truly let her baby be brought up by someone who couldn't see how indulgent it was.

Sure, she wanted her baby to be provided for, to have the stuff she never had, but she also wanted it to have a sense of humanity. She had thought as Ben had worked for MedSurg that he had that kind of compassion, but if he could come back to this and not feel tainted by the excess then maybe she was wrong.

Ben could feel his ire beginning to rise again. She was doing it again. Judging him. It hadn't mattered so much at MedSurg, his wealth had irritated her and he had exploited that role to the hilt because she had looked so cute when she'd been mad. But things had changed since then and her assumptions annoyed him. 'You think it's wrong? You don't approve of vanity?'

Katya schooled her features. Obviously she was letting her distaste show. 'I think all the bad stuff happening in the world is more important than whether your nose is too big or your tummy too fat.' She tried to keep the bluntness out of her voice but on this subject her passion ran deep.

Ben couldn't agree more. 'And yet you rang and asked me for a job. You knew what we do here. Why did you come if it was going to offend your sensibilities?'

His question caught her unawares. She wasn't ready to open up yet. Oh, God, how could she say, *Because I'm having your baby and I need to check out if you're worthy of raising it because I'm certainly not.*

'I told you, I want to change direction.'

'You? Leave MedSurg? I don't believe it.'

Neither did she! And as soon as this was all over, she was heading straight back to a workplace with some backbone. But for now, for the sake of her baby, she needed to suffer the whims of the wealthy.

'If you didn't want me to come you shouldn't have offered me a job.' Katya knew from long experience that the best defence was offence. 'But, then, you weren't really serious, were you? We both knew it was just a throw-away line the morning after.'

Ben felt her accusation hit him square in the solar plexus. His guilt from that morning came flooding back. She was right. He had handled the whole thing very badly. He had known it back then but his apology had been stalled by her scathing reaction to his job offer.

She was standing with her back to him, her hands gripping the railing. She reminded him of how she'd been that morning. Erect. Distant. He wanted to touch her but couldn't bear to see her shrink from his touch like she had that day also. 'About that morning…' he said.

Katya gripped the railing harder and held her breath. She had spent months trying to forget the incident, she didn't want to rehash it now, especially not when their child was already a constant reminder.

'Benedetto!'

Both Ben and Katya startled at the unexpected interruption and turned to see Gabriella, one of the nurses she had met earlier, come bustling in, a child wearing a blue theatre cap on her hip.

Gabriella smiled at Katya. 'Lupi has been asking for you.'

Ben smiled at the little girl, her bilateral cleft lip making it impossible for her to smile back, but he could see the happiness shining in her eyes. 'Has she, now?' he growled and reached out to take the child from Gabriella who went eagerly. 'Well, now, little Lupi,' he said kissing her jet-black hair, 'you found me.'

Katya watched as the girl bounced up and down excitedly in Ben's arms. Katya guessed the child to be about three but she was obviously malnourished so she could well be older. But there was no mistaking the look of adoration in the girl's eyes.

Katya swallowed as Ben grinned down at her and Lupi snuggled her head into his chest. Where did Lupi fit in at the Lucia Clinic? Someone had been remiss in their care for her

if her lip was only being repaired now. It didn't seem like
something someone with money, with choices, would do. Her
large almond-shaped eyes didn't look Italian either. Katya
looked at Ben with confused eyes.

'Katya, this is Lupi,' Ben said. 'Lupi, this is Katya. She's
going to help me with your operation today. We're going to
give you your smile back.'

The little girl looked at her with solemn brown eyes and it
took Katya a few moments to remember her manners. She
smiled at the little girl. 'Hello, Lupi.'

'She doesn't understand English,' said Ben, rocking. 'Or
Italian for that matter.'

'You're operating on her?'

Ben nodded. 'Lupi's is one of four operations I'm doing
in Theatre One today for the Lucia Trust.'

Katya was still confused. 'The Lucia Trust?'

'A charitable organisation I founded on my return home.
We perform operations on people, children mainly, with disfiguring conditions who don't have access to proper surgical
intervention because of their circumstances.'

Katya found what he was saying hard to take in. But as the
full implications sank in, she felt increasingly foolish. The
things she had thought! The things she had said! And he
hadn't corrected her. Just let her go on thinking the worst.

He chuckled. 'What's the matter, Katya? You're looking a
little uneasy.'

His laugh was sexy as hell and it scraped along her nerves.
He was rubbing his chin absently back and forth against
Lupi's hair in time with his rocking. He looked very male and
she felt her nipples peak despite her annoyance at him. 'You
could have said something,' she said, her voice low, the note
of accusation easy to detect.

He laughed again. 'And spoil your condemnation of me? Your problem, sweet Katya,' he said, tapping her on the nose, 'is that you are a reverse snob. You think everyone who has money isn't worthy. Is frivolous. You judge me because I'm wealthy and dismiss me as a rich playboy.'

A denial rose in her throat and died a quick death. It was true, she had. She did. But he had done nothing to dissuade her of her opinion. If anything he had nurtured it.

He leaned in close to her and said in a slow deep voice, 'Don't dismiss me, Katya.'

The words were like a caress and she swallowed hard. There was just something about his mouth, the way he stared at her from under half-closed lids, his eyelashes long and glorious. She could feel his slumberous gaze on her lips and could feel herself swaying closer before he pulled back and turned on his heel and exited, chatting to Lupi as he went.

Katya drew in a ragged breath and watched him walk away. She was too speechless to talk and too boneless to move so she stood and stared, trying to work out everything that had just transpired.

She wasn't sure who Ben was any more. She was so positive she'd had him pegged. With MedSurg he had been every bit the playboy count. Flirting and oozing sex appeal. Flashing his sexy smile and his diamond signet ring and managing to pull a packet of expensive chocolates or a tin of exclusive caviar out of thin air at the bleakest of times.

And yet this Ben was the opposite. He wasn't flashy or showy. He hadn't blown his own trumpet over the Lucia Trust and had cuddled Lupi to his chest like he had ten of his own children. She'd come to Italy to find out his suitability as a father. It was supposed to have been easy. But she was more confused than ever.

* * *

The theatre list got under way and right from the start Katya was aware of the differences between this and her MedSurg job. MedSurg dealt with major trauma. Big, ugly injuries. It was about saving lives, not delicate, intricate operations. It was fast, furious surgery. Patch 'em up and fly 'em out and start all over again. It was high-octane surgery.

This theatre was the exact opposite. There was no urgency, no sense of lives hanging in the balance, no adrenaline buzz. It was calm and ordered and relaxed, and Katya was surprised how nice that was for a change. She hadn't realised how much of an adrenaline junkie she'd become or how soothing a slower pace could be.

Maria, the nurse in charge of the operating suites, had put her on two days of scout nurse duty to ease her into the routine and familiarise her with the layout and had her down scrubbing from Wednesday onwards. Watching the preparations, Katya was surprised at how much she'd missed working. She'd been away from it now for a couple of months and she was itching to gown up again.

Ben winked at her over the top of his mask and she felt her skin flush beneath her mask, still embarrassed by her gaffe. So, now he felt superior to her, he was back to being flirty again? Well, at least she felt on firmer ground with this Ben. Flirty Ben she was used to. Serious, humanitarian, Lupi-cuddling Ben she wasn't.

'Do you want to have a closer look, Katya?'

Ben's words broke into her thoughts and she slowly met his gaze. *That's why I'm here, Ben—to get a closer look.*

'Katya?'

She blinked. 'Sure,' she said, ordering her legs to move. In fact, this operation had really piqued her interest. Not just because the little girl in question must have suffered so much with her disfiguring condition but because she was so relieved it wasn't someone voluntarily mutilating themselves, chasing some crazy beauty ideal.

She moved closer to the table opposite Ben, taking care to leave a little distance between her and the sterile drapes so she wouldn't contaminate them with any body contact. She wouldn't make herself popular if they had to redrape the patient.

'As you can see, Lupi's cleft is quite extensive,' Ben said, making his initial incision. 'She's lucky that her palate's not involved and that she only has a nasal deformity unilaterally on the left.'

'What's her story?' Katya asked.

'She comes from a remote village in her country that doesn't have access to health care. When she was born her mother and father thought she would die. When she didn't the village thought she was cursed. The villagers were too frightened to ostracise the family in case Lupi cursed them, too. But Lupi's mother has kept her hidden away in their dwelling for six years. The other children are very cruel.'

'Poor Lupi,' Katya said, a touch of anguish in her voice. She thought about how much Sophia, her own sister, had been through with her disfiguring injuries and how heartbroken she'd been whenever a kid from school had teased her. Katya's heart went out to this poor little girl. No wonder she seemed to be thriving with the attention she was getting here.

Ben flicked his gaze up from what he was doing. He'd heard the genuine distress in her comment. The little girl's plight had affected him, too. He couldn't imagine how awful it had been for her to be rejected by everyone around her and isolated from the normal life of a child.

At Lupi's age he and Mario had been inseparable, tearing around trying to outdo each other with more and more impressive deeds. He had been younger by a year but he'd never let that get between him and Mario and their hijinks. Poor Lupi had known none of that. She'd never been allowed to mix with other children.

'Indeed,' he said. 'She can't talk and has a very poor nutritional state because chewing and swallowing are so difficult with the bilateral cleft.'

Katya nodded. If Lupi had grown up somewhere with decent access to a good health-care system, she would probably have had several operations by now and had many specialties involved. Orthodontists, speech therapists, ENT surgeons, paediatricians, dieticians.

'Are you going to repair the nasal deformity in this operation as well?' Katya asked.

He nodded as he accepted his next instrument from the scrub nurse standing next to him. 'There are differing opinions on whether this should be done as a staged repair but Lupi's situation is very different,' he said. 'For a start, she's a lot older. Most children having this repair would be under a year old. And follow-up could be a problem. So I'll do both now. It may be that she'll need another operation in a few years' time as she grows and her facial structures mature but, as I say, follow-up could be a problem.'

Ben worked on the nasal defect, knowing he had to maintain symmetry and secure primary muscle union. He wanted to get the best outcome possible for Lupi, given everything she'd been through, but he was finding concentrating difficult with Katya standing a metre away.

He realised how much he'd missed being in the same theatre with her. It had only been a few months but he was looking forward to when she could scrub in with him in a few days. While she was close now, she could be closer and he wanted to be rubbing shoulders with her again.

Returning to Italy had put a very abrupt end to the 'thing' that had been happening between them. Oh, sure, Katya would have denied it but there had been a tension between them right from the beginning. He half suspected that was why she'd been so prickly, so feisty. Because deep down she'd also known something had been happening and it had scared her to death.

'Nearly done,' Ben said, asking for a suture.

Katya watched Ben's fingers as he operated, and allowed his deep husky tones to flow over her. He was concentrating, pulling the incised edges of the cleft together, preparing for closure. She studied his style and compared him to Gill Remy, the surgeon she had worked closely with at MedSurg.

Gill's fingers had been deft, his style understated and methodical. Ben's was different again. He was more flamboyant, his style entertaining. His movements were a little more exaggerated, his handiwork punctuated with an added flourish and touch of theatre.

It didn't affect his competency, she realised. It was more a reflection of his personality. Gill was a born surgeon, his skill and expertise defining him. Ben was a born count playing at being a surgeon. A rich man mixing it with the peasants and enjoying the freedom both worlds gave him. His style was…expressive, a bit like a conductor of a symphony orchestra, and Katya enjoyed watching him work.

The operation took an hour and Katya was amazed, as she always was, that time could pass so quickly when you were totally engrossed. Ben's handiwork was very impressive. The suture line dominating Lupi's now complete lip was obviously very prominent but Katya knew it would eventually fade to a ghostly white and the little girl that had been formerly shunned as a cursed child could now live a normal life.

And Ben had given that to her. For nothing. And if that wasn't true father material—then what the hell was?

CHAPTER THREE

ON FRIDAY morning, Katya finished breakfast a little earlier so she could stop by Lupi's room on her way to work. It was Lupi's last day and she wanted to pop in and say goodbye to the little girl who had won all of their hearts with her big brown eyes and beautiful new smile. Katya stopped abruptly at the door as she realised she'd been beaten to it.

Ben was speaking to her in Italian, their heads almost touching as they bent over a colouring book. Katya couldn't understand what was being said—hell, neither could Lupi— but the little girl giggled and beamed at Ben as he pulled funny faces while he coloured.

His rich deep voice traversed the distance between them and she almost sighed it sounded so good. Like the first coffee of the day, or a Sunday morning sleep-in or a crackling log fire in the middle of winter. She liked listening to him talk in his native tongue and she let her head relax against the doorjamb.

Lupi laughed and looked up at Ben with such trust in her eyes that Katya's heart skipped a beat. She knew in that moment that coming to Italy had been the right thing to do. That Ben was the perfect choice to raise their child. That if he could show this much compassion to a stranger, to a child he'd never even known until this week, his own child would be very lucky indeed.

It gave her a huge sense of relief, a sense of rightness, knowing that their child would look at him with the same measure of trust. Had she ever looked at her mother with such trust?

'You'd make a great father.'

Ben turned and saw Katya standing in the doorway. He looked back at Lupi, so defenceless, so trusting. He hadn't felt love for anyone or anything in a long time. Not a woman, not his country, not even his job. Not since Bianca and Mario. How could he give a child the love it deserved when he still felt so emotionally barren?

'No. I wouldn't.'

Katya felt a nudge of dread at the blunt rejection in his voice. 'You don't want to be a father someday?'

Ben returned to the colouring-in. Did he? Once upon a time he'd thought he and Bianca would have a tribe of kids. But he was older now, wiser. And still a little old-fashioned where children were concerned. It must be his mother's influence. His traditional upbringing.

He truly thought it was best that a man and a woman should be married before deciding to bring children into the world. That the parents should love each other and have made a binding commitment to be together for ever. Or at least he had anyway, before Mario and Bianca's actions had irreparably shaken his faith in love and marriage and family. He didn't know what the hell he believed any more, he just knew he wasn't ready for fatherhood.

'I'm too selfish,' he said dismissively.

Before coming to Italy, Katya would have agreed without hesitation. But looking at him now, sitting on a little girl's bed dressed in his scrubs, passing the time with her in the last few minutes before he had to start work, told her different.

'A selfish man would be enjoying an extra espresso or a few more minutes' sleep or relaxing over a newspaper,' Katya said quietly.

Ben stopped colouring and fixed her with a serious look. 'Don't read too much into this.'

He had to want to be a father. *He had to!* 'Sometimes we don't know what we're capable of until we try,' Katya said quietly, ignoring how much of a hypocrite that made her.

Ben put down the crayon he was using, turned back to Lupi and smiled. 'I'll be back later, little one,' he said, in English this time. Lupi smiled and waved as Ben eased himself off the bed and headed towards Katya.

He stopped in the doorway. He was close enough to smell her cinnamon scent. She was in her scrubs and the desire to see her out of them stormed through him. But talk of children dampened his ardour. Suddenly she'd made his life seem so bleak.

He placed his hand on the doorjamb above her head and leaned in, his mouth close to her ear. If he moved a fraction more he could pull the lobe into the wet cavern of his mouth, and fleetingly he was tempted. 'Children aren't something people should just *try, cara*. And my life is fine the way it is.' He pulled back a little and looked into her wide blue eyes.

Katya held his gaze, her heartbeat thundering in her ears. Fine? Just fine? Not happy, full, content? He didn't look fine. She could see a bleakness in his steady brown gaze. Here was the Ben she kept seeing glimpses of, the Ben that the contessa was worried about.

Ben could see Katya's keen gaze assessing him and he pushed away from her, not willing to share his deepest darkest thoughts with her. She was too damn astute and as he'd told her, his life was fine. Their arms brushed slightly as he passed her. *Fine, damn it!* If he could just stop thinking about her out of those damn scrubs!

Katya's stomach muscles contracted at the slight touch and she placed her hand protectively over her stomach as it looped the loop. So, he didn't want a baby? Well, neither did she. But whether he liked it or not, he *was* this baby's father. And he was a hell of a lot better equipped than she was to take care of it.

Katya inhaled swiftly as a sudden sharp pain flared in her chest. She ignored it, smiled and waved at Lupi then headed towards Theatre One. Some things in life were difficult. It didn't mean that they weren't right. She couldn't afford to think emotionally. She had to be practical. And luckily, thanks to her mother, Katya was a very practical person.

The morning cases got under way with Ben his usual jovial self again. She noticed he was always in high spirits while he operated and it was obvious that he thrived doing this kind of work. This morning they had a couple of children who had very bad burns contractures of their arms, making straightening them and their daily activities excessively difficult, limiting their independence.

One was a nine-year-old girl whose fingers on her burnt hand were being dragged into a claw shape due to severe flexion scar contractures, and the other was a four-year-old boy whose right arm was permanently bent up due to a contracture over his elbow joint.

They were brother and sister who had been involved in a tragic fire in their family dwelling that had also killed their mother. Both had had delayed and inadequate treatment of their burns, as so often happened in remote and poor communities. No burns protocols, no immediate grafting, no physio or splinting or pressure garments.

The Lucia Trust had been alerted to their cases through a charitable organisation in Africa and had flown them to Italy. It was Ben's job to debride the thickened scar tissue that was causing their problems and then cover the defects with a skin graft.

Katya could see he was totally in the zone, relishing the challenge, eager to make a difference to these children's lives. His excitement was palpable and the whole theatre was humming with anticipation.

Katya was excruciatingly aware of him today. It wasn't just his elevated mood but the memory of their earlier conversation, the way her heart beat had accelerated and her stomach had turned over at his closeness. She really needed some distance from him but scrubbing in with a surgeon always necessitated close contact and today was no different.

They both needed to see what they were doing, he to operate, she to anticipate his needs, and as much as she tried to distance herself it made very little difference to their proximity.

And despite her head telling her to keep it professional, focus on the job, her body had other ideas. When their arms clad in thick long-sleeved cotton gowns brushed together, it was if he had stroked her bare skin. When their gloved fingers touched as they exchanged instruments, it felt as if he had trailed them up her arm. When his low voice rumbled in her ear it felt as if he had feathered kisses down her neck.

Not even the music was a distraction. Ben liked to listen to classical music as he operated. Being Russian, she was quite partial to classical music herself, but it seemed weirdly intimate and she found herself pining for the dulcet tones of

Ella Fitzgerald who had serenaded them during her time with MedSurg, working with Gill Remy.

The CD that was playing today was Wagner. It was a poignant collection and she could feel her emotions see-saw with the rise and fall of the music. Wagner had been inspired by Ravello, Ben told her with pride, as he debrided scar tissue. The sexy timbre of his voice slid down her spine and ruined her concentration.

By the time Ben was satisfied with his work and the list came to an end she was eager to escape for a while. She needed to get as far away from him as was humanly possible. She'd come to her decision, there was no point buying into the attraction between them. All she had to do now was hang around until she'd had the baby and then get away—fast.

The list complete, Ben was just degowning when the wall phone rang. Being the closest, he picked it up.

'Lucia Clinic, Dr Medici speaking,' he said in Italian.

A woman replied. She was speaking in very broken, heavily accented English. 'I speak to Katya Petrova…please… I her…mama.'

Katya's mother? 'Of course,' he said switching to English. 'She is here. One moment.'

He looked up to see Katya just disappearing through the door. 'Katya,' he called after her.

She stopped and turned around. *What now?* She'd nearly escaped, damn it!

Ben held the phone out to her. 'It's for you. It's your mother.'

Oh, God! Had something happened to one of her siblings or was it just more of the usual? Katya covered the distance between the two of them quickly and practically snatched the phone from him.

'Mama?'

'*Da*,' her mother said.

'What's wrong?' Katya asked, slipping into her native tongue, gripping the phone, preparing for the worst.

'Katya,' her mother said reprovingly, 'can't I just ring and talk to my daughter without something being wrong?'

Since when had Olgah ever rung just to shoot the breeze with her firstborn? 'Everyone's OK, then?' Katya said. Her youngest sibling was now seventeen but that still didn't stop Katya fretting over them like a mother hen.

'*Da*, *da*,' Olgah said dismissively.

Katya breathed a sigh of relief and loosened her grip on the phone. She was conscious in her peripheral vision of Ben's blatant curiosity. He was sitting in the anesthetist's chair, pretending interest in a chart.

If there wasn't something wrong then Katya knew where this conversation was going to head, and she didn't want Ben to be privy to it. She turned slightly so she couldn't see him and leant heavily against the wall. She scuffed her feet against the floor, her head downcast, her free hand massaging her forehead.

'What do you want, Mama?' Katya asked, feeling herself tense.

'Katya! How can you speak to your mother like that?'

Katya ignored the indignation. 'How much, Mama?'

'I need a couple of thousand. I'm a little behind on the rent and I've just got the second notice from the electric company.'

The figure didn't even make Katya blink. Was it a new dress or a pair of shoes or a new man that had taken precedence over the rent and electricity? Katya sighed. 'Mama…'

'Please, Katya. It's expensive with four teenagers. And if you ever bothered to come home instead of tripping around the world, you'd know that.'

Katya gripped the telephone receiver and bit her tongue,

the unfairness of her mother's statement stinging. Like she'd been on a round-the-world trip! She'd been working her butt off in some of the world's hotspots so she could support her mother and four siblings. She knew how expensive it was, damn it. She'd been practically supporting the entire family since she'd started work.

'If it's too much for you maybe you can ask your rich count for a loan?'

'Mama!' Katya gasped.

Was her mother serious? She'd known the minute she'd told her mother that she knew a count and was going to Italy to work for him in the world-famous Lucia Clinic that she'd said the wrong thing. But her mother had been persistent in wanting to know why she was leaving MedSurg and a steady source of income and Katya certainly wasn't about to tell her about the baby.

And, just for once, she'd wanted for her mother to be impressed. Proud even. But, as usual, her mother didn't fail to disappoint her.

'Oh, don't be so shocked, Katya. You always were so high and mighty.'

'Well, somebody had to be, Mama.'

As soon as the words were out, Katya regretted them. Not because they were wrong but because she knew what was coming next. Katya held the phone and listened while her mother gave her the usual hard-luck story. How hard her life had been with five children and no man about the house. How she'd done the best she could with what she had. What an ungrateful daughter she was.

And then the real prize. 'You think you're better than me? Don't forget, if it wasn't for you, Katya, Sophia wouldn't be so horribly disfigured.'

No matter how many times she prepared herself for it, how many times she heard it, it still rocked her to the core. The angry little girl inside who had lost her childhood to her mother's reproductive irresponsibility clawed and begged and screamed to retaliate. To respond with righteous indignation. But the guilt, the guilt her mother knew how to manipulate so well, paralysed the words, froze them in her throat, every time.

She looked up and saw Ben watching her. 'I'll send the money, Mama,' Katya said, her voice shaky, her hands trembling as she cast her eyes downwards again.

'Good girl.'

No 'thank you'. No apologies for asking or lamenting her incompetence with money.

'You know, Katya,' Olgah continued, 'if you played your cards right, were nice to your boss, he might… I know from the magazines he's a terrible playboy but he might like a nice little Russian girl. We'd never have to worry about money again.'

Olgah was so matter-of-fact that Katya felt physically ill. She realised for the first time, as an emotion so vile injected its poison through her body, that she hated her mother. There had been plenty of times growing up—home alone, trying to raise her four siblings while her mother 'went out'—when she had felt rage and fury and frustration towards her.

But this? Suggesting first that she go to Ben for money and then that she ingratiate herself to ensure a lifetime of financial security for her family? This was truly corrupt, even for her mother. It became imperative to Katya right then and there that her mother never find out that the baby she was carrying was the heir to the Medici fortune.

'You owe it to Sophia to at least try, Katya.'

Katya gasped. The unfairness of her mother's words raged inside her but the overwhelming impotence she had felt from childhood neutralised her rage, her hate. It didn't seem to matter how far away she got from Moscow, her mother's ability to reach across the world and tap into her childhood psyche was astounding.

'Goodbye, Mama,' Katya said, swallowing hard as a rush of bile rose in her throat.

Katya replaced the phone, cutting off her mother's reply. She felt dead inside. Damn her mother. Damn her to hell.

She raised her troubled blue gaze and found Ben watching her.

'Everything OK, *cara*?' he asked softly.

Katya could see the concern in the depths of his eyes. She knew he had gleaned enough from the one-sided Russian conversation to know that it hadn't been a happy family reunion. His kindness was unbearable when she felt so raw inside.

She shook her head. 'Mothers.' She gave him a half-smile. He chuckled and Katya knew he was waiting for her to elaborate. To say more. But…she couldn't. If she'd needed to escape the theatre before the phone call, it was an absolute necessity now.

'See you after lunch,' she said, not waiting for a response.

Ben kicked at the aged paving stones of the Piazza Duomo. He scanned the outdoor cafés thronged with locals and tourists alike in the glorious sunshine, hoping to see Katya sitting at one of them. Gabriella had told him she was coming here and it was only the lunch-break so she couldn't have got too far.

Katya had covered well but he could tell that the phone call from her mother had upset her. He couldn't explain why he felt the need, but he wanted to check if she was OK. He remembered the look they'd exchanged in Lupi's doorway that morning, like she could see all was not well with him, and he wanted her to know that he was sensitive to her emotional state as well.

He decided to do a circuit. The day was nice, the sun beating down, and it felt good to be outdoors. He dodged some young boys kicking a soccer ball around the massive square, his mind preoccupied with Katya's phone call.

It was obvious that Katya had been arguing with her mother and even more obvious from her tone and her body language that she hadn't been happy about talking to her mother in the first place. But she had. And that was something Ben understood all too well. Doing something against your will for the sake of family. Family responsibility.

The *duomo*'s bell marked the hour with its deep chiming and brought him out of his thoughts. His eyes scanned the crowds and inside the different ceramic and tourist shops that bordered the square. Just as he was about to give up, he saw her inside the cameo shop.

He entered, his eyes taking a moment to adjust to the dim light. Katya was talking to a shop assistant, her back bent over the glass-topped counter, a cameo laid out on black velvet before her. She was wearing a gypsy-style skirt and a form-fitting short-sleeved T-shirt that emphasised the petiteness of her frame and the bony ridge of her spine.

Giovanna, the shop assistant, raised her eyes to his and instantly straightened. There weren't too many locals in Ravello who didn't know Count Medici on sight! He held his finger up to his mouth and smiled at her.

She smiled back and Ben saw the invitation in her eyes and wished he didn't feel complete disinterest. What the hell was the matter with him? Giovanna was a very attractive woman and he hadn't been with anyone since before he'd met Katya.

'It's so beautiful,' Katya sighed, unaware of Ben's presence. 'My grandmother had one very similar to this.'

Katya touched the chalky-white surface of the burnished orange cameo. It depicted a curly haired woman in profile, with bare shoulders and a strange, sad kind of smile. She remembered stroking her grandmother's as a child. There weren't that many memories that she recalled fondly but her grandmother starred in every one. Looking at the beautiful oval cameo and recalling the wonderful times it evoked was like a soothing balm after the vileness of her mother's phone call.

She remembered being held to the old woman's ample bosom, the cameo sitting snugly in her grandmother's cleavage, and she remembered feeling safe there. Feeling loved. She'd been seven when her grandmother had passed away and she still recalled how devastated she'd been.

Almost as devastated as the day Olgah had taken the cameo and pawned it. Katya had begged her mother not to, had clung to Olgah's leg as she'd tried to get out the door. But it hadn't stopped her. Katya remembered to this day how bleak and impotent she had felt as her mother had shut the door in her face.

If only she still had the cameo today, she knew what she'd do with it. She would leave it here with Ben, as a parting gift for her child. Something to connect the baby with its mother. And maybe her child could draw comfort from it over the years, as she would have done. Know, hopefully, that Katya loved him or her. Loved her child enough to give it the best life possible.

Ben could see Katya in profile and watched the flicker of emotions play across her face. His breath caught. He'd never seen her look so vulnerable. He could see fondness and happiness and regret mingling in her slight Mona Lisa smile. She looked wistful and sad and very, very young.

He'd never truly realised how shuttered, how in control she

was until he'd seen her like this. She looked vulnerable, uncertain for the first time since he'd known her. Like he was seeing the real Katya, the one beneath the bluster and the barbs.

Not even on that magical night that they'd shared had he seen her like this. What had made her the Katya she was today? The practical, tough, no-nonsense façade she hid behind. What had happened to this Katya, the one bent over the cameo, to make her seem so hard? Had that phone call had something to do with it?

Ben was intrigued as never before. Whatever the reasons, seeing her like this made him want to see more. This soft, female Katya was appealing on levels he'd never known existed. It made him want to make her happy. Put a smile on her face. Not a small sad little smile, but a big beaming one. He wanted to see her glow. And the way she was looking at that cameo, he knew just how to achieve it.

'We'll take it, thanks, Giovanna,' Ben said, striding over to the counter and winking at the shop assistant.

He saw Katya's back stiffen and she turned around slowly. She gave him a look that left him in doubt he was not welcome in the shop—very different to the warm, flirty welcome Giovanna had given him. Why the hell did that do more for him than Giovanna's blatantly sexual smile?

'No, we won't,' Katya said, placing a stilling hand on Giovanna's, not taking her gaze off Ben.

'You like it.' Ben shrugged. 'Consider it a gift.'

How many men had given her mother gifts? Seduced her into neglecting her children? Her mother's words rang in her ears—*if you played your cards right…we'd never have to worry about money again.* She felt bile rise in her again. She would not stoop to her mother's level. She'd never taken anything from a man and she wasn't about to start.

'I don't take *gifts* from men,' she said emphatically.

He blinked. She was angry with him—that was obvious. Her eyes glittered and her mouth was flattened into a thin line. Not the usual reaction he got when offering to buy women jewellery. He sensed he needed to tread carefully. 'It obviously means a lot to you,' he said softly.

'It's eight hundred euros,' Katya said, her voice blunt, her tone unmoved.

'Money is not an issue, *cara*,' he said, smiling gently, still hopeful of breaking through to her, the girl he'd caught a glimpse of. 'Can you wrap it for me?' he asked Giovanna.

'No. Do not wrap it,' Katya said, giving a severe look at the shop assistant. She would rather take cyanide than accept this from Ben. She felt raw on the inside from her mother's barbs and his persistence was rubbing salt into the wounds. 'And do not call me darling,' she snapped, and stormed out of the shop.

'Katya.'

She heard him calling her name but she was too angry to stop. Visions of the trinkets her mother's suitors had bought her flashed before her eyes. She remembered how exhausted she'd been each night, looking after four little ones while her mother had been out. She remembered Sophia getting burned, her sister's dreadful inconsolable screams. They reverberated around her head as she hurried away, they followed her now as they had haunted her for so many years.

She could hear her breath coming in short sharp gasps as she remembered the horror of that day and the crippling panic that had gripped her as her eleven-year-old brain had struggled with the enormity of what had happened. Images she'd thought she'd conquered a long time ago bombarded her as she walked blindly through the piazza, Ben's voice following her.

'Katya.' He caught up, grabbing her arm and halting her.

'Let go of me,' she yelled, blinking back tears she hadn't even known had formed.

Ben held onto her shoulders as she struggled against him. Something was really wrong, she was really upset. He'd never seen her tearful. 'Hey, hey, what's wrong? I'm sorry, OK? You seemed so taken with it. Don't worry about it, it's no big deal.'

She moved close to him, her heart hammering, her chest heaving. 'It is to me,' she said, her voice steely.

She saw the confusion and concern on his face. She could tell he was puzzled by her reaction. Hell, she was puzzled by it. One phone call from her mother and she was eleven years old again! But this was important.

Ben was relieved that she'd stopped trying to resist but he could still feel the tension in her shoulders. His fingers gently massaged the flesh coaxing her to relax. 'I'm sorry,' he said softly.

'I can buy my own jewellry.'

He nodded at her. 'I'm sorry,' he said again. He watched her watch him, her gaze assessing, as if she was searching for the truth in his statement. And then he felt her finally let go and her shoulders sagged against his hands.

'I'm sorry,' she whispered.

Ben gave her a tender smile. Piazza life careened all around them. The sun beat down, locals strolled, tourists snapped photos and shopkeepers touted for trade, but they were oblivious, locked in their own little bubble.

He pulled her gently towards him, half expecting her to resist, but she went without argument and he tucked her against him. She felt good against him, too good, and he wished for a moment that he hadn't done it. But instinct told him it was the right thing to do.

Katya Petrova was a complicated woman. A deceptive

woman. There were layers beneath her prickly surface that obviously ran deep. Holding her close, his heart thudding loudly in his ears, he realised he wanted to explore them. To understand what made her tick, what had made her the woman she was today. What had happened to cause such a meltdown just now? Would she let him in and why did he suddenly care so much?

Katya breathed deeply, inhaling his scent. He smelt like man, like Ben, and she remembered vividly how good it was to be held intimately by him. It was crazy, she couldn't buy into it, but for this moment, as her heartbeat settled down again, it was heavenly.

Soon she would have to pull away and repair the damage she'd done with her little performance. God knew what he thought. And she was going to have to tell him about the baby. Not right now, but soon.

She didn't want to leave it for weeks and weeks now she'd made up her mind. He had a right to know and as soon as she told him, there wouldn't be anything to hide from him any more. She didn't believe in deception, had seen way too much of it growing up, and he couldn't accuse her of a hidden agenda once the truth was out.

'We'd better get back,' Katya said, breaking the embrace.

They both turned towards the clinic and began to make their way back slowly.

'You want to come with me to my villa this weekend?' Ben asked. 'We can go out on *The Mermaid*.'

She looked at him. He had just handed her a golden opportunity. She nodded. 'Yes, thanks. Sounds like fun.'

So...tomorrow. It was set. She'd tell him about the baby tomorrow. And tonight she'd try and find the right words to deliver the shocking news.

CHAPTER FOUR

KATYA was awake early, having spent a night rehearsing the words she was going to use. She had a speech prepared and she hoped it was impassioned enough for him to understand that her motives were pure. That she was doing what she was doing for the sake of their baby.

She had no idea how he was going to react, none at all, and thinking about it, trying to second-guess it, was driving her crazy. Katya decided to get up and dressed and go and sit in the garden for a while. She doubted whether her thoughts would be any clearer, but at least she could stare at the Med rather than four walls.

The weather was beautiful outside and Katya could see it was going to be another gorgeous September day. She had a brown sundress on with shoestring straps, and she revelled in the early kiss of the sun on her practically bare shoulders. She could so get used to living here.

She bit into the plump flesh of a peach as she wandered around, trying to settle the nausea that had plagued her the minute she'd stood up. She hoped it wasn't going to be a bad morning-sickness day. If she was going to go on Ben's boat, the last thing she needed was a queasy stomach.

The gardens really were magnificent. She had spent most of her lunch hours outside, eating with the other nurses who chose a different terraced level each day to spread out on and soak up some sun. A lot of their patients also ventured out into the gardens and Katya liked the continuity of it all. So different from MedSurg.

She could hear the trickle of water and wondered if the fountains ran continuously or whether they were on timers. It felt good to be thinking inane things. Her mind had been preoccupied all night with such serious matters. Coming outside, getting up, had been a good idea.

Even high in the hills she could see the sun sparkling off the sapphire-blue Med and she drew a deep breath of clean air into her lungs. The beauty was distracting and she sat on a wrought-iron garden chair and soaked it in. She shut her eyes and tipped her face towards the early morning sun.

'Penny for them.'

Katya opened her eyes to find Ben looking down at her. Her heart skipped a beat. He looked so fresh and rested. His hair was damp and curling over his collar at the nape of his neck. The words she'd rehearsed all night spun around in her head. 'Good morning,' she said, in what she hoped sounded like a normal voice.

'*Buongiorno*, Katya. May I join you?'

Katya shuffled over, making room for him on the seat.

'You like our gardens?' he asked.

She nodded. 'They are very beautiful. Did you have someone design them for you or were they already like this?'

'The gardens have been here as long as the villa, for centuries, but they were very unkempt when we bought the property. Mario…' Ben's words trailed off, the familiar ache in his chest starting up at the mention of his brother.

Katya waited for him to continue. She'd been there the night Ben had received the news of Mario's death. She had witnessed his devastation firsthand.

'The gardens were Mario's baby. He had this grand vision for them and hired Europe's foremost expert on terraced gardens to help him design what you see today.'

'It must be kind of nice to have a lasting legacy like this, to remind you of your brother,' she said gently.

Ben just stopped himself from snorting. He rarely came into the gardens. Mario was everywhere and some things were just too painful. The last thing he needed to remember was how his brother had betrayed him. How he had discovered Mario and Bianca sharing a passionate kiss not far from here in these very grounds. Somehow the gardens had never seemed quite the same.

'He...did a great job,' Ben acknowledged through tight lips.

Katya looked at him sharply. She detected a slight bitterness to his tone. Maybe he didn't want to talk about his brother? Maybe it was too soon, too raw? Maybe that was what the contessa had alluded to on her first night?

Katya felt guilty that with everything she was going through she had totally forgotten that Ben's brother was dead. 'I'm sorry, Ben, I haven't asked. It's only been a few months—how are you coping with Mario's death?'

This time Ben did snort. 'Don't worry about me, Katya. There was no love lost between Mario and I. We were...estranged when he died.'

So? Did that make a difference when your own flesh and blood died tragically? Would she cry when her mother died? Of course. If for nothing else, over the wasted years, the wasted opportunities. If anything, being estranged made it worse.

'You seemed pretty upset that night.' He had looked completely shattered. Totally undone. Every female cell in her body had responded to his utter desolation.

He shrugged. 'It was a shock.'

'Well, of course, estranged or not, he was still your brother.'

'No.' Ben shook his head emphatically. 'He stopped being my brother a decade ago.'

Ben turned bleak eyes on her and she shivered despite the warm weather. 'I'm sorry. That's very sad,' she said.

Ben's lips twisted. 'That's life. Come on.' He stood. 'Let's eat and get on our way.'

Ben strode ahead of her and she followed him slowly. Was this why Lucia was so worried about her son? Something had obviously happened between Ben and his brother. Something that had been strong enough to drive a wedge between them for ten years. Something that had persisted, even through death.

Katya caught up with Ben a minute later. He had been stopped by Damul, the father of the two children they had operated on yesterday. The man had tears in his eyes and the biggest, broadest grin Katya had ever seen. He was shaking Ben's hand and gabbling away at him in his own dialect.

Ben spoke back to him in Italian as their hands remained clasped. Katya smiled at Damul, who bestowed another grin on her. She could see the joy behind his tears, how grateful he was, and her smile grew wider. Damul had been through so much. The loss of his wife and the injury to his children. Katya could only imagine how impotent he must have felt.

Damul patted Ben on the back and slowly withdrew, smiling all the way.

'A happy customer,' Katya said, still smiling from Damul's joy.

Ben smiled back. 'It's a good feeling.'

'Yes,' she said, 'it is, isn't it?' To be a part of Ben's grand dream had been extremely rewarding, even in the little time she'd been there.

He frowned at her. 'Really? I'd have thought it'd be a little too slow for you. I thought you liked the pace and the anonymity of the patch them up and send them on environment?'

So had she. And she did. The high turnover and hectic pace was exhilarating. She thrived on it. And the virtual anonymity of their patients was vital to keep burnout at bay. Being a body part rather than a whole person made the horror of it all easier to process. From a very young age Katya had learned to block her emotions so it was inevitable, almost, that she should gravitate to a work environment where there was no time for emotions.

But suddenly it didn't seem to be the be-all and end-all. Getting to know Lupi and Damul's children and the other kids had been surprisingly gratifying. Maybe it was just her hormones but for the first time in a long time she actually felt like a nurse.

She knew what she did at MedSurg mattered, that without people like her and Gill and Ben, many, many people might have died. But here at the clinic she was learning that making a difference to just one person, one child, could be intensely, intimately rewarding as well.

'Maybe I'm mellowing.' She shrugged.

Ben hooted with laughter, remembering their altercation yesterday. 'I can't quite imagine you mellow.'

She straightened. He was right. She was about to turn his life upside down. She couldn't afford to mellow until her job here was done. She shot him a withering look. 'Don't you forget, Count,' she said, and strode away.

He chuckled and followed her to the staff dining room where they had a quick breakfast. Half an hour later they were on the road to Amalfi and Katya was, once again, clutching the seat as Ben steered the Alfa expertly on the kamikaze roads. She was too frightened to even worry about what the rest of the day would hold, and in a crazy way it was a blessed relief.

When they arrived in Amalfi, Ben parked his car in the harbour car park. The sun reflected off the shiny surfaces of all the sleek white boats and Katya donned her sunglasses. She followed him past rows and rows of aquatic craft before pulling up in front of *The Mermaid*.

'Isn't she beautiful?' he asked.

Katya was pleased to see that Ben had shed his mood from the garden and she gave *The Mermaid* the once-over. She supposed it was beautiful but she was paying more attention to the way the boat bobbed in the water.

'Come on,' he said, grabbing her hand and helping her on-board. 'I'll show you around.'

Ben adored this boat. He'd had every intention of selling her when he'd sold the Ferarri—after all, he hadn't been out in her in a decade—but he just couldn't bring himself to do it. Maybe because it didn't have the same symbolism as the red car had had. Mario hadn't been interested in boats so *The Mermaid* was something that didn't represent his continuous rivalry with his brother. The boat had been truly just about his own pleasure.

As he sat at the helm and refamiliarised himself with the dials, ran his hands over the wheel, he lamented not having found the time to go out in her often. He'd been out in her once since his return to Italy and had been too busy with the Lucia Trust to go again. Maybe if Katya enjoyed herself this week-end, she'd come out with him again?

'Is there a bathroom on this thing?' she asked, her stomach already protesting the slight swell she could feel through the soles of her feet.

'Sure.' He grinned. 'Come on, I'll show you below.'

Katya didn't feel like she was going to vomit—yet. But she wanted to make sure she knew where to head if she did. This boat was shinier than anything she'd ever seen before, and she didn't want to foul it.

She climbed down the stairs, following his lead, and walked into pure luxury. Her feet sank into deep-pile carpet and her eyes took a moment to adjust to the muted light. They were in a lounge area with leather chairs and a coffee-table. A plasma screen dominated the wall the chairs faced.

Ben showed her the galley, which sparkled and shone like everything else. Then he showed her the cabins—two large luxurious ones equipped with huge beds. Beds you could roll over and over and over in. She had a vision of the two of them doing just that, the sheets tangling around their legs. She blinked hard to dispel it as he showed her the decadent *en suites* complete with spas.

'What do you think?' he asked.

Katya reeled. She'd never been amongst such luxury. The splendour of the Lucia Clinic faded in comparison. She felt gauche, like Cinderella at the ball. Her head spun and for a brief moment she thought she was going to lose the contents of her stomach immediately. 'It's like a…palace,' she said.

Ben chuckled. She looked all wide-eyed and he could tell she felt overwhelmed. 'Every woman deserves a palace once in a while, don't you think?' he asked.

Katya wasn't sure about that. It wasn't something she'd ever wished for. She'd wished they'd had more. That her mother had been home more often. That she could have gone to school more often. That they'd had food in their cupboards and a warm house all the time. She'd never even dared to wish for something like this.

And her child was going to be part of all this. Would grow up amongst all these amazing things. Would never know what it was like to feel hungry or cold. Or unloved. This wasn't a life she would ever feel comfortable living, but as much as it dazzled, even scared her, she was pleased that the baby would never have the sort of life she'd endured.

'I guess,' she said quietly. Doubtfully.

'I know you don't feel comfortable with all this,' Ben said, gesturing around him, 'but I swear, if you just let yourself, you'll have a great day.'

Katya looked into his earnest face. He wanted her to like his boat. He wanted her to enjoy herself. She could see it in his keen gaze. She smiled at him then and made a conscious effort to relax. Considering the bombshell she was going to drop at some stage, the least she could do was let him know how much she appreciated him trying to show her a good time.

'OK.' She smiled. 'Aye, aye, Captain.' And she saluted him.

Ben threw back his head and laughed. Somehow he couldn't imagine Katya ever being obedient. It was almost as absurd as her being mellow. 'Let's go back on deck and get under way.'

'Aye, aye, Captain,' she repeated, and joined in as he laughed again.

Katya's enjoyment soon faded as they moved out of the harbour. The Med was flat. It sparkled before them like a carpet of sapphires. Smooth as glass, beautiful blue glass. But the movement of the boat and her hormones were not getting along and they'd only been out for two minutes before Katya knew for sure—this was going to be a bad morning-sickness day.

'How long to your villa?' she asked, gripping the side of the boat, the faint whiff of engine fumes and the wake of another boat kicking her nausea up another notch.

'It's only half an hour from here,' Ben said, concentrating on navigating out of the busy area near Almalfi. 'But I thought I'd take you on a grand tour of the Amalfi coast. You've just got to see Positano from the ocean, it's an amazing aspect. Maybe we can even head to Capri, stay on the boat overnight, head back to the villa in the morning.'

Katya felt her stomach lurch. He looked at her for confirmation of his plans. He looked so excited, like a kid with an ice cream, and she didn't have the heart to ask him to turn the boat around. She nodded and smiled back. Maybe the nausea wouldn't last. Maybe it would be a day when the sickness only actually lasted the morning.

Pity she was feeling so wretched because the view inside the boat was just as spectacular as the view over the water. Ben was wearing some hip-hugging denim shorts. They had frayed hems, and showed off his magnificent long legs. A chocolate polo shirt completed the outfit, the sleeves fitting snugly around his biceps.

His hair blew in the breeze, becoming tousled, and a part of her wanted to walk up behind him, put her arms around his waist and snuggle her body into his. But she knew that any movement at the moment would be catastrophic both to her equilibrium and to her grand plan.

A speedboat passed them, rocking their craft in its wake, and Katya knew she was going to be violently ill. Ben shouted something in Italian but she didn't wait for a translation. She made a mad, rather inelegant dash for the stairs and just made it to the closest bathroom as the contents of her stomach rushed out.

Katya heaved and heaved into the bowl, wishing she was anywhere but here. Moisture welled in her eyes as she continued to retch. She felt cheap and nasty besmirching the beautiful luxury of the most elegant toilet she'd ever been in, but her stomach wouldn't let up and all she could do was cling helplessly to the porcelain and hope it would be over soon.

After what seemed an age she slumped back against the wall and shut her eyes. She could feel herself trembling all over and taste the bitterness of bile in her mouth. She waited until she felt strong enough to stand and clung to the wall as she pushed herself into a standing position.

She was grateful to find a boxed toothbrush and toothpaste in one of the marble vanity drawers and she brushed her teeth until her mouth felt minty fresh again. She looked at her face in the mirror. She looked like hell. Her pale complexion looked even whiter than normal and her blue eyes looked dull. But she felt better as each second passed and her spirits revived with the thought that now she'd vomited, the worst was over.

She could feel the powerful throb of the engine reverberate through her feet as she made her way back through the lounge and up the stairs.

'You weren't joking about the seasick thing, were you?' Ben said as Katya emerged from down below. 'Are you OK?'

'Sure. I feel much better,' she said, placing her foot on the deck. The breeze hit her face and a faint trace of engine fumes assaulted her nostrils. Nausea slammed into her gut and rolled through her intestines. She held up her hand to her mouth. 'I'll be right back.'

Katya made another mad dash to the toilet, again making it just in time. There was nothing left to bring up but it didn't stop her delicate constitution from trying. She felt like her hormones were ringing every last morsel of food from her entire digestive tract.

She vaguely heard the rumble of the engine cut out as she again slumped against the wall. The cessation of movement rallied her equilibrium but she felt as weak as a kitten. All she wanted to do was curl up on one of those heavenly looking plump leather couches she had now seen three times, shut her eyes and sleep through the trip.

'Katya?'

She opened an eye to see Ben standing in the doorway. If she'd have been remotely well, she would have worried about how bad she must look right now, but frankly she couldn't care less if she looked like she'd been dragged through a hedge backwards. 'I'm fine,' she said.

Ben looked down at the distinctly un-fine-looking Katya propped against the toilet wall. She looked like hell. Her blonde feathery fringe was plastered to her forehead, slick with sweat. Her normally pale complexion looked as white as the wall she was leaning against. So much for a great day on the water.

He turned to the vanity in the bathroom, removed a face-cloth from one of the drawers, wet it under the gold-plated tap and wrung it out. He crouched down beside her and pressed the cloth to her forehead. Her eyes flicked open briefly.

'I'm fine,' she mumbled.

'You look like hell,' he said. Ben mopped her sweaty brow with the cool cloth and trailed it over the rest of her face, across her parched lips and down her neck.

Katya murmured something in Russian and he felt as if she'd run her fingers over his stomach muscles. He'd never seen her helpless like this, so…docile. He'd never seen any sign of weakness from her, apart from yesterday afternoon in the cameo shop. It seemed he was seeing a different side to Katya the more time he spent with her.

The urge to sweep her up in his arms and protect her from her demons was overwhelming. Had she eaten something at breakfast that had been off? Was she actually really ill? Or was she really just not a seafarer? He needed to examine her in case she was developing a serious medical condition.

He tossed the facecloth over his shoulder and swept her up in one easy move into his arms. She barely protested. She felt floppy, like deadweight, even though he managed her slight proportions easily. He eased her gently down onto the leather couch and then went back to the bathroom to remoisten the facecloth.

Ben returned quickly and mopped her face again, folding the cloth and placing it along her forehead. She felt warm and he was worried now that this was something serious.

'Katya. Katya?' he said, speaking quietly, stroking his fingers gently down her arm.

Her eyes flicked open briefly. 'Mmm. That's nice,' she sighed.

Ben chuckled. She was right about that. 'I'm going to give you a quick once-over, Katya,' he said, 'just to check everything's OK.'

Katya was floating along in a nice hazy world. She could hear his voice and it was as sexy as ever and she wanted to wrap it around her like a feather duvet and go to sleep. She felt his long, lean surgeon's fingers at her wrist and felt sure he must be able to feel the flutter of her heart at his touch.

She felt his hands on her abdomen. They were deft, methodical, poking and prodding. 'Mind the baby,' she said, slipping into her native tongue as her hazy mind transmitted his non-sexual touch into a lover's caress.

Katya's eyes flew open. Had she said that in English or Russian? 'What are you doing?' she demanded, half sitting, displacing his hands, which were moving slowly and systematically lower. The baby! The baby! She was instantly awake.

'It's OK,' Ben said soothingly. 'I was just seeing if you had any abdominal tenderness.'

'I told you, I'm fine,' she said, removing his hands.

'You don't look so fine,' Ben said impatiently. 'You were out of it there for a minute. Did you eat something off this morning?' he asked, placing his hands against her stomach again.

'Nothing,' she protested, batting his hands away. 'We ate the same things. I'm not good on boats, that's all,' she protested weakly.

'Please, don't insult me. You couldn't get water any flatter unless you were in the bathtub.'

Katya watched as Ben started to pace and rattled off a number of things it could be.

'I don't think it's appendicitis. There's no rebound tenderness,' he muttered. 'No…you had the ham on your roll and I didn't,' he said, turning to her. 'Maybe it was off and you've contracted food poisoning.' Ben raked his fingers through his hair. 'Oh, God! How many staff and patients have had that ham today? This sort of thing doesn't happen at the Lucia Clinic. I'll have to ring the chef,' he said, striding over to the old-fashioned marble-handled telephone and dialing the clinic number.

Katya watched him in dismay. 'Ben, it's nothing.'

He held his hand over the receiver. 'Of course it is,' he said impatiently. 'People can't come to our clinic and get food poisoning. As soon as I'm done here, we'll head back to Amalfi and we'll go to the hospital. You may need rehydration.'

Katya couldn't believe how this was escalating out of control. She could see it becoming an international incident before her eyes. 'Ben, for God's sake, put the phone down. I'm pregnant, that's all.'

She hadn't meant to blurt it out like that. She had her speech all prepared. Had lain awake all last night, perfecting it. And in a matter of seconds she'd blown it out of the water. She watched his face as her words sank in.

'What did you say?' he asked, as he slowly replaced the receiver.

Katya sighed. She felt too wretched now to give him the whole spiel. She swung her legs around and sat up gingerly. At least with the boat now stopped, her stomach seemed to be more settled. 'I'm having your baby,' she said, her voice stronger now.

Ben stared at her, not even really seeing her as her words slowly filtered through. Baby? Was she insane? 'But…how?'

Katya could see she'd really thrown him. She'd never seen him look pale—ever. But he did now. And he was clutching the phone like he was going to fall over if he let go. She understood his question was rhetorical so she didn't bother answering it. She just sat and watched him, waiting for it to sink in further.

'Are you sure?' he asked.

Katya nodded patiently. It was a fair enough question. She'd spent a good week in total disbelief. 'I've taken three tests and been throwing up every day for two months.'

Ben blinked. This couldn't be happening. Him? A father? He didn't know how to be a father. He just couldn't get his head around it. 'Are you sure it's mine?' Thinking about it, they hadn't used any protection. It had been such a spontaneous act and he'd been so shaken that it hadn't even occurred to him. He'd just needed to be close to her, to hold her, to blot out the awful events and years of stupid, futile anger.

Katya felt the question slam into her even though it was delivered with no malice or accusation. The hairs on the back of her neck prickled. No way! He didn't get to question the paternity. 'I'm one hundred per cent sure,' she said rising, her hands curling into fists by her side. 'I was a virgin that night, Ben.'

Ben took the second body blow just as hard. His thoughts reeled. 'You were?' Shouldn't he have been able to tell? Had he been that caught up in his own grief and regret that he hadn't been paying attention to her cues?

'*Da*,' she said shortly.

'But…but I didn't… I couldn't… You seemed…'

'Oh, for God's sake, Ben,' she snapped.

That was it, Ben had to sit down. He walked over to the lounge opposite Katya's and sank into the plush leather. 'How do you get to twenty-seven and still be a virgin?' he asked.

Katya snorted. Growing up in her house, it had been easy. She'd lived with a woman who used sex as a commodity. Sure, deep down Katya really believed that Olgah had truly just wanted to be loved, but Katya had seen too many men come and go and leave her mother broken-hearted to trust any man. As a mere child she had picked up the pieces once too often. Held her mother, stroked her prematurely grey hair, while she had sobbed her heart out.

As a child, Katya had been frightened and bewildered by her mother's ups and downs. As an adult, her mother's example had taught Katya that weaknesses destroyed you. Consequently, she'd never let her guard down enough to have a relationship. Being intimate? Forget it!

Ben had been a complete one-off for her. A totally out-of-character thing for her to do but he'd been so shaken, so devastated that she hadn't even questioned her actions. She had just known on some intuitive female level that Ben needed comfort and had known how to provide it. The questions and the reprimands had come soon enough. The next morning, she had felt no better than her mother.

'Upbringing,' Katya said dismissively as she sat, wanting to rehash that night as little as possible. 'Anyway, that's not the point. The point is I'm pregnant. I'm sorry, I didn't plan to tell you this way.'

Ben shook his head to clear it. She was right. The point was, he was going to be a father. The thought was no less horrifying than it had been minutes ago. But something was clearer. 'That's why you're here,' he said. 'You came to tell me you were pregnant?'

'*Da.*' Katya nodded.

Ben could feel his thoughts coming back on line now. Things were starting to make sense. And yet they weren't. 'Why? You could have just rung me.'

'Because I don't want the baby.'

Ben took a moment to absorb her answer. It seemed they were back to not making any sense. 'So why didn't you just have a termination?' When he thought about it, it was exactly the thing that practical, sensible, no-nonsense Katya would do. Why not, if she didn't want the baby? Want his baby. *She didn't want his baby?*

Katya shook her head. 'Tried. Couldn't.'

Ben's brow puckered. He felt like he was running in quicksand and sinking. 'What do you mean, couldn't? You couldn't get in to a clinic?'

'I mean I made the appointment, I sat in the waiting room, they called my name and I just couldn't go through with it.' Katya rubbed her stomach. She remembered the moment—the precise moment. The nurse calling her name again and again and knowing, just knowing that she couldn't do it. For better or for worse she had given this baby life, and she couldn't take it away.

Ben heard the husky note to her voice and noted her hand movements. The quicksand solidified a little. How many pregnant women had he seen repeat the same action? Katya's stomach was still flat, no baby bump at all, yet she had the action down pat. She sounded surprised by the turn of events and he could imagine how her inability to see something she'd organised all the way through would have turned her neat, practical world upside down.

But nothing changed the fact that growing inside her was his baby. His flesh and blood. He felt a strange sense of possession and found himself thankful that Katya hadn't been able to go through with the termination.

'So where do we go from here?' he asked.

Katya took a deep breath, forgoing her speech for the direct route. 'I want you to raise the baby.'

Curiouser and curiouser. 'Me?' he said, trying to wrap his head around everything that had come out of her mouth in the last couple of minutes.

'Well, you are the father,' Katya said bluntly.

The father. He was going to be a father. He felt the enormity of that simple statement hit him. How could they have been so careless? He couldn't be a father. He hadn't even been a good brother. Surely a much lesser role? He'd ignored all Mario's overtures, closed himself off to a relationship he'd invested in since birth. He'd closed himself off to any kind of love for so long now. Did he even have the capacity for it any more?

'And how do you envision that will work?' he asked, as his brain madly tried to keep up with the ever-changing plot.

Now, this was a topic she could talk on. This was what she'd been planning for over a month. 'I have a plan.'

She did? 'OK then.' He rubbed his hands through his hair. 'Let's hear it.'

'I'll stay here until the baby is born. After the birth, you can take over the baby's care.'

Ben could see her face become animated. She'd obviously put a lot of thought into this. 'And you?'

Katya shrugged. 'Back to MedSurg, of course.'

Just like that? She could seriously just walk away from her own child? His reticence he could understand. But, Katya? She was the mother. Wasn't that innate? How could she reject their child? 'Why don't you want the baby?'

Katya shook her head emphatically 'Why doesn't matter.'

Ben had the feeling, watching her caress her stomach, that 'why' mattered very much. 'It does to me.'

Katya wrestled with how much to tell him. He didn't need to know all the gory details, just the basics. She sighed. 'From the age of eight until I left home at twenty, I raised three sisters and a brother. I'm mothered out.'

Ben absorbed her stunning statement silently. He caught a brief glimpse of the eight-year-old Katya before her shutters came down. 'Your mother?' he asked.

'Left it up to me,' Katya said, and stared at the floor, not daring to elaborate. How could someone who had grown up with everything—emotionally and financially—ever understand the gritty reality of her childhood?

Five little words spoke volumes to Ben. They were brief and clipped and he noted she couldn't even meet his gaze. Suddenly the whole Katya persona was making so much more sense. Her practicality, her harshness, her bluntness. She would have needed to be all those things to mother four children as a mere child herself.

And her conversation with her mother on the phone yesterday was another piece in the crazy Katya puzzle that was becoming clearer. But looking at her as she cradled their baby with her protective pose, like a lioness protecting her young, he knew he was just scratching the surface. Obviously her childhood had left scars.

'At least you know how,' he said in a soft voice.

Katya saw a flash of Sophia's terror and pain and clamped

down on the memory before it developed sound. 'Trust me, Ben. I wouldn't be any good for this baby.'

'What makes you think I would be any better?' Sure, he could provide for it. But giving himself up completely to another human being, as babies demanded, was a terrifying thought. He'd done that once already and he too had been left with scars.

'Because you have Lucia. You had a fantastic role model and an idyllic childhood—none of which I had. And I see that reflected in the way you've been with Lupi—it's innate in you. I've watched you with Lupi, Ben. You're good with her. And she adores you and so will this baby. And you can give it things I can't.'

'I can't give it a mother's love,' he said.

Katya gripped her abdomen more firmly his words penetrating like bullets, shredding her fortitude. As long as it had love, did it matter whether the source was from the mother or the father? 'I meant material stuff.'

'Like Ferraris and Learjets?'

Katya shook her head, feeling her ire rise. He made her feel like a gold-digger. 'You think I give a damn about expensive status symbols? You think I got pregnant to bleed you dry?'

'I'm sorry,' he said, holding up his hands. 'That was uncalled for.' Ben massaged his forehead. He hadn't meant his words to sound so judgmental. He just couldn't believe his life was suddenly spinning out of control. He'd left Italy a decade ago to get back control over his life and feeling that all slip away again was frustrating.

And he'd be damned if he'd let it take over a second time. He needed to take it back again. And not by running but by staying and taking the only option open to him. The one thing that his traditionalist background demanded. Katya was having his baby. Wanted him to raise it. Then it had to be on his terms. He wasn't going to let another woman turn his life upside down.

He looked at her, her blue eyes still glowering at him, her hand still firmly in place on her stomach. She said she didn't want their baby but her body language said differently. And despite his shock, he couldn't suppress a tiny faint glow deep inside that already connected him to his child. Maybe they'd both been given a chance to overcome their pasts?

'I think we should get married.'

CHAPTER FIVE

KATYA blinked. Her hand stilled on her stomach. 'What did you say?'

Ben couldn't blame her for her shocked expression. He was kind of shocked himself. The whole morning had been one mind-bending revelation after the other. He certainly hadn't come away this morning expecting to ask Katya to marry him. But his old-fashioned values, beliefs ingrained into him by his mother and his upbringing, overrode everything.

They were having a baby—it deserved to be legitimate. Even though his faith in marriage and family had been destroyed a decade ago. Even though Katya wanted nothing to do with the baby. The baby hadn't asked to exist and it deserved no less than any other child. It deserved the right beginning.

'I said, we should get married.'

Katya was lost for words. *Had he gone completely mad?* He was looking at her calmly—no signs of obvious insanity. He wasn't frothing at the mouth or going cross-eyed. What the hell did marrying him have to do with the baby? The thought was as horrifying as it was tantalising.

'You?' she spluttered. 'Bendetto Medici, the playboy count? Get married?'

He shrugged. 'You're pregnant. The baby's mine. It may be old-fashioned but it's the right thing to do.'

Katya blinked again. Old-fashioned? *Try archaic!* 'In the Dark Ages, maybe.'

'I'm a traditionalist.' He shrugged again.

Katya felt bitter laughter bubble in her chest and it was out before she could check it. It sounded harsh in the confines of the cabin. 'This from the man who famously spent one of his leave periods from MedSurg dating every swimwear model he could locate?'

Ben could have been deaf and blind and still wouldn't have missed her mocking tone. Her harsh judgment of him rankled. He was far removed from the man he used to be. 'Dismissing me again, Katya?'

She stood up and pushed herself away from the lounge, putting some distance between herself and the dark, dangerous glitter of his eyes. She paced over to the window and looked out. This was crazy. Crazy! The Med shimmered and stretched out before her and she turned back lest her now settled stomach decided to change its mind.

'No.'

She'd decided long ago, after witnessing her mother's emotional destruction every time a relationship ended, that she'd be far better off without a man. She'd learned the hard way that true commitment and love were elusive and rare and she'd sworn to never settle for less. Never marry for less. Certainly not someone who felt it was his duty and responsibility. *All or nothing.* It had to be all or nothing. And she wouldn't compromise, not even for the baby.

Ben wasn't surprised. But he wasn't deterred either. 'Yes.'

Katya shook her head emphatically. He looked so sexy, pinning her to the deck with his brown-eyed stare. She shivered. She was pregnant and had just thrown up her entire stomach contents but when he looked at her, her toes curled. 'No.'

The more she resisted, the more determined he became. 'So, let me see,' he said quietly, observing her hand-on-tummy stance, 'you expect to have our baby then leave it with me with no legally binding contract? Nothing to say that the baby is mine? Do you want our baby to have my name, Katya?'

Katya let his words sink in. For all her planning, she hadn't got that far. Did she? Did she want their baby to have its father's name or hers? What was the point of Ben raising the baby, of her baby growing up in Italy with its father with all the financial security she could dream of, if the child had her name? Whether she liked it or not, she was having a Medici. Wasn't it this baby's birthright to claim its father's name?

'We don't have to marry to give this baby your name.'

'No, but it makes everything a hell of a lot easier. It legitimises this baby's birth better than any other legal process. Both in the eyes of the people and the law. I don't want there to ever be any questions about this baby's paternity. It has rights to my title and the Medici fortune. Everything has to be above board and a marriage is the simplest, easiest way to achieve this.'

Ben finished, congratulating himself on such clear thinking. He wasn't actually sure of the legalities concerning illegitimate children and the line of succession but considering how rattled he was he was surprised he'd been so comprehensive. So concise. But suddenly every word he spoke was important. Part of him, the one per cent that wasn't horrified, the one per cent traditionalist, was already completely committed to this baby.

Katya Petrova was pregnant with his child. *His child.* The Medici heir. And whether it was the male in him or the Italian in him, that meant something. When he had been young and foolish and in love with Bianca he had imagined himself with many children. Had anticipated it, eagerly. Then life had happened and his dream had been destroyed but now, whether he liked it or not, his dream was becoming a belated reality. And he had to face his responsibilities.

Katya blinked. She knew the words he had spoken were the truth. She wanted her child to be legitimate too. She didn't want there to ever be any doubt or whispers. She thought about the whispers she had grown up with. The neighbours who had disapproved of her mother's lifestyle. Five children with no fathers. The gossip. The judgmental stares.

Marrying Ben would tidy up any nasty loose ends. But a marriage would be harder to walk away from. And she couldn't stay. For the sake of her baby, she had to be far, far away.

He had to know that her being involved with this baby was not going to happen. She raised her head and looked him straight in the eye. 'A marriage would mean a divorce. I can't stay after I've had the baby,' she said.

Ben saw the finality in her blue gaze. For some reason she truly believed that this baby would be better off without her. 'Why, Katya? Would being married to me be that awful?'

Oh, God! Awful? On the contrary. She shut her eyes briefly and thought about waking up to his beautiful face every morning. Having his lazy smile and slumberous gaze the first thing she saw every day. It was a delicious thought. A seductive thought.

'I can't be a mother.'

'Because you're mothered out,' he said. Somehow he didn't think that was it. There had to be more than that. As prickly as she could be, abandoning a child just didn't ring true.

She heard the disbelief in his voice. It sounded like such a paltry excuse when he said it like that. But he hadn't lived her life. If he could have just walked a mile in her shoes, he'd understand. But if you're born with a silver spoon in your mouth, how could you possibly understand a life of poverty?

'*Da*,' she said. *Let him think what he liked.*

'I don't believe you,' he said. 'You may not be the softest person I know but underneath your hard exterior, there is a deeply compassionate woman, Katya. I know that because you showed me that woman the night I heard about Mario. The one night I needed comfort and you gave it to me. Unquestioningly. I know that woman could never walk away from a child. Especially her own child.'

Katya just stopped herself from gaping. One night of passion and Ben had seen the person beneath the surface. The Katya she was deep down, beneath the blunt, unemotional façade. The Katya she'd been before her mother had decided to give her responsibilities beyond her years. 'You wouldn't understand,' she said dismissively

'Try me,' he countered.

Katya sighed. 'It doesn't matter, Ben.'

Ben snorted. 'I'm sorry, Katya, it does. You want me to take on a child that you're not prepared to. Give years of my life that you're not prepared to. Convince me.'

Katya looked at him helplessly. How could a man of Ben's background understand? Her hands shook. Baring her soul, telling him everything was too exposing.

'I'd be bad at it.'

'Rubbish.'

Katya's head shot up at his tone. She shook her head. 'You don't know me,' she said. 'You think one night in your arms and you know me?'

He ignored her. If he kept at it, he was sure she'd tell him the real reason. 'I know you're strong. I know you're tough. I know you're capable enough, stubborn enough, fierce enough to do this by yourself.'

Katya shook her head emphatically. 'I've seen how hard it is for a single mother. What a struggle it is to raise a child and juggle work and home commitments. I know how hard it is financially and emotionally. I don't want to be that kind of mother.'

He noted her look of grim determination. Katya's life had obviously been very hard. But despite that she obviously cared about the quality of her mothering. That didn't strike him as someone who didn't care. He sensed he was getting closer and closer to the real reason. 'What kind of mother do you want to be?'

Katya glared at him. She was not going to fall for that. 'I don't want to be any kind of mother.'

'Why?' he persisted.

Why didn't he just leave it alone? 'Because,' Katya said exasperated, 'I'd be really bad at it.'

'Why?' Ben asked again. 'You said yourself you've already raised four babies, one would have thought you'd be highly experienced at it.'

Yeah, right. Katya was sure Sophia would beg to differ. 'I did what I had to do,' she said. 'Doesn't mean I was any good at it.'

Ben watched Katya pluck at the leather beading on the arm of the lounge. Her gaze was downcast, her movements seemed agitated and he suddenly wondered if something bad had happened. 'Katya,' he said, 'talk to me.'

Katya was lured into looking at him by the raw inflection in his voice. He was looking at her with a soft compassionate gaze and she wanted to crawl into his lap and tell him everything. About all the hard years and the guilt.

The terrible guilt she still felt today over her sister's injuries. Even though Sophia was leading a happy and productive life.

She shook her head. 'It's OK for you, Ben. You had a great role model. Lucia is loving and supportive. You probably even had a father at some stage.'

'Not really,' he said. 'My father died when I was one. I never really knew him.'

'I bet your mother adored him, though, right?'

Ben smiled and nodded, remembering the many happy memories his mother had recounted over the years. 'They were very happy. My mother misses him very much.'

Katya nodded. 'I can tell.' The contessa looked like a woman who had been well loved. 'My mother's not like that. She's…different. Life hasn't been so good to her and really, as role models go, she was lousy. So I don't know how to be a mother. Not a good one, anyway.'

Ben was getting a clearer and clearer picture. Katya was the product of her upbringing. But he couldn't get past her hand still absently stroking her abdomen. She may have talked herself out of it but there was something in her actions, in the way she was launching into this crazy plan, that told him she didn't want to walk away from the baby. And if he agreed to Katya's proposal, if raising their child became his responsibility, then surely he'd be remiss if he didn't demand the best? And surely that was two parents?

'You don't have to do it alone, *cara*. I'll be there to help you.'

Katya stared at him, captivated by the promise in his words. But how often had she heard her mother's men say the same thing? Years of ingrained mistrust couldn't be undone so easily.

If she stayed, if she married him, what would happen to the child when it all fell apart? Like her mother's relationships always had? Would their child be forced to pick up the pieces as she had done? Did she want to inflict that on her baby? Repeat the cycle?

Katya shook her head again before she did something stupid like say yes. 'No.' She must not let a count with long eyelashes and silky promises ruin her focus. 'But I'm pleased it will have a father,' she said, rubbing her tummy again. 'I didn't have a father...I missed that. No doubt you did, too.'

Yes, he had. But he'd had a mother. Probably the only person more important than the father in a child's life. 'Yes, I did. But a child needs a mother more. What about breast-feeding? Don't you want the best start in life for our child?'

Katya swallowed as an image of her with Ben's baby snuggled in close rose before her. She could see its dark downy hair and almost feel the pull of its hungry mouth against her breast. 'Plenty of babies are bottle-fed in this world. If that's the worst that can happen, it'll be doing OK.'

Try as he may, Ben just couldn't get his head around a woman rejecting her baby. 'Don't you want this baby, love this baby with every cell in your body?'

Katya felt his words claw at her soul. She didn't expect him to understand her motivations. She cleared her throat. 'This is not about me not loving the baby, Ben. Why do you think I couldn't terminate the pregnancy? But I love it enough to know that I can't look after it. Trust me, it will be much better off without me.'

'All this baby needs is for you to love it, Katya. Nothing else.'

He made it sound so simple. But she'd loved Sophia. And ultimately that hadn't meant anything. It hadn't stopped her getting hurt. Nearly dying. Being permanently scarred.

'No, Ben, trust me, babies can't live on love alone.'

Ben clenched his hands into fists. He was getting tired of

her vague insinuations. He knew she wasn't deliberately trying to frustrate him, that there was something deep down that she couldn't share, that was too horrible for her to talk about. And he knew how that felt. How guilt and anger and circumstances in life made you someone that you didn't want to be or never thought you would turn into.

'What are your other options?' he asked. 'If I say no, what's your plan B?'

Katya felt her heart pounding in her chest. He wouldn't. Would he? 'Adoption,' she said.

Ben felt as if she had slapped him. His head was filled with a mix of emotions all whizzing around, clashing into each other until he didn't know how he felt any more. But he knew how he felt about this. Would she seriously give his baby away to complete strangers? Not that he had a problem with adoption, but his baby? 'Really?' he asked.

She heard the incredulity in his voice. 'It's not my preferred option, Ben. But you have to understand—I can't do this.'

Ben nodded slowly. Suddenly, he believed her. He got it. He really got it now. She was deadly serious. It was him or some stranger raising his child. He rejected it immediately, the traditionalist emerging again. This was his baby. *His baby*. He couldn't let anyone else raise it.

For some reason she really thought she couldn't do it. Some reason that she couldn't tell him about. It was frustrating but maybe she just needed a bit of time. Maybe the marriage would give her a different perspective?

He nodded slowly. 'OK. I'll do it. But only if you agree to marry me.'

Katya felt her body rock with a maelstrom of emotions. Ben had said yes. She had accomplished her goal. But at what cost? She knew everything he said made sense but if she married him, she'd be walking away not just from her baby but from a marriage, too.

'Why,' she asked, 'why do you want to complicate your life by marrying me?'

'Oh, and you think a child won't complicate it?'

She gave him a frustrated stare. 'Don't you think marrying for a child is wrong?'

He shrugged. 'Plenty of couples do it.'

'And plenty of them fail,' she pointed out. 'Don't you want to marry for higher ideals? Like love?'

He snorted. 'Love? What's that? I don't believe in it. All love does is make you blind to things you should see and makes you see things that aren't there.'

Katya blinked. *And she thought she was cynical?* Could she marry a man who didn't believe in love? Even for a few short months? She may have grown up in the gritty reality of life but somewhere beneath her tough exterior there was still a tiny part of her, a remnant of a romantic eight-year-old, who still dreamt of a Prince Charming on a white charger. Who demanded it.

'And what do we tell people when I leave the marriage after the baby's born? If we marry, we give everyone involved a false promise. Can you lie to everyone about that? Can you lie to your mother?'

Ben hesitated. Could he? Could he look his mother in the eye? 'Married or not, they're going to have an expectation that our relationship is going to last longer than a few months,' he said. 'I'm a Medici, they'll have expectations.'

Katya shrugged her slim shoulders. 'Let them.'

'People around here will expect us to marry.'

'I can't, Ben. I won't. I'll do whatever else you ask. I'll sign anything you want to grant you legal recognition as the father of the baby. You can get a paternity test. I'll stay here till it's born. Hell, I'll live with you, if that helps. But I will not marry you.'

Ben heard the finality in her voice. And he believed her. She looked grim and solemn and resolute. 'You're making a mistake,' he said grimly.

She shook her head emphatically. 'No, Ben, I'm not. This is probably the only thing I'm doing right. You see, I have no control over being pregnant. Over this situation. Not now. And if this hadn't have happened, we'd probably never have seen each other again. But I do have control over this. Over who I marry. My faith in marriage is fairly non-existent, I'm afraid. But I do know that I can't settle for less than one hundred per cent love and commitment. I've seen firsthand how that can destroy someone.'

'I can promise you, you will have one hundred and ten per cent commitment from me, Katya.'

Katya laughed harshly. 'What, until I leave?'

He nodded. 'For as long as you stay.'

And then what? Back to the swimwear models? 'Can you promise me love?'

Ben blinked and felt his heart pounding in his chest. An image of Bianca and Mario locked together in a passionate kiss swam before him. Love? What the hell was love? 'Maybe…over time…'

Great. Just like her mother. Waiting around, wasting her life in futile relationships, hanging on for those three magic words? 'Relax, Ben, it's OK. You don't love me. I don't love you. We're just two people who were irresponsible and are facing the consequences. But that only gives you the right to this baby. It doesn't give you the right to me.'

Katya raised her head and held it up proudly. The tradition-alist in him might be forcing him to be noble but the eight-year-old girl in her, the one who'd had all her dreams crushed into the dirt, was stubbornly shaking her head, refusing to give away her last childhood fantasy.

Ben took a moment to digest her words. She really was serious about leaving the child for him to raise. He could see the determined jut of her chin. This was obviously a deal-breaker for her. He quickly weighed up his options. If he insisted, forced her hand, would she leave taking his baby with her? Go through with her plans to have it adopted?

Or could he pull back and try and convince her in the time between now and the baby's birth that their child needed a mother as well as a father? Gently, slowly, surely work away at her, get to know her and help her to see that she *could* be a mother to the baby? Even if they never married, surely Katya staying was the best scenario possible? He had about six months.

He nodded. 'OK, fine,' he conceded. 'We'll play it your way.'

Katya watched his face, searching it for any insincerity, any hesitancy. All she saw was openness and acceptance. She felt all the tension that had been holding her upright since she'd found out about the baby leave her body. Katya gratefully sagged back into the soft leather of the chair. She had done it. She had secured the best possible outcome for her child. What happened from now on didn't matter.

Now it was done, there was a moment of awkwardness. 'If you want to get a test organised and some papers drawn up, I'll sign them,' she said.

He nodded. 'I'll see to it. I'll make sure you're provided for as well.'

Katya felt her heartbeat slow for a few seconds before it sped up and a spurt of anger surged through her bloodstream. This was the second time he'd try to buy her. 'Like payment, Ben?' she asked, her voice low.

'No,' he protested quickly. 'No. I just meant…I don't want the mother of my child to have to struggle.'

Katya could see his good intentions written all over his handsome face and her anger dissipated. She sighed. 'I don't want anything from you, Ben. I never have. Not money or property or anything else. I'll be just fine. I was fine before you and I'll be fine after you.' *Hopefully.* 'All I need is your assurances that you will love and care for our child.'

Ben believed her. She truly was a woman who didn't seem to need anyone. Sincerity oozed from every pore of her body. Katya Petrova was a proud woman. Even a legitimate chance to improve her status was rejected. 'On my family's honour, Katya,' he assured her, 'I will be the best father I can be.'

'Thank you. That's all I want.'

Silence stretched between the two of them. Katya wasn't sure what they should do next. What did people do after they'd haggled over the future of their baby and their lives? Shake on it?

A few more moments passed. Ben roused himself from his still spinning thoughts. 'How are you feeling now?' he asked. 'Do you think your stomach could stand the trip back? We may as well get the ball rolling. We'll go to Positano and tell Mamma.'

Ben stopped and grinned for the first time since Katya had flipped his world on its head. 'She'll be ecstatic.' *Until she finds out about the whole no-wedding thing, anyway.*

Katya felt a ghost of a smile flit across her lips as she imagined Lucia clapping her hands in glee.

'How about your mother? Have you told your family?'

Katya heard her mother's words again about being nice to Ben and she shuddered, thinking about it. She wasn't going to tell her mother about the baby ever. Olgah was not going to get a chance to ingratiate herself with a rich Italian count.

'No.'

Ben regarded her seriously for a few moments, her expression shuttered.

'Katya, she's our baby's grandmother.'

'No.'

He nodded. 'OK.' Now was not the time for pushing. 'Do you reckon you're up to taking the boat to Positano or do you want to head back in to Amalfi and drive?'

Katya looked at both alternatives disparagingly. Neither was particularly attractive. But her stomach was feeling much more settled now and at least on the sea they had more room than on those narrow twisting roads.

'You really have to see Positano from the sea. I think it's the best aspect. It gives you a true appreciation of its magnificence.'

'OK,' Katya agreed, following him up on deck. Whatever. She couldn't believe that after all that had transpired that Ben could calmly talk about other things. Her head was spinning, barely able to formulate a coherent thought.

But he was right, the sea aspect was amazing. She sat on one of the side seats, the breeze blowing her hair, and watched the world go by as the powerful boat ate up the distance. Her stomach never quavered once and Katya actually enjoyed the warm sun on her face and arms.

He pointed out different areas of interest as they passed by and Katya took in the incredible edifices of the villas lining the cliff faces. They clung to the craggy rocks, some new, some almost as old-looking as the mountains themselves. The sun beat down, bathing the scenery in an impossibly bright light, the villas almost glowing.

Each house seemed to have stairs cut into the stone of the cliffs that zigzagged their way down the rock face until they reached concrete platforms at the bottom. Many of the residents were availing themselves of these private balconies, using them not just for sunbathing but as a springboard into the inviting blue of the Med. Some of the people even waved at Ben as the boat sped by.

'That's mine,' he said, raising his voice to be heard over the engine as he pointed to an impressive white villa dominating the rock face.

Katya stared at it. It was huge, sprawling along the cliff top, its clean white lines and arched windows elegant. Purple bougainvillea crept along the façade on one side, a colourful foil to the stark whiteness. It too had steps that led down the cliff to the sea below, with more bougainvillea creeping along the iron railings, blazing a trail of colour down to the sea.

'That's where we'll live,' he said.

She turned and looked at him. He returned her searching stare with an unflinching brown gaze. So, he was taking her up on her offer to cohabit? She turned back quickly, her heart beating a mad tattoo. What would it be like living in this beautiful white home? It looked like a palace sitting atop the cliffs in all its dazzling white glory and Katya found it difficult to digest. In a couple of short months her whole life had been turned upside down and she wasn't sure about anything.

She had a moment's yearning for her previous life as the villa passed from her direct line of sight. At least she'd known who she was before she'd become pregnant. She'd been her own person. Now she was having a baby and was about to live in a palatial villa in Italy with a one-hundred-and-eighty degree view of the Mediterranean in the company of a devilishly good-looking count. She knew how to be Katya Petrova, poor Russian nurse. She didn't know how to be this Katya. *Ben's Katya.*

The scenery continued to dazzle her as the boat sped on.

Positano appeared in the distance, nestled on the shoreline at the feet of the soaring mountains behind. As it grew bigger she could see the alternating orange and blue lines of the deckchairs adorning the front, a striking contrast to the black stones of the beach.

Rows and rows of villas clung to the two main cliffs in a haphazard, colourful display, each one on top of the next, crammed in so the rock of the cliff wasn't visible. Just buildings. Private homes sharing space with tourist hotels. The impressive *duomo* nestled between, dominating the seafront. People, locals and tourists alike, cluttered the beach, swam in the sea or sunned themselves.

Katya had a moment of complete disconnectedness. She was really here. In a beautiful Italian seaside resort village. An Italian count beside her. It seemed too incredible to be true. Never even as child had she dreamed this big.

Ben cut the engine and dropped anchor a little way from the shore. Katya watched as he shaded his eyes from the sun and searched through the crowd of people. He spotted who he wanted on the short rickety wooden pier, then put his fingers in his mouth and let out a short sharp whistle. 'Hey, Marco!'

A man turned and Ben waved at him. The man dived into the sea and swam quickly to one of the many small boats that bobbed calmly nearby. He hauled himself in, pulled up the anchor and started the motor.

'You ready?' Ben asked, turning to Katya as Marco's small boat with the outboard motor grew closer.

She nodded and stood just as Marco reached *The Mermaid* and pulled up alongside.

'Hey, Marco, my friend. Thanks for the lift,' Ben said in Italian.

'Anything for you, Count,' Marco replied, grinning.

'This is Katya.' Ben introduced them in English and Marco held out his hand to help Katya into his boat.

Marco said something in Italian to Ben and they both laughed. '*Bella*,' he said to Katya and grinned. 'Benedetto is a lucky man.'

Ben roared with laughter and said something else in Italian and they both laughed again as Ben stepped into the boat as well. Katya sat on one of the wooden cross seats and Ben plonked himself beside her and placed his hand on her knee and smiled down at her.

It was such a dazzling smile, Katya forgot to breathe, and she certainly forgot to tell him to take his hand off her. It seemed that Ben wanted to portray them as a young, in-love couple and Katya gave him a small smile back. If he thought it was important to pretend to be something they weren't then she could go along with that. As long as he remembered that their act had a definite end date.

They reached the jetty a minute later and Marco helped her out.

'Do you know everyone in Positano?' she asked ten minutes later when they hadn't even left the beach area, continually stopped by people greeting Ben.

'Nearly.' He grinned.

He took Katya's hand as he led her up the steep stone stairs that took them past the *duomo*. Mario and Bianca had been married here with all the church trappings. He had been far away in Asia at the time but he had seen the pictures in a magazine somewhere. Mario with his arm around the woman who had been betrothed to *him*.

He tightened his grip on Katya's hand. 'Mamma's house is a bit of a climb from here, I'm afraid,' he said.

They made their way up the hill through the narrow

twisting alleys haunted by throngs of tourists. T-shirts and other items of clothing and shoes were hung on walls and placed outside shopfronts on tables. Ceramicware hung from every available surface. Artists displayed their paintings and local craftsmen hawked their jewellery in bougainvillea-draped lanes.

Bakeries and restaurants adjoined boutiques and gelaterias. Fruit and shoes and olive oil and wine and exclusive one-off dresses were sold in one vibrant clash of noise and colour. A multitude of languages and accents assaulted her ears.

Lucia was waiting for them at the front door when they'd finally made their way up the hillside.

'Somebody rang?' He laughed as he kissed both the contessa's cheeks.

'Three people,' Lucia confirmed, with a twinkle in her eye.

Ben's mother turned to Katya and clasped her hand. 'How lovely to see you again,' she said, and embraced Katya in a tight hug.

Katya closed her eyes and felt Lucia's warmth and sincerity surround her.

'Come,' Lucia said, breaking away and taking a hand each. 'Tell me why you have come to visit an old woman on such a beautiful day.'

Ben laughed at his mother's tired joke. 'We came to tell you you are going to be a grandmother.'

Lucia gasped, dropped their hands and turned, looking from one to the other. She launched herself at Ben and let loose a string of rapid-fire Italian as she kissed his cheeks repeatedly. When she was finished with Ben, she turned to Katya and rained more kisses on her, still speaking in Italian.

'Enough, Mamma,' Ben chuckled, looking at Katya's slightly bewildered look.

'Yes, yes,' Lucia said, finally pulling away, her cheeks damp with tears, and grabbing their hands again. 'Come, we'll celebrate on the terrace and we can discuss the wedding.'

Katya's step faltered and she looked over Lucia's head at Ben. He chuckled and winked at her. *Was she ready for this?*

CHAPTER SIX

A MONTH passed. Katya felt like her life was now flying along out of her control. A rather unsettling feeling for someone who had been steadfastly in the driver's seat from the age of eight. September became October, their work continued, her stomach remained stubbornly flat, but other things changed.

News of her pregnancy slowly leaked out and then snow-balled until everyone on the Amalfi coast seemed to know. Lucia, after her initial disapproval of their non-wedding plans, accepted their decision graciously and fussed round Katya like a broody hen. People regarded them as a couple. Her colleagues treated her differently. It was subtle but she definitely felt like the boss's girlfriend around the clinic.

And, the biggest change of all, she moved in with Ben. As she had promised. It was a surreal kind of life to be living, real and fake at the same time. But it was her one concession to legitimise the baby and Katya knew she would do whatever it took to instill into the collective consciousness that the baby she carried was Ben's.

They developed a routine. They would finish their theatre list for the day, spend time with their post-op cases and then Ben would take her out to dinner.

Ravello had many wonderful restaurants and she enjoyed

exploring and getting to know the charming Italian village that would be her home for the next few months.

Ben was an interesting and lively tour guide and she'd certainly never eaten so well in all her life! The locals got to know who she was very quickly and she couldn't go out of the clinic without being recognised.

After dinner they would return to the clinic and their room. And their bed. The bed that they shared. She dreaded that moment. Was even getting really good at stalling. Because climbing into that bed next to a man that would tempt a nun and then having to platonically go to sleep was an impossible task. And when she did manage to grasp the elusive tendrils of slumber, she'd dream about him. About their night together.

Was it just her stage of pregnancy? Was it just her hormones that made the images so erotic she'd wake up with a hum in her veins and a buzz deep down inside? Was it them that caused her heart to trip when she glanced at his sexy sleeping profile? Or dared her to reach out and touch him, run her finger down his cheek, so much so that her palm would tingle and she had to clamp it between her thighs to stop it from following through?

And why did she have to dream in such agonising Technicolor detail? Why was her mind blowing it up into a scene of such amazing proportions? In reality, in the grand scheme of things, it probably hadn't been that good. Really, what comparison did she have? In fact, it could have been fairly average. Probably was. She'd been a virgin after all, so what did she know?

And then she'd wake in the morning, tired and irritable, only to find a heavy male arm slung across her belly or her head snuggled into his chest and his lazy morning smile grinning down at her. Sharing a bed with Ben was a particularly exquisite form of torture.

Katya lived for the weekends when they went to the villa and had separate rooms. It was strange and lonely, the bed big and empty, but by the time Friday night came around she was just too tired to give it more than a fleeting thought.

Consequently, needing a major distraction, she threw herself into the Lucia Trust work. Every day they operated on a growing number of unfortunate patients as their work became better known. They were children mainly, some born with disfiguring deformities, others having acquired them through horrific accidents. They also did a lot of burns-related surgery, releases of contractures mainly, as well as removals of several large benign disfiguring tumours.

It was rewarding work, seeing kids with such a poor quality of life have their lot improved so dramatically. And the whole surgical team was proud of their work. Katya even started to take an interest in the behind-the-scenes work of the foundation.

Ben introduced her to Carmella Rossi, the foundation's field officer, who was infectiously exuberant about her work and explained to Katya all the ins and outs of working with myriad charities and government agencies to identify patients, and the intricacies and red tape involved with getting them to Italy.

Katya soaked it up, asking questions, even going to the control room after surgery had finished for the day. Anything, anything to take her mind off Ben and that bed.

A week later Katya found herself standing next to Ben, gowned up ready to repair a severe bilateral cleft lip and palate. She yawned behind her mask as she daydreamed about Ben's lips. The last few nights her imagination had started to embellish her dream. The Ben in her dream had told her he loved her and the Katya in the dream had confessed her love too and they'd gone on to make love again, this time even better than the first. The joining more intense, the passion even deeper.

'Katya!'

Ben's impatient exclamation cut into her fantasy. She looked at him startled, her brain taking a few more seconds to shed the heavy cloak of the fantasy and focus on the present. 'What?'

'I *said* are you ready to start?'

Above his mask Katya could only see his eyes and for a moment, as he looked at her, they were the eyes from her dreams. Deep and dark and brown, and getting darker and stormier the more he kissed her. Those incredible drugging kisses that made her lose track of time and place.

'Katya?'

She saw his eyes widen fractionally and heard the slight husky tremor in his inquisitive voice. She blinked to dispel the images in her head. 'Right, yes.' She cleared her throat. 'Okey-dokey.'

Ben chuckled at her use of slang. It seemed so strange coming in her accented English. But it was a distraction from the look he had seen in her eyes. The frank sexual hunger there was startling and he was pleased to have an operating table and a scrub top to hide his instantaneous reaction.

Sleeping in the same bed every night, her warm body and cinnamon scent temptingly close, especially when he knew what delights her body held, was becoming increasingly difficult. Even more so when he kept catching brief glimpses of that look he'd seen again just now.

Mostly she was polite and friendly but from time to time, like just now, he could see she wanted him. And, God help him, he wanted her, too. It had been months since they had made love, since she had given herself so freely and completely, and it had fuelled his every night-time fantasy since.

That look had just completely shot his concentration and he knew it didn't bode well for this morning's theatre list. Each night was an exercise in self-control. And Ben prided himself on it. She had made it clear that their cohabitation would not be sexual and he had given her assurances that he would respect her wishes. But he was just a man, just flesh and blood, and he was damned if he was going to keep his hands to himself if she kept looking at him like that.

'Good, let's start,' he said. 'Scalpel.'

The list was as frustrating as he'd thought it would be. Katya could barely meet his gaze. She seemed tired and distracted, yawning frequently. Consequently their timing was off so things took longer, and he dropped an instrument, which he'd never done before, and they couldn't get his CD to work, and the op turned out to be more involved than he'd bargained for. So the list finished later than scheduled and by the time he closed the last patient he was in a foul mood, his staff were on edge and Katya was visibly annoyed at him.

'I want to talk to you,' Ben said as they left the theatre and stripped their gowns off.

'Go to hell,' she said, dumping her gown in the linen skip.

One of the theatre nurses nearby gasped and Ben smiled, despite his mood. Only Katya would dare to tell Count Benedetto Medici, Director of the Lucia Clinic, to go to hell.

'Lovers' tiff,' he said in Italian, and shrugged dramatically as he watched Katya stride away.

He caught up with her a few minutes later as she grabbed a cup of coffee from the dining room. 'Are you OK?' he asked.

'Sure,' she said abruptly. *Nothing that a spot of sex wouldn't fix.*

Ben put a hand under her chin and noticed the dark circles under her eyes. 'You look tired.'

'That's because I *am* tired,' she said irritably, annoyed at the tingling of her skin where his fingers were resting.

Ben castigated himself. 'Why didn't you say something, *cara*? You're pregnant, for God's sake!'

'I'm pregnant Ben, not dying.'

He took the cup from her hands and gave it back to the waitress.

'Hey, I need that!' She needed something to pep her up for the afternoon list.

'No.' He shook his head. 'Caffeine is no good for the baby. You need sleep, not something that's going to keep you awake.'

'Ben—'

'Go to bed, Katya,' he ordered, placing his hand on her shoulder and priding himself on how steady his voice sounded when his mind was full of images of her going to bed. And him joining her. Kissing her neck, stroking her back. Caressing her hip.

'We have an afternoon list,' Katya said, her voice husky as he lightly massaged the muscle that sloped from her neck to her shoulder. It felt so heavenly, somewhere between asexual and erotic, and she could feel her eyes closing in response, her body swaying towards the source of pleasure.

'It will be fine, *cara*,' he murmured. She looked done in, out on her feet. Why the hell hadn't he noticed how tired she looked until now? Spending hours behind a mask every day was no excuse.

'Come on,' he said, putting an arm around her shoulders and leading her to their quarters. 'I don't want to see you in Theatre again today,' he told her as he unlocked their door and pushed her gently inside.

'Thanks, Ben,' Katya murmured.

He nodded and then shut the door and got the hell away before he was tempted to go back and join her.

Katya had a quick shower, doubting whether she'd be able to sleep with her skin still tingling, her shoulder still burning from his touch. She stepped into a towelling robe that had come with the room—the Lucia Clinic thought of everything—and pulled on a pair of knickers. She gave her hair a quick rub with a luxuriously fluffy towel. The beauty of her fine, feathery locks was that they only took thirty seconds to dry off.

Katya eyed the bed as she wandered out of the bathroom. It was exactly as they had left it that morning. Neat and tidy, the duvet smoothed of any lines. A bit like their relationship—straight and orderly. Not messy and passionate.

The thought of lying on it without Ben was strange and yet it beckoned to her, her tired brain hopeful that, without a sexy male dominating it, she might just be able to sleep. She sat on the edge and then lay back, turning on her side and tucking her knees up.

She had a fleeting moment of indecision as sleep claimed her that maybe she should change into her pyjamas in case Ben came back. But she was so tired and what if he did? The gown covered her from neck to toe. *He'd seen her naked, for crying out loud.* And, realistically, she could probably only manage a nap.

It was her last conscious thought for five hours.

Ben opened the door, ready to greet her, when he completely lost his train of thought. Katya was fast asleep on her back on the bed, a vision in white towelling. The belt at her waist had loosened and the lapels of her robe gaped slightly to reveal delicate collarbones and pale, milky skin. His eyes followed the gaping fabric, which showed a glimpse of the curve of her waist, the rise of one bony hip and the dip of her flat stomach. Her legs were almost totally exposed and he could see the scrap of white cotton hiding her modesty from him.

The whole room smelled of cinnamon. Like her. His frustrations from the day, from the last God knew how many days, all surged to the surface and he was overwhelmed by the urge to completely part the robe and just look at her. All of her.

He walked across the room to the bed, as if drawn by an invisible force, and sat on the edge. The way she looked, relaxed and peaceful, like a sated woman, made the air hard to breathe, and the room shrank until there was just him and her and the bed. His hand shook as he lifted it and hovered it over her stomach, over the place his baby was calling home.

He gave in to the urge to touch her there, cradle his baby as he had seen her do so often. He laid his hand against her flat stomach, her skin warm to touch.

Katya's eyes flew open. It took her a few seconds to break free of the clinging folds of the best, dreamless sleep she'd had in weeks. She was disorientated, momentarily confused by her surroundings.

'Ben?' Had she conjured him up?

He withdrew his hand. 'Sorry, I didn't mean to wake you.' He could see the slight rise of the inner curve of her breast, the creamy skin taunting him with its perfection.

There was an awkward silence.

Katya's head was still filled with cotton wool. 'Did you want something?'

You. Under me. Now. He couldn't think of something to say that didn't involve the damn bed.

'Ben?' Katya searched his face in the gloomy late afternoon light of the room. The heavy cloak suddenly evaporated and she was captivated by the desire in his eyes. She'd seen that look before. Still remembered the pleasure that had followed.

His brown gaze was hot. He wanted her, she could see it. She felt her own eyes widen as a flare of heat seared her pelvic-floor muscles. She felt them contract and the rub of cloth against her sensitive nipples was so excruciating she thought she might faint if he didn't soothe it with his hot, wet mouth.

He looked sexy as hell in his scrubs and her mind was full of images of how much sexier he looked out of them. She became acutely aware of her own state of undress. Nights of erotic dreams had left her ripe for this moment.

'I just came to check on you,' he said, his voice husky.

'Oh.'

Ben willed himself to move away but didn't seem to be capable of anything more vital than breathing. 'Have you been asleep all this time?'

She nodded. If he didn't get out of there soon she was going to scream. Or combust. Or demand that he make love to her.

Ben saw a blaze of desire in her blue eyes and knew his choices were running out. He should move away, leave the room, immediately. Or maybe he could just kiss her? They were hardly strangers. They'd slept in this damn bed every night for weeks. She was pregnant with his child. She looked like she wanted him to kiss her.

Just then Katya felt a quick sharp jab down low. 'Oh!' she said, fanning her hand across her stomach.

'What?' Ben asked, his brow puckering.

It happened again. Was it? Could it be? 'The baby,' she said looking up at Ben, 'it's…moving. I think I can feel it moving.' She looked at him uncertainly, the sexual haze disappearing. She was eighteen weeks gone. She'd felt the odd fluttering sensation a few times this last week, dismissed it as nothing, but this was a definite jab.

Ben's frowned slowly disappeared and a big grin split his face. 'Really? Can I feel?'

She nodded and reached for his hand, guiding it beneath hers, placing it down low. Despite the lifting of the sexually charged atmosphere, it was somehow suddenly more intimate than earlier. His heart pounded as they waited, staring at her tummy, at their linked hands.

'We scared it away,' Katya whispered. She felt strangely disappointed. The feeling had been difficult to describe. She'd felt…connected to the baby for the first time. And she'd been surprised to find herself eagerly anticipating the next one.

Ben was about to remove his hands when the baby kicked again. Katya gasped.

'There! I felt it!' he exclaimed.

Katya saw the excitement and wonder on his face and found it contagious. She smiled back at him, feeling incredibly close to the baby, like she knew it suddenly. They waited again, eager for another kick.

'I think the show's over,' Ben said a few minutes later, reluctant to remove his hand. The tiny foetal movements had been thrilling to be part of and he wished suddenly that it was he carrying their baby. To be able to play a more intimate role in their baby's development.

It was one thing feeling its first movements through his hand, but to feel it from the inside must be truly wondrous indeed. The baby had gone from being an abstract, slightly terrifying idea to being a real live little human in an instant.

Ben felt a rush of emotion rise in his chest. They were having a baby. He became aware again of his hand on her stomach. Her soft, warm skin, his hand grazing the line of her hipster knickers. He couldn't remember a time when she'd looked sexier and he wanted her even more than before. Wanted to feel her beneath him, around him. He trailed his hand up the milky path the parted robe afforded him, stopping when he reached the valley between her breasts.

He saw the desire flare in her eyes again. 'I'm going to kiss you,' he said.

Katya heard the rough texture of his voice and felt a rush of desire heat her belly and tingle between her thighs, the baby forgotten in the overwhelming urge to have his mouth against hers. Her nipples beaded again, his hand so close and her mind begged him to slip his hand beneath the fabric and touch one.

'You shouldn't,' she said quietly, her gaze flicking to his full mouth. At least her head was still grounded in reality. They really, really shouldn't. She had been adamant about the rules of their cohabitation.

'I want to,' he said as he edged closer.

'It'll complicate things.'

'You want me to, too.'

Katya swallowed, her mouth suddenly dry. Was it that obvious? She watched in fascination as he slowly lowered his head, his mouth creeping inexorably closer. 'No,' she said softly, with absolutely no conviction.

There was silence as Ben's lips inched nearer.

'I keep thinking about that night,' he said, his voice a husky whisper, his fingers sliding slowly beneath the fabric of her gown.

'So do I,' she admitted, her teeth biting into her bottom lip, her breasts aching for his touch.

'I want to look at you,' he groaned, his heart thudding as his mouth zeroed in on his goal, his fingers finding her scrunched nipple, the pad of his thumb stroking it impossibly higher.

Katya felt a moan escape her lips and arched her back involuntarily, pushing herself into his hand, moaning again when his hand cupped her entire breast. Her face flamed at her wantonness and she licked parched lips. 'I want to look at you too,' she whispered.

'Katya,' he groaned and closed the whisper distance between their mouths. The smell of her skin was intoxicating, the taste of her mouth divine. Ben groaned again, his hand tightening against her breast as he lavished her mouth with sweet, slow kisses that burned his mouth and seared his soul. He wanted to touch her, kiss her all over, know every inch of her skin, possess every inch of her body.

At the touch of his lips Katya flamed with passion, ignited by his taste and his smell and his deep erotic groans. She could feel the glide of his lips and the prickle of his stubble and the tease of his fingers at her nipple, and she opened her mouth wider, wanting to feel him deeper, closer. She lost track of time and thought, caught up in the all-consuming sensation of his mouth and his hand and their increasingly desperate kisses. She felt wanton and female and when he yanked her gown completely open she felt a surge of heat and desire pulse between her legs.

A knock on the door was a sharp intrusion into their passion and they broke off, shocked both at the interruption and at their recklessness. It was if someone had walked in and thrown a bucket of cold water all over them.

'Benedetto? Carmella is asking for you,' someone called in Italian.

Ben closed his eyes and rested his head against Katya's shoulder, sucking in air, his hand still resting on her breast, the nipple still temptingly hard. He noted with some satisfaction the harsh rise and fall of her chest and was pleased to see she was similarly affected.

'*Momento*,' he called out, and was grateful to hear the retreat of footsteps.

Katya lay very still, his hand hot against her aching flesh, struggling to come out the other side of the sexual fog and regain control of her breathing. God, what had she been thinking? This was not going to make their cohabiting any easier.

'I'd better go,' Ben said pushing away from her. He grasped the lapels of her gown and pulled them gently together, covering the temptation of her aroused breasts. He stood up reluctantly, already dismayed to see her heady sexual stare from moments ago retreating. He wanted to throw caution to the wind, forget about Carmella and stay, kiss Katya until it came back again.

Katya nodded, too aroused and shocked at her behaviour to speak. She watched him walk out the door and then rolled on her side, pulling her knees up and her gown around her to try and ease the hot, deep ache between her legs. How on earth was she going to sleep next to him now?

Ben rang an hour later to tell her he was going to be caught up for a few hours with Carmella. They were working on trying to get a patient to Italy and had run into bureaucratic red tape. He was hitting the phones, calling in favours. He was very brisk and businesslike, for which she and her still raging hormones were grateful.

Any other day Katya would have gone and helped or at least watched, but she knew it was best to be apart from him at the moment. So she ate tea with some of the live-in staff and retired back to their quarters early, pleading a headache.

She feigned interest in a book but by ten, and much to her surprise, she was falling asleep. Ben still hadn't returned and she was relieved she'd be asleep when he got back.

She was up early the next day and didn't see him until the theatre list was due to start.

'Avoiding me, Katya?' he asked in a low voice as they scrubbed up together.

'Yesterday was a mistake,' she said, paying an inordinate amount of attention to scrubbing her fingernails. 'Let's just forget it, OK?' She placed her soapy hands beneath the tap, the automatic spray clicking on and rinsing the suds away.

Forget it? How the hell was he supposed to forget it? He'd hardly slept a wink, thinking about it. The first thing he'd wanted to do when he'd arrived back at the room had been to pick up where they'd left off. Glide his hand around her stomach, pull her into him, see if he could feel the baby moving again and then take it from there. Instead, he'd turned his back to her, clamped his hands between his thighs and balanced precariously on the edge of the bed, not trusting himself to get any closer. There was no way he was going to last the next few months. No way.

Katya was conscious of Ben's weighty stare as he joined her at the table and was grateful for the routine as the first operation got under way. They had months to get through yet and Ben needed to know that one slip-up didn't mean that she was losing focus.

The first case was four-year-old Ten-ti. The child was, without a doubt, one of the cutest little girls Katya had ever seen. She had gorgeous huge brown eyes, a gappy grin and soft black hair that fell in crazy layers around her face.

She was a happy little thing, chatted away merrily at

everyone in her native tongue and had a giggle that was wickedly infectious. She had taken a particular liking to blonde-haired Katya and in the two days she'd been at the clinic Ten-ti had drawn at least a dozen pictures of her favourite nurse.

Katya had taken Ten-ti down to the garden with her that morning and the little girl had crawled into Katya's lap and laid her head against Katya's chest and waved and smiled at everyone who had come past as if to say, look at me, look how important I am.

The foundation had found Ten-ti at an orphanage. She had been abandoned at the age of one by her family when her condition had shown no signs of improving. It was hard to believe that the little girl was so happy. When Katya thought about how abandoned Ten-ti must have felt, it broke her heart. At least she wasn't going to give her baby a chance to get attached.

Katya looked down at the defect now as Ben made his first incision. The haemangioma was impressive. The vascular benign tumour protruded from Ten-ti's skull over her temple. It was quite large, about the size of a grapefruit, and its typical bright red colour was marred in the centre by a large, ugly, grey-black patch where it was badly ulcerated.

It looked like something out of a science fiction magazine. Like a maniacal cartoonist had dreamt it up—a beautiful child with a mushroom-like growth protruding from her head. A soft spongy mushroom. The nuns that ran the orphanage had been told that it would gradually get smaller and disappear, as the majority of hemangiomas did, but Ten-ti's had shown no such propensity.

At the age of four there were no signs of the tumour involuting. And the ulceration, with its associated bleeding and pain, had made her a perfect candidate for surgery.

The actual excision of the haemangioma was relatively

easy and Katya watched as Ben expertly sliced and slowly divided the tumour from the scalp. She handed him a metal kidney dish as he performed his last slice and he dropped the spongy mass into the metal receptacle.

Katya stared at it. On Ten-ti's head it had looked huge. A nasty, poisonous-looking, disfiguring mass that had isolated her and flawed her pretty features. And now, after four years of marring her life, causing her to be abandoned, it lay there, looking incongruous. Impotent. Forlorn almost.

Katya turned slightly and placed the kidney dish on her trolley, draped with sterile towels and returned her attention to the procedure. There was now a sizeable area on Ten-ti's head, about six centimetres across, where there was no skin to cover the skull.

'Closure device,' said Ben.

She had already anticipated his needs and he held out his hand at the precise time she was handing him the instrument. The transfer was seamless. No pauses or fumbling, just smooth and flawless. Textbook. A well-oiled team.

Katya had never seen these devices until now. There hadn't been much call for them in the MedSurg environment. Ben used them quite a bit and she'd even seen him use them under local anaesthetic at the bedside. They looked a bit like a fancy can-opener to her but the results were fantastic.

Ten-ti's wound was too wide for normal closure. The wound edges were too far away from each other to sew together and would normally require a skin graft. But this tricky little device was designed to stretch the skin so the margins could be brought together and then safely sutured or stapled. It worked by applying a controlled amount of tension evenly along the wound margins and exploiting the elastic properties of skin while minimising its tendency to recoil.

Ten-ti's head had been shaved around the tumour site to allow easy visualisation of the wound edges and Ben now applied the device to them. When he was satisfied with the placement he locked the device in place and started to turn the tension knob, beginning the stretching process. After twenty minutes Ben was satisfied with the approximation of the edges of the wound and he sutured it closed, using the conventional method.

'There,' he said, turning to Katya. 'She'll be as pretty as a picture.'

Katya couldn't wait to see Ten-ti's reaction when she woke up and realised that the disfiguring growth, which had bled and caused her so much pain, was no more. That was going to be a smile worth seeing.

Almost as good as the one that sparkled in Ben's eyes. His excitement and satisfaction at a job well done was palpable. He so obviously thrived on how his brainchild, the Lucia Trust, was making a real difference. She grinned back at him under her mask, struck by how different he was from the man she'd known before.

He was still as handsome, as toe-curlingly gorgeous, but at MedSurg he'd been cocky and arrogant and conceited. Overly confident. He'd matured in a few short months and she wondered about the catalyst for that. Had it just been Mario's death? She had the feeling, the more time she spent in his company, there was so much more she didn't know about him. Would never know about him.

A few hours later, Katya hurried from the theatre to visit Ten-ti. A wizened old woman with no teeth and a navy blue nun's habit smiled at Katya as she entered the room. The foundation always paid for a carer to accompany the patient and one of the nuns from the orphanage had escorted Ten-ti.

'Is she still asleep?' Katya asked, sitting on the opposite side of the bed.

'Yes,' the nun said serenely.

Katya had been surprised to find that Mi-tung had a smattering of many languages and spoke quite good English. The old nun had kind eyes and Katya was pleased that Ten-ti had known this woman's kindness.

Ten-ti stirred at the sound of Katya's voice and her eyes fluttered open. Her gaze fell on Katya, and Ten-ti gave her a weak smile. Katya smiled back and stroked the little girl's hair. There was a small dressing covering the suture line but that was all there was to remind everyone that a few hours ago a large growth had disfigured this little girl's beautiful head.

'It's amazing,' Mi-tung said in her quiet voice. 'Thank you,' she added, bowing to Katya. 'We thank you from the bottom of our hearts.'

Katya saw the old woman had tears in her eyes and felt humbled by her emotion. She reached across the bed, over Ten-ti, and held out her hand. Mi-tung didn't hesitate and took it immediately. The old woman's hand felt soft and wrinkly in Katya's and they kept their hands clasped as they watched Ten-ti sleep.

Ben found them there a few minutes later. He watched silently from the doorway for a moment. It was rare to see the softer side of Katya. She looked just like any mother sitting by her child's bedside. Concerned, dedicated.

His mind skipped back to yesterday afternoon. The memory was so vivid he could almost taste her lips, hear her moan, feel her hard, scrunched nipple against his palm.

'Here you are,' he said, deliberately interrupting his thought processes, not giving his body a chance to become any more aroused. He walked up behind Katya's chair and casually placed his hand on her shoulder. He felt her muscles tense and gently stroked her skin there so she would relax.

For a moment Katya wanted nothing more than to lean back against him and purr at his touch. But she held herself erect, very conscious of his fingers trailing a path of fire from her shoulder to her neck.

'How's she doing?' Ben asked.

'Sleepy,' Katya said, wincing at how blunt it sounded.

Ben smiled at Mi-tung and removed his obviously unwanted hand. 'I'll check back later,' he said, and withdrew.

He went to his office and shut the door. He sat behind his desk, removed his theatre cap and rubbed his hands briskly though his hat hair. He'd forgotten how infuriatingly stubborn Katya could be.

Yesterday, and on other occasions, he'd seen plainly that she'd wanted him. But right now she obviously couldn't even bear him touching her. Couldn't he even lay a hand on her without it becoming something more than it was? He drummed his fingers on the desk, frustrated beyond words.

The very last thing he wanted to do was stand beside her this afternoon and operate. Her cinnamon scent was driving him crazy, taking him right back to yesterday. To their night together. They couldn't go on like this. Something had to give.

CHAPTER SEVEN

AFTER another tense night Katya was pleased to get out of bed and away from Ben's brooding presence. She made a beeline for Ten-ti's room and was happy to find the little girl awake and sitting on the balcony with Mi-tung. For a moment the breathtaking view distracted her and she took a deep calming breath, expelling the pent-up tension caused by another platonic night.

The Mediterranean stretched into the distance, the early morning sunshine warming the cliff faces of the craggy coast-line. The gardens stepped down below in all their colourful splendour. From the nearby lemon grove she could smell a faint tang of citrus waft towards her on the light breeze.

Ten-ti lifted up her arms and Katya picked her up off Mi-tung's lap and settled with her in the other chair on the balcony. The little girl chattered excitedly and pointed to her head.

'I know, I know.' Katya laughed.

Ten-ti said something to Mi-tung and Mi-tung got up and went inside. She came back with a mirror and Ten-ti pointed at it and then at her head and stared at herself in the mirror in amazement. She angled her head from side to side and primped and preened like a teenager on a first date, and Katya laughed at her utter joy.

The little girl put the mirror down and threw herself at Katya, her little arms clinging around Katya's neck. Katya hugged her close, a lump rising in her throat. What would her child look like at four? Would he or she take after her or Ben? Would he or she have her blondeness or Ben's dark Italian looks? Would he or she ever wonder about her?

The desire to hold her own child was suddenly overwhelming and she quashed it as she squeezed Tent-ti closer. Just because she was feeling the baby move all the time now, it didn't mean anything. Other than that the baby was growing normally. Which was good. It didn't mean she was developing any motherly yearnings.

Katya felt a pang of guilt and hugged Ten-ti harder. She didn't protest and Katya was grateful, for this little girl gave her hope. Here in her arms was living proof that a child didn't need to have a mother to grow up happy and loved. It just needed someone to love it and to grow up in a loving environment.

Ten-ti justified Katya's position and Katya held onto that dearly. The last few days had been a confusing time for her with the Ben incident and the baby's first movements. There had been a lot of unexpected emotions and feelings which could threaten her plans if she allowed them free rein. Ten-ti was tangible evidence that her plan could work and Katya really needed that reassurance.

Two weeks later Ben and Katya waited in a small anteroom for Dr Rocco Gambino, the Clinic's radiologist, to finish an X-ray. It was their lunch-break and Rocco had arranged to do Katya's first ultrasound. Ben had told Katya with great pride that at one time Rocco had been one of the most experienced obstetric sonographers in the country.

Things were a little easier between them now there was some distance from the passionate kiss they'd shared. The nights were still hard but a new routine had developed. After their evening meal, Katya would go to bed and Ben would go to his office for a couple of hours and do paperwork. She would be asleep when he finally made his way back to the room and on a couple of occasions he'd even slept in his office. It wasn't perfect but at least it had taken the pressure off.

A thought that had never even occurred to Katya before, so preoccupied had she been with her plans for the baby and her attraction for Ben, popped into her head as they waited. 'What if there's something wrong with it?' she asked.

She felt a wave of dread rise over her. What if the baby was deformed or had major congenital problems? What if the fates had decided that as she didn't want the baby, she didn't deserve a healthy one? She clutched her stomach. It was still fairly flat but she could feel the bulge of her hard uterus beneath.

'It'll be fine,' Ben said.

His dismissive answer was irritating when her active imagination was already conjuring up a dozen different dire possibilities. 'Are Medici babies immune to congenital problems?' she asked.

Ben looked down into her face and saw genuine fear in her eyes. He took her hand. 'There is nothing wrong with our baby,' he said, emphasising the words carefully.

'Do you promise?' she asked.

Ben nodded. 'I promise.'

Dr Rocco Gambino came out, interrupting them, apologising for his tardiness. Ben translated as Rocco was one of the few people at the Medic clinic who wasn't bilingual. He ushered them into a cubicle and helped Katya onto the high, narrow bed.

Ben went around to the far side so he wasn't in Rocco's way. He could have easily performed the ultrasound himself but obstetric sonography was a specialised field and Rocco was the best. And, anyway, he wanted to be the father in the room, not the doctor.

Katya knew the moment the screen flickered to life and her baby appeared in a grainy black and white image that the ultrasound was the worst thing she could have agreed to. She held Ben's hand and barely heard Rocco at all. Or Ben's translation. She was totally and completely mesmerised by the tiny little life she could see on the screen.

It was no longer 'the baby' or 'it' or 'he' or 'she'. It was a real, living, breathing, kicking, squirming baby. Her baby. *All this baby needs is for you to love it*, Ben had said. And she did. Right now, her love for this tiny human being filled her completely. Overwhelmed her.

She felt connected, truly connected with her child for the first time. Feeling it kick had nothing on this. She was actually seeing inside her womb. Actually looking at her baby. It had been so easy to think of it, make decisions about it when all she'd had to confirm her pregnancy had been a pink line on a test kit and greeting the toilet bowel every morning.

But this? Actually meeting her baby. Seeing its ten fingers and ten perfect toes. Watch it as it sucked its thumb. Follow the curve of its perfectly formed spinal column. See its tiny, fragile-looking heart beat sure and steady. This was real.

Rocco pushed a button and the room filled with a magical pulsating. Whop. Whop. Whop. It was like a symphony to her ears. A concerto. There really was a baby inside her. It wasn't an abstract concept any more. An inconvenient hiccup in her life plan. It was real. She was a mother.

'Rocco says the baby is a good size and that your dates are spot on. He says everything looks fine.'

Ben could feel Katya's grip on his hand. He looked down at her, her eyes glued to the little screen. She had a strange intense expression on her face. 'He wants to know if we want to know the sex?'

Katya nodded distractedly but she hadn't really heard him. She couldn't take her eyes off her baby. She was mesmerised by the tiny central flicker in its chest.

'Katya?'

'Hmm?' she said, dragging her eyes away reluctantly from the screen. 'What?'

'Do you want to know if the baby is a boy or a girl?'

Katya blinked. Did she? She hadn't thought about it in any real sense until now. The baby's sex was just another one of those things she'd blanked out of her mind. Hadn't permitted herself to think about too much.

And if Rocco had asked her yesterday she would have given him an emphatic no. She would have classified that as information not necessary to her goal. But now, her baby on the screen in front of her, she was overwhelmed with the urge to know. 'Do you?' she asked.

Ben smiled at her sheepishly. 'I wouldn't mind,' he admitted. He had also been surprised by the power of the tiny image on the screen. Feeling the baby kicking had been amazing but this was so much more incredible. He was going to be a father and his curiosity to know everything about this tiny precious human being was incredibly strong.

Katya nodded at Rocco. He smiled at her. 'Ragazzo,' he said. 'A boy.'

A son. Katya looked back at the screen again. She was having a baby boy. She felt Ben's hand grip on hers tighten and saw his crazy grin in profile. He seemed as taken by the image as she. Would he look like his father? Would he have dark brown eyes, killer eyelashes and a quick lazy grin?

Rocco said something to Ben and Ben nodded.

'Rocco has to go,' Ben said to Katya.

No! She wasn't finished looking yet. The baby was still moving around, his tiny movements endlessly fascinating. She didn't want Rocco to switch the machine off. She wanted to watch her baby for ever.

'Katya?' Ben prompted.

Katya nodded reluctantly. She reached forward and touched her hand to the cold screen to prolong contact with her baby boy for just a little while longer. Rocco removed the transducer from her abdomen and the image went blank. She kept her hand flat against the screen, not ready to break contact. Her baby. Her son.

'There, see,' Ben teased as Katya slowly withdrew her hand, 'I told you the baby was fine.'

'He,' Katya corrected.

Ben nodded and grinned at the wonder in her voice. 'Our son.' She looked absolutely smitten. For the first time he felt a little ray of hope. Had seeing their son's image been the key to connecting Katya with her inner mother?

It had certainly helped to put things into perspective for him. He had been worrying deep down about the kind of father he would be. Bianca and Mario's betrayal had soured him to the whole meaning of love and family. And a decade of freezing them out, ignoring their pleas for reconciliation, had made him doubt whether he was capable of either.

But seeing the ultrasound had been curiously empower-

ing. The rush of feeling that had flooded through his gut and
bubbled in his veins had been too powerful to ignore. This was
the meaning of love. A grainy ultrasound image blinking on a
screen.

He may have been immunised against the love between a
man and a woman but his heart soared knowing he was
capable of a different love. The love of a father for his child.

They travelled to Ben's villa after work that night, both lost
in their own thoughts. Ben watched Katya go to her room and
shut the door. After the high of seeing his son today her actions
were depressing. More than anything, tonight he wanted to
hold her. It wasn't even about sex. He just wanted to lie beside
her, pull her into him and cradle them, her and his baby. He
was falling in love with the life they'd created and he wanted
to share this time with her. Be as much a part of the baby
growing inside her as possible.

He didn't want to be kept on the outside. He wanted to be
able to touch her belly freely, feel the baby move, lay his head
against her bump when they were in bed together at night. And
not have to worry about her stiffening or rejecting his moves
or looking at him as if he'd violated some pact.

He rustled up a fruit and cheese platter as his mind mulled
over how he could achieve his goal and still keep things
platonic, which was her goal. He imagined laying his head
against her stomach and not wanting to make love to her and
knew there was no easy middle ground.

'Katya,' he called, knocking gently on her door. 'I've fixed
us something to eat.'

He heard her muffled reply and retreated to the terrace to
wait for her. It was mid-November and the nights were much
cooler. They wouldn't be able to stay out for long. He took a
sip of some local Chianti and felt it warm him through.

'Mmm, this looks good,' Katya said, approaching from behind and plucking a slice of apple from the selection.

He smiled at her and handed her a glass of sparkling water. They indulged in some idle chit-chat, Katya asking him about the budget meeting he had attended with the foundation's financial directors that afternoon after the ultrasound. He was still wearing the suit and he looked sexy and powerful and it was taking all her willpower not to flirt. Or touch.

'The ultrasound was pretty amazing,' Ben commented lightly after a few minutes of financial talk.

Katya caught his smile and smiled back. 'Yes,' she admitted.

'Thank you,' he said. 'Thank you for letting me attend.' He knew Katya hadn't thought it necessary for him to be there.

Katya shrugged. 'It's your baby, too.'

There was a momentary silence as they both sipped at their drinks. 'I think I fell in love today,' Ben said into the quiet night air.

Katya stopped in mid-chew, startled momentarily. Her heart tripped crazily. But the look on his face put his comments into perspective. He was talking about the baby.

'You sound surprised,' she said lightly, sipping her water to cover the commotion inside.

'I didn't expect for it to be so powerful so soon.' He shrugged. 'After years of avoiding it I didn't think I'd ever feel love again in any capacity. But this just seems so…easy.'

She nodded. Her love for their baby was the one constant in her life. That and her desire to give him the best chance in life.

'You avoided love?' Katya asked, looking up at him. He was staring out over the water. Had he been hiding the real Ben behind a playboy façade?

He nodded. 'Just like you.'

He turned back and pierced her with a searching look and

Katya felt as if he'd seen inside her soul. She felt on shaky ground and needed to turn this conversation away from her. 'Someone break your heart?'

'Once.' He gave her a sad smile. 'A long time ago. I was young and stupid.'

Katya shivered at the bitterness in his last words. Someone had hurt him very badly. She felt a brief pang of sorrow for the younger Ben. It must have been awful to still be screwed up about it now.

'What about you, dear, sweet Katya? Have you ever been in love?' he asked.

'No.' Katya's answer was quick. Definite. There had been no-one in her life. She had been determined to be the exact opposite of her mother and hadn't had a moment's regret. Until one night in Ben's arms.

Ben could see the honesty in her frankness and envied her escaping the clutches of love. He'd been battered and bruised by the emotion and permanently scarred.

'Wise girl,' he muttered, and took another sip of wine.

'Until now,' she admitted, covering her tummy with her hand, the baby moving as if in agreement.

'Guess that makes two of us,' Ben said, reaching out his hand and placing it on top of hers.

Katya adjusted their placement so Ben's was snuggled close to the baby's activity. It was kicking a lot and they both stared down at her stomach and smiled at its antics.

'How can you walk away from him, Katya?' Ben asked after a minute had passed and the show seemed to be over.

Katya closed her eyes and sighed. She stood and Ben's hand dropped away. She walked over to the railing, watching the moon bathe the coast in a silvery shimmer, her back to him. She ran her hands briskly up and down her arms, the evening getting cooler as each minute passed. She had jeans and a top on but the night air had penetrated, making goose bumps on her skin and beading her nipples.

Ben rose, removing his jacket from the back of the chair. He joined her, placing it around her shoulders. Katya felt the warmth instantly and was enveloped in a snug, Ben-smelling pheromone cloud. His jacket smelled so good and she knew if she buried her face in his neck he'd smell the same, only better.

She turned to face him. It was time for honesty. He had opened up to her a little tonight and she wanted him to understand why she couldn't stay.

'When I was eleven, I was changing Leo's nappy—he was one—when my sister Sophia pulled the heater down on herself and her clothes caught light. She was very badly burned. She nearly died. To this day, she has these really horrible scars down her side and arm. Scars that I'm responsible for.'

Katya was surprised to discover tears had built in her eyes as she recounted the story. 'I'm not fit to be a mother, Ben.'

'Katya,' Ben said softly, aching for the frightened eleven-year-old he'd just caught a glimpse of. He could only begin to imagine how terrible she must have felt. '*Cara,* you were eleven years old. You were a child.'

She shook her head as a tear squeezed out and tracked down her cheek. 'I was in charge.'

Ben saw the guilt in her eyes and it clawed at his gut. He wiped the tear away gently. 'How old were your siblings when it happened?' he asked softly.

'Leo was one, Sophia was two, Marisha was three and Anna was four.' They'd all been so young. So dependent on her and she had let Sophia down.

Ben shut his eyes and dropped his forehead gently against

hers. 'Sophia's accident wasn't your fault, Katya. It was your mother's fault.'

Not according to Olgah. Katya still remembered her mother's rage when the hospital had finally tracked her down.

'I can't do it, Ben,' she said, shifting back from him slightly, his soft words very persuasive. 'I can't risk being careless and having this baby get hurt. Sometimes as I'm drifting off to sleep I hear Sophia's screams, I can smell her burnt flesh.'

Ben stroked his hand down her spine and Katya shivered. She wanted to step closer into the circle of his arms, where he was warm and male and tempting, but she had to make her point.

'I don't know how to be a good mother, Ben. I had a lousy role model and my sister nearly died because I failed in my duty of care to her. And I won't subject this baby to my inadequate mothering. I can't.'

Ben nodded. Her conviction was obvious. What had happened with Sophia had obviously had deep, long-lasting effects. She truly believed she couldn't be trusted with her own baby. Another tear trekked down her face and before he could stop himself he leaned forward and gently kissed it away.

Katya sighed and gave in to the desire to lean against him. His chest was broad and he smelled like man, like the smell that pervaded her pillow and her sheets. Suddenly the atmosphere turned sexual. The moonlight glowed on the Med to her left, stars winked down at them from above, and in front of her was a gorgeous, sexy man, holding her close. Suddenly it all seemed terribly inevitable. Fated, even.

Katya lifted her head and got a brief impression of square jaw and dark stubble and hooded eyes and then Ben's mouth was shutting it all out. His body surrounded her, pushing her back against the railings. Nearer, closer, harder. Her head spun as her senses filled with his heat and his smell and his touch.

His mouth left hers and tracked kisses down her neck and she gasped for air, her heart beating frantically. He moved with her, walking her backwards away from the terrace. Her fingers grasped his shirt for stability until a wall pressed firmly against her back. She had a vague notion he had her up against the doorjamb where the French doors separated the villa from the terrace but they could have been floating high above the Med for all she knew.

Then he was helping her out of his jacket and she was stripping off his loosened tie and unbuttoning his shirt and finally, finally laying her hands on his naked chest. His skin was hot and he moaned against her neck. The mat of hair covering his bulky pectorals trailed down his flat abdomen and felt springy and tickly against the palms of her hands. She could feel his muscles twitch and react to the path of her hands and it emboldened her to undo his belt buckle.

'Katya,' he gasped, and reclaimed her mouth as his hand trailed down from her face to claim one firm breast. She moaned and his erection surged but it wasn't enough. He was half-naked and she was still fully dressed. Her clothes looked fantastic, tight in all the right places, but he knew they'd look better crumpled in a heap on the floor. 'I want to look at you,' he groaned against her mouth.

Katya laughed. It felt good to be finally letting go, her head spinning from the pleasure rocking her body.

Ben cut off her laughter with a deep searing kiss, stripping off her top in one swift movement. Her jeans zip followed and she wriggled her hips as he pushed them down, stepping out of the denim with relative ease.

He pulled away and got his first look at her near naked body. The light from the lounge room and kitchen illuminated her body enough for him to know it was just as he remembered. Petite and feminine. Her stomach still flat despite her twenty-week pregnancy. Her skin milky. Her hips looked slightly rounder, though. And her breasts were considerably fuller. He stared at their lushness spilling out of her bra.

'Ben,' Katya begged, the look in his eyes, the roving of his gaze pure erotic torture.

'Shh,' he teased, 'I'm looking.'

Much to her amazement, Katya blushed. She had no idea why. He had seen her with fewer clothes than this. But she was conscious of her body's changes due to the pregnancy. Her hips were a little fuller and her breasts had practically exploded. She'd always been an A cup. Her breasts had been small but pert, the nipples rosy-tipped and perfectly central. But the baby had expanded them considerably and darkened the nipples to a deep dusky hue.

'You're beautiful,' he said, stroking the skin from the hollow of her throat down into her cleavage. He zeroed in on the front bra clasp and popped it, watching fascinated as her breasts sprung free. Full and lush and perky.

He noticed the prominent bluey-green veins standing out like a road map against her creamy skin. He traced the biggest one with his finger from the centre of her chest down over the swollen flesh of her left breast, to the edge of her areola. Her nipple puckered.

Katya tried to cover herself. She hated the big veins that had sprung up as her breasts had grown. 'Don't,' she said. 'They're horrible, I know.'

Ben shook his head in awe. 'No, *cara*. They are the most beautiful breasts I have ever seen. They are ready for our baby, they are all woman.'

Katya was about to protest again but he lowered his head

to a nipple and sucked it into his mouth, and she swayed against him, her knees nearly buckling at such pure sweet erotic agony. His hand covered the other breast and she closed her eyes and let her head loll back against the doorjamb.

When he lifted his head several long drugging moments later Katya opened her eyes and gazed into his. They looked glazed, drunk with passion, and she felt heady with power. She smiled at him and he smiled back before lifting her quickly away from the doorway, hauling her up into his arms and striding through the house with her.

She revelled in the smell of his neck and the scratch of his whiskers against her nose and the way he moaned and stumbled when she licked at the pulse beating madly in his neck.

'Hurry,' she growled as she pulled his earlobe into her mouth.

Ben eased her down on the bed and stood back to admire how good she looked against his sheets. He saw the glitter in her blue eyes and noticed the uneven rise and fall of her naked breasts. He smiled and ran a finger down the centre of her chest, directly down the middle of her stomach to the edge of her undies. He continued the trek and pulled the white lacy fabric down as he went. He saw her teeth bite into her soft full lip and he didn't have to ask. She lifted her hips and he pulled the scrap of fabric all the way down.

Now she was totally naked before him and she was so beautiful and sexy he didn't know where to look, where to touch first.

'Ben!' She squirmed.

He chuckled. 'I'm just looking,' he said. 'I like to look at you.'

'What about me? Maybe I like to look at you, too.'

Ben grinned. 'Your wish is my command.' And he quickly stripped off his half-undone trousers and followed them with his designer jocks. His erection sprang free and it felt good to have no constraints.

Katya had thought she'd had him fairly represented in her

dreams, that her imagination had conjured him up perfectly. But looking at him now, the fantasy paled in comparison. Ben was all male. Every hard, strong, Italian inch of him.

She reached her arms up and almost fainted from pleasure when he covered her body with his solid male frame. 'Yes,' she whispered just before he kissed her.

Their passion ignited. His kisses grew hotter, longer deeper. His mouth left hers and found a nipple and she bucked against him like a bolt of electricity had coursed through her. She whimpered as he created pleasure and pain in equal parts. 'Please, Ben,' she begged, grinding her hips against his.

He chuckled and looked up at her from her wet nipple. 'No, Katya. I want this to be slower this time. Like I should have done it last time. Like I would have if I'd known you were a virgin.'

Katya gave a frustrated growl. 'My virginity is gone. Get over it.'

Ben laughed at the appearance of blunt Katya but his eyes widened as he saw a fierce light burn in her eyes.

'If I don't feel you inside me now, I'm going to scream.'

'Katya, *cara*,' he said soothingly,' I want to make sure you are ready.'

Katya laughed. 'Oh, God, Ben. I am, trust me. Can't you tell?'

He could. His senses swam with a heady mix of cinnamon and aroused woman. Ben saw the desperation, the sexual frustration glittering in her eyes. She was lifting her hips and his erection was rubbing against her hot moist core. He held her gaze as he trailed two fingers down her stomach. They continued through the downy hair and teased her slick entrance.

A wave of heat surged through his body at her readiness, almost blinding him with intensity. 'Katya,' he groaned.

'Ben, please,' she whispered, her voice hoarse with need. 'I promise after this you can impress me with your tricks but, please, I need you in me now!'

Katya lifted her hips, trying to catch his erection and guide him inside. 'Please, Ben,' she begged.

'Katya,' he groaned lowering his head to kiss her as he gave in to his base urge and hers and entered her tight, hot core.

'Yes,' she said. 'More.'

'Katya,' he moaned, again, moving inside her beyond any semblance of control.

Katya had been hot and ready for this for weeks. Nights fuelled by erotic dreams had primed her for this moment and it took only a few strokes of his rock-hard erection to tease the sensitive flesh into blast-off. 'Ben. Oh, God, I can't hold this back…it's too…much,' she panted, enjoying the build-up as it undulated through her internal muscles.

Ben knew the feeling. Katya's readiness, her eagerness and erotic dreams of his own were powerful catalysts. He could feel her trembling under him. He could feel her tighten around him further and he knew that as she let go and her muscles milked him that in a few more strokes he would join her.

She was raking her nails down his back as his orgasm erupted. His muscles tensed, his breathing stopped, his heart skipped a beat for a few seconds and then it came and he pounded into her again and again, urged on by her cries and his powerful, all-encompassing release.

And somewhere, up there, while she was out of her body, shattering into a thousand pieces, Katya realised the awful truth. That she had fallen in love with Ben. That she was no better than her mother. She'd thought she was above such emotions, immune after years of her mother's dramas but ultimately the old adage, like mother like daughter, had proven true.

She had fallen for someone who couldn't love her back.

* * *

Katya woke a little later to find Ben staring down at her. He was tracing the veins on her breast again and she realised her nipples had been responding even in her sleep. He gave her a lazy smile and a surge of love welled up in her chest.

'I love these,' he said quietly, following a green pathway. 'I love them because I know they're making you ready to nurture our child. Are you sure you won't reconsider?' His hand moved lower, to her stomach, and he cradled it.

Katya looked at him and knew it was more important than ever now to leave. She had done the dumbest thing on earth, fallen for a man who didn't believe in love. So that was two reasons she couldn't stay. The baby and being with someone who couldn't—wouldn't—ever love her back.

Her life stretched before her, a long lonely corridor of time. She felt a tear escape. Katya closed her eyes as Ben dipped his head to kiss it away as he had done earlier. He was gentle and reverent and she thought her heart would burst it ached with so much love for him. His hand felt heavy and warm on her stomach and she felt completely possessed.

Surprisingly the thought didn't fill her with dread or revulsion. My how things had changed! She had been resisting a man's ownership for years but now she was here, she knew her life would never be the same. Was this how her mother had felt with each of her men? For the first time in a long time Katya felt a strange link with the woman who had given her life.

Ben pulled her in close, spoon-fashion, one hand cupping her stomach. One tear became two, became three until she was crying a river in the bed. Ben hushed her and kissed her hair and she cried even more. It felt like heaven to be safe in his arms and he held her till she fell asleep.

CHAPTER EIGHT

BEN and Katya spent the weekend in bed. In fact, they spent a lot of their weekends in bed over the following months. Either in their villa or on *The Mermaid*. By some kind of unspoken agreement, they both knew denying themselves was stupid. They didn't question it, they didn't even speak about it, they just let it happen.

Katya was surprised at how easy it was. How easy Ben made it. Loving him and knowing that he wouldn't love her back hurt. But walking away now wouldn't help her love him any less. She still had a goal—the baby. And she had to finish what she had set out to do.

So, was there something wrong with having a few brief months where the eight-year-old Katya's romantic fairytale played out? Was it wrong to make the most of her time with Ben and just enjoy it? Life without him, without her son would go on. It would be hard, her heart would be well and truly broken, but she knew she was strong enough to do it. Was it wrong to want this for a little while?

Still, living in the lap of luxury was hard to get used to. Years of being poor and living frugally were harder than she'd imagined to overcome. She was enjoying the perks but the wealthy mindset that was inherent in Ben was still a foreign concept to her. She kept thinking she'd do or say something to embarrass him, show her lack of breeding. And despite his inclusion of her in every part of his life, she felt like an interloper, like Cinderella waiting for the clock to strike twelve.

Ben was great. He took her out and showed her all around the Amalfi coast. To Priano, Minori and Sorrento. He took her over to Capri on his boat, to the Blue Grotto and the Emerald Grotto. And one memorable afternoon he drove her to see the ruins at Pompeii. They dined with his mother and Katya loved going to Positano for their visits. Of all the places he'd taken her, she loved Positano best.

He took her to fabulous restaurants, way off the beaten track, where the tourists didn't go. She ate amazing dishes, like Parmigiana Melanzane and mussels caught fresh from the Med cooked in wine, lemon juice and pepper. And bruschetta. Katya developed a real craving for bruschetta.

But it had to be Taddeo's. Taddeo owned a restaurant not far from Ben's villa and they often ended up there for Katya's favourite food. Taddeo had told her the first time he'd served it up to her, 'When you go home tonight, *bella*, you will dream of my bruschetta.' She had laughed but he had been dead right. It was divine with just the right blend of basil and onion and the final touch—a drizzle of olive oil. And she had asked for seconds and had made Taddeo's day.

The weeks flew by. Christmas and New Year passed. Her belly grew into a decent-sized bump. Ben loved watching her grow with his child—her stomach expand, her breasts flower. He rejoiced in every kick, every somersault. Every day that passed he fell further in love with his son. And Katya fell further in love with him.

Work was great as well. They worked well together, probably better now sexual frustration wasn't making them edgy and tense. And Katya was surprised every day by how much she loved the work. It was so different to the madness of the frantic get-them-in, get-them-out world of MedSurg. At the Lucia Clinic there was time to follow a patient through, to get involved.

And that surprised her, too. The MedSurg environment had suited her emotional state for many years. The insanity of war and senseless violence became blunted in the frantic atmosphere, but as her pregnancy advanced and her hormones bloomed and she fell deeper in love with Ben, the emotional involvement the clinic afforded her gave her job satisfaction she'd never dreamed of. The old Katya would have scoffed at such human sentiment, shied away from it even, but she was softer these days.

Was it love or the baby? She suspected a bit of both. One thing was for sure, she had a lot to thank Ben for. If she'd never fallen pregnant and never come to Italy, she would never have known this other side of herself existed. Never known she could be this…female. Sure, she'd always looked like a woman, but perhaps now she was thinking and feeling more like one.

She was even developing an understanding of her mother. Maybe they'd never be close but Katya was starting to appreciate that sometimes things weren't so black and white. She could see her mother's choices through the eyes of a woman now, instead of those of a child. How love and duty for your child could war with the love you could feel for a man. Did that excuse her mother's neglect? No. Did it make it a little more comprehensible? Yes.

She was thirty weeks before she knew it. Her bump was soccer-ball-sized now. And she was tired. A lot. And her feet had started to swell at the end of each day from standing for hours and hours at an operating table. Ben would massage her feet each night and tried to persuade her to finish work early. But Katya refused.

Working with Ben was the one thing that helped keep their relationship in perspective. It gave it a professional aspect that she needed to keep from surrendering her heart completely. It gave her a different view of Ben for eight hours a day. Ben the surgeon. Not Ben the father of her baby. Or Ben her lover.

It was a daily dose of reality and she didn't want to lose that sitting at home all day waiting for Ben, the man that she loved, to come home from work. That definitely smacked too much of happy families and she was determined to keep working until the day she went into labour.

But in her thirty-first week, the baby pulled rank. Followed closely by Ben.

'Are you OK?' he asked her quietly at the end of a particularly long day. Ben had noticed her rocking on her heels quite a lot throughout the long operation and moving from foot to foot.

He was repairing a severe burns contracture of the face and neck. The ten-year-old boy had sustained his initial injury through a kerosene explosion several months before and inadequate treatment had led to the current grotesque disfigurement.

The contractures involved the eyelids, face, neck and chest, the resulting downward pull leading to the boy's inability to shut his eyes or mouth. There was a fixed flexion deformity of the neck so that his chin was sitting against his chest, with the front of his neck not visible at all. Looking at the poor boy it was as if his skin had melted from his face and fused his head to his chest.

So it was a big repair job, involving skin grafting and complicated by difficulty gaining and maintaining anaesthesia. Four hours in, Katya's back ached, her legs ached, she was starving and feeling exceedingly light-headed.

'I'm fine,' she dismissed, knowing that they were on the downhill run and she could sit and eat something very soon.

They were stripping off their gowns fifteen minutes later, Ben chatting away excitedly about the op. He'd done a fantastic job and given a little boy back his face and neck. Katya could hear him vaguely, her rebelling stomach and a surge of nausea distracting her from his words.

Her ears started to ring and then she couldn't hear him at all. She could see his mouth moving but the words were lost in the noise coming from inside her head. Her vision started to go next. Ben was shrinking before her eyes as a black fuzz slowly encroached on her field of sight. And then everything went black and she fell.

'Katya? Katya!' Ben caught her as she slumped against him. He gave her a shake and she flopped like a rag doll. He swore in Italian and swept her up into his arms. He strode down the corridor, past surprised staff, getting angrier with each footstep. He kicked the door to his office open and laid her down on the double sofa.

She murmured and he let out a pent-up breath, his heart hammering madly. 'Katya?' he said again.

Her eyes fluttered open and he was so relieved for a moment he wanted to kiss her instead of strangle her.

'What happened?' she asked, half sitting.

'You fainted.' He pulled a blood-pressure cuff out of a desk drawer, wrapped it around her arm and took a quick reading.

'Eighty over thirty-five,' he told her disgustedly.

Katya returned his told-you-so look with a baleful glare. 'My blood sugar got a little low,' she said, ripping the cuff off and sitting up. Her head swam for minute and she shut her eyes briefly, willing it to stop.

When she opened them Ben was looking at her with raised eyebrows. 'What?' she said crankily. 'Pregnant women faint from time to time.'

Ben swore again in his native tongue. She'd scared the hell out of him. 'I will not have you jeopardising this baby's health because you want to be some kind of super-nurse.'

Ben's blunt reminder that to him she was just a life-support system for their baby stung. But it was a good reminder to her foolish heart of her purpose here in Italy, which seemed to get more and more blurred the longer she stayed.

'I am not giving up work,' she said stubbornly.

'Oh, yes, you are,' he countered, rising from his crouched position to sit behind his desk.

'You think if you sit behind that desk that it makes you more important? That I'll suddenly realise you're the count and I'm the commoner and I'll bow before you?'

Ben chuckled. Hardly! Katya was not like any other woman he'd ever known. Fawning and flattery just weren't part of her persona. She had her own opinions and spoke her own mind. She'd certainly been a refreshing change from all the others.

'Would you?'

'Not a chance.'

Ben chuckled again. It was good to see a glimpse of her prickliness. She had lost a lot of that edge to her personality over the weeks and it was reassuring to still see flashes of her old spark. The Katya who had never given him an inch.

Too many women had hung on his every word once upon a time and he'd soaked it up. Even Bianca had been a major ego trip for him. Being with someone who afforded him no such adulation had made him see that about himself. In fact, Katya made him work for his compliments and he was surprised at how much more rewarding it was.

A knock on the door interrupted them. It opened to reveal Carmella. 'I'm sorry,' she said, looking from one to the other, 'I'm interrupting something?'

'Yes,' Ben said.

'No,' Katya said, glaring at Ben.

'Katya's giving up work,' he told Carmella.

'No, Katya's not,' Katya denied hotly.

Carmella looked from one to the other, as if she was watching a tennis match. 'Right…maybe I should come back later,' she said, backing out the door.

'No,' Katya said. 'Go ahead. Ignore me.' She lay back on the lounge. In truth, she'd have liked to have risen from the couch and stalked out of the room with her head held high, but she still felt a little dizzy.

Ben and Carmella slipped into Italian and Katya let it swirl around her as she shut her eyes and waited to feel more grounded. She heard papers rustling and realised that she kept hearing a word she was familiar with. Mulgahti.

She sat up. 'What are you talking about?' she asked.

Ben and Carmella stopped what they were doing and turned to her. 'There's a baby girl in a remote village that has been brought to our attention, but her extraction is proving difficult due to internal politics.'

'Mulgahti?' Katya asked. 'That's the village?'

Ben frowned. 'Yes. Do you know it?'

Katya nodded and rose. A wave of dizziness swept over her and she swayed momentarily. Ben stood and was at her side in an instant. 'Katya!' Exasperation laced his voice.

She leaned against him briefly. 'I'm fine,' she mumbled,

pushing away from him and walking on shaky legs to the desk. Carmella offered Katya the chair she'd been sitting in and Katya felt too weak to refuse.

'I was stationed not far from Mulgahti a few years ago,' she said, locating it easily on the map that had been spread on the table. 'MedSurg spent six months there, treating victims of the local civil war.'

Carmella glanced at Ben. 'Do you have any contacts there still?' she asked Katya.

Katya thought for a moment. It was a difficult area, controlled by local warlords, one of whom they'd patched up after he'd taken a bullet to the shoulder. 'Maybe,' she said. 'Gill would be the best contact. I can make a few phone calls.' She looked first at Carmella then at Ben.

Carmella looked at Ben then back at Katya. 'Any help you can give would be welcome,' Carmella said.

Ben saw the smile that Katya gave his field officer and the spark of interest in Katya's eyes, and an idea started to form in his head. 'Why don't you two stay here in my office and see what progress you can make?' he suggested. 'Carmella can help you with any information you might need,' he said to Katya.

Katya nodded, feeling a tremor of excitement course through her, knowing she might be able to help get a child in need of medical attention to the Lucia Clinic. 'It's the middle of the night in Australia—Gill's not going to be happy.'

She grinned at Ben and he grinned back. 'He'll be fine when he realises why you're ringing.'

Katya nodded and picked up the phone.

'Can I get you ladies something?' he asked.

'Food,' Katya said, dialling the number.

He chuckled. 'Anything in particular?'

She shook her blonde head. 'As long as it's fast. I'm starving.'

Ben returned fifteen minutes later with a plate laden with bruschetta. Carmella was sitting in his seat, talking into her mobile in Italian and Katya was sitting where he'd left her, speaking in Russian. He plonked the plate on the table between them and they both automatically reached for a piece while they continued their conversations.

He placed his hands on Katya's shoulders and lowered his head to whisper in her ear. 'I'm sorry its not Taddeo's.'

Katya turned her head and smiled at him, still talking in rapid Russian. He stood and massaged her neck for a few moments. He smiled as she relaxed back against him. He could see the rise of her burgeoning belly from this vantage point and he just wanted to let his hands slide down her front and link them together under her bump.

Katya dropped her head to one side and he concentrated on the exposed muscles of her neck. He realised suddenly that he could also see down her scrub top to her lace-covered, full, ripe breasts, and he wished Carmella was somewhere else. He pictured cupping them, kneading them as he was her neck, until the nipples peaked in his hands. Spinning her around in the swivel chair, lifting her top and tasting them.

A knock interrupted his fantasy.

'Here you are. Benedetto. We're waiting for you,' Gabriella reprimanded in Italian.

Ben looked at his watch. He'd lost track of the time completely. 'Sorry. I'll be right there,' he said.

He dropped a kiss on Katya's shoulder, where the scrub top gaped and exposed the creamy skin.

'Later,' he murmured.

They were sitting on their terrace that evening, enjoying a candle-lit dinner. Katya was excitedly relaying how she and

Carmella had successfully managed to organise safe passage for the Mulgahti patient. The baby girl would be at the Lucia Clinic in two days.

'Carmella is very busy. She's been complaining for a while that she needs another staff member,' Ben said, keeping his voice very matter-of-fact.

Katya stopped in mid-chew. 'Ben…' she said, a slight warning in her voice.

'Katya, it's perfect.'

'I don't want to give up work,' she said.

'You won't be. You'll still be working. But you'll get to sit instead of standing on your feet for hours. You'll be able to eat regularly and take regular breaks.'

Katya looked at him, the candlelight throwing warm shadows on his dark features. He made the offer very attractive. Being on her feet all day was more tiring then she'd ever admit to him or even herself. Plus she'd be out of Ben's company, too, which would be an easier transition for her when she had to leave in another couple of months. It was time she started withdrawing a little. But what if she missed being a scrub nurse?

Ben could see her wavering. 'Look, just think about it for a few days, OK?' He reached across and placed his hand over hers.

She looked at him and smiled. 'OK, I'll think about it.'

He grinned triumphantly and she shook her head at him and rolled her eyes and returned her concentration to the food in front of her. Now that she had told Ben all about her day, her thoughts returned to something that Carmella had said at one stage. It stewed away in her brain as she ate some of Taddeo's gnocchi.

Ben noticed her getting quieter. 'Penny for them,' he said.

Katya looked at him, startled. She toyed with her food and eventually took a bite. 'It's nothing,' she said, shrugging her shoulders.

'Katya,' he said gently, 'you can tell me anything.'

Katya wasn't so sure about that. But he looked like he believed it anyway. She took a deep breath. 'I was just thinking about the girl who broke your heart. You never talk about her. Or Mario.'

Ben swallowed his mouthful of food, surprisingly without choking. This was not what he'd been expecting. 'It was a long time ago,' he said abruptly.

Just as she'd thought. She felt a nagging sense of regret that Ben didn't think he could talk to her about his feelings over his brother's death and the mystery woman who had broken his heart. He knew all her secrets now, all about her dirt-poor background, her mother's neglect and the incident with Sophia. Surely he should be able to tell the woman he made love to every night some of his past too?

'Mario's death wasn't.'

'Katya.'

She held up her hand. 'Carmella commented today that this was the happiest she'd seen you since Bianca. I didn't even know that was her name. I guess I suddenly realised that I don't know much about you. Your past, your secrets. It seems odd to be…' Katya chose her words carefully '…living with you and not know you.'

'You know me.'

Katya shook her head, the candle flame dancing in the light breeze. 'I know the man you were when we were with MedSurg is very different to the man you are here, in Italy. I mean…you are the man you are today because of the things that have happened in your past.' *You can't love me because of her.* 'I'd just like to be able to understand, that's all.'

Ben could see her sincerity. She wasn't asking out of some ghoulish curiosity, she genuinely wanted to understand what made him tick. He sighed. 'It's hard for me to talk about Bianca. Or Mario. I was angry for so long. And proud. And then they died. And I was ashamed that I had rejected any attempts at reconciliation. Mario had tried. Bianca had tried. Mamma had tried.'

Katya frowned. So Bianca had died, too? She was confused. Were his ex and his brother not two separate issues? 'I'm sorry,' Katya said. 'Bianca is dead, too? Were their deaths linked?'

Ben gave a bitter laugh. 'You could say that.' He saw her puzzled look and stopped being cryptic. He was so used to everyone knowing, he'd forgotten that she didn't. 'Bianca and I were engaged to be married. I was totally besotted with her. I was twenty-four…young, foolish. I found her and my brother together, in the clinic gardens. They were kissing. He had his hands on her…she was half-naked. That's when I left Italy. I ran away as far as I could go and Bianca and Mario got married.'

'Oh, Ben, how awful.' Katya heard the emotion in his voice. She could only imagine how devastating such a betrayal must have been. Now she understood the estrangement Ben had talked about. Now she could see why he was sworn off love. He was obviously in no hurry to risk his heart again after it had been battered so soundly.

Katya, better than anyone, understood how things like that could affect you for ever. And she knew that any hope she was harbouring that Ben might grow to love her would never come to fruition.

'The irony is Mario and I were so close until then. Oh, we were rivals. In everything. We were always trying to best each other with the biggest and the best, the latest and the greatest. But it was good-natured. He was my older brother, there was only twelve months between us, I hero-worshipped him and our rivalry pushed me to be the best I could be. But he took our one-upmanship too far when he took Bianca.'

Oh, dear, Katya thought. It seemed they'd both been victims of their idols developing feet of clay. Ben had just been much older before life had turned on him.

'Did you ever speak to each other again?' she asked.

Ben shook his head. 'He tried to extend an olive branch. They both did.'

'Bianca was in the car crash with your brother?'

Ben nodded. 'I may not have respected him, may have wanted nothing to do with him, but I didn't wish him dead. Either of them.'

Katya could see the truth of his words written all over his face. He was looking at her earnestly, his eyes begging her to understand. And she did. As much as she disliked and didn't respect her mother, Katya knew she would be devastated when the inevitable happened. No matter what, Olgah was the woman who had given her life.

'It's funny how a decade of hostility and self-righteousness can suddenly seem so churlish,' he said quietly, mesmerised by the flame.

Guilt. Another emotion Katya knew intimately. 'It sounds to me like they didn't do it to hurt you, Ben. Maybe they just fell in love? It happens sometimes. They say forgiveness is good for the soul.'

Deep down he knew he needed to be able to forgive them. But the image of Mario and Bianca in the garden was etched into his memory. And after years of it, absolution was a big thing to ask. 'Like you've forgiven yourself?' he said, fixing her with a hard stare. 'Forgiven your mother?'

Katya felt his accusation hit her in the solar plexus and

blinked at the sudden turn in the conversation. It struck even harder because she knew he was right.

Ben saw her eyes widen and immediately castigated himself. 'I'm sorry,' he said. 'That was uncalled-for.' He rubbed his hands through his hair. 'This topic drives me crazy.'

'Because it's unresolved?'

'Because Mario and Bianca are everywhere I go here. At the clinic, at Mamma's, in the streets of Positano, in the piazza at Ravello. I bought this villa so I could get away from memories of them. This is my sanctuary from the past. Coming back to Italy to fulfil my family duty has been made so much harder because of all the memories. And everything I do here has Mario's stamp on it. All of it makes me crazy.'

Katya nodded. It must be hard for such a proud man to have to continually face ghosts from an incident that had driven a wedge through his family for a decade. 'Maybe it's time to make some new memories?' she suggested.

He looked at her and realised suddenly that, thanks to her, he had a whole host of new memories. Very, very pleasant ones at that. And with the advent of the baby, his son, even more to come.

He nodded. 'Hence the clinic,' he said. 'Coming back from MedSurg and the poverty-stricken countries I've worked in, the opulence and the luxury here seemed so disproportionate. And I kept hearing your voice, nagging in my head, about hedonistic pampered rich people.'

Katya smiled. 'Nice to know you thought about me.'

'Oh, I thought about you,' he said, and chuckled as Katya blushed. 'Getting the Lucia Trust up and running and finding someone else to take over the management of the rest of the clinic has given me something to focus on that's truly mine. I've been able to blend the old direction with a new one and put my own stamp on it. Made it something other than a vanity clinic for the rich and famous. Made it mine. And I'm proud of that.'

'As you should be,' Katya murmured.

Her quiet confirmation meant more than any effusive display. He could tell from her earlier excitement and her involvement with their clients that the clinic had come to mean a lot to her as well. That she was also proud of the work they were doing with the foundation. He was surprised to find that it mattered to him. What she thought of him.

'But then I go into the gardens and I see Mario everywhere. He loved those gardens. Every nook and cranny reminds me of that day…rounding a corner to see Bianca with Mario…her shirt unbuttoned…'

Katya felt sick at the dread in his voice. He may say he had sworn off love but he must still be in love with Bianca if a decade later he couldn't even bear to say the words. Was he still in love with her? A dead woman? Who'd betrayed him? Something squeezed her heart and the hopelessness of her love was brought into sharp focus.

'Are you angrier with him or with her?' she asked.

Ben blinked. No one had asked him that before. And if they had, he probably would have said Bianca. But being forced to confront it now, he realised he was angriest with his brother.

He sighed. 'Mario, I guess. There are just some lines you don't cross.' It felt amazingly cathartic just to admit it.

Katya nodded. She understood a little better now that people were only human, with human failings. 'Of course, Ben, he was your brother. You idolised him. And he let you down. And then you had to go from hating him to grieving him with no time in the middle for reconciliation. But you can't get over it by denying he ever existed. Running away from the memories. You need to be able to accept he was human and celebrate his life.'

Ben frowned. 'What do you mean?'

She shrugged. 'I don't know.' She groped around for an idea. 'How about some kind of memorial for him and Bianca in the gardens somewhere? Put your own stamp on them, too?'

Ben regarded her seriously and nodded slowly. 'Maybe.' He was beginning to think that Mario and Bianca had done him a favour. Had they never betrayed him, he wouldn't have ever known Katya. And suddenly he couldn't imagine being without her.

CHAPTER NINE

A WEEK later Katya stopped midway up the clinic's grand stone staircase for a breather. It had been long day in the operating theatre and everything ached. Ben's offer to move her into the administration side with Carmella was looking more and more attractive as standing for long periods of times was becoming very wearying.

She looked down at her belly and wondered how it could possibly get any bigger. And she still had eight weeks to go! The baby seemed to have had a growth spurt and she felt uncomfortable and was sure she was waddling. Ben reassured her that she wasn't, which was sweet, but she knew he was lying.

Katya had never known it was possible to be this tired. The baby's size was even making it uncomfortable to sleep so she was back to being an insomniac again.

'You OK?' Ben asked, coming up behind her. One hand automatically reached for the muscles at her neck and started to knead them. The other automatically caressed the bulge of her tummy. He dropped a kiss against her neck.

'A few months ago I could take these stairs two at a time.' She grimaced, closing her eyes as his fingers worked their magic.

Ben could see Katya was looking more and more exhausted each day. '*Cara*,' he said softly, 'I think it's time to give up work.'

Katya's eyes flew open and she stepped away from him. 'I'm fine,' she said testily.

'*Cara,*' he said, looking at her reprovingly.

'What happened to working with Carmella?' she asked.

'I think it's becoming obvious that you just need to put your feet up and rest.'

And sit around thinking about you all day? She shook her head. 'No. I like working. I like working here particularly. Don't you understand? I didn't expect to but I do. If I sat around doing nothing all day I'd go mad.'

God, she could be exasperating. 'Katya, think of the baby.'

She heard the reproach in his voice and wanted to kick him in the shins. *Well, as long as the baby's OK.* 'The baby is fine,' she said, and turned on her heel.

Except somewhere in the execution of her about-face she tripped herself up and before she knew it she'd slipped and fallen and was bumping down the stairs, flailing around like a beached whale, trying to stop, trying to protect the baby from the fall.

'Katya!' Ben lunged for her but couldn't grab her in time and he rushed down the stairs, reaching her as she came to a stop in a crumpled heap at the bottom.

'Katya. Katya!' His heart was galloping in his chest. 'Are you all right?' She was lying very still and he turned her over, a dozen dreadful scenarios marching through his brain. God, please, let her be all right!

Katya's eyes fluttered open. She moaned. Now she really did ache everywhere. Her arms and legs felt battered and she lifted her hand to the back of her head and gingerly prodded a rapidly growing lump.

'What?' Ben investigated the bump. 'I think you need an X-ray.'

Like hell. She wasn't exposing her baby to any unnecessary radiation. '*I*'m fine, Ben,' she protested weakly, pushing herself up.

'No, we need to get you checked out,' he said, supporting her into a sitting position.

Katya looked into his eyes. She could see the concern in his brown gaze. Was it for her or for the baby? 'The baby's fine,' she said, and stood up, shaking his hands off her.

'The bump on your head needs looking at. You took a big tumble.'

'I feel fine,' she said again, pushing away from him feeling irritated by his concern.

Ben watched her go and raised his eyes heavenward. *Give me strength!* If she thought he was just going to let her walk away and not get checked out then she didn't know him at all.

Katya hurried away, knowing she was being unreasonable, but loving him and knowing that his only interest in her was the baby and some latent sexual chemistry was harder than she'd thought.

She felt a sudden warmth between her legs and stopped abruptly, looking down. 'Ben!'

His eyes flew open and he ran to her side as she stood stock-still in the corridor, her hand clutching her stomach.

'I'm bleeding,' she said, staring at the growing red stain on her scrub pants and then looking at him. The baby. Had she hurt the baby?

Ben felt his heart in his mouth when he saw her blood-stained clothes. He swore and swept her up into his arms.

'Where are we going?' she asked, clinging to him, trembling all over, biting her lip to stop the tears that were building in her eyes.

'Rocco.'

Katya lay very still as Rocco ran the transducer over her belly. Her mind was frozen, fear for her baby bringing up all the horrible possibilities. How could she have been so stupid? Why had she insisted on working? If she'd been sitting at home with her feet up, this would never have happened. *I'm sorry, baby, I won't put you in danger again.*

Ben and Rocco were talking in Italian over her, pointing at various things on the screen, but she wasn't listening. Her eyes were fixed on the image. At the baby's strong heartbeat and its vigorous, healthy movements.

He was OK. The baby was OK. Her relief was immense. As was the sudden clarity that descended on her. She could no more hand her son over to Ben than fly to the moon. She touched the screen as she had done at her first ultrasound. *I promise to protect you from everything. I promise to be vigilant. I promise to give you everything I have. I promise to love you above all else.*

'Rocco says the baby looks good. The fall seems to have caused a small area of the placenta at the margin to come away and bleed. But the rest of the placenta looks healthy.'

Katya nodded, a surge of relief bringing her thought processes back on line. 'Thank you,' she said to Rocco.

'As the bleeding's now stopped Rocco recommends bed rest for a couple of days and then he'll scan you again. But if you notice any decrease in foetal movements or any more bleeding, he wants to see you straight away.'

'Of course,' Katya said eagerly. She would have lain in bed for the duration if that's what it took for the baby to be OK.

Rocco left and Katya sat on the narrow couch, letting Ben do a full neuro assessment on her. It was making him feel better and she was still so relieved to see the baby was OK, she didn't even think to protest. After it was done he walked her up to their quarters, stood outside the cubicle while she showered and then tucked her into their bed.

'Do you want me to stay?' Ben asked. It had been a frightening couple of hours and the last thing he wanted to do was go back to work. But there was still one more case to complete.

'No.' Katya smiled reassuringly, lying on her side and hugging her belly. 'I'll be fine.'

'Page me if you need me,' he said, dragging the bedside phone closer to her. 'I'll bring us some dinner when I finish.'

Katya nodded and was grateful when Ben finally left. Her mind was whirring around despite the classical music that Ben had switched on before he'd left. She knew what she had to do. She couldn't stay any longer.

She knew now there was no way possible she could hand this baby over to Ben and walk out of its life. Those awful moments when she'd thought she was losing the baby or had harmed the baby had been the worst of her life. Worse than discovering her pregnancy. Worse than admitting her love for Ben. Why had it taken a threat to the baby's life for her to realise the truth? It was her destiny to be a mother to this child.

What kind of a fool had she been? Yes, she had been scared. Scared that she'd make a mess of it. Scared that something awful would happen to him as it had happened to Sophia, as it nearly had today. Scared that she couldn't provide for him like Ben could. Scared of the single-parent life she was about to embark on which her own mother had failed at so miserably.

But all that paled in comparison to her love and desire to be with this baby. Ben's son. Her fear of never seeing her child far outstripped her fear of failure. She was just going to have to be the best damn mother she could. The safest. The most vigilant. The most loving. Because she'd known, looking at that screen, her baby strong despite the trauma it had been through, that she couldn't give her baby up. She'd known it as surely as she'd known that day that she couldn't terminate the pregnancy.

The revelation had been unexpected. It had been much simpler before today. Pregnant with baby. Don't want baby. Have baby. Leave baby with father. Simple. Straightforward. Uncomplicated. Although as each day passed and the end drew nearer and she felt a deeper and deeper connection with the baby, the lines were blurring. And falling in love with Ben had complicated it further.

And now things were as sticky and mired and complicated as they could get. And that meant only one thing. She had to get out. Leave Ravello. Leave Positano. Leave Italy. Leave Ben. Get as far away as possible. Because she couldn't hand her son over and she couldn't stay either. Ben had made it very clear that he wouldn't love again. Couldn't love again. And she couldn't live with him, loving him, knowing that she'd never hear those words.

Sitting in their house, waiting for him to say them, hanging on, getting more and more desperate every day—like her mother. Becoming old and bitter, like her mother? Seeing him heap love on their child. Growing jealous of that? No, she would slowly wither and die. There was no choice. She had to cut her losses now.

Loving Ben these past few weeks had been a surprise and a complication she could have done without but she was a big girl, a practical woman, and she'd known she could bear a broken heart to achieve her goal. But today, with the fall and the bleeding scare, the lie of the land had completely changed.

So now she was stuck with two choices. Leave the baby with Ben, as their deal currently stood, and go on her merry way.

Impossible.

Or stay in their one-sided relationship and raise their child together. And die a little each day.

Also impossible.

But there was a third option. Take the baby and run.

Possible. Plausible. Essential.

But could she do that to Ben? As painful as it was to admit he didn't love her, the same couldn't be said for their baby. Ben was besotted with him. He spent ages each day talking to his son. First thing in the morning and in bed at night he would stroke her stomach and place his lips against her bulge and whisper sweet nothings to it. In two languages.

He talked about the baby non-stop. Told her the things they were going to do together and the places they were going to go and the things he wanted to show his son. At the moment he was going through three different name books, hoping to find a good balance between the baby's Russian and Italian ancestry. He was completely and utterly committed to their baby. Head over heels in love with him. How could she take away the one thing Ben wanted more than anything? The one thing that had started to restore his faith in love? In family?

But how could she stay and keep herself whole? How could she stay and not turn into her mother? This was her dilemma. She couldn't leave her son behind, neither could she stay in a relationship where she was never going to be loved, hoping for some crumbs of affection. She knew Ben was going to be hurt. Angry, probably. But she couldn't stay.

Her childhood memories of her mother's emotional destruction were still too vivid. She'd fought all her life to escape the scars of her upbringing, determined not to repeat her mother's mistakes, and she wouldn't compromise on that because Ben might get hurt in the process.

She could only hope that he had enough compassion in him to understand her motives.

Katya stayed in bed for two days, going slowly stir-crazy. Ben was attentive to a fault which made her cranky and irritable and guilty, knowing what she was about to do to him. She had no further bleeding and the baby was as active as ever. Rocco was pleased with the second scan but cautioned Katya to give up work and take it easy for the rest of her pregnancy.

Katya promised she would and she could see Ben's visible relief in the periphery of her vision. Poor guy. He had taken her moods on the chin the last two days and been the absolute soul of patience. Her heart swelled with love and she felt like a hot knife was being jabbed into her side at the thought of leaving him.

Katya went back to the room and packed her bag, taking only the things she'd arrived with. There was much more stuff she was leaving behind but she had all she needed. Her plane ticket and her clothes. She placed a hand on her stomach—and the baby. Her heart was heavy as she paged Ben.

Ben arrived a few minutes later and she turned and looked at him, her lover, her heart, and tried to memorise every feature. He looked so male and sexy in his scrubs, her chest swelled with love and eyes blurred with tears. If only it didn't have to be this way. If only he could love her like she loved him.

Ben looked at the bag at her feet and the tears shining in her eyes. 'What's all this?'

Katya dashed the tears away and searched for the hard woman who had arrived here some months ago. She'd thought this through enough times in the last two days. Now was the time for action.

'I'm l-leaving.'

Ben stared at her vacantly for a few moments, letting her announcement sink in. He felt as if he'd taken a punch to the solar plexus from a world boxing champion. He felt short of breath. He felt his stomach drop. His mind reeled. What the hell did she mean? 'I'm sorry? What do you mean, you're leaving?'

'I thought I could do this…I really did, Ben. But the other day, when I was bleeding and I thought I was losing the baby, I realised I couldn't. Couldn't walk away from him.'

Ben looked at her earnest face. She didn't want to give the baby up? But that was…perfect. 'So don't,' he said. Ben could tell she was just holding herself together, that one wrong word could see her walking out the door. 'Stay here with me and we'll raise the baby together. My offer of marriage still stands.'

Katya bit her lip to stop the sob that rose in her throat at the casual offer. 'We don't love each other, Ben.' The lie hurt so much she had to gulp in a big breath to ease the pain.

'No, but we love this baby, and that's a good start.'

She stared at him eyes blurry with tears. What had she expected? That he go down on one knee and admit his undying love? She took some deep breaths. How, how could she marry him? She'd never be able to trust his motives. She'd question every aspect of their life together, everything he did, everything he said, not knowing if it was her or the baby motivating him. She couldn't—wouldn't—marry someone who didn't love her.

She shook her head. 'I can't give him up and I can't marry you either.'

Ben felt his heart beat louder in his chest and a slow steady burn rise in his chest. 'So, what? You're just going to leave?' His voice was low and menacing. 'Cut me out of my own child's life? Because you'd better know—I won't take that lying down.'

Katya swiped at a tear that had finally escaped to splash down her cheek. She heard the threat in his voice and knew it wasn't an empty one. She knew he had the power and the means to follow through. Knew that he'd move heaven and earth for his child. 'No. I won't cut you out but I need some time away to think about how we can handle this.'

'Where do you propose to go?'

'London,' she said. It was a good distance but not too far.

Ben could see all his hopes and dreams for the three of them crashing down around him. Katya had been very adamant that she wasn't ever going to be part of their lives, but he had built up that fantasy anyway, convinced she would change her mind. And she had, but she'd also completely changed the rules.

He felt like he had that day with Mario and Bianca. Like the rug had been pulled from under him. 'Like hell you're going to London. You've just had a bleed, it's not safe for you to travel.'

She flinched. Again, his concern for their baby was total. 'Rocco assured me it would be OK to travel.' She had enlisted Gabriella's help as an interpreter after Ben had left.

'No.' Ben shook his head, clenching and unclenching his fists.

Katya raised her chin. 'Are you telling me that you plan to physically restrain me?'

'Don't be ridiculous,' he snapped.

'Then I am going to London.' Katya's heart banged loudly against her ribs. Her hands trembled slightly but she was pleased to see the old strong-as-steel Katya was still there when she needed her.

Ben regarded her seriously, his mind frantically thinking of a legal way to keep her in Italy. Anything he could organise through a court would take a few days. He looked at her stomach full with his child. There had to be a way to keep her here. To convince her to stay.

'I have rights to this baby, too,' he said, injecting steel into his voice.

'I'm not denying you your rights, Ben. Please…I just need some time.' Everything was so mixed up in her head and she couldn't sort it out living here.

Ben could see her torment. Could see this conversation wasn't easy for her either. Maybe some time away would help her see the wisdom of his suggestion? 'How much time?' he demanded.

For ever? 'A few weeks.' She shrugged.

'You can have two.'

Two? She felt like she would do nothing but cry for at least the first two weeks. 'No. Four,' she said.

Ben did a quick calculation in his head. She'd be thirty-six weeks. Still a good month until the baby was born. 'You promise you'll get help if anything else goes wrong with the baby?'

Katya ground her teeth. 'Hell, Ben, of course. Don't worry,

your baby will be well looked after.' *Its mother, on the other hand, will be a mess but don't concern yourself about that.*

'Four weeks, then,' he said, pulling his wallet out of his bedside table drawer, pulling out a credit card and scribbling on a piece of paper. He handed them both to her.

'My card and its PIN number,' he said.

Katya looked at them blankly and then threw them on the bed in disgust. 'I don't want your money, Ben.' She picked up her bag. 'I've never wanted your money.'

She opened the door, unable to believe they were parting like this.

'Keep in touch.'

Katya stilled with her hand on the doorknob, the quiet warning putting a chill up her spine. 'You know my mobile number,' she said, her heart breaking as she walked out of the room without a backward glance.

CHAPTER TEN

Two weeks later, Katya sat in a glass bubble high above the Thames as the London Eye slowly completed a revolution. She hadn't really seen any of the capital spread before her. Big Ben and the Houses of Parliament were directly below her now, but their architectural beauty didn't register. She sat on the central seat staring out aimlessly, while tourists walked around the car, snapping photos.

She didn't even know how she'd ended up here. She'd just had to get out of the flat. Being alone gave her too much time to think, to reflect. To be miserable. She was annoyed with herself that she couldn't just shake it off and that after a fortnight away from Ben she still didn't know what to do.

She yearned desperately for the old Katya to make an appearance. The one who had gone to Italy. The one who had seen her through years of hard times. The one who had ruled her life with an iron fist. But being with Ben, falling in love with him, had softened that woman. His support and understanding had dispensed with the need for her. And furthermore, she couldn't get her back. Loving Ben, having his baby, had changed her for ever.

The ride came to an end and Katya stepped out of the slowly moving car with the other passengers. She pulled her coat collar up and did up the buttons over her baby bump. She was grateful for the warm, knee-length wool as the crisp March air enveloped her. Where to now? She didn't know. Just walk, be among crowds, wander along Oxford Street maybe or around Covent Garden.

Wherever, just not back to the poky little flat in Islington which she was house-sitting for a MedSurg colleague. She almost wished she'd taken Gill and Harriet up on their offer of a bed in Australia. But it was too far away from Ben. And he had made it very clear from his text messages that he wanted to be part of his child's life.

And she knew that if he'd really wanted to play hard ball, he had the money and the means to provide for their son better than she did. And the money and the means to ensure he got his way.

Going back to Italy was inevitable. She knew that deep down. Unless she could persuade Ben to come to London. But ultimately where they lived didn't matter. It still involved seeing him regularly. Seeing him and knowing he could never be hers. Watching him with their child. Maybe even with other women. The newer, softer Katya wasn't strong enough for that.

She was fairly sure, though, that Ben would insist on Italy. He had the Lucia Trust, his pride and joy, still in its infancy, and also his heritage. It may have been one he hadn't wanted but he was embracing it more and more, determined to put his own stamp on it.

So it was either go to Italy willingly or face a court battle for their son. Something she wasn't up to financially or emotionally.

Katya's mobile rang and her heart skipped crazily in her chest. *Ben.* They hadn't spoken since she'd left, communicating by text only.

She flipped the phone open. 'Hello.'

'I'm in London.'

Katya gasped. She wasn't ready yet. Even though every cell in her body ached to see him again. 'I have another two weeks.'

'We need to talk, *cara*.'

Even being brisk and businesslike, his voice was still as sexy as hell. She swallowed.

'I couldn't wait.' His voice was softer this time. She shivered and her toes curled at the sensual, husky purr of his voice. Heaven help her, his voice was stroking all the places that had ached for him this last fortnight.

'Meet me for dinner at seven tonight. One-fifty Piccadilly.'

She heard the disconnected tone and folded the phone away. She should have been annoyed at his presumption but hearing his voice again after so long had obliterated everything. And in a few hours she'd be actually seeing him.

At least he hadn't insisted on coming to the flat. It was small, the entire thing not much bigger than their quarters at the clinic. The bed took up three-quarters of the available room. And they didn't have a very good track record around beds. If she was going to survive with her heart intact, they could never cross that line again.

Ben waited impatiently at the table. She was late. If she didn't show soon he was going to go to her temporary dwelling and drag her out, kicking and screaming. OK, he'd changed the rules but, then, so had she. She couldn't turn his whole world upside down and then just leave and expect him to take it on the chin.

Waking up without her the morning after that fateful day two weeks ago had been the worst moment of his life. Worse than finding his brother making love to his fiancée, worse than the news of Mario's death. Worse than watching her walk out the door. Because he'd realised in that moment, with an empty space in the bed beside him, that he loved her. That he'd fallen in love with her the night they had first made love. He'd just been too stubborn to see it.

And from then on, he'd just been plain mad. The first time he'd risked his heart in a decade and it was being ripped to shreds all over again. It was *déjà vu* and he'd be damned if he would take that sitting down this time. Last time running had been his way of coping. This time he would fight.

But he wouldn't fight for Katya. Yet again it had been proved to him that women only brought heartache. Obviously if she could just walk away from him, she didn't return his feelings. Had only sought him out in Italy when she'd been convinced she couldn't raise the baby herself. To use him.

But he would fight for his child. He'd gone from potentially being a sole parent to no baby at all, and if she thought he'd take that without a fight, like he'd taken Mario and Bianca, then she was wrong. He *would* play a role in this child's life and she either agreed to that or he would make it his life's purpose to seek it through any means at his disposal.

He just wished there was a way to make her love him. That he could take her to court and have a judge order her to love him. But he knew it didn't work like that. That love was either there or it wasn't.

And it obviously wasn't for her. And he was going to have to deal with that for the next however many years. It would be exquisite torture loving her and not being able to tell her. Watching her give birth to their baby. Breast-feeding him. Laughing and talking in Russian to him. Maybe having to put up with another man in her life. In his son's life. It would all be unbearable—but he'd do what he had to do to be a father to his son.

Ben gripped a fork absently, concentrating on his anger. He'd need it to harden his heart. She mustn't know the power she had over him. One woman with the power to crush his heart had been more than enough in his life. And he wouldn't give it to another, not when his child was in the middle.

Because that had to be his focus now. Their child. Their son. This was what being in London was about. To convince her to return to Italy. To hash out a mutually satisfying parental agreement. And if she didn't agree? He'd find a judge to force her to do it.

Katya sat on the back seat of the black cab, watching the lights of London flash by. The taxi pulled up outside the Ritz.

'No, I'm sorry, there must be a mistake,' Katya said, staring at the opulent building. 'I said 150 Piccadilly.'

The taxi driver nodded. 'The Ritz. One-fifty Piccadilly.'

Katya felt her shoulders slump. *Of course. The Ritz. Where else?* She paid him and alighted from the vehicle. It was a chilly night and she hoped she was dressed well enough for such a swanky restaurant.

The doorman opened the heavy gold and glass door for her and she stepped inside nervously, cursing Ben silently. He knew she didn't feel comfortable in places like this. If he'd wanted to put her on the back foot, he had certainly achieved it!

Ben wasn't anywhere in the foyer and she peered into the elegant French-influenced surroundings to see if he was waiting for her further along the vaulted gallery that ran the length of the building.

'Miss Petrova?'

Katya turned to find a concierge in a dark suit with gold braid on his epaulettes addressing her. 'Yes?'

'Count Medici is waiting for you in the dining room,' he said, gesturing down to the end of the gallery.

'Oh, right… Thank you,' she said. It seemed like a very long walk.

'May I take your coat' he asked.

'Ah…yes.' Katya shrugged out of the dark wool. The temperature inside was toasty compared to the chilly night air outside.

Her hands shook and she buried them in her pockets as she walked on equally shaky legs towards the dining room. She passed the elegant Palm Court on her left, where glasses tinkled, crockery clattered and muted laughter mingled with piano music. She continued on until she reached the entrance to the dining room.

'Miss Petrova?' a waiter enquired.

Katya nodded.

'This way, please. The count is expecting you.'

Katya followed the waiter into the glamorous room, her eyes searching the tables, oblivious to the Louis XVI-inspired decor. Her heels sank in to the plush carpet of muted pink, green and cream. Above her head chandeliers linked by gilt garlands cast a subdued glow.

The ceiling from which they hung displayed an amazing fresco. The large floor-to-ceiling windows that faced Green Park were hung with heavy formal drapes. A four-piece band was playing and some couples were dancing.

Katya felt exactly how she'd felt the first time she'd seen inside the Lucia Clinic. Smothered. Stifled. And more and more annoyed. She'd rather be eating a BLT sandwich on a park bench. She felt like she'd been naughty and the principal was summoning her. Trying to impress her with his stature and power.

Trying to intimidate her? Well, she'd never scared easily and if Ben thought he was going to lord it over her, he could think again. She had as much right to this baby as he.

The waiter stopped at a table set for two and pulled out Katya's chair. She ignored it. Ben stared up at her. Her heart slammed madly in her chest. He looked tired and haggard. He had a three-day growth and his jaw looked a little gaunt. He looked utterly gorgeous.

'The Ritz, Ben? How predictable,' Katya saw the waiter discreetly melt away.

'Sarcastic, Katya? How predictable,' he mimicked. 'You're late. Sit.' He could smell cinnamon. She was a sight for sore eyes and as she twisted to sit he saw how much more the swell of her stomach had increased. He suppressed the urge to stand and embrace her, feel her belly pressed against his.

Katya felt rather than saw a waiter pushing her chair under her. Ben ordered a Scotch for himself and some iced water with lemon for her. It irritated her that he hadn't even asked. She wasn't used to seeing him like this. He seemed to be playing Count tonight and she didn't doubt it was another power ploy.

He certainly looked every inch the aristocrat. He was wearing a suit that shrieked of class and money. His shirt was blue with a blue pinstripe and his tie was navy. He looked...wealthy. There was just something about the way he held himself that spoke of old money.

He passed her a menu.

'I'm not hungry,' she said.

He looked at her over the top of the menu. 'I'll have the snails. The signorina will have the quail,' he said, snapping his menu closed and handing it to the waiter.

The last thing Katya wanted to do was sit there and make

small talk over birds and disgusting slugs. She just wanted to get this over with so she could get the hell away. Away from the oppressive opulence in a place she'd never belong. Away from his brooding presence. She'd missed him. So much she ached all over.

'Just say what you need to say, Ben.'

I love you. My life is awful without you. 'What the hell happened to the plan, Katya?'

I fell in love, that's what. With you and our baby. 'I'm sorry,' she said. 'I can't just hand him over to you. I thought I could. Then I took that fall and nearly lost him and I felt so awful, so wretched…I just knew I couldn't give him up.'

'I would never have asked you to.'

No. But you'd ask me to commit to a loveless marriage. 'Once I realised I could do it by myself, I had to get away. It's all this,' she said gesturing around her at the palatial dining room. Waiters with different-coloured jackets fussed over each table under the watchful eye of the head waiter, who wore tails. 'This isn't me, Ben.' It wasn't the real reason but it was another aspect of their relationship that had always made her uneasy.

'It isn't me either,' he denied.

Katya snorted. 'Tonight you look like you were born at this table.'

Ben could feel his patience wearing thin. 'So it was OK for our child to have all this when it was me raising him. But now you want to raise him, all this is too rich for you?'

Oh, God, it sounded so awful when he said it like that. She shook her head. 'You said it yourself, Ben. All a baby really needs is love. It just took me a little while to realise that.'

'Well, whether you like it or not, this child is the heir to the entire Medici fortune, Katya. You think I should let you raise him in some grubby little Islington bedsit?'

Katya gasped. 'How did you…?'

He shrugged. 'As you pointed out, I'm a wealthy person. I have ways.'

The whole time she'd thought he'd been giving her space, respecting her independence, he had known where she was? Had she been watched the entire time? Tonight she was seeing a Ben she didn't like or know. She'd seen glimpses of him in the past, but he was front and centre at the moment.

'What do you want, Ben?' She wanted to get away from him. Every minute she spent in his company was torture. Even through her anger she wanted him to kiss her again.

He regarded her seriously. She sounded tired. He would like nothing better now than to take her up to his suite, undress her and rock her to sleep with his hand cradling her stomach. 'You. Back in Italy. I'll set you up in a flat in Ravello. But we share the parenting half-half. It's that or I take you to court and get full custody. And I will win.'

Katya felt as if he'd thrown knives at her. She knew he was right. What hope did a Russian nurse from a poor background with an average income have against a rich, titled surgeon? Even if she was the mother.

'So I'll be like your kept woman? Like a whore? Like how you offered me a job the morning after we slept together for the first time. Payment for service?'

Ben shut his eyes. He'd known that morning, from her vehement rejection, that he had made a gaffe but he hadn't realised that he'd hurt her quite so much.

'No. I'm sorry, I handled things badly that morning. I didn't mean to make you feel cheap. I was going back to a world and memories I didn't want to confront. I was trying to get my head around all that and I spoke without thinking.'

Katya could hear his sincerity but was too angry to cut him

too much slack. 'I am not my mother,' she said frostily. 'I can get my own place.'

'Don't be ridiculous,' he snapped. 'You're the mother of my child.'

She folded her arms mutinously against her chest. 'You want me back, this is non-negotiable.'

'Places are hideously expensive, Katya.'

'I'll manage,' she said tightly.

Ben realised they could argue the logistics later. The important part was that she was agreeing to return. 'So, you're coming back? And you agree to equal parenting?'

'Yes,' Katya said, removing the napkin that an attentive waiter had placed on her lap and throwing it on the table.

How could she still love him? Because she knew he was just doing whatever it took to be with his baby. Just as she was doing. She had no doubt that he would love and dote on their son with every breath in his body. She felt a streak of jealousy and knew it was wrong. Knew it was twisted.

All the fight suddenly left her. 'I'll be back this time next week. I'll let you know when I'm getting in.'

She stood to leave. There was no point in staying. Her heart was breaking in two and she might just do something stupid, like tell him she loved him.

'Katya.' Ben stood and put a stilling hand on her arm.

He looked at her, trying to read her thoughts. She looked sad and defeated and exhausted. Tears shimmered unshed in her eyes. And something else he couldn't put his finger on. He almost told her then. He hated himself for being so harsh. So cold. All he wanted to do was pull her into his arms. Kiss away the tears. Tell her he loved her. But he couldn't make the words come out of his mouth.

She looked down at where he was holding her arm and he

slowly let her go. She walked away without looking back and he stood and watched her go until her figure completely disappeared from sight.

'Everything OK, Count Medici?' the head waiter asked anxiously.

'No. May I have another Scotch?'

Ben ate his meal. He had won. Why didn't it feel like a victory? Seeing her all pliant and docile had left a bitter taste in his mouth. He preferred the Katya who had first arrived at the table. Maybe once the baby was born and she was too busy to resent him, they could eventually be friends. Even though it would be very hard to pretend there wasn't more.

Hard? It would be impossible. He'd almost told her just then. How long did he think he could hold out? Could he go along loving her from afar for ever? Did he want to? It would kill him, slowly but surely. He knew how it was to hold her, to make love to her. How could he see her every day, want her every day and still stay sane?

That's why he'd left Italy over the Bianca fiasco. Having to face his brother and his ex every day would have been too hard. And his feelings for his long-ago ex were nothing compared to the depth of his feelings for Katya. She had showed him so much in the time he had known her. He had matured and his ability to love had matured, too.

And she had given him the gift of a child and he loved them both dearly. Was he going to let what had happened a decade ago ruin his happiness now? He had let Bianca go, had run. But he was older now, and wiser, and Katya had taught him the meaning of true love. Surely he had to fight for her as well, not just their child?

A woman laughed and Ben looked around. There were a lot of glamorous bejewelled women there that night. But Katya outshone them all. And he'd just let her walk out the door.

His thoughts crystallized for the first time in two weeks. The last time he'd had his heart broken, what had he done? He'd run away. Felt sorry for himself. Played the victim. Well, not this time.

Mario's death had been the catalyst for a lot of change over the last few months. But when he thought about it, it had been Katya's gift that night that had had the most effect on his life. Her recognition of his distress and her unquestioning generosity had shaken and humbled him. He'd fallen in love with her that night.

And not the love of a young man obsessed with perfection and finding the right woman to show off to his brother and the rest of the world, but that of a man with a damaged spirit who had found his soul mate. So, she didn't love him. And that hurt. But it was time to fight for her. To declare his intention of wooing her, wining her over, making her love him.

And in the end, if he failed, then he could hold his head up high and know that he had given it his all. When Bianca had thrown his love back, he'd fled. But Katya wasn't Bianca. Katya wasn't some young man's fancy. She was the woman for him. The only woman for him. A lot had changed in a few short months. And if Bianca and Mario had been alive today, he would have thanked them for their betrayal for it had led him to the woman of his heart. His old bitterness paled into insignificance beside what was now at stake.

He threw back the rest of the contents of his glass, paid his bill and left. It was time to stop running away.

* * *

Katya was lying in bed, crying, when the banging on her door started. She was in her pyjamas, staring unseeingly at the television.

She knew it was him. 'Go away,' she croaked.

'Damn it, Katya, open the door.'

'Go away, Ben. You got what you want. Leave me alone.'

'Katya! So help me, I'm going to break this door down if you don't open it.'

Katya felt another stream of hot tears spill down her face. She believed him. She got up, dabbing at her eyes with a tissue and blowing her nose. She undid the deadbolt and the chain latch and flung the door open.

'Go away,' she yelled at him, and attempted to slam the door in his face. He looked like hell. His tie was gone, his collar unbuttoned, his shirt half hanging out.

Ben brought his arm up to block its closure. 'I need to talk to you and I'm not doing it in the corridor.'

'Afraid you'll catch a disease?' she snapped, and turned on her heel, leaving him standing in the doorway. She got back into bed and pulled the covers up to her chin.

Ben felt a surge of frustration well up inside. Sometimes she was so maddening he wanted to pull her across his knees and smack her bottom.

'You've been crying.'

'Don't flatter yourself,' she said, pointing to the television. 'It's a sad movie.'

'Since when have you cried at movies?' Katya was one of the most unsentimental women he knew.

'Since I got pregnant,' she flared.

Ben picked up the remote from her bedside table and switched the television off.

'I was watching that!'

Ben pulled up a chair and placed it beside the bed. 'Katya, I want to talk to you. I don't want things to be like this between us.'

'Oh, I suppose you want us to be friends after your little threat before?' she sneered. She knew she was being unreasonable but he was so close and he looked so sexy with his hair all tousled and his three-day growth and his shirt half-undone. It had been two weeks and she'd missed him.

'No, I don't want to be your friend.'

'Well, that won't—'

'Katya, shut up,' Ben interrupted harshly. 'I have something to say and I'd really appreciate if you could just keep your shrewish tongue still until I've finished. Do you think you can do that?' he demanded.

Katya blinked at his masterful tone. 'Do you promise to leave as soon as it's said?' she asked.

He sighed. 'Yes.' Ben figured she'd probably turf him out anyway.

'OK, then,' she said, drawing her knees up and placing her hands protectively across her abdomen.

Now he had the opportunity he wasn't sure where to start. 'I realized something big recently, after you'd gone. I realised that I loved you.' Katya opened her mouth to speak and he held up his hand and shot her a warning look.

'I was angry, too, of course. In fact, it's been anger that has got me through this last two weeks. Because I realised that it was all one-sided. Because if you loved me, you wouldn't have taken my baby away.'

Katya tried to interject again but again he hushed her. 'It was like Bianca all over again. Loving someone who didn't love me back. And that hurt and it brought back some painful memories. But it's worse this time around because I was so

immature last time. I didn't know the true meaning of love.
I was selfish. Thinking that it was all about me and my
feelings. You helped me see that it wasn't some great conspiracy against me, that things like that happen in life sometimes. You showed me a mature form of love. A selfless love.
By letting me seek solace in your body when I needed it so
badly, even though you were a virgin, and by being willing
to give up your baby because you didn't think you'd be a fit
mother.'

Katya's hands trembled as his words sunk in. He loved her?
Was it possible? Her heart thundered in her ears. She lay
stock still waiting for the but.

'But…'

Katya held her breath, waiting to hear how her running off
and her behaviour tonight had totally destroyed his love.

'Tonight I decided I wasn't going to lie down and take it
like I did with Bianca. I've decided I'm going to fight for it.
I know you don't love me back, that you may never love me,
but I'm declaring my intention to woo you.'

'But—'

Ben held up his hand again. 'I know my whole lifestyle
makes you uncomfortable. But I can't change who I am,
Katya. I know that because I spent a lot of years fighting it.
And it was you who made me see that I could be the version
of me that I wanted to be, not the one everyone expected. And
this title allows me to do so much more good in this world.
But I don't need or care for any of its trappings. We'll stay
home every night and eat bruschetta from Taddeo's if it means
that you'll grow to love me.'

'Ben—'

He shook his head. 'No. I haven't finished yet. And if you
never love me, at least I'll know that I tried and that there'll

be honesty between us. Because if we're going to raise this child separately, we're going to need that.'

Katya felt tears build in her eyes and one roll down her cheek. He had said the words she had never thought she'd hear from his mouth.

'What about Bianca? Don't you still love her?'

Ben rubbed his hands through his hair. 'No, no, no. I've been hanging onto my bitterness not because I still love her but to protect myself from getting hurt again. I was a fool. You're the one I love. You were right there in front of me and I didn't realise it until you were gone. I'd been so used to emotional isolation I didn't recognise that you'd brought me back into the fold.'

Katya felt the baby move beneath her hands. He gave her a couple of hefty kicks and she grimaced. She looked at Ben, his face so earnest, so hopeful. She picked up his hand off his knee, brought it across and laced it under hers down low on her bump where the baby was partying.

Ben felt the strong movements and dropped to his knees beside the bed, burying his face against her abdomen, his cheek resting against the bulge. He kissed her gently there, where the baby was somersaulting, and cinnamon suffused his senses. He wanted to pull back the bedclothes, remove her pyjamas and just stare at her pregnant body. He had missed her so much.

Katya stared at his downturned head. Felt his lips sear her abdomen even through layers of bed linen and pyjamas. Her heart swelled with love. She had put him through hell. 'Do you remember the moment?' she asked quietly, her hand creeping down to push involuntarily through his hair.

Ben looked up at her. 'What moment?'

'That you fell in love with me.'

Ben nodded. 'The night we made love for the first time. I didn't realise it at the time but, looking back, I know I've loved you since that night.'

Katya smiled. 'Me, too.'

Ben stilled. 'You, too?'

Katya nodded. 'I didn't realise it until the night we made love at the villa. But I fell hard for you the night Mario and Bianca were killed. You were so devastated, so intense, so… different. You flipped the switch on every feminine cell I possessed that night.'

He grinned slowly. 'It was an amazing night. I'm so sorry about the next morning.'

'Don't,' she said dismissively. 'I reacted badly, too. I was angry with myself for being so irresponsible, so like my mother.'

They grinned at each other for a few more moments, letting the revelations sink in.

'Hop up,' Katya said, moving slightly and displacing Ben from his position.

Ben straightened up and looked at her questioningly. He'd liked that spot. She pulled back the covers and held them open for him.

'Well?' she said. 'You want to get closer?'

Ben grinned at her. He stood and shucked his shoes off and then joined her under the covers, fully clothed. She went into his arms eagerly and with her head against the steady thump of his heart, she knew she was where she wanted to be for ever.

'I'm sorry about these last two weeks, Ben. Once I realised I couldn't give up the baby, I couldn't stay. I didn't want to live with a man who could never love me back.'

'Hush,' he said revelling in their bodies pressed together again. 'I know. I understand. I didn't know how I was going to face you every day either, knowing I loved you. Knowing you didn't love me.'

Katya sighed. What fools they'd both been. 'I love you, Ben.'

He looked down into her eyes. 'I love you too, Katya. Marry me?'

She looked at him solemnly. 'Anywhere. Any time.'

Ben lowered his head and captured her mouth with his. He could taste her tears as they tracked down her face and mingled with their meshed lips. 'Don't cry,' he whispered. 'I'm going to make you happier than you've ever been in your life. And it starts right now.'

As his head swooped again, Katya heard the conviction and sincerity in his voice and gave herself up to his delicious promise.

EPILOGUE

KATYA reclined back against the pillows, weary but content, Mario Ivan Medici snuggled in her arms, sleeping peacefully. His cherubic face was gorgeous, his features a mirror image of his father's.

Ben, sitting on the chair beside the bed, smiled at her—the most beautiful woman in the whole world. Watching her give birth to their son had been the most humbling experience of his life and he bowed to the amazing power and control of his wife-to-be.

He pulled a flat square leather box out of his inner jacket pocket and handed it to her. Katya looked at it without touching it, noticed the company motif and felt tears well in her eyes. Her heartbeat picked up its tempo. She could hear the sound of her breathing loud in her ears.

He opened the box for her and she gave a soft gasp, even though she'd known the minute he'd produced it what the box contained. The cameo they'd fought over sat nestled in the silky lining.

Ben could see the play of emotions across her face. The same look he'd seen in the shop that day. A glimpse of the little girl she'd been before she'd lost her childhood. A glimpse of the yearning that she'd suppressed so hard.

He'd had the cameo attached to a two-strand red coral choker and he lifted it over her head and placed it around her neck. She didn't protest, just sat very still while he latched it at her nape.

She brought her fingers up slowly to stroke the delicate chalky white carving of the curly-haired woman with the bare shoulders and sad smile. It felt firm around her neck but also, strangely, like it belonged there. Katya felt an instant connection with her grandmother and knew she would treasure it for ever.

'Thank you,' she said quietly, her eyes meeting his. 'It's beautiful.'

'I want you to wear it on our wedding day,' he said.

Tears shimmered in her blue eyes. 'I'll wear it with pride.'

He dropped a kiss on her blonde head and she raised her face to claim another on her mouth. The baby stirred and Katya broke off, hushing and rocking him gently.

'We were supposed to speak to the mayor today,' Katya said after her son had settled. 'Do you think he'll reschedule?'

Ben chuckled. 'I think when he knows we were a little busy, he'll fit us in another time. He's as eager to marry us as we are to marry each other, *cara*.'

'What about the sundial? Will that be done by the wedding date?' she asked.

Ben eased out of his seat and went to the balcony and looked down at the gardens, the Med sparkling like a jewel in the distance. Two workmen were installing the heavy masonry ornament down on the bottom tier of the garden.

Ben had decided to honour his brother with a sundial. It had been the one thing Mario had always wanted to see in the garden and had never got around to doing. The process had been cathartic, to say the least.

Their wedding was taking place next to the sundial, and

Ben felt like he was finally claiming the gardens for himself while still acknowledging his brother's contribution. Both to the gardens and his life. And he had Katya to thank for it.

'They'll be finished tomorrow,' he said.

He walked back into the room and sat back on the chair.

'Did you speak with your mother?'

Katya smiled at him and nodded. 'She and Dimitri are both coming.' That her mother had married two months ago had come as a complete surprise. That a bridge had finally been built between mother and daughter, even more so. It was new and rickety, and Katya wasn't sure they'd ever be really close, but she'd never heard her mother so content, and it was a start. Katya knew she had Ben to thank for it. 'They arrive at the weekend.'

In fact, thanks to Ben, her whole family was going to attend the wedding. Sophia, Anna and Marisha were all going to be bridesmaids.

Katya linked her spare hand with his and they both sat watching their newborn son sleep.

'Thank you,' Ben said. 'Thank you for making me the happiest man in the world.'

Katya smiled at Ben, her heart filling with joy and love. 'Thank you,' she replied. 'For him. For this.' She touched her cameo. 'For being patient. For helping me reconnect with my mother. For loving me.'

Ben rose and kissed Katya lightly on the mouth. 'I'm going to spend the rest of my life loving you.'

And then he kissed her properly. Today was a wonderful day. His son was healthy. Katya was happy. The Lucia Trust was thriving. Life was perfect. Just as they both deserved.

0211/05a

We're thrilled to bring you four bestselling collections that we know you'll love…

3 in 1 ONLY £5.99

Claiming His Secret Love-Child

Melanie Milburne
Cathy Williams
Maggie Cox

By Request

3 in 1 ONLY £5.99

In Bed With Her Tall, Sexy Handsome Boss

Natalie Anderson
Anne McAllister
Anna Cleary

By Request

featuring

THE MARCIANO LOVE-CHILD
by Melanie Milburne

THE ITALIAN BILLIONAIRE'S SECRET LOVE-CHILD
by Cathy Williams

THE RICH MAN'S LOVE-CHILD
by Maggie Cox

featuring

ALL NIGHT WITH THE BOSS
by Natalie Anderson

THE BOSS'S WIFE FOR A WEEK
by Anne McAllister

MY TALL DARK GREEK BOSS
by Anna Cleary

MILLS & BOON

On sale from 18th February 2011

By Request

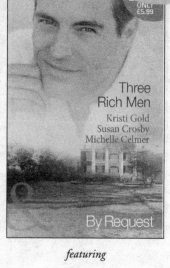